Loving Arms

Melissa Mikesell

Contents

RAE

Fifteen sets of eyes stared at me as my focus came back sharp and clear. I was sprawled on the couch, a middle-aged Sleeping Beauty. But instead of a tiara, I had an ugly Christmas sweater, now splattered in cranberry juice and reeking of vodka. I sat up too quickly. The world started to blur and swirl at the edges again. Dean grabbed my elbow, steadying me.

"Whoa, whoa. Sit back. You passed out. Take a second."

To the side of me, Cami Peterson flitted about her immaculate living room. She was undoubtedly conflicted about attacking the stain on her plush carpet or playing her proper part of the concerned hostess. Wringing her hands, she moved at warp speed, fetching napkins and seltzer. She darted away, returning with a bottle of water.

I sat up again, slower this time. Then I stood, moving through the crowd gathered around me. The room was silent except for Mariah Carey shrieking about what she wanted for Christmas at top volume.

"I'm fine, really. I'm okay. Thank you."

Even as I said it, my eyes sought out the card on the mantle, the one that had caused me to become the sideshow attraction at this party. My eyes found it, and I felt my knees begin to weaken. I locked them, lurching forward almost imperceptibly.

Dean's hand shot out at the exact moment Patti stepped forward, her face softened by wine and concern. I ignored both of them, my singular focus on that card. As the glossy surface skimmed my fingertips, Cami's shrill voice drifted into my ear.

"Cute, isn't he? That's my niece Rebecca and her son Dustin."

I turned to her. A fine sweat broke out on my back. My sweater stuck there, like the front already was, stiff with the sugar from my spilled drink. My heart was pounding. My voice came out in a burst.

"Adorable. Dean, look."

My husband skimmed the photo, still worried about me.

"Cute. Come on, let's go. You need to get in your own bed." He spoke.

The crowd parted as he led me out. Patti emerged, our coats in hand, pressed her lips to my cheek, and murmured she would check in on me later.

And then we were out in the cold, my head still haunted by those eyes, staring out at me from the card. We were home in less than three minutes, our house just a few doors down from Cami.

I peeled my clothes off robotically and stepped into the shower. Dean was already mid-shower, absentmindedly humming "Rudolph the Red-Nosed Reindeer."

"What happened tonight? Other than the fact that Cami had the damn heat cranked to 150. Hotter than hell in there."

Dean turned to face me, the water showering down and coating his beard with fine droplets.

"Did you see the picture?"

"Yeah, I looked at it."

"No, you didn't LOOK at it."

My voice rose slightly in frustration, slapping my bare chest as I soaped myself.

Dean heaved a heavy sigh.

"What was so special about a damn Christmas card?"

"The boy, Dean! That boy! He looked just like Sean!"

He stilled. The soap and water coursed from his hair down his back and forehead. If it stung his eyes, he did not betray it. I could see the pain that had sprung to them and how carefully he was choosing the words he wanted to speak.

"Rae…" His hand looped around my wrist, and he stroked the skin there softly.

I jerked my hand away, my temper- my fatal flaw- flaring again.

"No!" I yelled, my voice bouncing off the white tiles.

Dean had painstakingly installed them as a distraction from the horror of our life four years before.

"Don't look at me like that! Don't act like I am a lunatic. He looked EXACTLY like him."

"Maybe your mind just wanted to see him in that little boy. You know, this time of year. Well, we want him here more now than most days. We want to see his stocking on our mantle. His presents under the tree." Dean choked up, breathed. "Him."

"It wasn't my brain playing a cruel trick. His eyes. Those were Sean's eyes. Hell, his whole face!"

"It's not possible. You know that." Dean traced a drop from the shower down my cheek with his thumb. "Now, come on. Let's go to bed. It was just a weird coincidence."

Five minutes later, my husband was sound asleep; his arm splayed across my waist. I took his hand in the dark. I traced the nails, the rough skin, the calluses on the pads of his fingers, the hard metal of his wedding band.

These hands had held mine through all the stages of my life. Prom, heavy with oversized and over fragranced corsages. The day he proposed, down on one knee in my college dorm room. Our graduations, twirling the colored tassels. Our wedding day, trembling and sweaty. The day two lines on the test appeared, his hand clenched over mine in a tight fist of triumph and excitement.

They had cradled mine when I had broken my thumb hanging drywall in our home. I had sobbed like a baby, stomach hugely pregnant and my overalls busting at the seams. They had held Sean so tenderly, moments after he was born, yowling and pink.

And four years ago, they had been steady and strong. Those hands had been the one constant as the world was upended, never to be set right again. Dean's hands had been the ones clutching the phone, white-knuckled when we got the call from the police in Boston. There had been an accident. A drunk driver had hopped the sidewalk. Our son, our only child, was gone.

My tears came then, hot and silent, soaking my pillow. I cried with practiced restraint, careful not to shake the bed with my sobs. Finally, I began to drift into sleep. But it was not Sean's face I pictured as so many nights before, but the little boy from the Christmas card.

I woke up early, with the sun barely peeking around our thick curtain. Dean still snoozed next to me as I balanced on the edge of the bed to slide my feet into sneakers. He stirred as I pecked his cheek and exited our bedroom. I followed the familiar path down the stairs and out the door, breaking into a leisurely run as I began my daily run through our neighborhood. I lost myself in my workout for the next hour and a half, trying hard not to let my thoughts drift to the night before.

Finally, I stopped on the sidewalk in the front of our house, stretching and breathing, letting my heart rate return to normal.

"Heyyy Rae! How are you feeling? Better today?"

Cami approached fast, her rail-thin frame encased in an all-black workout ensemble, ready for her own morning run.

I whirled around, hair falling from my bun and sticking to my face. My heart started to race again, and my mouth went dry.

"Oh, good morning, Cami. I'm feeling better, thanks. A few too many cocktails!" I laughed, but it sounded empty and foreign.

Cami either didn't notice or didn't care. She nodded sympathetically as she began her run. She was almost past me when I reached out and grabbed her elbow. She stopped abruptly.

"Thanks again for having us over. It was so fun. And the house looked wonderful, as always! I was thinking about that little cutie on the Christmas card. It was uncanny how much he looks like our Sean when he was a baby."

I paused, not sure how to proceed. Cami blinked and shifted foot to foot, half-listening, probably calculating how many miles she had to run to burn off the cocktails and appetizers she consumed last night.

"Isn't that funny? I know how terribly you miss him."

Her mouth turned down, as best her Botox would allow, in an attempt at empathy.

"Do you know anything about his father? I didn't see one in that picture."

Cami leaned forward conspiratorially. "One-night stand. My sister, Bernie, was scandalized. Rebecca was in her thirties. Single. Great job in the city. Went out with some friends to celebrate a birthday or something. Met a guy. One thing leads to another. Sperm meets egg. Decided to keep the baby since she was getting older, and it may be her only chance."

"What city does she live in?" I asked, attempting to sound nonchalant.

"Boston. Can you imagine raising a baby in the city? Ok, well, I'm off!" Cami trotted off, leaving me with me wavering on the sidewalk.

Without knowing how I made it back into the house and started breakfast. It wasn't until my finger grazed the hot skillet that I jerked back to reality.

"Damn it!"

"That good of a day already?" Dean said, smirking as he shuffled into the kitchen.

I whirled around, spraying the front of his shirt with the cold water I was running my finger under.

"I burnt my finger," I said, feeling pathetic, as he nuzzled my neck. "I'm all sweaty. Oh, and I ran into Cami on her run."

"And how is the Queen of Crandall Drive?" Dean asked, sitting at the table with his coffee and picking at the bowl of fruit I had sat there.

"Oh, you know. Nothing is ever wrong. We got to talking about that boy."

The mood in the room became hostile instantaneously. "I thought we talked about this?"

"They're from Boston, Dean."

Dean dropped his head into his hands. He rubbed his hands over his hair briskly, a sure sign of the impact my words had on him. "What are you thinking?"

"I think we have a grandchild out there somewhere," I exclaimed, feeling desperate, crazed. Off-balance.

The feeling of the world being off-kilter was one I was familiar with. It had dominated my days since Sean's death. "It doesn't make sense. Sean was 19. Cami said her niece is in her thirties. It was a one-night stand. In a bar. Sean couldn't even get into a bar." I continued.

"Well, it wouldn't be the craziest thing in the world for a college kid to have a fake ID. But, Rae, who she is and where she lives doesn't really matter. We can't just barge into this woman's life because you feel a connection to a photo."

"I don't feel a connection to a photo. I feel a connection to the child in the photo. Because I know that he is our son's child, and nothing you say will change my mind."

"Rae, I'm just trying to help you. I don't want to have to cart you back to…" His voice trailed off, and the past sat between us, heavy and dark like a boulder.

"This is different, and you know it. That was Sean." My voice broke, and I couldn't hold the tears at bay.

"And this is still about Sean. I know you, babe. You've already decided this child is his, with no information to support that. You're building dreams for this boy. Just like you did with Sean. And I am not convinced that you won't crumble just like before when those dreams are taken away. You're stronger, but you're not bulletproof."

"I'm telling you; I know I won't be disappointed. I won't have to fall apart. Because that's Sean's son."

Dean sighed, a sigh filled with defeat, sadness, and maybe even a little wonder.

"What can I say to change your mind and put this to bed?" He asked quietly.

"Nothing," I said. "I already know the truth."

His jaw worked, and I knew how hard he must be biting his tongue. He shook his head slowly back and forth and stared at me.

"Penny for your thoughts?" I asked.

"Honestly, I'm torn between committing you and hoping you're right. God, how I wish you would be right." He said, bowing his head.

I heard him sniffle discreetly. I reached my hand out and put it on his forearm. Often, my own grief and pain were so immense, so consuming, so solitary that I didn't always remember Dean's. Before Sean's death, we had been partners in every sense. Now, it seemed the balance of power and control swayed and shifted as we tried to find our footing, occasionally stumbling but mostly free-falling through the stages of loss, never quite syncing.

"I am right, Dean. I feel it in every part of me. Please, just let me prove it." I said, urgency flooding my voice.

"How would we even track this girl down? And what happens if we did? Just knock on her door and swoop her son away for a DNA test on one of those crazy talk shows?" He asked.

"I haven't thought that far. But we have to try. Sean has a baby out there somewhere."

I lifted my head so he could see the tears on my cheeks.

In a whisper, I said, "We could have him back."

"Nothing, and no one will bring him back, Rae." His voice was hard but softened as he spoke again. "No matter how bad we want that. Leave this be. Don't go chasing heartache."

"But— "

"Enough. Let's just get through the holidays. We can figure this out later."

While Dean was upstairs and I was cleaning up the breakfast dishes, my phone chimed.

ARE YOU FEELING BETTER? The message read.

Drying my hands, I thumbed out my response.

COME OVER.

In less than a minute, my front door opened, and the only person who knew me longer than Dean bounded into my house with her normal overabundance of energy.

"Goooooood morning! A little hair of the dog?"

Patti held up a clear tumbler with a straw in it, filled with what appeared to be a mimosa.

"No, thank you. Sit down." I replied.

"Well, you look like hell. Hungover? You barely drank. Ohhh, long night? That's why Dean wanted to rush you home. That snowman sweater had him all hot and bothered."

Patti threw her head back and laughed the whole body laugh she was famous for.

"I wish," I tried to laugh, but it was tinny. Patti snapped to attention, in tune with me wordlessly.

"What?" In an instant, she turned serious, sliding into a chair and staring intently with her head balanced on her hand.

"You know why I fainted? It was because I saw the card on Cami's mantle."

"What card?" Patti looked confused.

"It was a Christmas card from her niece and her son. That little boy, Pat, he is Sean's spitting image." I plunged ahead, the years between us emboldening me. "I know it is his son."

"Wait, what? Listen, honey. I know you miss Sean. We all miss Sean. And it's a rough time of year. But he's gone. The little boy probably just reminded you of him." Patti said.

"I talked to Cami this morning. Her niece is from Boston."

Patti's mouth snapped open and shut a few times. "I don't know what to make of that. That doesn't prove anything, though."

"I have to find out. I have to know. Come to Cami's with me. I need to get some information so that I can find this girl."

Patti paused. She sipped from her tumbler slowly and deliberately, not meeting my eyes. She swallowed, then sighed.

"Rae, I love you, but this is nuts. It's one thing to be reminded of him and wish he were here. But to start poking around in a stranger's business with nothing but a hunch? That's different. And to align with the Ice Queen to do it?" She shuddered at the mere thought of Cami. "One whiff of good gossip, and she'll have it around town by the end of the day."

11

"I'm not nuts." I retorted.

"I said THIS is nuts. Not you."

"And what other choice do I have but to involve Cami? She's the common denominator between us."

"But what if you just didn't contact the mother?" She asked softly. "Just let Sean rest in peace."

"I can't believe you would even suggest that. You know me. You know what losing Sean did to me. Is still doing to me. I'm in Hell. In agony. Every moment of every day. My heart is broken." I stopped, my body wracked by sobs. "And there is someone, a little boy with my son's eyes and hair and Sean's blood rushing through his veins. Pushing blood to his beating heart. Alive and waiting for me."

I paused, still struggling to compose myself.

"Rae, I know how hard it's been. It kills me watching the hell you're going through. I can't fathom your pain. God, it's hard on me, and I didn't carry that boy. I can't…." She trailed off, composed herself. "…but Sean is gone. And what happens when you chase after this boy and find out he's not your grandson? Rae, what happened when Sean died could happen again."

"I'm better now. You know that." I said, irritated. "And what happens if it is my grandson? Does anyone think about that?"

"Even if he is, don't you feel like it's a violation of this woman's privacy to track her down? She may not even let you see him. And you're not thinking about what happens if it's not. I think it's best if you just move on. You need something to look forward to. Do you want to help me plan Liv's graduation party? And when I say help me, I mean plan entirely."

"What if this was Liv?" I looked at her square in the eyes, my stare unbreaking. "What if Olivia had died instead of Sean? Wouldn't you do anything in the world to get a piece of her back?"

"Rae…" She sighed, a defeated, heartbroken puff of air. "I love you. And I love Sean. And there's nothing I wouldn't do for either one of you. But you terrified me when Sean died. I can't lose you again."

"You didn't lose me. I'm right here." I paused. "Please, Patti, I have to know. Please, just tell me you'll help me."

She sat quietly for a long time. She sighed several times, then shook her head. Finally, she spoke.

"I will bring the celery, and you bring the protein shakes."

Despite my mood, I laughed. A real laugh, for the first time since seeing that picture.

"There you go!" Patti said, smiling.

Later that afternoon, we found ourselves in Cami's all-white kitchen. The three of us were seated at her kitchen table with steaming cups of green tea. I wasn't close with Cami. In fact, she was often fodder for my daily gossip sessions with Patti, which made me reluctant to lay all my cards on the table.

I rubbed my chest. My heart literally ached for my son. It had for four years. And now it ached for that little boy staring at me from the card, who I knew in my soul was connected to me through Sean. A boy who could give me back bits of the boy I cried for every night and longed for every day.

"Thanks for the tea, Cami. We wanted to ask you some questions about Rebecca and Dustin." I began.

Cami's face closed slightly, and her body language became guarded. I sighed, impatient but wanting to tread carefully. I plunged forward.

"you said Dustin's father was a one-night stand. And that Rebecca lives in Boston. And I know that boy looks just like Sean. I know that boy is his child. But now I need you to help me prove that."

"Why are you so sure this is his child? People can look alike. Sean had that curly brown hair. A lot of boys— "

Cami stopped short as I produced a picture from my purse of Sean at roughly the same age as Dustin in the holiday card. I put the two photos next to each other. When we finally looked up at one another, tears covered all our faces.

"This is crazy." She paused and dabbed her eyes. "You deserve some peace, Rae. Either the peace of closure or the peace of having a small part of that sweet boy of yours back."

Cami pushed back her chair. I heard her rustling around some papers in her office. She came back a moment later with a small slip of paper in her hand.

"Here, this is Rebecca's email address. Good luck. I hope this works out for you." She said, extending a pink post-it to me.

Once on the sidewalk, Patti and I hurried to my house and into the living room, where my laptop sat on the coffee table. I fired it up, then looked at my best friend expectantly.

"What do I say?"

I could see her warring with herself. I knew she had an opinion about what to say. And it was probably perfect. But if she told me, that would mean she supported my crazy plan, and she most definitely did not. Finally, her natural-born bossiness won out.

"Here, give me that. This doesn't mean I support this insanity, but you've come this far, and you can't fuck it up."

Patti's tone conveyed her usual air of authority. Shielding me from the screen, she tapped the keys efficiently. She paused, scanning her work, then handed the machine to me.

I read aloud:

"Dear Rebecca,

You don't know me, but I am a neighbor of your Aunt Cami. I saw a photo of you and your son Dustin at her house. Your son is the spitting image of my son, Sean, who I lost four years ago. I would like to talk to you about the possibility of Dustin being Sean's son, as your aunt tells me he was conceived after a one-night stand."

Before I could hesitate or over-analyze, I hit SEND.

"And now we wait," I whispered.

Patti rose wordlessly and went into the kitchen, emerging moments later with two glasses and a bottle of wine. She set them down, flicked on the tv, and settled back on the couch, pulling the throw blanket over her in one swift motion. We sat together in silence for a long time, the television the only noise.

Night had fallen, and the bottle of wine had long been empty when the computer signaled a new email was in my box. I sat up quickly, sending an asleep Patti tumbling to the floor.

"Gee, thanks," Patti said, sitting up and untangling herself from the blanket.

My hand hovered over the mouse, trembling. Taking a deep breath, I clicked. Patti came to full awareness and grabbed for my hand.

The email was brief. "Dustin is two. If your son died four years ago, he couldn't possibly be his father. Don't contact me again."

My eyes filled with tears and my breath came in jags.

"This doesn't make sense. Patti, I know that is Sean's son, as sure I have ever known anything. I can't explain it."

"Sweetie, he's two. Sean's been gone four years. It's not possible. I think we need to let this go." She said soothingly.

Outwardly, I agreed with Patti and wished her a good night. Inwardly, I was already crafting my next plan to get to the truth about Sean's son and how he came to be in the world.

I googled "Rebecca Malone Boston" and sat back, learning all I could about Cami's niece. The sun was starting to peek over the horizon when I snapped the cover closed to the computer. I knew what I was going to do.

In the morning, after Dean left for work, I left a note on the counter, along with lasagna in the freezer he would have to throw in for dinner. I double-checked that I had everything I needed and locked the door behind me. I was headed to Boston to find out what answers waited for me. After stopping for gas and coffee, I merged onto the highway.

A little over two hours later, I was in Boston. I stopped for a moment, pausing to take in the sights and smells I had always loved. Though I lived in suburbia now, complete with the white picket fence, I favored the city. Always had. In another life, I had thought I would live there, in a stylish apartment positioned above the bustling city streets, where I would wear the trendiest clothes and go to the hippest places with the cutest men.

But Dean's pull had been too strong. Even when we had tried to separate, we had gotten back together. I had given up my big city plans for a quieter life with the only man I had ever loved, who hated the city in equal measure with how deeply he loved me. I had settled into life without complaint, especially once Sean came and my days were filled with baby smell, giggles, crayons, and wonder. I had loved my life. But secretly, I was pleased when Sean asked me to escort him to Boston to look at colleges.

Dean wanted no part of the city, so Sean and I had packed up the car, a cooler full of snacks, gas station Big Gulps and some mix CDs and headed out together. We stayed in a hotel right in the heart of Boston, on the 23rd floor, with the entire city spread before us. It cost a fortune, but the look on Sean's face when he looked at the view from those windows, the wonder and excitement- the joy- was all worth it.

"This is where I want to be, Mom! Let's see how many colleges we can hit before we have to go home."

He had bent his head over the thick book of colleges he had lugged with us. Along with a map of Boston, he spent half the night highlighting and making notes. In the morning, we had hit the ground running. We had visited five schools that weekend, one blurring into the next for me.

We had sampled all of Boston's tourist attractions, from the Duck Tours to Newbury Street. We enjoyed the museums and parks. We cheered on the Sox at Fenway. We rode the T over and over as Sean tried to memorize the stops so he wouldn't be pegged as an outsider when he moved.

He became more and more enchanted with each passing minute. My eyes welled now with tears, but I smiled, remembering the memories we made that weekend. It was the first time I ever saw my son as more than just my child, but also my friend.

We came home to Dean and the quiet of our neighborhood and the only house Sean had ever known. Sean didn't pause for breath for the first half-hour, showering his father with all the details of what we had done and seen. He ended his tale with the proclamation, "I'm going to school in Boston!"

And true to his word, we had dropped him and all his belongings off in what seemed like a blink of an eye. We navigated to his dorm in Boston, Dean swearing and cursing the traffic the whole time. I had hugged Sean goodbye bravely, but once we got back into the car, I had sobbed for nearly the entire trip home. Dean had been solid and stoic.

Sean called often, always sharing adventures he had with me and places he wanted to take me when I came to visit. I walked around our empty house, lost and listless. I had never worked, never gotten any life experience to create a resume with, so I couldn't get a job to occupy my time. To assuage the boredom of an empty nest and ease the way my chest hurt with missing my son, I had taken to jumping in the car and making the two-hour trip to Boston during the week. I hung out in the Commons or the Public Library reading until Sean got out of class, then having lunch or dinner with him, going to a show or movie, or even a game.

For a long time, after Sean died, I would climb into the car, all ready for a trip to Boston, when reality would hit me again, hard, and I would be rendered breathless. Patti had come home more than once to find me sitting in my car in my driveway sobbing. She always had gently steered me back inside, rubbed my back, and kept an endless supply of tissues coming.

So here I was, assaulted by ghosts of a life I had previously lived, a childless mother. A grandmother, whether anyone else believed it to be so. The thought of my grandson being in the city, close enough for me to touch, to look at and see Sean in, fortified me. I snapped back to reality. I gained my bearings and set about finding the office Google reported Rebecca had been employed at since before she had gotten pregnant with Dustin.

After about fifteen minutes, I found the address I was looking for. It was right before noon. Hoping to catch Rebecca on her way to lunch, to buy some time, I entered the lobby and waited to spot her. Cami's Christmas card and various Facebook photos were my memorized visual aids.

It wasn't long before Rebecca emerged, head down, her face illuminated by her phone screen, thumb busy scrolling. She was dressed professionally but not trendy: black dress pants, a white button-down, and a pretty raspberry-colored cardigan. Her hair was pulled into a bun, curls tumbling out to frame her round face. She looked stressed and not well-rested.

She went out the door, and I slid out behind her. She stopped at a small restaurant a few doors down. I followed her in. She chose a table after ordering at the counter and sat down, still engrossed in her phone. I made my way to where she sat.

"Rebecca?"

She looked up, distracted by whatever held her interest on the phone screen. "Yes?"

"I'm Rae Baxter. I received your email last night."

In an instant, her attitude changed. Her blue eyes snapped with intensity. She bristled. "What are you doing here? I told you not to contact me."

"I know. And I'm sorry. But I just have to know about Dustin. He is Sean's son. A mother knows—look."

I pulled from my purse all the photos I had removed from their plastic sleeves in the early morning hours, my defense for this insane argument. My words tumbled over themselves as I tried to get her to see, to listen. I shoved picture after picture in her hand.

At first, she turned away, but then one hit the ground near her feet. Almost reflexively, she bent to pick it up. Sean, a round-bellied two-year-old, sandy curls and limbs, on the beach making a sandcastle, his head tossed back and his mouth open wide in a laugh. Her face softened, and she ran her finger over the image. Rebecca turned to look at the other photos before her then, carefully picking up each one. After a while, she gestured for me to sit down.

When she spoke, she never took her eyes off the pile of pictures in between us.

"I don't know why I am telling this. It's the biggest secret I have ever had in my life. No one knows the truth. Not my best friend, not my mother."

She paused. Her eyes filled with tears, but she swallowed them back. She took a deep breath and whispered so softly I had to lean forward to hear.

"I was artificially inseminated."

She waited for my reaction, looking everywhere but my eyes, but the only thing I could manage was stunned silence. She continued, louder but in an almost pleading tone.

"Even though my mother was mortified, I told everyone I had a one-night stand with a handsome stranger in a bar. It seemed easier to explain than the desperation I felt as a woman in her early 30s with no boyfriend or husband, whose biological clock was ticking so loud it as keeping me up at night."

Now, her words tumbled out over each other in her haste to unburden herself of this secret.

"I wanted so badly to be the type of girl a man would have a one-night stand with. Instead, I'm the friend who holds her friend's purse while they dance with the man who THEY will have the one-night stand with. I wanted it to be plausible that I would be able to get accidentally pregnant from a dangerous stranger. Instead, I am the woman who had to create a baby on my dirty bathroom floor with a vial of a stranger's sperm, holding my feet in the air for hours, completely alone. When no one questioned it, I was shocked. So, I stuck with the lie. Dustin's dad is a stranger, whether I chose him from a profile in a book or over the brim of a glass." She looked at me then, her eyes softer. "I have no details at all about Dustin's father, other than the profile I picked him from at the bank, but the chances of your son being the donor are slim. I don't know if those kinds of odds even exist."

She rocked with a nervous laugh, unburdened finally.

My heart sank. Why would a 19-year-old boy donate sperm? It didn't make any sense. My head played against my heart as logic told me that Sean was not the father of this boy, while my heart continued to tell me otherwise. I knew what had to be done to quiet the noise.

"Would you be willing to get a DNA test for Dustin?" I said. As you said, the odds are slim. But I just look at your son, and my heart just connects to him in the way it only ever has once before-with Sean."

Rebecca paused, her face unreadable. She looked hard at the pictures one last time. She stroked one of Sean naked except for a diaper, covered in red paint, a clump spiking his curls. Finally, she spoke, again so quietly I had to lean over to hear her.

"Don't get your hopes up. And you'll have to foot the bill." She whispered.

I wanted to jump up and down and scream at this small victory, but I didn't dare move or breathe. I trained my eyes on the ground to avoid spooking Rebecca and taking back this olive branch she had extended.

Rebecca stood up, swept her bag off the chair next to her, and brushed past me without another word. I reached down to gather Sean's photos from the sticky tabletop. Her business card sat on top of the stack of photos. I punched in her cell phone number and typed simply, THANK YOU.

A few hours later, Rebecca texted me back with details for an appointment to get a DNA test the next day, including that both

Dean and I had to be tested, in the absence of the father- a phrase which pierced my heart anew. I picked up the phone, filled with dread.

"Rae, what the hell?" Dean's annoyance and anger were evident as he greeted me.

"Babe, I'm sorry. I had to."

And then, slowly and carefully, sparing no detail, I told Dean the circumstances of Dustin's conception. I told him what the next steps were and asked him to come. He assured me he would be there in the morning. We said good night. I was just about asleep when there was a knock on my hotel room door.

When I opened it, there stood the person who had always been my strength and my soft place to fall.

Dean smiled. "You know I can't sleep without you, and I figured you would be lonely in that big hotel bed."

I fell into his arms, and together we fell into bed, not daring to hope or anticipate what tomorrow may bring.

"How do you always know when I need you most?" I said, snuggled against his chest, the place that always felt like home.

"Because I love you, and as such, I make it my business to know what you need. Now go to sleep, my love."

The shower was already running when I woke, steam rolling out from under the door. I stretched; my brain was still not sharp as I slowly became aware of the morning's events. The shower turned off, and I went to the bathroom door, surprising Dean as I flung it open.

"Sorry! I just want to get going. Get dressed while I hop in the shower." I said.

Dean shook his head, amused at my enthusiasm. I reached behind the shower curtain to turn the water back on, pausing to rest a palm on my husband's damp, handsome face. I kissed him slowly.

His body responded, his chest pressing into mine and his hands reaching between my thighs. I felt his lips curled into a smile as he kissed my neck. My body began to hum, still putty in this man's hands after all these years.

Wordlessly, trailing kisses all over my upper body, Dean reached over and turned off the shower. I laughed, throwing my head back like in the first days of our relationship when I wanted to inflate his ego as he cracked mediocre jokes.

"There's my girl."

Dean murmured into my neck, tugging the flimsy material of my underwear aside as he teased me with his fingers. I was almost over the edge when he stopped abruptly, leaving me panting and frustrated.

I tilted my head back, silently imploring him to continue. He looked back at me, his eyes dancing with lust and confidence in his ability to play the familiar rhythms of my body. He spun me playfully, catching me in his arms and dancing me across the small hotel room to the bed. He pushed me down, throwing his legs on either side of me, and the weight of the day faded away as we moved together.

Later, after my breathing returned to normal and I untangled myself from the sheets, I took a shower. I washed my hair with a grin, Dustin's round face in my head. I couldn't wait to meet him—my grandson.

Don't get your hopes up; Rebecca's voice suddenly echoed in my head. I stilled. I needed to manage my expectations somehow, though that seemed impossible. The odds of this boy being Sean's son were minuscule. Even more improbable because there was no reason Sean would have had to be a sperm donor. Nothing pointed to the result my heart so desperately wanted. That I needed to believe.

The rest of the morning passed quickly. Dean and I ate brunch in a small restaurant, our words coming in an endless stream. We finished each other's sentences and then were reduced to giggles when we did. We talked about everything but what we were about to do and who we were about to meet.

I recalled silently how nervous Dean had been to meet Sean. He had been plagued with insomnia in the weeks before his birth, but not from a huge belly and heartburn like me. After the tumultuous relationship with his own father, he was so anxious about having a son. He had gotten down on his knees the day we found out I was pregnant and asked God for a girl because he doubted his ability to parent a son.

When an ultrasound confirmed Sean was a boy, Dean took a week off work and went fishing. He never shared with me what changed for him during that trip, but he came home with a tiny fishing vest, which he hung in the nursery closet without another word about wanting a girl. He was invested and excited after that, but his fears crept back in as my belly grew, buzzing under the surface like an electrical current.

On our last child-free nights, we ate fruit and ice cream in bed, watched the baby kick the bowls as they balanced on my bump, and indulged in fantasies about adventures we would have as a family. I felt sick suddenly, as I remembered our talks about what songs we would dance to at Sean's wedding and what kind of grandparents we would be.

My throat felt thick as I realized I could get one of those dreams back. I could be Dustin's grandma. A small scrap of one of the plans I had given up the day I buried my baby crept back in and wrapped itself around my heart in the form of delicate baby fingers.

Dean sat oblivious as he scanned the restaurant for the waiter to bring us the check. When he finally flagged him down and turned to me, his face changed from cheerful to instantly concerned. Dean took in my flushed cheeks and almost overflowing eyes. He patted my hand. I managed a weak smile.

"Let's go get this done." He said.

We stood up, and holding hands, walked into what I prayed would be the next chapter of our lives. Lives that had stood suspended for the last four years. Weighed down and ugly. Empty.

Would this be the thing that filled them up again, I wondered, winging up another silent but fervent prayer.

We found ourselves gazing up at a nondescript, gray office building just a few minutes later. We took an elevator up to the third floor. I eagerly scanned the waiting room for Rebecca and Dustin. I yearned for this little boy I had never met.

I wanted to feel the weight of his hug around my neck and smell the unique scent of a baby mixed with a big boy: diaper cream and graham crackers, dirt and perspiration, and cloying sweet fruit juice. My stomach lurched when I didn't see them. *Manage expectations*, my inner voice chided.

"We are here with the Malone appointment. Do you need the first name?"

Dean was calm and efficient.

"Thank you, sir. We have the name, no worries. A tech will call you back in a few minutes." The receptionist assured us.

I tried to read a tattered copy of *People Magazine* while we waited, but the words and pictures all swam together. I flipped too fast through the pages. Finally, the door leading to the exam rooms creaked open, and a tech appeared. Where was Rebecca? Was she blowing us off?

"The Malone party?" She called, consulting a clipboard almost absentmindedly.

We followed her. As she waved us into the room, I noticed her nails were long and polished with neon green nail polish and tiny rhinestones.

"You need anything while you wait?"

Her accent was Boston, with something else mixed in, and conveyed that she often kept her guard up.

"Could you tell me what room Rebecca and Dustin Malone are

in? I would love to say hello." I asked.

She sighed deeply, as though my question aggravated her. "They already came and went."

"What? We were supposed to meet them here to complete a DNA test." I said, my temper stirring.

"We don't need you here together. They came in about an hour ago, we collected the swab from the boy, and they left. Anything else?" She asked.

"No, thank you," Dean spoke from behind me.

I whirled around as soon as the door shut, furious suddenly.

"She was supposed to meet us here. Why…why… would she do this? She better not be trying to pull a fast one on us." I ranted.

"Calm down. I am sure there is a logical explanation, Rae. Just call her." Dean soothed.

"Oh, I am going to call her all right."

I rooted around in my purse for my cell phone. I pounded the screen.

"Hello?"

"Hi Rebecca, it's Rae. We are at the DNA lab. You were supposed to meet us here."

Rebecca hesitated. "Rae...we got the swab done. But I decided not to stay. I was up all night thinking about this, and I decided I don't want Dustin to meet you guys."

The world began to blur and spin. "What? Why?"

Dean stood up quickly, grabbing my elbow.

"Rae, sit down."

"It's too confusing for him. I don't want people in and out of his life. We already discussed how slim the chance even is that he is related to you. Surely you can understand where I am coming from." Rebecca explained.

"We wanted to meet him. We didn't do anything wrong. Please."

Grief flooded in, sharp and quick, replacing the rage. My voice was verging on hysteria.

"I don't owe you anything." Rebecca spat. Then, softer, "Let's see what the test says. If, and we both know, it's a big if, if it comes back that you are Dustin's grandparents, then we will talk. But for right now, there is nothing left for us to say. If you will excuse me, I have a little boy very eager to see Santa. Merry Christmas."

Before I could manage another word, Rebecca hung up, leaving me with only silence. I shoved my phone in my purse.

"I heard," Dean murmured, rubbing my shoulder. "Maybe she is right. This is a long shot. We shouldn't confuse the boy if we don't have to."

I knew he and Rebecca were both right. I would have made the same choice with Sean. And I would never want to hurt or confuse Dustin. It wasn't fair. But selfishly, I felt it was unfair not to get a small glimpse of the boy who could be my son's child.

I was deep in thought and self-pity when the tech came in.

"Hi, Mr. and Mrs....Baxter? I am here to collect some DNA from you. It's straightforward, won't hurt a bit. I am just going to swab the inside of your cheek with this. The lab is a little backed up because of the holidays, so that it could be a little bit of a wait. We try to get results out within a week, but it could be up to three. Open up, please."

Dean and I both did as we were told. The tech was quick and efficient. In minutes, we were out at Reception, where the receptionist swiped our credit card.

The light-hearted mood of the morning had vanished, replaced by the emptiness that had come to define our world. Dean had made a shrewd decision in taking the train the day before, so we didn't have two cars to contend with. Though I craved the silence of my thoughts, I was glad for the company.

He took the wheel, despite his hatred of city driving. I stared bleakly out at the city, with its holiday decorations and people rushing to finish last-minute shopping, bundled up like Eskimos against the biting New England air.

As we navigated our way through the city, it started to snow. Usually, there was nothing better than the promise of a white Christmas, even as an adult. But right now, I was too upset to be excited. My head throbbed with a million thoughts and questions. Then suddenly, everything quieted as one thought rose to the surface above all the others.

REBECCA

"Shhhh, shhh, Dusty. Come on, lay down. It's time to sleep."

I rocked so vigorously in the glider I thought we would take flight. Dustin became all limbs and wild curls at bedtime, a baby soap scented dervish, water-seeking, and endless bedtime stories. Usually, his boundless energy didn't bother me. But tonight, my head pounded, and all I wanted was a glass of wine and a moment to think.

"Mama." He whispered.

His little hand snaked up to my ear and began to rub, a sure sign I was winning the bedtime battle. Soon, I felt his body go limp and his breaths even out. Slowly and methodically, as if diffusing a bomb, I slid him into his crib. I froze and held my breath, then tiptoed out of the room. I paused for a minute outside the door, waited to hear any stirring from the other side. As I stood there, a framed photo hanging on the wall caught my eye.

Dustin, last summer, on the beach, his red swim trunks sagging under the weight of a wet and sandy diaper, his fist closed around a shovel. Caught mid-laugh, eyes dancing with glee as he looked out over the water. Almost a replica of the photo Rae had shown me yesterday. The one that had turned everything upside down. The one that hasn't allowed me to take a full breath since I saw it.

My heart started to pound in rhythm with my head at the thought of what the implications of today's cheek swab results could bring. Anxiety flooded me. I headed to the kitchen and pulled out a bottle of sweet wine to calm myself. I chuckled as I poured.

Not that I hadn't tried to refine my palette. In my thirties, with a child, I still preferred the stuff teenagers drank in fields, or college students chose because it was the cheapest. On weekends, I had gone to wine tastings to vineyards and even taken a sommelier course to no avail. My mother, a lover of decadence in all areas of life, was horrified. Yet another mark on the well-annotated list of my flaws she seemed to keep tucked in her purse for the perfect moment, ready to weld as lethally as her Chanel lipstick.

I sank back onto my couch, tucking my legs under me. I scrolled through Netflix, trying to find something mindless to watch. I settled on a romantic comedy, hoping the light-heartedness would lift my mood. Several hours later, I woke up, my hair covering my face and Netflix asking if I was still watching. I flicked off the tv and padded to my room, pulling up the covers and falling into a deep sleep. For the first time in a long time, I dreamed a dream where Dustin and another boy danced together in the sand, mirror images of one another.

I woke with a start, light barely peeking over the city's skyline and Dustin on the baby monitor.

"Mama mammmmmma mammmmmmmaaaa."

Instantly, I was awake, and there was no more time to think about my dream and the boy that looked just like my son.

"Hey there, beautiful boy." My heart cracked open as Dustin reached out his arms to me from his crib.

"Morning!" He intoned into my neck, his arms squeezing me.

I lay him on the changing table, and so began the morning frenzy. A diaper change and outfit later, we were at the table, eating breakfast. Dustin ate his oatmeal heartily, making raspberries and a spectacular mess all at the same time. I picked at my fruit, still plagued by my dream. While Dustin played in the safe confines of his playpen, I took a quick shower, the door open in case he needed me.

As I got dressed, I heard him singing to himself. I smiled as I tugged on my pants. Dustin had shown me a joy I had never known ever since the day I found out I was pregnant. The thought of being forced to share him caused my heart to speed up again. I shook my head, angry at getting ahead of myself. There was no way the DNA test would come back with the Baxters son as Dustin's father. Then they would go away forever. And the circumstances of Dustin's conception would be kept a secret, just as I had always intended. I swallowed hard, slid my feet into my heels, and went to tackle the day.

Why do children come with so much stuff? I mentally scolded myself for falling asleep last night and not restocking the diaper bag of the ever-growing arsenal of products required to keep Dustin happy and healthy. I dashed around, replenishing the supplies. Finally, I strapped Dustin into his stroller and navigated it through the door, balancing the bulging bag and my purse on either shoulder. I was exhausted before the day even officially began.

I was fortunate to have a sitter in my apartment building, an elderly lady named Betty who had lived two floors up since she was a child. She had inherited her parent's apartment. Her babysitting rates reflected her dedication to remaining in the "golden days," as she often called them. We met when she had approached me one day when I was getting my mail. She had put her hand on my belly and invited me to her apartment for dinner. Betty enchanted me with stories of Boston and her family, growing up there herself, then raising her children in the two-bedroom apartment. When she showed me the closet door where first her father and then she had painstakingly recorded their children's heights and ages, I tearfully asked her if she would consider watching my baby. Since then, we had become like family. Betty was like the grandmother Dustin deserved, the one I imagined for my son, but the one my mother would never be.

Before I could even knock, the door creaked open, and Betty's smiling face greeted us. Dustin kicked his legs in approval.

"Good morning, handsome boy!" She sang, pressing a kiss onto my cheek and taking the diaper bag off my shoulder. "It's going to be brutal out today. Make sure you bundle up! He will have a good day; his girlfriend will be home soon."

She winked, and I laughed. Betty's granddaughter, Mia, had started college at Northeastern last year and moved into the spare bedroom of Betty's apartment, where her father and uncles slept as boys. Betty had been delivered in that same room, sliding with a gush onto a sun-drenched patch on the floor.

Since moving in, Mia had developed a deep and unexpected bond with her grandmother and Dustin, who equally adored her. She had become indispensable for both Betty and me. She was young and energetic enough to help out Betty when Dustin became a handful and was always willing to babysit if I needed it.

"Sounds good! Kiss me, baby. Mama has to go!" I smacked a loud, playful kiss on his cheek, and he squealed with laughter. "I love you, my whole heart!"

In moments, I was out on the sidewalk, jarred by the biting December wind. I pulled my hat down tighter on my head and made a mental note to take it off in the bathroom to do appropriate damage control to what would most certainly be a severe hat head situation. I navigated the icy, salt-pocked sidewalks and around the ever-mounting snow piles to the T and hustled onto the train. A quick ride and a short, freezing walk later, I was inside the lobby of the building that housed my office. I was shaking off the cold when strong, thin arms came from behind me. They scooped me up, twirling me to face their owner, my best friend, Kieran.

"Becky with the good hair!" He enthused, a wide grin making him even more attractive than he already was.

"What are you even talking about?" I laughed. "There is no good hair under here, trust me."

"Uh, Beyonce...Lemonade...any of this ring a bell?" He analyzed my face for any register of meaning.

"I got nothing."

"Do you live under a rock?" He looked shocked.

"The only lemonade I know about comes in juice box form, and the musical variety in my house runs more Barney than Beyonce these days."

"Tragic. Come on, let's go. We can't be late."

After a quick trip to the bathroom to address the hair situation, which was even more dismal than I had anticipated, I settled at my desk, checking my emails and drinking my coffee.

I was responding to the many messages my boss had sent marked High Importance, as mostly all of her messages were. She marked them this whether they were as mundane as "Can you please order copier paper?" to actual matters of importance, like "Correct permits didn't get filed for the new project. We need a status update ASAP so all building can proceed on schedule." She was great to work for, but her tendency to panic about every detail of every day made for challenging times if I didn't reign her in. Apparently, my early departure the day before had caused a reaction, and she was in full panic mode. Halfway through my fourth response, my phone vibrated. As if summoned by the noise, Kieran's head popped over my cubicle, eyebrows raised in question. I had to laugh at him.

"No love connections, Chuck Woolery. You can sit back down."

I tapped my screen to make my phone come alive and held it up to him. "Just Mommy Dearest, see?"

With a deep sigh, he sat back down, and I heard his typing resume. My mother wanted to know about plans for Christmas, which was fast approaching. The thought of spending a week in a house with her made me want to hide under the covers until Ryan Seacrest counted down the ball drop in Times Square. But Dustin deserved to be around family for Christmas, and it had been months since we had seen my mother. So, even though my head screamed NO, I told her we would be coming by

Christmas Eve and staying for a few days after the holidays. I had to be back at work on the 3rd. Her reply was almost immediate.

Are you bringing anyone with you?

Just your adorable grandson...the only man in my life.

It was going to be a long holiday.

Before thinking of any strategies to get out of Christmas with my mother, I heard Megan, my boss, calling me from across the office. I stood up hastily, sloshing coffee on myself. I dabbed at it with a tissue as I scurried across the room to see what she wanted.

Megan Gallagher stood all of five foot nothing, but her long hair that she always coiled into a tight bun directly on top of her head afforded her another couple inches. When I got into her office, she was pacing, a sure sign she was already agitated about something. I had worked for her since I graduated. I certainly hadn't planned to be a personal assistant, but here I was. I had wanted to leave once upon a time. Still, the prospect of starting over in a new position and career was too menacing, especially when I started hearing the deafening tick of my biological clock. I never was a gambler, and this position was no different. I doubled down on the sure thing and was patiently biding my time until a promotion came my way.

"How are you, Megan?"

"Not good, not good at all." Her thin arms flitted about in their usual anxious way as she paced. "I need you to contact Joe and find out the status on the Rockwell project. I just have such a bad feeling." She stopped moving and paused for dramatic effect, a favorite of hers. "Like building has stalled."

"Sure thing, right on it. Anything else?"

"No, thanks. How was your appointment yesterday? Everything ok with Dustin?"

The abrupt change of topic caught me off guard. I felt my face get hot and stammered through a response she only half heard. By the time I was done, she was looking at me expectantly, waiting for me to get to the assigned tasks.

"So, what's the verdict? Does she need a Xanxy?" Kieran peered around his cubicle again, this time shaking a pill bottle.

I couldn't help but laugh. "No Xanax yet, but close."

"Well, you just let me know when you need me, your friendly pharma rep! Your phone was going off again. Someone's popular today."

I picked up my phone, already annoyed by my mother's endless nonsensical texts about the menu and decorations and family gossip. To my surprise, it was Rae. My hand quivered involuntarily.

We have gone back home. I really wish we could have met Dustin. It would have made our Christmas quite a merry one.

Anger flared within me. How dare she! There was not a shred of evidence except her hunch that Dustin was their grandchild. I was not going to be introducing him to strangers based on suspicion. And I was about one hundred percent sure that the Baxter's would remain just that, strangers, once the test came back. It didn't matter what they wanted. Dustin's best interest had to come first.

Bitch, please! My inner voice called me on my bullshit. If I was honest, my secret had to be protected. With the Baxter's in the picture, that would be impossible. And until *and unless* I had to, that was a chance I was unwilling to take.

I was so caught up in trying not to explode via text back to Rae; I didn't even notice it was time for lunch. Kieran stood next to me, tapping his debit card on my desk impatiently. I stood up, and we made our way to our usual sandwich shop, where the servers had our orders waiting for us. Kieran chatted away as he devoured his food, oblivious to my dark mood. He had launched into a tale about his latest dating dud when he stopped abruptly.

"Okay, what gives? You haven't said two words, and this is some pretty good material I am giving you here."

"Nothing, just my mom."

I couldn't tell him about the truth without revealing Dustin's story, and I was going to the grave with that.

"You know how she gets under my skin. I just can't stand the thought of playing the charity case single mom another year."

I sat my sandwich down and raised my hand like I was being sworn in. "I shouldn't even be eating this. Carbs,

Rebecca! Heaven on the lips, straight to the hips. And if she says, *'alternative lifestyle,'* so help me, God. It's so much."

"Well, I certainly have the alternative lifestyle market cornered in my family too, but you know my mom. Pretty much the exact opposite of yours." He replied.

And it was true. Where my mom was cold and distant, Kieran's mom Dianne was loving and super involved in every aspect of his life. She was the mastermind behind our trek to New York City to participate in last year's Pride. She had scoured the internet discount travel sites and booked and paid for our rooms. She got custom tee shirts printed with a photo of her and Kieran wrapped in a giant rainbow flag. She made sparkly signs roughly the size of an NYC studio that knocked several people over on the subway ("Fucking deal!" she had snarled at anyone who dared try to complain.) Each sign was loudly proclaiming her love for her son and her belief he deserved the same rights as all of us heteros. Dianne was a force, a champion for gay rights who had once been a meek housewife. She left her husband after Kieran came out, and he refused to accept it, insisting she disown her only child. Instead, she filed divorce papers.

Her most recent endeavor was learning how to use dating apps so she could find some decent prospects for Kieran, which amused and horrified him in equal measure. It was common for him to get 20 or more texts from Dianne a day. They were screenshots of men in various stages of undress and from all sub-sets of the gay community. Sometimes it was a This or That? with two pictures next to each other. Sometimes questions about Kieran's likes, dislikes, or deal breakers for her to compare to theirs, as she vetted the potential sons-in-law. Her Round One questions ranged from tame to so blisteringly X-rated holding the phone looking at the screenshots made my palm feel greasy and dirty. Once they passed her no holds barred "audition," as she referred to it, she gave them Kieran's information, made them a date, provided the restaurant her credit card for their meals, and let Kieran take over.

His Round 2 was also an audition but of a vastly different variety. Few moved beyond the Second Round, but many had attempted. Kieran was becoming well known for having a matchmaking mother and used it to his advantage. Whoever Dianne didn't find for him, he found for himself. To say Dianne was invested in her son's happiness was an understatement. I yearned to have but also strived to be the unwaveringly devoted mother she was.

Kieran's phone trilled as we finished our lunches and headed back to the office, then mine one second after. As if our discussion had summoned her, Dianne sent several rapid-fire messages in our three-way group text.

IS IT POSSIBLE TO DO A PRIDE TOUR?

HOW MANY PRIDES CAN WE DO THIS YEAR?

I GOT DUSTY'S TICKETS. DO WE LIKE THIS?

Several rounds of children's Pride tee shirts, accessories, and rainbow-striped pants followed her one-sided exchange.

"For the love, Dianne!" Kieran mumbled under his breath as we sat back down at our desks. "And all capitals. The audacity."

The rest of the day was a blur of managing Megan's anxiety and trying to reign in Dianne from booking a countrywide Pride Tour. I was patting myself on the back for negotiating her down to just adding Miami onto our Pride schedule when the workday ended. I didn't rush home from work. Mia had texted me and assured me she had made dinner for Dustin and Betty already.

I'll give him a bath and bring him down after a story from Betty. Relax!

I let the T rock me into a half stupor. Sleep had been a precious enough commodity before a grief-stricken woman claiming to be Dustin's grandma arrived in our life. Now, it eluded me as I worried what the DNA test would show, if my secret would be exposed, what my mother would say.

The speaker crackled and announced the stop loudly and mechanically. I rose without thinking; muscle memory perfected after so many years. In my apartment, I ditched my restrictive work clothes for shorts and a worn tee shirt. I caught my reflection in the full-length mirror hanging on the back of my bedroom door as I changed.

Thin had never been a word associated with me, but pregnancy and childbirth had taken the thinner parts of me to full and the already full features to near overflow. Stretch marks traversed my hips, stomach, and breasts, which also hung lower after breastfeeding. My body was a road map to a suddenly foreign land slowly becoming familiar, shot through with silver and purple, detailing our journey- Dustin's and mine.

I remembered vividly the months after his birth. It was the only time in my life I can remember loving my body. I felt powerful and badass, strong, fierce. I had grown and birthed a human. I gave life, damn it!

But eventually, the voice of doubt crept back in, cataloging all my faults. Too fat, crazy hair, acne, frumpy, permanent luggage under my eyes. Average. Nondescript. Nothing special at all. Unworthy. Not enough. The voice sounded a lot like my mother's.

Sighing, I pushed the negative thoughts out of my head. Sweeping my hair up, I ordered in Chinese. While I waited, I put on an old Friends episode. Right about the time Ross and Rachel went on a break, my food arrived. I ate to excess, eating my stress about the Baxter's. *About your big fat lie coming out, bitch.* My inner voice really needed to stop. I laid down on the couch, shaking off the ever-present thought that I should be multitasking every moment of every day and ignoring the two (okay, three) baskets of laundry that needed folding. Dustin would be home soon, ending my last moments of solitude.

When I woke up, it was very dark, and there was no movement. The tv was off. A white note glowed in the darkness. I fumbled for my phone in the cushions. Finding it, I hit the screen and immediately squinted as the brightness punctured the dark. Clicking the lamp on next to me, I read the note.

D is fed, washed, read to, and passed out! I put him in his crib. You looked too peaceful to wake up. See you guys tomorrow!

P.S. I took your keys so I could lock up. Grab them from Betty in the AM.

M

God bless that girl; I thought as I folded the blanket on the back of the couch and headed to bed. I checked in on a lightly snoring Dustin. As I looked at his sleeping face, my thoughts abruptly drifted to Rae, a mother without a son to parent. I thought about what losing Dustin would feel like. I couldn't imagine a life without him. That was Rae's reality every day. No wonder she was trying to find any shred of connection to her son. She was searching for a bond she needed as much as breathing but would never have again. For a split second, I almost wished for the DNA test to come back that Sean was indeed Dustin's father.

Dustin stirred, and I held my breath. He settled again, and I shook thoughts of Rae and Sean out of my head. I checked to ensure the monitor was on, closed the door, and went to my room. I slept a peaceful sleep for the first time since I read Rae's email.

The next few days passed quickly. Last minute shopping, a holiday party outfit crisis, and packing dominated my time. Before I knew it, I was navigating Dustin's stroller through Logan International, Florida, bound to my mother's for the holidays. We went through security with time to spare. I grabbed some way over-priced airport snacks and settled into a chair. Dustin was starting to doze, so I pushed the stroller lightly with my foot. I smiled as his breath slowed and evened. I checked emails as he napped, reassuring Megan that I would be back on the 4th, and her travel plans for the holiday had been triple-checked and confirmed by me personally.

As I was checking Facebook and feeling a bit jealous of my college friends lined up in front of their Christmas trees with handsome husbands, and adorable kids in matching pajamas, a text from Rae popped up.

MERRY CHRISTMAS! I HOPE YOU AND DUSTIN ARE HAVING A HAPPY HOLIDAY. I DO HOPE WE WILL BE ABLE TO SEE DUSTIN ONCE THE TEST COMES BACK.

I didn't know whether to be irritated by her brazenness or impressed by her unwavering conviction that my son was part of her son. It was like she didn't recognize how improbable that seemed. What would I do if the test confirmed Rae's gut instinct? Rae and Dean weren't going to go silently into the night. Would I be comfortable with them spending time with Dustin? What if I didn't want them around? Oh my god, what if they tried to take my son from me? A replacement for their dead son?

Terror and panic coursed through me and made me shoot from my seat like a rocket. Several other waiting passengers' strange looks brought me back to reality, and I settled back down onto the seat. Dustin continued to doze peacefully. My breath came in jagged spurts, but I willed myself to calm down. Being this anxious would not bode well with a flight, especially with a toddler. As I waited the last few minutes before our flight started to board, I typed" family attorney Boston" into Google and started to scroll.

RAE

I used to love Christmas morning. There is truly nothing like seeing the magic of Christmas through the eyes of your child. And there is no holiday more painful than those you spend alone, yearning for the child who showed you the magic of Santa. Dean was trying so hard, pulling immaculately wrapped gift after gift from under the tree for me. *Presents won't make me forget him;* I wanted to say. *You can't distract me from missing him with stuff.* Instead, I smiled and showered praise down on him.

" This sweater is lovely!" I said in what I hoped was more than a halfhearted tone.

" Rae, it's only us. You don't need to put on the show for me." Dean's voice was soft, and he put his hand on mine.

" I miss him." My voice broke.

My vulnerability beckoned Dean's out of hiding, and he cried too. We knelt together, crying, for the Christmases past, for the Christmases we would never have, and for our son, his brilliant light extinguished. After a time, we gathered ourselves and moved to the kitchen for coffee. While we sat, we tried to make each other laugh with silly Christmas escapades from our youth. Our laughs felt tinny and forced.

I took a long drink, swallowed, and said," I wonder what Santa brought for Dustin. I wish we would have been able to see him at least."

" Oh, Rae. Sweetheart, you need to prepare yourself. That test will be back soon, and if it doesn't say what you want, you will be crushed. I don't want to lose you to that dark place again, my love. I couldn't bear it."

He pushed my chin up, forcing my eyes to meet his eyes.

" It's not what I think. It's what I know, Dean."

I paused, hesitant to let him know the full scope of what I was thinking. Against my better judgment, I plunged ahead.

" And if Dustin was born from a sperm donor, and Sean is that donor, do you know what that means? It means there could be more children of his out there. Our grandchildren. Little pieces of our son waiting to come back to us. And I'm going to find them all."

My words tumbled out, fast and reckless. When I was finished, I slumped down, empty of the thoughts that had consumed me since we left Boston.

Dean's hand, now clammy, slid off my arm. I was afraid to meet his eyes. Was this silence surprise or anger? Sadness? I wasn't brave enough to raise my face to see. I heard him trying to regulate his breathing. His hands slowly clenched and unclenched.

Finally, he spoke. His voice was steely, distant, and cold.

"Listen. Don't go putting all your eggs in this basket. You could find a thousand children from our son's sperm, and not one of them will be him. Nothing will bring him back to us. He's gone. Every damn day, we go through the motions, waiting to wake up. Well, we aren't going to. This is our life. We are the parents with no child. We visit our son on a plot of land. We don't get any more Christmases. And we won't get anymore. Because I am quite sure this test will tell you what the rest of us already know, that Dustin just bears a striking resemblance to our son who died. The connection ends there. Even if, by some miracle, he was our grandson, he is Rebecca's son. We have no claim. She doesn't owe us time or a relationship with him. She did it on her own and in secret for a reason. If Sean did donate sperm, he did it that way for a reason too. It's not for you or me to understand. We just have to honor the choices they made. If there are more out there, they aren't our family. They are their own families who may not welcome the intrusion of two broken strangers trying to fill the void their dead son left with them and their children."

He spat out his last words like the bitter pills they would always be.

Now it was my turn for my voice to be icy.

"How dare you."

With that, I stood up and went to our bedroom, where I cried myself into a dreamless sleep.

I woke up many hours later, as twilight was starting. I didn't hear anything in the house, not even Christmas Vacation, which

Dean ran in rotation every Christmas Day, always laughing uproariously at the same parts every time. I didn't hear him doing dishes or puttering around. I ventured out into the house. The remains of breakfast I had left out this morning were gone. The dishes were washed and in the drainer. Dean's keys, wallet, and phone were gone from their usual bowl. *Merry Christmas*, I thought. In all of our years together, this was the first time we had spent any amount of time apart on any holiday.

I drank a bottle of water, trying to tamp down the uneasiness that gnawed at my belly, but it was not sated. I poured a bowl of cereal and ate it standing over the sink—*some Christmas dinner*. I finished quickly, washed my bowl, and added it to the dish drainer. I wandered into the living room, still sprinkled with bits of wrapping paper and wayward bows that had escaped the trash bag.

After I was done cleaning up, I brought our garbage to the curb. As I was turning to head up our short driveway, I noticed headlights coming towards me. I recognized Dean's car. I lingered in my spot, waiting for him. He met my eyes as he pulled in and did not break the stare as he turned off the engine and opened the door.

"I'm not going to apologize. I'm not losing you to this shit again. I can't do it." He said before I could say anything. "Besides, I am pretty damn sure sperm donations are confidential and finding out who received what from who is breaking the law. And baby girl, you're too pretty for prison."

He smiled then, the mischievous grin of much younger days. Days before marriage and mortgages. Before Sean. Before we ever knew the pain of living in a world where a perfect child, half me and half him, did not. Despite myself, the lowest part of my belly flickered, and heat rose from my center. *Damn it. Weak bitch,* I scolded myself. Dean immediately became attuned to my body's responses and started to smirk.

"Damn it. You know it's not fair when you use that look on me!" I teased.

"Hey, when you got it, you got it." He did a playful spin on his heels. "And no Viagra, baby!"

He wiggled his eyebrows, and I dissolved into laughter.

The laughter ignited the flickering flame of desire that he had already started. Suddenly, I was on fire for this man. It was like I was 20 years old again, literally craving his touch while his hands were still on me, crying out for him to make love to me again while he was still moving inside me. I wanted him all the time. I felt that strong pull to him now.

"Come on." I grabbed his hand and threw him what I hoped was a sultry look over my shoulder.

"Don't have to tell me twice," he mumbled and slapped my ass.

In the bedroom, his hot and fevered touches worked expertly to make me forget my yearning for any grandchildren that came from Sean. I surrendered as Dean created a delicious tension within me. I went over the edge. And then again. Dean followed soon after. We laid in each other's arms, my head on his bare chest. As his heart rate returned to normal and the sweat dried on our skin, Dean praised himself. "Not bad for an old guy."

"Not bad for any guy," I whispered, lifting my head and looking into his eyes. He kissed me long and deep.

"Round two?" He questioned.

"Oh my, it really is Christmas!" I joked.

"Now, that's just about enough of that, Mrs. Baxter!" His eyes twinkled. He covered my mouth with his.

The second time was slow and sensual. We made love instead of the feverish coupling of the first time. We finished together, whispering each other's names. When he pulled his head away from my shoulder and looked at me, I saw the tears.

"Oh, my love," I murmured, using my thumb to trace the salty trails. "It's okay."

"I'll be damned if I don't want it so much, Rae." He buried his head back into my shoulder and sobbed. "But I need you more than grandbabies—even more than I need Sean. I've lived without him this long. It's terrible, but I can do it. But I'm not sure I can live without you. You're the only damn thing that makes sense. I can't bear to watch you lose him again, lose yourself again when this test comes back when no more babies are waiting for you to love them. When Sean is really and truly gone."

"Look at me." I tugged his hair, starting to go salt and pepper, and lifted his head from my shoulder. "I'm not going anywhere. And the test will show us what I already know- that there are more kids out there for us to love. Sean's story isn't complete yet. I have felt that ever since he died. But now, I feel like this was the thing that was missing. This was Sean's legacy. He sent these babies, wherever they are, to us."

"How do you do that?" Dean asked, smiling.

"Do what?"

"Make me love you more and more every time you open your mouth."

"I'm just *that* good, sir."

"Well, I like it. And baby, however this all turns out, we are in this together. Every step of the way. I love you."

"I love you too. Now go to sleep."

Dean was asleep in under a minute. How he managed to fall asleep so quickly always astounded me. It took practically an act of God or a plain miracle for me to fall asleep, even before Sean died. Now, I slept so little and spent a lot of time roaming our house at night.

When Sean had first died, I sat in his desk chair for three days straight, not talking, eating, or drinking. Dean had taken me directly to a hospital where I was held on the psychiatric floor for 72 days. I slept heavy, sedated sleep. I cried. I wailed. I talked. I came home with a prescription for antidepressants and a referral to a therapist. Dean had packed Sean's whole room up while I was away, his belongings in neatly labeled boxes in the garage and attic. He had painted over the burgundy Sean had lobbied for and about which I caved almost instantly, never able to deny him anything.

He had turned the space into an office. I had begged for an office space for years. If it had been anywhere else in the house, I would have jumped for joy.

Instead, I curled into the fetal position in the center of the carpet and sobbed.

Dean had been patient and caring. He bathed me when the depression overtook me, and I laid in bed for days. He fed me. He cleaned. He went to work and paid the bills. All while working through his silent grief about losing Sean. And slowly, the intensity of his love healed me. He didn't make me not coming back to him an option, and so I came back.

When I emerged in the kitchen showered and clothed in regular clothes, Dean's smile lit up the room. That was the only indication of how he felt.

And every day since that one has gotten better. Most days were bearable if I kept busy. And now, I knew just how to fill that time.

The following day, Dean greeted me with a steaming mug of tea.

"Thank you for the lovely Christmas."

His eyes sparkled over the rim of his own mug.

"Likewise, sir."

"But Rae, you can't screw me to distract me. You also cannot try to find out people's private medical information if this test even comes back with anything. Leave it alone. Please. I'm begging you."

"I can't make that promise," I said.

"You can, and you will. We can't keep ripping the wound open." His voice was thick. "We have to stop bleeding, Rae, or we'll die."

Test processing was slower due to people taking time off for the holidays. Waiting was nearly impossible. It had only been a few days. How was I expected to wait an entire week, possibly more? I wanted to text Rebecca, but she hadn't replied to my last text. Should I call the testing center office? A text from Patti filled my screen.

Coming over with lunch. Do you also need me to bring wine?

I typed back, **This is more a vodka day, and we have plenty.**

Ok, on my way.

As I was still reading the text, my door burst open, and Patti came in, a cloud of chaos and noise as usual.

"I made a new pasta salad recipe. I don't know if it's good, so you're my guinea pig. I also brought the one I know we like, in case it sucks."

She shook a Tupperware container in each hand vigorously.

"Always glad to be your test subject. Cranberry vodka?" I asked.

"Oh dear, we're at that stage in the game already. But also, yes, please." She said.

"I just have so much on my mind, Pat. This test can't come back soon enough."

Patti paused almost imperceptibly as she spooned our two plates of pasta salad.

"I know you're anxious for them. It will be good to know once and for all. Give you the final closure to move on to the next chapter."

Her tone was measured and guarded, two things she rarely ever was. Patti was honest to a fault. Not rudely, just confident and comfortable with herself and being an opposing voice. As a result, it just plain didn't occur to her to change her tone. Knowing this and hearing how much concern was in her voice made me uneasy.

"You don't think the test will prove me right either?"

My tone was nasty, accusatory, but I couldn't curb it.

"Honey, I would love nothing more than for that test to give you the answer you need. Hell, the one you deserve. But you need to prepare yourself for the very real possibility that you won't get it. Dean and I— "

"Dean and I? Were you talking about me with my husband behind my back? Terrific! Just wonderful. Why were you alone with Dean?"

My temper, a trait born into me by my hot-blooded mother, my worst trait, a hellfire that had burned my world down around me more than once, flared. I saw a flash of red, then black. The words tumbled out, reckless and heavy.

"Are you fucking my husband?"

Patti's fork froze mid-air as she glared at me. When she finally spoke, her words were carefully chosen.

"Rae Baxter, I have loved you like a sister for most of my life. It's for that reason alone that I didn't just haul off and deck you. But you have lost your goddamn mind if you thought I would EVER violate our friendship and take up with your husband. You know me better than that. And as you also well know, your husband has only had eyes for you since he was a boy. Dean came to me because he is worried to death about you and wants to know how he can help you."

The logical part of me knew that Dean would seek out Patti's counsel as my oldest friend to try and save me. He had done it a few times when Sean died. But the part of me that wanted to hurt someone, anyone, as much as I was, was still overpowering me.

I felt like I was outside of my body when I snarled, "And I bet you were all too happy to talk about his crazy wife and how terrible I am. I bet you were happy to comfort him. Did he like that lingerie you got a few weeks ago when we were shopping? Was he your date?"

"You know what, I'm not going to sit here and be accused of shit I didn't do. I know you're upset. But that doesn't give you the right to treat me like crap. I'm outta here. Call me when you find Rae, the woman who knows I would never touch her husband.

Who knows what a friend I have been. I was there to hold you up when Sean died. I don't know who the hell you are right now, but I don't like her."

The door slammed behind her, and all I could do was stare into my plate of pasta salad.

REBECCA

Is it over yet? That was the first thought that sprang to mind as I came into alertness. The lumpy mattress had my back objecting in pain. It had been a long few days, and a few more loomed on the horizon. Hell Week was almost behind us, my once-a-year obligation fulfilled.

I looked around my mother's guest bedroom. It was the room in her house that least reflected her personality or lack thereof. This room was also the least used, so it had been neglected in the major overhaul Bernie had done when she moved into her condo right on the beach.

The rest of the house was covered in tones of greys and whites. Very neutral and bland, just like my mother, who only had a mind for lunches and spa dates, fast cars, and men with fat wallets. She wasn't particularly well educated, but she was well-bred. And for her, that meant never having a genuine opinion or feelings about anything and making sure to be the dutiful, accommodating wife, mother, and host at all times.

My father's death about 15 years ago had catapulted her into a mid-life crisis of sorts. She spent a hefty chunk of his insurance on cosmetic procedures. She had procured the whole catalog: a breast lift and augmentation, Botox and other fillers in every inch of her face, a facelift, her ears pinned and her eyes un-hooded, head to toe liposuction, and even a damn butt lift. When she had come home from the hospital, swathed in bandages like a mummy loose from the tombs, I had been tasked with caring for her.

I was forced to miss a road trip with my only two childhood friends. I took a part-time job at TJ Maxx and worked after school and weekends for a year to save up for it. My mother hadn't paid any attention or care when booking her surgery. Nor did she entertain the idea of asking my Aunt Cami to fly in from Connecticut, where they had grown up in a sprawling estate with manicured lawns, to nurse her.

"Of course, you'll do it! I'm your MOTHER!" She widened her eyes and waved her hand around as hot tears spotted my thighs as I begged her to reschedule or ask someone else to help.

That trip was the first time I had asked for independence. It was our last summer before life became too busy and big for all of us to see each other regularly. We had made so many plans. And she had taken it all away, for what, a fucking facelift? So, she could snag a man to replace my father?

Thinking back, even now, years later, hot anger rose in my throat. I shrugged it off and sat up. My eyes were drawn to the most un-Bernie-like part of her condo. I loved it almost exclusively for that reason.

A giant mural of the dining room scene in Beauty and the Beast where they sing "Be Our Guest" spanned the entire wall. Those very words were sprawled across the top of the mural in an elegant font. The cast of characters, cutlery, and vivid splashes of color filled the rest of the space.

"A must-have for any Florida home!" The realtor had trilled at closing.

"A garish monstrosity," my mother had mumbled under her breath.

Dustin loved it and spent most of the time when we visited with his cheek pressed to the wall, his arm stretched over his head with his palm resting flatly on Mrs. Potts.

For the moment, Mrs. Potts lay exposed as Dustin was still sleeping soundly next to me. I stood up slowly, so I didn't disturb him and padded into the en suite bathroom. I kept the door open a crack so I could hear him if he stirred. I didn't need to, though, because I enjoyed a long, hot shower for the first time in a long time. Dustin woke up as I was finishing my hair.

Breakfast at Bernie's was never a dress-down affair, mainly because you were highly likely to encounter a male visitor at the table and "A lady is never caught unawares,"

Bernie had drilled into my head since birth. A lady probably also doesn't have a bedroom with as much traffic as an international airport, but I guess that was beside the point.

I changed Dustin's diaper, got him dressed, and headed out to the dining room. My mother looked up from her phone, which she was scrolling through enthusiastically, her long, baby pink acrylic nails tapping away.

"Oh, look who decided to wake up!" She teased.

"Mom, we're on vacation. I work 60 hours a week. I can sleep a little. And it's only 8 am, not noon." I snapped.

My mother held her hands up.

"So defensive! It's just a beautiful day. Shame to not get out and enjoy it before you have to leave."

For once, I didn't have a snide comment in me. Mom was right. It was sunny and warm—perfect weather to swim and enjoy making some memories with my son. Savoring every moment with him had been nagging on my mind more and more since the day at Logan. The test was probably sitting in my mailbox, and our whole lives could be in freefall. All the bricks could be tumbling down right now, and I wasn't even aware yet. I gulped and pasted a smile on my face.

"You know what, Mom. You're right. Do you want to come to the pool with us?"

My mom looked surprised, as surprised as one can get with a face full of fillers. Her voice became softer, less shrill.

"That would be lovely." She sounded touched by the invitation.

We finished a quick breakfast, and I began to get Dustin ready. As I wrestled him into a swim diaper and his trunks and slathered him with sunscreen, my mom packed a small cooler: fresh fruit salad leftover from breakfast, tuna sandwiches on white bread, chips, and some jellybeans as a special treat for Dustin. I also noticed her placing a large thermos of juice and one of what I suspected was spiked lemonade in the cooler. Her domesticity and sudden awareness for others were off-putting, but I ignored it. I had never once seen her pack a picnic, just simply order whatever cook we had at the moment "to whip up a little something."

"Is that what you're wearing?" My mom asked as I burst into the kitchen hot on the heels of Dustin.

"Slow down, please!" I called breathlessly. "Yes, why? Don't you like it? I bought it because I thought you would." I looked down at the striped high waisted bikini I had ordered online.

"I was just going to say I liked it. It's very complimentary. You look lovely." She smiled, a sincere smile that she did not often do.

"Thanks. I like it too. And on that note, are there any cute, single men into overworked single moms in this complex? Maybe we can find me a love affair!" I popped one hip out playfully.

I saw her face light up. She smiled the genuine smile again, as much as the fillers would allow. "That's the spirit! Do you want me to set you up on Tinder?" She started tapping away on her phone. She looked up over the top of her screen.

"Are you keeping it right and tight?" She asked seriously.

I burst into laughter. Was my mother really asking me whether I was keeping up with my Kegels?

"What? I've been told- repeatedly- that tightness matters. Just like size."

At that, I blushed and shushed her. "Real nice talk for a grandmother," I teased.

She pulled a face and adjusted her giant straw hat, slinging the cooler over her shoulder. I grabbed the bag I had packed with and held Dustin's hand. We spent the day at the pool, laughing and splashing. My mother ducked out early, having made a Tinder match by the pool earlier in the day. They were meeting for drinks.

We were just getting home as she headed out. She glowed, her dark tan accented by her form-fitting white dress, baby pink pedicure, and hot pink sandals. Her hair was piled high, with some soft curls falling. She looked innocent and seductive all at the same time.

"You look like a million bucks, Mama. Have a great time. I'm getting this boy in bed." I motioned to Dustin, fast asleep and sweaty from the sun on my shoulder.

When he settled in next to me, smelling like sunshine and soap, I curled up with my book. I couldn't concentrate, though. My mind kept drifting to what a pleasant visit this had been so far. My mother was acting like the mother I had always wanted. She hadn't criticized my weight or my lack of a boyfriend. She hadn't made a dig at me getting accidentally pregnant and raising a baby alone. It was highly suspicious. I lay there for a few minutes more, trying to read, unsuccessfully. Unease nagged at me. I couldn't shrug it off, so I headed to the couch to watch old reruns of Full House without disrupting Dustin. As I headed out into the living room, the door opened.

"Just drinks, my ass, Mom!"

I laughed but suddenly stopped when I saw her slumped against the wall, her hand on her chest, and her face glistening with sweat. The loose curls she had pulled out of her up-do were plastered to her head. She was panting. She looked up at me, fear in her eyes. Before she could say anything, she came to alertness and dashed to the bathroom, where I heard her vomiting.

" Mom, you ok?"

My heart throbbed in my throat. Maybe she just had too much to drink. The door opened a crack. I peered through to see Mom sitting on the floor hugging the toilet. Her makeup has run, and her hair was a mess. Her white dress had a small splatter of vomit on it. She looked vulnerable and frail, two things she had never been in all my life. I sat down on the edge of the tub and rubbed her back.

"I'm sick, Bec." She rested her head on my knee and looked up at me through thick false eyelashes.

"It's ok. You probably just drank too much. It happens."

"No, baby. I'm SICK." She paused and visibly shuddered. "I have cancer. I've been doing chemo. That's where I was yesterday."

My whole body flashed hot and cold. I felt dizzy. Now, I gripped the toilet for balance.

"Mom, what are you talking about?"

Panic and fear made hard edges in my voice.

"I found out about two months ago. It's in my ovaries, and it's a bit more advanced than they are comfortable with, so I am doing chemo and radiation. They wanted to do a hysterectomy, but I won't allow it. I would go straight into menopause."

"Jesus, Mom. You're almost there anyway. This is your life!"

"The dryness, Rebecca! I'm on the scene!"

Her dismayed expression generated a fit of laughter in me. *She has cancer, but really, the priority is some vaginal dryness.* She remained shocked as I laughed and laughed. Then, as suddenly as I began laughing, I was sobbing, curled into the fetal position on the rug, my head in my mom's lap.

She let me cry for a while. When I was calm, we settled on the couches, and I brewed some tea. We talked until almost dawn about her diagnosis. She had underplayed the severity of the situation. Her prognosis was bleak, even with chemo, radiation, and a hysterectomy. There were more tears, some yelling, and some late-night phone calls to her oncologist.

By the time Dustin rose in the morning, I had decided to postpone our trip home for a few weeks while Mom had a hysterectomy. This time, I didn't mind being her caretaker. I called Megan, and she fretted for a full five minutes before transferring me to HR to start my leave paperwork.

The next few days were a chaotic blur. Bernie's surgery was scheduled for the new year, which she took as good luck, a big believer in the "New Year, New You!" credo. It may be cancer surgery, but it was a kind of transformation, and she was grasping onto it, damn it. When it wasn't Bernie or Dustin or the doctor's office, I was trying to answer or delegate my boss's emails and increasingly frantic calls and messages. With each passing moment, my body hummed louder and louder, using physical energy to fuel the anxiety pulsing through me relentlessly about Bernie and always Rae and Dean, their presence an undetonated bomb in the corner waiting to blow my life to pieces.

One afternoon I found myself bathed in silence after a long, exhaustive phone call with Megan. Immediately suspicious, I checked the living room. Mom and Dustin lay curled together, a Ying and yang of her light hair against his dark curls. Impulsively, I decided a dip in the pool would be just the way to end this day. I was floating in the water, nearly asleep in the hot sun, when my phone trilled.

I floated over to the side of the pool and reached for it. It was an email from the DNA testing facility. My heart stopped and dropped into my stomach. I swallowed thickly and clicked it, willing it to deliver a zero-probability match.

Your testing results are available. Please make an account and sign in to your patient portal to view your results in a secure browser. Thank you.

Jesus Christ, can nothing be simple? I hadn't even remembered providing my email to get electronic results. I decided to enjoy the rest of my scarce alone time. After Dustin went to bed, I would check. No rush. *Coward,* my inner voice challenged.

When I got back, the pair were still asleep on the couch. Dustin stirred as I heated leftovers and worked up the nerve to check the results. He slid out from Mom's grasp and padded over wordlessly. Still half asleep, his curls were matted on one side. He reached out to me, and I swung him up on my hip.

He was increasingly independent and resisted being picked up most of the time now, so I leaned into him, soothed by his warmth and heft. He snuggled into me, pushing the curve of his chin into my neck. He sighed and dozed on my shoulder. I shoved my phone into my pocket, took my pizza in one hand, and maneuvered us into the bedroom.

Dustin lolled back against the pillows when I laid him down, rolling to one side of the bed leisurely. I crawled into the other, eating my pizza while texting Kieran.

I tried to convince him I didn't need him to come to save us and take us back to Boston. I reassured him that for the first time in a long time, maybe ever, things with my mom were great. Sadly, it took cancer to soften the hard edges of her. I liked this version of her.

I decided to take a shower to get all the chlorine off. *Or avoid checking the results,* that bitch of an inner voice chimed in. As I was running the water, my phone emitted a beep, indicating a text message.

" Can you believe it? I knew it all along. I know you have a lot of adjusting to do, but we would love to see Dustin as soon as possible."

I became immobilized with anxiety and fear. Rae's texts came one after another. I didn't look at any of them. I just sat on the rug and let the anxiety wash over as the water ran cold beside me.

RAE

It was a cloudless but bitingly cold afternoon almost two weeks after our cheek swabs. Time seemed to be at a standstill, not only from the winter doldrums that come from an oppressive cold but from living a life suspended- before the test results and after.

The holidays had come and gone, leaving either the promise of a new year and its new beginnings or the emptiness of another year being a parent with no child. Finally, one day, I reached into the mailbox, and there it was: a letter from the DNA testing center. My breath hitched in my chest, and I felt dizzy.

"Dean! Dean!" I shouted, running into the house.

"Jesus, Rae. Your yelling could wake the dead. What are— "

He stopped short when he saw the envelope in my hand. "Did we finally hit the Publisher's Clearinghouse?"

"Even better. It's the DNA results."

Quiet but insistent, he held out his hand and said, "Give it to me, Rae."

I relinquished the envelope, knowing he wanted to know first if it was bad news so he could pad the blow for me. My protector.

The battering ram to every storm that tried to fell me. He opened it slowly. I wanted to rip it out of his hands and tear into it, but I restrained myself.

He read silently. "I'll be a son of a bitch." He whispered. Tears pooled in his beard. "I should know better than to doubt you, Rae. 99.9% match."

He paused for a few minutes, rereading the letter. Then he ran a single fingertip over the paper.

"Sean." He whispered, like a fervent prayer.

I was frozen. Fireworks were going off inside me, but I couldn't speak. My vision grew tunneled, then black.

"Rae! Breathe baby! Breathe! Here, sit." A chair materialized at the back of my knees, and I sat without thinking.

I sat, Dean buzzing and flitting around me like a moth next to a lightbulb. I tried to breathe, but my entire body felt like it was in an ever-tightening vice.

Finally, after what seemed like forever, I felt my lungs relax and then fill. My body unknotted. I felt myself coming back into consciousness.

I was right. Sean has a child. I was right; it repeated in my head in a loop. All I could think was that I wanted to meet my grandson. Right now. It seemed as urgent a need as breathing, as water, as food.

"Holy shit," I mumbled, fully back in my body.

"I'll say. I can't believe this, Rae. It makes no sense at all, but it's true. We have a grandson." His voice broke a little.

"I have to call Rebecca. We must see Dustin right away. The sooner, the better."

"Whoa, whoa. Slow down, my love. The first thing you need to do is apologize to Patti. You know damn well she didn't deserve being accused and treated that way. And you surely know you have been and always be the only woman for me."

My cheeks flamed instantly. I hadn't really thought Patti would just shut up and let me abuse her, but I hadn't banked on her telling Dean, or at least not so quickly.

"I really was a jerk, huh? I was so anxious, so scared, waiting for these tests. I wanted someone to hurt like I was- like I have been for years."

"But still- "

I held up my hand and cut him off. "It's no excuse for treating people like shit. Now, excuse me while I go mend a fence."

I held out my hand, where he placed the letter, delicately and carefully. I opened a drawer, tucked a white dish towel under my arm, grabbed a bottle of tequila from the pantry, and was out the door without another word. Patti's car was in the driveway, and judging from the light on upstairs, her daughter Olivia was home too.

I went around to the side door, off the kitchen, the one only family used. I heard sounds of cooking within, but they stopped when I knocked. I opened the door a sliver and stuck the white towel through with my hand, and waved it around.

"Truce! Don't shoot! Truce!"

Patti's big laugh started almost immediately. "Get in here. What took you so long?"

I breathed a sigh of relief and opened the door fully.

"I am the worst friend ever, Pat. I am so sorry. You should never talk to me again, but I hope you will because I have news."

Patti's big smile and joking demeanor instantly changed.

"News news?"

"Yes. Pat- it's a match. He's Sean's son."

And at those words, in the safety of my best friend, my chosen sister, I crumbled. I went to my knees. Patti fell to hers too and caught me before I hit the floor. Our tears mingled together. I smoothed the letter out, and we read it over and over again, our heads together until we memorized it word for word. We alternated between laughing in wonder at the miracle and crying for Sean. The meal on the stovetop had long scorched, due in part to the celebratory tequila shots we had downed every few minutes when the news struck us dumb once again.

"Mom! What's for dinn— "Liv burst in. "Uh oh, looks like we're having pizza."

"Sorry, Liv. I distracted your mom and ruined your dinner. But we're celebrating. I'll text Uncle Dean and order the pizza, and we can all eat here together."

"So, you and Mom aren't fighting anymore? Thank goodness. I need your opinion on prom dresses. You know Mom has the sense of style of the mom in Rugrats who wore a sweatband 24/7."

"I beg your— "Patti tried to object, but I placed a finger over her lips to silence her.

"I would love to, sweetie. What kind of pizza are we in the mood for?"

"Hmm, how about pepperoni and pineapple? What are we celebrating anyway?"

"Pepperoni and pineapple? Ok, if you say so. You're eating it, not me. And Uncle Dean and I got some good news today."

I looked at Patti to see if she wanted me to try and explain this complicated situation to her daughter. She shrugged, indicating it was up to me.

"Well, it's kind of crazy, but we found out that Sean has a baby."

Her eyebrows shut up. "Whoa! Wasn't he, like, really young to have a baby? Who is the mom? Who is it? How did you find out?"

"He didn't have the baby when he was alive. He donated sperm, and someone used it. I saw the baby's picture at Cami's house and just knew they were related. So, your mother and I tracked down the girl, and we did a DNA test which came back today."

You could see her brain working, trying to process something so huge and unbelievable.

"Honey, us adults don't even understand this situation, so it's okay if you can't wrap your brain around it." I soothed her.

"No, I mean, it's weird that he donated sperm. But how cool that you guys get to have a grandkid now. And he looks like Sean." Color rose on her cheeks, and she struggled to hold back tears. The kids had grown up like brother and sister. For Olivia, losing Sean had been like losing her sibling. She had been inconsolable for weeks after his death and still had photos in tribute to him on her walls.

She cleared her throat and said, "I am so happy for you guys. When do we get to meet him? Is he going to come here? What's his mom like?"

"Hold on, girl, I will answer all your questions. But first, let's get your uncle over here and get this pizza on the way."

The four of us spent hours around the kitchen table, eating and talking. The adults all drank more tequila, blurring the edges of all the feelings the results brought. Liv brought out a deck of cards, and we started playing card games. Soon, we started remembering all the nights we had spent with Sean at one table or the other playing cards. All the kids' memories tumbled out, each of us one-upping each other. Laughter filled the house. Soon, it was the middle of the night.

"Ugh, it's 2 am!" Liv said, examining her phone screen.

"Ok, ok ladies, let's pack it in. Thank you for the hospitality. We're outta here. Unless you need help cleaning up?" Dean stood and wobbled, the tequila making him a little unsteady.

"No, we used paper. Just toss it." Patti hiccupped. "I can barely keep my eyes open. Rae, I'm glad you came to your senses. Congrats again, guys. We'll see you tomorrow."

"Good night!" I sang, floaty and loose-limbed from the liquor.

As we crossed the street, the light from a streetlight caught Dean's face. He was still the most gorgeous man I had laid eyes on (except for maybe Sam Elliott, but who didn't love Sam Elliott?) Overcome with emotion, a good dose of tequila, and hormones, I grabbed his face and kissed him hard.

"Do you know how much I love you?" I said breathlessly, the freezing air making my breath show in filmy clouds.

"I have an inkling. Most gorgeous grandma I ever did see!" He said, grabbing my face and kissing me back even more deeply than I had him.

Our kiss turned into a mutual shiver, our teeth clanking together. We pulled apart, laughing, and made our way across the slick street to our house.

The next morning, I rose with a thumping head and a filmy tongue. The sun was much too bright through the windows, but I couldn't bear to move to shut the curtains. I rooted around with one arm in my nightstand. I was trying not to move so that nausea would stay at bay, but I needed the eye mask I thought was in there.

79

As I was attempting to sit up, with great effort, Dean came into the room with a tray. The tray was laden with all my breakfast favorites- coffee with real sugar and cream, fruit salad, French toast, and bacon, and filled to nearly overflowing. There was even a vase with a single rose. Under his arm was tucked a bottle of water.

He sat the tray down in front of me, handed me the water bottle, and fished into his robe pocket. He produced a bottle of Advil. I could have cried, anticipating the relief from my banging head.

I held out my hands like a child wanting to be picked up.

" Ooh, gimme, gimme!"

"I figured you are feeling about the same as me. Every time I drink tequila, I am reminded I am not 20 anymore."

"Oh yes, definitely not 20. Could you close those curtains, please?"

"Oh, someone really tied one on." He teased as he moved to pull the fabric closed.

"Watch it, Grandpa!"

At that word, Dean stilled.

"Wow. We have a grandchild. I'm a grandpa."

He looked at me.

"I had made as much peace as you can with not being a grandpa."

"Well, my love, you don't have to make peace. Our son sent us a gift. I have to get in touch with Rebecca. I'm sure she must have the results by now."

I grabbed my phone off the nightstand. I was surprised to see I had texted her in an alcohol-induced haze last night about the results. I was relieved to see I didn't seem drunk in the texts. That would be an excellent impression for Rebecca of her son's grandmother.

I noticed she hadn't texted me back. I was conflicted. I wanted to meet Dustin. In fact, I was desperate to. But I didn't want to overstep or do anything that could spook Rebecca. After all, she had a lot to lose.

I sighed, not content with doing nothing. I laid back on the pillows and finished my breakfast. I was watching an old Golden Girls rerun and scrolling through my phone aimlessly when a message filled the screen.

ARE YOU ALIVE? BECAUSE I BARELY AM. WHY DO YOU MAKE ME DRINK TEQUILA?

MY HUSBAND MADE ME BREAKFAST IN BED AND BROUGHT ME ADVIL. I CAN STILL BARELY MOVE. WE'RE OLD AS HELL.

I'M COMING OVER. I HAVE SOMETHING FOR YOU.

Not even five minutes later, I heard my door open and footsteps trudging up the stairs. The door opened, and a flood of blue balloons burst through the door, followed by Patti quickly. Light blue confetti sprayed across the room as she twisted a paper tube. I couldn't even be irritated at the mess. All I could do was laugh.

"What's all this?"

"This, my dear, is an impromptu baby shower. Liv dragged my ass out of bed to pull off way too early and when I was way too hungover."

"We even have a cake!" Liv followed hot on her mother's heels, a sheet cake spread across her forearms. The blue icing read, "Congratulations, Grandma and Grandpa." A blue gift bag dangled off her elbow.

"Oh, my goodness! Liv! Dean, grab that cake before she drops it!" Dean quickly swooped under her arms as he joined us for the celebration. As soon as her arms were free, she pounced onto my bed, just as she and Sean had done so many mornings before.

"Here! Open it!" She thrust the gift bag towards me.

I opened it, my eyes filling at the sweet gesture. Inside was a pair of jeans. Next were tiny bundles of socks. A book. The last two items made all of us fall silent.

In the bottom of the bag, folded over a box, was a tiny black tee shirt. The shirt was a mini replica of one of Sean's shirts, a simple Ramones band tee-shirt he wore almost daily. He had loved music and had amassed quite a collection of band tee shirts, both from shows he had gone to but also from vintage shops and online. He never wore anything else. But this particular design, the one in my hand, was practically his signature look if men can have such a thing.

Once, a teacher had snarled at him, "I'd like to see what you even know about the Ramones, kid." He had leveled the man and earned detention for disrupting class with his extensive and creepily detailed knowledge about the group.

"Mom. I'm the son of an old punker. I was practically listening to them as lullabies."

Dean would always chime in, "I got news for you. You WERE listening to them as lullabies."

I looked to Dean out of the corner of my eye, with my head down, not wanting Liv to see. He had set the cake on the dresser next to him and was dabbing the tears that flowed freely down his face. I reached into the bag and pulled out the box. As soon as I saw the logo, my stomach dropped, and my throat thickened.

"Converse?" I choked out.

I opened the box, all of us crying together, and saw the tiny black high tops in the paper. I cried with abandon, crushing Liv with a hug, falling back into my pillows.

In my head, I heard Sean. He had always taken a lot of heat from kids at school for wearing his beloved Converse since they weren't "cool."

"You know what? Screw them! I like them! What's not to like? Colorful- check! Comfortable- check! And what other criteria do you need in shoe wear? Give me Verse or give me death! When I am a father, my kid's having a whole closet of these suckers, just like his old man!"

"Just like his old man," Liv whispered into my ear as we lay cuddled together in the pillows. I felt her tears slide onto my cheeks and squeezed her again, hard and long.

"Ohh, what would I do without you? Oh, my girl! Thank you so much. You're the best. Thank you for starting the collection! Sean would very much approve!"

She turned shy all of a sudden. "I miss him a lot," she mumbled.

"We all do, baby," Patti said, moving onto the bed and hugging her. "Now, let's go eat some cake and figure out when we can get that boy here to wear his new Converse."

"Sounds like a plan to me!" Dean said, picking the cake back up and leading the parade down the stairs.

I brought the rear, but before I did, I tapped out a quick text to Rebecca. It was time to meet Dustin.

I was in the kitchen finishing dinner when a knock sounded at the back door. Olivia's head appeared in the window. I motioned her in.

"Hey there, girlie! Come in, sit down! What are you up to?" I asked. "Are you ready to talk prom dresses?"

"No. I have something to tell you."

Olivia didn't meet my eyes. My stomach lurched. Instantly, my mind flicked through a catalog of scenarios, each worse than the next. Drugs? Eating disorder? Pregnancy?

I took a deep breath. A baby wasn't the end of the world. At least at first, Patti would think it was, but I would be here for them both. Instinctively, I reached out and covered Olivia's hand with my own.

She took a deep breath as well. I let her work up her nerve in her own time, staying quiet. Finally, she spoke.

"Do you know Chad?" She asked.

"Sean's roommate?" I asked.

Chad and Sean had been matched to room together through the university. When we saw them standing next to each other for the first time, the stark contrast in their appearances was evident.

Sean was tall and thin, all angles and energy, with dark curls falling into his eyes perpetually. Chad was a compact ball of muscle, a bulldog of a boy, almost as wide as he was tall. He had a shock of red hair cut into a spiky crew cut and a wide grin that made him resemble the Mad Magazine cartoon cover boy. He was a football player for the university who had been the star of his high school team.

"It's like the nursery rhyme. Jack Sprat could eat no fat, but his wife could eat no lean." Chad's father, Kevin, a good ole boy from Texas raising his son alone after his wife's death, drawled, laughing uproariously.

The last time I had seen or spoken to either Chad or Kevin was the day of Sean's funeral. They had arrived in black suits with matching, red-rimmed eyes.

Kevin was clutching Chad's hand tightly. It was as though if he let go of his child's hand, Chad would disappear into a puff of purple smoke, dancing away from Kevin's fingertips then gone. They had both given me bone-crushing hugs, making me feel alive for the only time that day.

Olivia broke into my thoughts.

"Huh? Sorry, sweetie. I got lost in my head for a minute." I said.

"Did Chad do something to you?" I asked, horrified. "Olivia, I can't help unless you tell me."

"As if he would sleep with me." She mumbled, tightening her ponytail aggressively.

I realized that Olivia had liked Chad. Something had happened, but I wasn't sure what. I fixed my gaze at Olivia, hoping I looked understanding instead of judgmental.

"This isn't about me and Chad." She snapped.

"Are you sure?" I prodded gently.

Anger danced across her face, but it was gone as quickly as it appeared.

"If you must know, he was the first person I ever gave...you know...." She trailed off, but her hand worked near her mouth pantomiming oral sex." When it was done...."

She stopped and blinked back tears. *I'll murder that meathead,* I thought.

"And when it was done, he patted me on the back and said...."

"Said what?" I asked, my temper already flaring.

"Th-thanks, pal!" She finished, her voice wobbly. "It was humiliating."

"Liv, I'm sorry. That must have made you feel terrible. Did this happen the weekend you went to visit Sean?"

She nodded. Patti had fretted the whole weekend about Olivia going on that trip. She was sure she was getting gang-banged in a frat house basement. A blowjob seemed innocent in comparison.

"But anyway, that's not the point." She recovered, back on her agenda.

I almost smiled because she resembled her strong, no-nonsense mother at the moment, a comparison they would both roll their eyes at.

"I sent him a message and told him about Dustin. I wanted to know if he knew Sean had donated sperm and why."

My anger evaporated almost instantly, replaced by curiosity. I leaned forward, hungry for this new insight into a part of my son's story that I would never truly know the words to.

"What did he say?" I asked.

She pulled a face as she answered.

"Those idiots both donated. It was fifty bucks for every donation, so they donated when they had dates or needed things."

"Things like what? Was Sean doing drugs?" I was simultaneously devastated and pissed at my son and his stupidity.

"No, nothing like that. Beer money, Auntie." She pulled another face and shook her head. "Condoms. That's it. Maybe pot. But you can't even get mad at that. You and Mom and Uncle Dean all smoke it."

My eyes widened in horror, not at the accusation, but that Liv knew what was in the vape pen we all passed around from time to time. She smiled, pleased at having caught us in the act.

"Okay, little girl. That's enough of that." I joked. "You didn't have to talk to stupid Chad, you know, but I am happy you did."

"Yeah, he said Sean knew you would send him money if he asked, but he didn't want to burden you guys. He was just trying to help."

I smiled, knowing that he had helped me by donating his sperm without Sean ever planning to. His sperm had created Dustin, who would carry his father in his body forever. Then he would pass it down to his children and them to theirs and so on, Sean never truly forgotten.

"He did help. His donation made Dustin, and I can't imagine anything more helpful to help me with missing Sean."

"Life is nuts, huh?" She said. "The thought of him doing that didn't make sense to me. But when Chad explained it, I got it. There's no one Sean loved more than you guys. And it looks like

Fate knew better than everyone what was going to happen and how to help you through it." She paused, a bit emotional, then whispered incredulously, "I can't believe I just told you that story."

She put her head in her hands, her hair over her face, and shook her head back and forth.

"He just got me mad all over again talking to him. Just thinking about it…." She stopped, then looked at me and smiled her beautiful smile. "I should have bit it off when I had a chance."

I threw my head back and cackled.

"You truly are your mother's daughter!" I sputtered out, wiping away tears of laughter.

REBECCA

"Mamaaaaaaaa! Maaaaaaaammmmmmaaaaaaa!" Dustin trilled, trying to sing me awake.

I didn't need the wake-up call. I had been up all night, staring at the ceiling, trying to decide what the hell I was going to do now. Dustin was Sean's son. Rae and Dean wanted to see their grandson- badly- and my secret would be exposed.

The timing couldn't be any worse. Every day, a little more of my mother's spark went out. I feared the end was coming soon despite her reassurances to the contrary. Could I let her go to her grave thinking her daughter was still just a drunken slut and not a loser? Or did she deserve the truth, as she had given me? My thoughts had raced all night, playing out so many scenarios and never settling on one. It was an impossible situation created entirely of my own design.

"Come here, bubby," I said, twisting to pull Dustin over to the front of me.

He curled into the front of me, his head right under my chin. His baby shampoo and little boy smell, mingled with sweat from sleeping and detergent, wafted to my nose. This smell was God in its purest form. His heart thumped under my arm. He was warm. Squirmy. Ready to get up and live.

Live a life Sean would never be able to, I thought for the millionth time. I wanted to give Rae and Dean back a piece of their son. They seemed so nice. Certainly, no one should have to face the loss of their child. *But what if they wanted to take Dustin away? What if they would remain a secret if I let them have some time with him? Is that bribery? Surely, Dustin has a right to know them too?* My mind swirled and swirled. I sighed. Clearly, I had made no more headway with this than when I was frozen on the floor of the bathroom with "sun poisoning," as I had told my mother. She had knocked long after midnight after seeing the light still on under the door.

I went through the rote motions of getting Dustin ready. Today was a chemo day. It was also my first time meeting Mom's doctors and nursing team in person. I needed to be present and clear-headed. I pushed the results to the back of my mind as best I could. I opened the door to the guest room, and Dustin bounced out, resembling a tiny tornado.

Mom was already in the kitchen, making coffee. She smiled as Dustin plowed into her legs. She winced slightly as she steadied herself on the counter.

"Oh Dus! Buddy, watch out for Grammy. She has an owie in her belly, and she's a little sore."

Dustin stopped moving and looked up at his grandma somberly. "I sowwy." He said.

"I'm just fine, sweet boy. Don't worry!" Bernie said, patting his upturned cheek. "How are you feeling, Bec? You looked pretty miserable last night. I was up late, worrying about you."

"Mom! Don't lose sleep over me! I'm fine! Feeling much better." I managed a weak smile.

"Well, as you well know, losing sleep over their children is a mother's lot in life. Are you wearing that to the doctor?"

She gestured to my pajamas.

"No, I was just going to ask you to feed him some oatmeal so I can get ready, and we can head out."

"Of course! Go ahead!" She shooed me away and grabbed a package of oatmeal out of her pantry.

I went back into the room, beelining for the bathroom. I felt nauseous and leaned over to vomit, but nothing would come. *This secret is poisoning you*, my inner voice inserted.

"Shut up!" I mumbled under my breath as I flipped the shower on.

I took a quick shower, then coiled my hair in a tee shirt and toweled off. I decided on a palm-printed romper some plus-sized influencer Kieran followed had designed, and he had insisted I needed. I added a calf-length white duster and a pair of flat espadrille sandals with straps the same color as the palm leaves.

I brushed my teeth, grabbed my bag and my sunglasses, and called out, "Let's hit it, gang!"

Mom and Dustin were all ready to go. We made a quick stop at the neighbor's house, who had offered to supervise her granddaughter as she babysat Dustin. The arrangement made me ache for Mia and Betty back home in our cozy Boston apartment building. Once he was content with a coloring book, some new crayons, and a juice box, we hit the road.

Mom began to wilt in the car. It was like she was recharging for her next performance for the nurses and doctors we would see today. I was the only one allowed to see her vulnerable. She slumped against the door, her what I affectionately called her "Mean Girls mom" velour tracksuit almost growing in size as she shrank into herself.

"I'm just going to close my eyes for a bit." She said sleepily. "Just follow the GPS. I already have the address programmed."

Before I could respond, she leaned her head against the window and was out. I listened to the radio, finding a 90's and 00's station that brought me back to my teen years. To no avail, I tried to lose myself in the saccharine sweet lyrics of pop songs and recapture the carefree existence of being 16. I couldn't block out the sirens going off in my head, blaring the news of the DNA test, of my mother dying, of my secret shame being found out.

I felt the familiar fingers of a panic attack start to grip me, but I fought it hard. A busy, strange highway with my cancer-filled mother in the car was not the time or place for this. I tried quickly to do a grounding exercise as best I could while navigating a vehicle and found that it worked. My breathing returned to normal as I was pulling into the hospital parking lot.

"Come on, Mom. Wake up. We have to go in. It's time for your appointment."

And just like that, my mother came alive before me. Her feet started tapping like they were generating the energy to propel her forward. She shook out her arms and rolled her neck. She went from asleep to fully awake, with a Stepford Wife smile on her face, in under 10 seconds.

"Let's get the show on the road!" She cooed.

"Oh, there she is!" I teased.

"Who?" She looked around, confused.

"The mother I knew my whole life. This new version of you is wonderful, but it's not the one I know. So, it's a little weird for me. This one is the "character" you played most of my life. I'm intimately familiar."

She paused and sighed. "I WAS playing a part for a long time. My whole life practically. Young ladies act like this. Women are expected to be that. Well, where did it get me? A daughter and grandson I barely know, no friends, no husband, and a body full of cancer. Being a good daughter and obedient wife and mother didn't get me shit. And I'm done playing by those rules. I am going to be the real me for whatever time I have left." She paused and looked directly into my eyes. "And that starts with us. I want to know you, Rebecca. I want to teach you things. I want to tell you things. I want to leave this earth knowing you and knowing that you know me. That you will share me with Dustin. With anyone and everyone who will listen. I don't want to leave and just be thought of as frivolous arm candy for rich, powerful men. I mean, that's nice." She fluffed her hair proudly. "But there is more to me. And I need you to know it all."

I placed a gentle hand on my mom's arm. "Don't worry. The very last thing anyone will do is forget Bernie Malone. I'll make sure of that." I paused. "And I can't wait to meet who you really are."

Mom wiped a tear away. "Enough, enough! I don't want my makeup smeared all over."

And with that, we linked arms and walked into the hospital.

The rest of the day was a head-spinning blur of medical talk that my Grey's Anatomy medical education had ill-prepared me for. The chemo was a quiet opportunity for my mother and me, a bubble of refuge bookended by chaos. We sat, as the medication was administered, talking. She started at the beginning- a childhood she never spoke of in all the years I had been alive. As she recalled story after story, I ached to tear my skeleton out of the closet, but I was still unsure if she could handle it.

She was uninhibited and passionate, vivacious and animated. Her words tumbled out as fast as the drugs dripped into her veins. My cold, stand-offish mother was transforming before my eyes. I was an enchanted girl watching a princess blossom into a queen.

After we finished getting her medication, we met with her oncologist. He was a tall, white-haired Ichabod Crane named Dr. Price. He was friendly and warm. He explained the severity of the situation with gentleness.

"It's advanced. I don't like to deal with numbers and stages because they can be misleading. What I will say is, we are in a fight for Bernie's life. That's not a secret to her or anyone else on her team. But we all believe in the power of positive thinking and have put on the gloves to fight. If you're ready to be on the team, we welcome you. If not, get back on that plane and let us help your mother."

"I am 100% on Team Bernie," I assured him. "Just tell me what I need to do."

"What you're doing right now is huge—being with her, supporting her, taking care of her. A lot of responsibility will be falling on you after the surgery. But you'll have some visiting nurses coming, and I want you to continue to reach out to my office if either of you starts to feel overwhelmed or anxious or anything out of the ordinary."

I was happy to hear how invested he seemed in helping my mother. We discussed her upcoming hysterectomy. I was trying to take notes, but my phone kept going off with text messages. A glance told me they were all from Rae. My heart was pounding. I couldn't deal with this right now. But I couldn't *not* deal with it either.

As we were leaving, Mom paused and whispered something urgently to the nurse ushering us out. Without a sound, she disappeared into a room and appeared with a basin. Mom vomited twice.

The nurse opened the bathroom, emptied the basin into the toilet, then cleaned and sterilized it. As she handed it back to Mom, she enveloped her in a firm hug. She pulled away, one hand on one shoulder as she fished a candy out of her pocket.

"Ginger candy will become your new best friend throughout this process. At least, it helps most patients. Or anything sour. Here, won't know till you try."

Mom popped it into her mouth. She paused for a few moments, then smiled. Her authentic smile, not the Botox-enhanced version most people received.

"Yes, that's a little bit better. Let's go! Thank you for everything."

When we got home, Mom was still not feeling well and wanted a nap. The neighbor's granddaughter took Dustin to the playground on the property while I made dinner. I decided on a ginger and broccoli stir fry with chicken. I had read that protein-rich food could help combat nausea from chemo.

As the recipe simmered, I decided to scroll through my phone. Fifteen missed texts from Rae. The tone of all of them swung wildly from friendly, then pleading, then almost intimidating, then back to nice. I had to respond. This was cruel to them. But how do you say, *I need you to slow the fuck down and back the fuck off because you're going to make my world explode, and I need a minute* nicely?

After some deliberation, I typed out: *I am so sorry for the delay in getting back to you. While I was home for Christmas, I found out that my mom has cancer, and it's fairly advanced. I took a leave from work to care for her, so Dustin and I are here in Florida for the time being. I don't know for how long. Still trying to get my bearings with her news and now this news. I just need some time. Please. I know you want to see Dustin, and you will, but I need to figure out some things first.* I took a deep breath and hit send.

Her response was almost immediate, *Oh no! That's terrible, Rebecca. We are so sorry to hear this. Please let us know what we can do.*

I breathed a sigh of relief. Rae seemed to be satisfied for the moment. Crisis averted. *You still have to come clean, bitch.* My inner voice chided me. *Sooner rather than later.*

I was contemplating how to go about telling my mother about everything when she started calling for my help. She needed her nausea pills and some water. I helped her to the bathroom.

As she took her pill, she examined herself in the mirror above the sink. She used a wipe to remove any makeup still clinging to her face after her nap, then washed with cleanser and smoothed on some face cream. She had an obscenely wide terry cloth headband with an enormous bow on one side that she wore to wash her face, and she appraised herself in the mirror.

"Do you mind if I keep this on? It feels so good to have all my hair up off my neck and face."

"Mom, this is your house. You can wear whatever the hell you want to dinner. We can have naked dinner if that will make you feel better."

"I hardly think my grandson seeing my nipples will help how I feel," Mom laughed. "I am just going to get out of these sweats. I am burning up."

I texted the babysitter while she changed. They must have been on their way home anyway because Dustin ran in at full speed.

"Hi, Mama! I'm a plane!" He shouted, with his hands tight against his side and extended behind him like makeshift wings.

"Hi, my love! Slow down! It's dinner time! Are you hungry?" I steered him towards the bathroom to wash his hands. "Thank you for everything! Here, this is for you." I handed the girl two twenty-dollar bills. "Will you be around tomorrow? I may need you if my mom isn't feeling well."

She nodded enthusiastically. "Wow, thanks! Yeah, just text me if you need me. They're doing movies and sundaes under the stars here tomorrow night. Maybe I can take Dustin? If you don't want to, of course."

"Ohh, that sounds fun. Let's see what tomorrow looks like before we make any plans, though."

"Sure thing! Night Dustin!"

Mom emerged, her head still punctuated by her giant headband. Dustin settled in his chair and happily munched on the stir fry and rice. He giggled, something he did when he enjoyed what he was eating. My mother stared at him in wonderment.

"I've never seen anyone giggle while they eat. He looks just- I don't know- joyous."

"That's one of his quirks. He's done it since he was a baby."

"He's amazing. Dustin, do you want to watch a movie with Grammy in her bed tonight? We can have popcorn!"

"Nem a nems too?" He asked, still at last waiting for the answer.

"M & Ms?" I laughed. "Who gives you M & Ms?"

"My Mia," he said simply. "Only dis many dough."

Dustin held up one chubby hand with all fingers extended, then counted to 5. I couldn't even be aggravated with Mia for sneaking junk food to him if it taught him to count.

"Yes, sure. We can have whatever you want. And you can pick the movie." Mom assured him.

"Otay," Dustin replied.

After dinner, the pair retired to Mom's room with a giant bowl of popcorn mixed with chocolate chips in the absence of M & Ms. I heard the distinctive sound of a Disney movie starting. Mom had agreed to come to get me or text me to move Dustin once he fell asleep. I finished the dishes and settled on the couch. HGTV played in the background as I texted all the people I was missing in Boston.

I texted Mia, asking her to give our love to Betty and let her know Dustin had spilled the beans about her sweet bribe. I checked in with the group text with Dianne and Kieran. Dianne appeared to be debating with herself about whether my mother's illness would exclude Dustin and me from participating in Pride.

I thumbed out, *Just count us in. If you prepay anything, let me know so I can reimburse you. If we end up not coming, I will make sure to get you my share anyway for all the trouble.*

She answered not to worry about it at all. She was just asking to make sure we would be included if we wanted to be. We went back and forth for a while. She reassured me everything would be okay and asked what she could do to help. I didn't have an answer. *Can you help me tell everyone I have been lying to them? Can you take away my mom's cancer?* I wanted to ask.

My eyes were growing heavy after such a long, emotional day and no sleep the night before. I checked in with my mom and Dustin before heading to bed. They were asleep together, Winnie the Pooh blaring on the television.

Mom rested her chin on the top of Dustin's head. Her mouth was curled into a peaceful smile. I tiptoed over to him and started to untangle him from her. Mom stirred and opened her eyes.

"No, leave him. He's fine. I'll call you if I need you to move him."

I was surprised, but pleasantly so. This tenderness and affection were something that I had wished for my son and my mother since he was born. But Bernie had always cared most about Bernie, so I didn't push it. Again, cancer had smoothed the rough edges of her into a person I loved more and more.

"Ok, I'm right down the hall. I put a water bottle on the nightstand for you. Love you."

I bent down to kiss Dustin. As I stood up, my mom caught my wrist.

"I love you, Rebecca." She whispered, looking right into my eyes.

"I love you too, Mom," I whispered back, pulling up the covers around them. "Good night."

As I padded across the house to my room, my phone went off. Maybe Kieran had finally caught up with all the texts. I checked the screen. Rae.

Dean and I are coming to Florida. I found out from your aunt where your mother lives. I emailed you our flight and hotel information so you can check your schedule and plan some time for us to meet Dustin. We just felt like we needed to come to support you, Dustin, and your mom.

Fuck. My legs didn't even feel like my own as I moved into the room. I lunged for my purse, grabbed out my Ambien prescription, and swallowed a pill. I needed sleep. Maybe when I woke up, this would all be a bad dream.

As I lay waiting for the pill to take hold, I marveled at the current state of my life. Tuesday, my mother would be getting the cancer scrapped out of her body, and her stomach hollowed. At the same time, Dustin's grandparents would be touching down, ready to meet their grandson and ruin my life simultaneously.

How the hell did this happen? How in the hell was I going to deal with this? *Moron*, my inner voice chided. It echoed as I slid into the blackness of sleep.

I came to awareness, flailing and being shaken awake. "Wake up, Rebecca! You're having a bad dream. Wake up!" Mom loomed over me, her face concerned.

"What? Huh? What?"

I was disoriented. My heart was pounding, and I was sweaty.

"You had a bad dream. You were screaming so loud it woke me up. Dustin's still in my bed asleep." Mom said softly, perching on the edge of the bed and rubbing my back. "Do you remember it?"

An image of Dustin slung over a man's shoulder, running away from me as bombs dropped and exploded behind them, destroying everything in its path, popped into my mind. I shuddered.

"No," I lied to my mom. "I'm going back to bed." I rolled, turning my back away from her, and tunneled under the covers, away from her comforting touch, which only served to make me feel even more guilty than I already did.

Morning came without further incident. Mom was flitting about, too achy and unsettled from chemo to get comfortable, but also too nervous about her impending surgery to focus. Dustin was his usual ball of energy. I felt weighed down with my secret and was snappy to them both.

By my fifth explosion, Mom had enough and shuttled Dustin off to a matinee. I was alone with a list of things to do before the surgery and my thoughts- which had turned from anxious and fearful to angry. *Why the hell were Dean and Rae so pushy? Couldn't they wait a few weeks until we came back to Boston? My plate was already full enough as it is. I did this anonymously for a reason. They had no right to strip the confidentiality away from me.* But then, another voice rose to the surface. *They just want to help. If you lost Dustin, you would be doing the same thing. They have had to go years missing their son. This is the last link to him. Of course, they are coming. And a dead son trumps your precious secret. They win. They got dealt the shit hand. You have your son. They don't. They win.*

I had to reach out to Rae. I had to let her know that I was unprepared for this meeting. I had told no one about the test even happening, let alone the results. Dustin wouldn't have any idea who they were and what they were to him. My mother had no idea of the actual circumstances of her grandson's birth. Not to mention, she definitely would hate an audience in the "hour of her greatest need," as she kept saying whenever she thanked me.

"Thank you for staying and caring for me in the hour of my greatest need," she would say unprovoked at random moments throughout the day, her voice breaking and my hand sandwiched between hers.

It was all a little melodramatic for my taste, but that was one thing the old and new Bernie shared, a flair for the dramatic. I didn't even know if she could physically handle another shock.

I was really surprised to hear you are coming to visit Florida. My mother is scheduled for surgery the day you arrive. Maybe you can get settled from the trip, and I can meet you for breakfast Wednesday. I think we should talk before you meet Dustin.

I hit send and bent to set the phone down on the table. As I was setting it on the table, Megan called with a "crisis of epic proportions," which occupied my time until Dustin and my mother returned home.

"We're back! And hopefully, your good mood has returned!" Mom teased. "He probably won't eat dinner. He ate all the way to the bottom of the bottomless bucket."

"Mom!"

Just like with the M & Ms, I couldn't be mad. Matinees and bottomless popcorn were one of my very favorite treats when I was a child, and it thrilled me that Dustin now shared that same memory.

Looking back, movies with my mother were one of my few happy memories of childhood, a delicious excursion where calories and sugar weren't monitored. It was a moment in time where Bernie smiled and laughed. Where once or twice, she had held my hand and kissed my cheek. Once, she had laughed at my opinion about a movie. That day was my second-best day, ousted from first by Dustin's birth. Her opinion had always mattered too much, even when she never cared.

"You know, I'm not super hungry either. I'm going to go lay down for a while." Mom said.

"Okay, then I'm not making dinner for no one to eat it. I'll scrounge up some leftovers. But before you go lay down, can we make some time to talk later?"

She tilted her head like a pug when they are observing something interesting. "Is everything ok?"

"Yes, Mom. Everything's ok. I just want to talk." I assured her, knowing I was lying through my teeth.

"Ok. Sure, honey. I will take a nap; you get Dustin to bed, and we will talk when I wake up."

"Perfect." I pressed a kiss to her cheek and moved past her to go track down Dustin.

I located him asleep, propped against the wall, his hand outstretched, touching his beloved Mrs. Potts. I carefully scooped him up and changed his diaper, grateful that he was such a sound sleeper. He rarely stirred once he snoozed.

I changed him into pajamas and laid him down on the bed next to me. I needed him next to me to fortify me for the conversation ahead. Well, the many conversations that would be ahead. But not all of them would be had tonight.

I changed into my pajamas and watched a Netflix movie while waiting for my mother to wake up. Finally, I heard a light tap. I imagined that waiting for that knock is much like the feeling a death row inmate has as they wait for the executioner.

I opened the door, and Mom stood close to the door, trying to listen.

"Sorry! I wasn't sure you heard me. I didn't want to knock too loud and wake up Dustin."

"Dustin can sleep through anything. We could drive a train through this living room, and he would stay asleep."

"Good to know. Not that I have any plans to turn the living room into a train station."

"Does that mean you took down your Tinder profile?" I teased.
She huffed and puffed and pretended to be insulted.

"Okay, wise guy! Sit down. You want a drink?" She stood at the fridge with water in her hand.

"Do we have any vodka?" I asked, feeling the need for liquid courage.

"Jesus, is it that bad? It's late!"

"Mom, it's 8. Bars don't even open this early!"

She thumped a shot glass down. I poured, filling it nearly to the brim. We looked at one another. She clinked her water bottle with my glass, and we drank in sync.

I poured a second shot and gulped it down. My mother's eyes were wide with surprise behind the raised bottle. I sighed, let the warmth spread through my body, and began.

"Mom, let's talk about Dustin."

"Oh my god, what's wrong with Dustin?" Panic filled her voice.

"Nothing, nothing at all! And let's remember that. Let's be grateful and remember that he is an amazing blessing. I am thankful every day that he is here."

"Yes, of course. Get to the point, Rebecca."

"Ok, ok." I took a deep breath and plunged in, head down, refusing to meet her eyes, "I always wanted a child. But I was in my thirties, and I didn't even have a boyfriend, let alone anyone who wanted to marry me, even on the horizon. And so, I decided to have a baby on my own."

I didn't dare look up as I finished.

"So, I took a second job and saved up and bought some sperm. I learned from lesbians at my gym who inseminated themselves how to do it. But I didn't want anyone to know. I felt like such a loser. I couldn't even find a man to get me accidentally pregnant. So, I invented him. And I lied to everyone. And I am sorry. And I am ashamed."

Tears dripped onto my lap as I hung my head. My mother remained silent for a long time. I looked up, and her mouth hung open in shock. Then, I realized that I still hadn't told her the part of the story that had caused me to reveal this secret in the first place. I was about to explain about Rae and Dean when she spoke.

"You're ashamed? I'm ashamed." I braced for the impact of the words, *of you,* that I was sure were going to follow. "Of myself. For failing as a mother so badly that you thought you had to make such a huge life decision alone. That you had to hide it. That I ever made you feel worthless enough to create a story where you are the victim and not the heroine. You're an independent, wise, amazing, courageous woman who saw what she wanted and forged her own path to get there. I am ashamed that I have never fully seen you until this moment." She paused again for a long time.

When she spoke again, her voice was thick. "Ashamed that I would have been mortified about the truth of my grandson's birth just a year ago, that I would have preferred you had a one-night stand instead of knowing the truth. Ashamed that I had never even noticed it or tried to guess what was really going on. God, baby, you must have been so scared. So alone."

She started to cry hard, her shoulders contracting violently with each sob. She kept mumbling, "I'm so sorry," repeatedly.

She finally stopped, then stilled. She cleared her throat. "I wish you had told me sooner, but I understand why you didn't. But this trip has been so different from your others, and I am trying so hard…" she faltered for a moment. "I had just hoped you would let me in for once, that's all."

My voice caught in my throat. I was speechless from the words she had spoken, weightless with her praise, her absolution.

I felt almost giddy with that secret off my shoulders. My mother was okay. Better yet, she wasn't in physical shock or dead. She accepted me. And she was sorry. She really was a new person. For a moment, I felt a deep and strong pang of grief over the impending loss of a woman I loved more and more by the second.

"You don't know what this means to me. I've been terrified. The mom I knew my whole life would never have been okay with her daughter getting artificially inseminated. She was barely able to accept me as a single mother. She surely didn't savor her role as grandma. But this mom, the one I met on this trip, she's a beautiful, open, accepting person. The new Bernie made this a warm memory instead of a traumatic experience. Thank you, Mom." I smiled at her, love and gratitude for her and this moment radiating from my core. But there's a little more you have to know."

"What else? I can't take any more. Are you pregnant again?" Her eyes lit up hopefully, and I had to laugh.

"No, I didn't manage to score another vial, so no more grandchildren for you. Sorry to disappoint. However, the donor is kind of what I want to talk to you about. Mom, the donor's parents contacted me a few weeks ago."

"His parents? How in the world did they get your information? How did they even know about you? Aren't there Hippo Laws that protect you?"

"HIPAA laws," I corrected her. "And the clinic didn't tell her anything. Your sister did."

"Cami? They're from Connecticut?"

"Apparently, the donor's family is her neighbor. Their son went to college in Boston. The donor's mother saw Dustin on our Christmas card at Cami's party, and he looked so much like her son that she just knew he was his. She got my information from Cami, came to Boston, and convinced me to do a DNA test. I was so skeptical. I thought she was insane. And I was so scared that my secret would be found out. And we got the results back, and their son is Dustin's father. I don't even know how to wrap my brain around this, but it's true."

"Where does the donor stand on all this? Obviously, his parents seem to want to be involved. Where's he at?"

"His name was Sean, and he died in a car crash four years ago."

My mother's hands flew to her throat. I knew it had constricted sharply, just like mine always did when I heard about a mother losing a child and that vicarious pain shot through me.

"Oh no. Oh, dear. Those poor people."

"He was 19 when he died, and Dustin is his spitting image. She showed me a picture of Sean. I immediately thought of an identical one I had at home with Dustin. That's kind of what sealed the deal with me to agree to the DNA test. I didn't expect ever to be found out. I certainly didn't think the test would ever come back positive. I thought she was insane. Nice, very nice, but insane. But you'll meet them. You'll like them, I am sure."

"I would love that. Dustin has more family! What a blessing, Becca! What a blessing. More people to love children is never a bad thing. It's a miracle!" She smiled and clapped her hands, childlike.

"Well, I'm glad you feel that way because they'll be here tomorrow."

She startled. "Tomorrow?! On the same day I am getting everything womanly about me stripped away; they will be flying here to meet us all for the first time? I mean, the timing is less than ideal."

She paused and stilled. She thought for a moment.

"But then is ever an ideal time for cancer? I wonder if I can get a wig that fast. My hair isn't gone yet, but once the hormones and the chemo hit, there's no telling what could happen."

She began to scroll through her phone in search of a wig shop.

"How long are they staying?"

"You're not pissed off? I was. We have enough going on without adding them into the mix. It's pushy just to invite yourself several states away to visit strangers."

"Rebecca, they lost their child." She stopped, overcome. She composed herself. "Nineteen years old. My God. Just a baby. They shouldn't have to wait one more minute to meet his son."

She paused again, this time for a long time. I could see the wheels working. I would have laughed, but her expression was so serious, I held back. Her eyes filled with tears, then she smiled and nodded her head, responding to some internal conversation I wasn't privy to. She slapped her thighs.

"Yup! Here's what I am going to do. I am going to open my home and my heart to them. We're family now."

"What do you mean, your home? They're staying at a hotel."

"The hell they are. They need to be around Dustin. Rick converted the attic when he was trying to write the next great American novel. They can stay up there. It has a full bathroom and office space and a guest room. Go look."

I opened the door to the walk-up attic and went up the stairs. The former storage space had been transformed. Skylights and large windows on each end had been installed and flooded the room with light. The floors had grey stained laminate floors. There was a desk with a computer and some shelves above it on one end of the room. The other side had a king-size bed, two dressers, and nightstands. There was a large tv suspended on the wall. I opened the door and discovered a giant, luxurious bathroom.

"Well, damn. I'm kind of offended I wasn't invited to stay up here." I joked, emerging back downstairs.

"You know Dustin loves that damn Be Our Guest mural. You can't stay in any other room in this house, and you know it."

"You speak the truth. So, should I tell Rae and Dean to cancel their hotel? They're rooming with us."

"Of course!"

I quickly texted Rae, hoping it wasn't too late and that I would be disturbing her.

Hey there! Sorry to text so late, but my mother and I talked, and she would be honored to have you and Dean stay with us while you are in Florida. She wants to make sure you can have as much time with Dustin as possible.

Her reply was instant. *Wow! Thank you! You can't understand what this means to us. We can't wait to meet Dustin! See you tomorrow! WOW!*

"They're excited to stay here. Thanks again, Mom. This is above and beyond."

"You sound unsure."

"Oh no, I'm sure it's above and beyond! I am so thankful you are so great about this. I just feel uneasy about Dustin meeting them. What if they try to take him? Like what if they want to replace their son with mine? What if he likes them more?" I started crying and hiccupping simultaneously.

"And there's the vodka shots! Listen, none of that is going to happen. Dustin adores you. You are a wonderful mother. But you know they deserve to spend time with him too. I know this isn't how you planned it. How you thought it would be. But just maybe, this will be better than you ever dreamed." She paused, stood up, and placed her hand on my shoulder. "But you take it at your pace. You're the mom. You call the shots. But right now, I am YOUR mom, and I am calling the shots. Go to bed! It's almost midnight. We have a big day ahead of us tomorrow. It's my sterilization day!"

"Glad to see you're coping with it so well," I said dryly.

"Good night, drunky!" She giggled, pushing me into my room. I climbed in next to Dustin and began to cry silent, hot tears of relief, of thanks, and fear.

RAE

"Patti! You won't believe this!" I burst through her back door. It was nearly midnight, but I was too excited to wait.

"Rae! What the hell?" Patti's head popped up from over the top of the couch.

The room was dark except for the glow of the tv and a few strategically placed candles that usually only appeared when Patti...had a date. Oops. I had just walked in and interrupted an intimate moment.

"Oh, my goodness, sorry! Sorry! I'm sorry!" I shielded my eyes. "I'm going to go."

"No point now. You've effectively killed the mood."

She stood up, readjusted herself, and made quick introductions. Her date sat up and laughed at the awkward moment instead of being upset, which scored him some brownie points in my book.

"Rae, Bryan. Bryan, Rae. What's up?"

"Bryan. Nice to meet you. I'm sorry to interrupt. But Patti, Rebecca just texted me."

Both Patti and Bryan leaned forward, invested in my next words, which led me to believe Patti had been regaling him with the whole tale over dinner.

"Her mother invited us to stay with them when we're in Florida! She told her mom the truth, and she took it so well that she wants us to have as much time as possible with Dustin. She's having her surgery tomorrow. I know the last thing I would want is strangers around while I am recovering. But how incredible is that?"

"Do you think her being sick has inspired a change of heart? From what Cami has always told us about her, they both sound like matching ice queens. Maybe the cancer is thawing the icicle up her ass. Whatever it is, it's amazing and generous, and you should take her up on that offer."

"Oh, you bet we are. I sent Dean out for a gift to bring to say thank you."

Bryan brayed loudly and suddenly, startling Patti and me.

"You know he's coming back with booze and tube socks, right? Men can't pick gifts for shit." He said.

We all started laughing.

"And on that note, I'm off. I have to finish packing...and go to find the best thank you gift the 24/7 Walmart has to offer." I said.

Patti stood up and came over to me. She looked me in my eyes and then pulled me into a tight hug. "You got this, girl. Go meet Sean's baby."

The alarm's blare at 5 am was early, but we both leaped up as soon as it sounded, wide awake and eager to start our journey. Dean flicked on the light, and we both stood there, eyes bulging from the shocking brightness, giant grins plastered on our faces. We brushed our teeth quickly and threw on the clothes we had laid out the night before when we had booked the Uber. We were out the door in under thirty minutes, whizzing to the airport in the back of an SUV heated against the cold New England morning.

My stomach lurched with a mix of emotions. In a few hours, I would be meeting my grandson—Sean's son. I would get to see his eyes again, alive and dancing. I looked up at the sky brightening with brilliant colors and sent a silent prayer up to God that this trip would be a good one.

As if in answer, Dean squeezed my hand.

"I can't believe this, Rae. This is really happening. Did you take your pill yet?"

"No, not yet. I'll take it when we get to the gate. I don't want to be a zombie going through Security."

My fear of flying had been well documented over the years. My doctor prescribed anti-anxiety meds for every flight. This time, however, I didn't think I would need it. Nothing would keep me from making this trip.

We moved through the airport and passed through Security quickly as if in a dream. The building was too hot and stuffy for the constant movement within. We found our gate and sat to wait, well ahead of schedule. I took my pill and leaned my head on Dean's shoulder. I was sure I would be too excited to sleep, but I was shaken awake by Dean to board sometime later.

"Come on, sleepyhead. Your grandson awaits."

The plane ride passed uneventfully, thankfully. It was a shock to my system to go from the bone-chilling cold of New England to a balmy 60 degrees. I stripped off my sweater while we waited for the Uber to shuttle us to the hospital to get the keys to the condo we would be staying in from Rebecca.

As we rolled through the town, so lush and vibrant and alive compared to our gray, slushy suburb, it felt like a rebirth.

I leaned back and remembered the day Dean had whizzed down streets, narrowly missing mailboxes and other cars, to get me to the Maternity ward the day Sean was born.

The anticipation mingled with fear of that moment felt the same as this one. I didn't have to withstand the physical pain of childbirth this time, but the pain I had endured to get to this place had been worse than even that of labor.

The pain of missing my son had been a soul gripping pain that never went away. With childbirth, the pain was sharp and shattering, but temporary, with a sweet, scented bundle to love at the end.

Losing your child, there was only unrelenting anguish and all-consuming regret and sadness. I hoped meeting Dustin would ease the constant pain of losing Sean, but I feared it would only evolve into resentment for a life that could never be, where my son and my grandson existed together.

The Uber swung into the hospital, and I gathered all our bags. Dean tapped on his phone, paying the bill, and then moved to take our suitcase out of the trunk.

"You need me to stay?" The driver asked, his heavy accent making him difficult to understand.

"No, we'll be a while yet," Dean said.

With that, he was off. We looked at one another and took a deep breath. Rebecca had seemed okay about us coming when we had texted, but it was hard to assess what she thought without speaking to her.

We had made an impetuous decision, but one that felt right and necessary. Rebecca has already dealt with so much alone. She shouldn't have to deal with this too. And Dustin was our flesh and blood, and now, Rebecca and her mother were too. This is what you did for your family. *And sometimes, you must be pushy to get what you want,* my inner voice intoned.

Dean's eyes twinkled as he looked at me. "You ready, my love? No time like the present."

I reached my hand to his rough cheek, sprinkled with stubble, and gave him a shaky smile.

"Right now, you look like the boy who I fell in love with. I haven't seen him in a long time."

"I thought he died the day Sean did. But Rae, you brought him back. You knew. You believed. You didn't give a shit about odds or nay-sayers. Thank you for not listening to your foolish husband. You gave me back something I never dreamed I would have. I love you."

The staying power of our love wasn't lost on me. We had not only been in love for most of our lives, a feat rare enough, but we had also survived losing a child. So many marriages didn't remain intact after the partners experienced the loss of a child. But for us, it had never been even a thought. I had struggled and tested him, but he grew stronger. When he cried, his tears fortified me to support him. I was so blessed to know the love of this man. I took a deep breath, readjusted my purse on my shoulder, and grinned.

" Here goes nothing!"

We approached the Information Desk as soon as we came into the hospital. The elderly volunteer directed us to the Surgical Waiting Room. The room was filled with people, some with swollen eyes and looking shell-shocked, others muttering their annoyance at having to wait for news or for a procedure that had run over. A few rambunctious kids tore through the room, running over people's legs and knocking magazines off the tables. None of them looked to be Dustin.

As the door closed behind us, I surveyed the room for Rebecca. I saw her almost instantly. Her head was bent over her phone, texting, I guessed. She looked up when she heard the door click and locked eyes with me. She stood up, gathered her purse off the chair next to her, and strode over to us. I was immediately taken aback by her appearance. She hadn't looked incredibly well-rested when we had met in Boston, but now her eyes were ringed with dark circles, and she walked wearily like she carried a belly of cement.

Her work clothes had also de-emphasized her exhaustion, but you could tell she was dressed for comfort today. She wore black slides, her French manicured toenails peeking out over the thick band, black Capri leggings, an oversized tee-shirt emblazoned with" Nevertheless, she persisted," and a tattered denim jacket to protect her against the freezing air conditioner. Her hair was a burst of wild curls gathered on top of her head and barely contained by the elastic wound around them.

She reached us and halted abruptly. She weaved back and forth, lifting her arms up and down. She was clearly fighting with herself about how best to greet us. A handshake? A smile? A hug?

I didn't give her time to debate. My motherly instincts won out, and I enveloped her in a hug. Her body was tense in mine for a moment, but I could feel her relax as I squeezed a bit tighter. Finally, we pulled away, and I was surprised to see tears in her eyes.

"Thank you. I needed that. It's nice to see you, Rae. I assume you're Dean?"

She turned her attention to Dean and flashed a smile that reminded me of Cami's, a hollow, fake smile fraught with self-doubt.

Dean nodded, a smile lighting his face. He embraced her, lingering as I had. Though Rebecca never knew Sean, she felt like a link to him as much as her son did. I knew Dean was feeling it too.

"It's so wonderful to meet you, Rebecca! I can't even believe this! Nuts, right? How's your mom?" Dean asked.

Tears sprang back into her eyes, and her chin quivered.

"Well, they said it could take an hour with no surprises and longer if they found anything. So far, she's been in there for about two hours. My nerves are shot."

"Well, we can't have that! Come on, darling, let's get something to eat down in the cafeteria, and we can talk. Get your mind off things."

Dean took her by the elbow. For a moment, I saw the father he would have been to a daughter, the father-in-law to a wife Sean would never marry.

He was always solicitous and charming to women, a true gentleman raised by a Southern debutante transplanted in Connecticut who was determined to raise her son like the suitors who had called upon her at her parents' farm, a Rhett Butler mingling with the Yankees.

Rebecca looked gratefully at him and nodded. I asked the receptionist to hold our bags for us while we went to eat. She issued us a pager that would go off if they had any updates about Rebecca's mother. I thanked her and joined Dean and Rebecca, who chatted easily as we waited for the elevator.

Rebecca held me at arm's length. The instant comradeship between them made me happy but also jealous. I hoped that would change in the coming days.

Their conversation barely stopped as we waited in the lines for food. It was still early, and breakfast was being served. Smelling the food made me realize how hungry I was. I hadn't eaten before our flight. My stomach growled loudly, joining in my one-sided conversation.

"Couldn't have said it better myself!" Dean laughed, hearing the growl. "I'm starving. How about you?"

He looked at Rebecca, who was eyeing a stack of pancakes on a passerby's tray with reverence. She was almost drooling. Dean exchanged an amused look with me and started laughing.

"Guess that answers the question!"

"Sorry!" Rebecca snapped back to reality, looking sheepish. "Yes, I'm starved. I haven't eaten out of solidarity for Mom."

We set about filling our trays. I chose a breakfast sandwich and a bowl of fruit, and some tea.

Dean had selected eggs, home fries, sausage, and a bagel with coffee. Rebecca, not surprisingly, chose a large stack of pancakes and sausage. She balanced it out with a banana and some apple juice.

We paid for all three meals, despite Rebecca's protest. We found a table together. Rebecca looked sheepish again as she made quick work of preparing her pancakes and beginning to eat.

"I'm sorry. I've been up since about five and just realized how hungry I am. And I am super anxious to know what's happening with my mom. So- pancakes," she gestured with her plastic fork, grinned, and popped a triangle covered in syrup and butter in her mouth.

"Don't worry a bit about us. We've been up since then, too, and I am right behind you."

Dean's hand moved back and forth quickly between his plate and his mouth. Rebecca laughed.

"Me too!" I chimed in, spearing fruit.

Rebecca and Dean both chuckled politely, but it was a flat gesture. Jealousy sprang up again. I continued to eat in silence.

As we all began to fill up, conversation resumed more readily. It was all small talk, none of us willing to address the elephant that loomed larger than life in the room. The longer the meaningless conversation dragged on, the more impatient I got. Their voices and laughter grated on me until I couldn't eat anymore. Dean, usually so attuned to me, wasn't paying attention.

"When can we see Dustin?" I blurted out, cutting Rebecca off mid-sentence.

She and Dean both looked at me with surprise on their faces. I tried to keep my own surprise off my face. I hadn't meant to say that out loud.

Dean mouthed, *What the hell?*

I shrugged.

"I just want to see my grandson."

Rebecca looked sick, either from the pancakes or from the prospect of us meeting Dustin. I thought we had given her some time to adjust to the idea. She knew why we traveled here. She said she wanted us to spend time with him. Was she changing her mind now?

I felt desperate and furious at the same time.

"Of course, you do, Rae. And you will. But let's set some ground rules first. First, I am his mother. I have raised him and loved him alone for a reason and what I say goes."

She looked like the courage she had mustered up to say that was faltering.

I reached out and placed my hand on top of hers on the table. "Dustin is lucky to have a mother like you. We don't want to replace or contradict you or spoil him. Well, maybe spoil him a little. We just want to have a relationship with him. With you both. We know this is a shock. I know we may come on a little strong. Okay, a lot strong in my case." I reassured her.

Dean chuckled under his breath next to me.

"We pictured our son getting married and his wife coming to tell us with tiny baby booties that we were going to be grandparents. Then we lost Sean and had to cope with the idea that we would never have grandchildren. Then this crazy serendipitous moment set all this into motion. But it has happened, so now we make the best of it."

Dean nodded, putting his hand over mine.

"Rebecca, I can't be anything but grateful and appreciative of you. You have given us such a gift. I know you didn't mean to, but I am so happy you did. And I don't intend to do anything to lose that gift. So, run through the rest of the rules. We'll follow them." He said.

I could see Rebecca visibly relax before us. She smiled and laughed.

"I worked on that one little piece for hours. I don't have anything else." She confessed.

"Does he know who we are?" I asked. "Can he call us Grandma and Grandpa? I know you may not be comfortable with it right away, but it's important to us." My voice caught. "It's a title we never thought we would have."

Before Rebecca could answer, the pager on the table went off. All of us jumped. Rebecca shot out of her seat and grabbed her bag.

"Come on. There's news." She commanded.

"I'll clean up. You go ahead with her," Dean said.

I caught up with Rebecca, pacing and rubbing her stomach while waiting for the elevator.

"Ugh, I should know better than to eat hospital cafeteria pancakes. I feel like I swallowed a bowling ball." She complained.

"Would you like some Tums?"

I fished a small bottle out of my purse.

Rebecca chuckled.

"I thought I was the only out toting around antacids in my purse."

"Age hasn't been kind to me. I need them pretty much after I eat or drink anything. I keep avoiding mentioning it to my doctor in case he recommends surgery or something."

"Isn't that why you should mention it? If surgery could help you, why not?" She asked.

"Surgery at my age is riskier than at your age. Besides, Tums do the job just fine." I replied.

She waved my bottle away and fished her own out of her purse. We clinked bottles, giggling, as the elevator slid higher to the Surgical Waiting Room. She popped a few in her mouth as the doors opened.

We hurried to the reception desk. Rebecca stuck the pager out wordlessly. The girl at the desk looked up.

"Who are you here for?"

"Bernie Malone."

She clicked her long nails on the computer keys. She twirled her fingers over the mouse.

"M...M...oh, ok, there she is. The doctor wants to speak to you. Come this way."

She came out from behind the desk and led Rebecca down a hall. She glanced over her shoulder, her face a mask of terror.

"I'll be right here waiting, Becca. It's going to be okay!"

I tried to soothe her without really knowing if I was telling the truth.

REBECCA

My stomach was in knots as I was ushered into a conference room. I was hoping against hope that the many medical dramas I had indulged in were wrong when they brought people into rooms like this to tell them their loved ones were gone. I began to shake involuntarily. Mom couldn't be gone yet. I had just started to know and love her.

I rose to my feet. Tears were starting to fall as Dr. Price, and a middle-aged woman in a camel-colored pencil skirt, low heels, a black blazer, and a turtleneck walked into the room. Dr. Price looked like he had changed scrubs from the blue ones he had worn pre-surgery to a pair of teal green ones. I didn't want to think about what would have caused him to need to change his clothes. The woman next to him stared ahead, radiating sympathy but also a professional distance.

"What's going on? How's my mom?"

Dr. Price sighed. "Let's sit down, Rebecca. First, your mom made it through surgery. She's in Recovery, and she will be in ICU in about an hour. When we are done here, you can go see her."

"Why does she need to be in ICU? You said she would likely be in a regular patient room to recover."

"Let's let Dr. Price talk," the woman said. "Let's all sit."

I did, reluctantly, as did the doctor and the hospital staff person.

"Rebecca, we completed the hysterectomy successfully, but we have some additional concerns we didn't anticipate. First, she lost a lot of blood. She tried to hemorrhage all over me, but I won."

He started to chuckle, then read the room and bit it back.

"We have had to give her a blood transfusion."

He paused for a moment and then began again before I could jump in. My palms felt clammy, and I felt short of breath.

"Also, the cancer is much more advanced than our tests showed. I am so sorry, Rebecca, but your mother's cancer is terminal. I would recommend discontinuing her chemo and focusing on managing her pain until her time comes."

Dr. Price paused again to let me absorb this information. A cold numbness started to spread through my body.

"This is Barb Chambers, our hospice liaison. She wants to give you information about what to expect in the coming weeks and how their program can help your mother, as well as you, cope with all of this."

Barb began to speak, but I cut her off.

"Dr. Price, how come you didn't see this on all the tests you ran? And how can you just give up? A hysterectomy was bad enough for my mother. She won't be able to handle a terminal diagnosis."

Then, I paused and drew in some shallow, hiccupy breaths. I could feel the tears coming but tried to get them to stop falling. I was unsuccessful as I looked into Dr. Price's kind, sad eyes.

"How much time does she have left?"

Dr. Price raked his hands across his head and took off his glasses to rub his eyes.

"It's hard to say. We're doing scans to see how far along it is. But every lymph node sample I tested came back positive."

"How. Long."

"If I had to put a time on it, I would say six weeks, a month. Maybe less. Having the hysterectomy as I recommended when she was first diagnosed would have dramatically improved her odds of survival, but that was a risk she took willingly."

Barb jumped in then.

"We don't like to focus on the quantity of time left in a patient's life, but the quality. We can keep your mother comfortable. We can give her rich experiences and leave your family with happy memories. We can make the next transition in your mother's life an easy and peaceful one if we work together."

Dr. Price pushed his chair back as his pager went off. I became overwhelmed and laid my head on the desk, and sobbed. Barb moved to rub my back, her musk-tinged perfume enveloping me like a comforting hug.

"Ms. Malone, I have to go. Please excuse me. I am terribly sorry about your mother. I will check in on her before I head home tonight. You have my number if you need anything."

We said goodbye, and I sat with Barb as she outlined the purpose of hospice and how they would become involved as my mother got sicker.

Finally, she was summoned away too. She hugged me tightly and quickly before she left. She handed me her business card and a brochure.

"You can stay in here as long as you need to. Do you have anyone here to support you?"

I was startled, remembering Rae and Dean waiting for me.

"Yes, I guess I do," I said as she was halfway out the door.

I took some deep breaths and fished a compact out of my purse. I didn't have any makeup on, but I wanted to see how swollen my eyes and face were.

I swiped some powder over my skin, but my tears mingled with the makeup and made it look muddy. I gave up, figuring it was a lesson in futility and hurried back to the waiting room to find the Baxter's.

I emerged into the waiting room. Rae was standing right by the door I had gone through, nearly where I had left her. I guess she kept her promises. She had said she would wait right there.

Dean paced the distance of the waiting room. It looked like he was setting quite a few visitors on edge. As soon as Rae saw me, she threw her arms around me.

"Dean!"

She yelled, and he materialized almost instantly.

"Come on, Becca. It's ok. Come sit down." She murmured.

"Outside... I need to go outside." I choked out.

They wedged me between their shoulders, and we moved through the room and into the elevator as one, a fused wall of pain. Rae and Dean handled pain with action, like those that have survived unspeakable tragedy always do. They ushered me outside to a garden run by the hospital auxiliary club, where I sat sobbing in the humid air.

I felt gutted, and every time I tried to speak, tears drowned out the words. They sat on each side of me, rubbing my shoulders. They knew this pain, a pain that transcended words. I took deep breaths and started to calm down. Finally, I was still.

"She's terminal. They're giving her a month. She's going home on hospice care." I said it in a slow monotone.

Dean squeezed my shoulder, his calm steadiness soothing me. Rae let out a small gasp.

"I have to stay here with her. There's a lot of things I need to know. Papers to sign. Oh, my God. Dustin! The neighbor can't keep him forever. I have to go grab him." I prattled on at loose ends.

Dean stood up.

"Okay, one thing at a time right now. Your mom needs you. Why don't you and Rae go back upstairs and check on her? Stay as long as you need to. If you give me the key, I can head to the condo with the luggage and get Dustin from the neighbor. I don't have to tell him who I am if you don't want me to. I can take him swimming or bowling or something, grab some burgers for dinner." Dean said, taking charge.

Usually, alarm bells and sirens would be going off in my head at a stranger offering to babysit my child. But in the short time I had known Dean, I had seen what a kind, genuine, and incredibly good man he was. I trusted him already, especially with Dustin, our mutual gift. And he wasn't quite a stranger anymore.

For whatever reason, I had no qualms about him meeting Dustin or about Dean's ability to care for him. I also knew Dustin would love him. He would also love some guy time, as there were no solid male influences in his life despite my best efforts. Kieran just didn't cut it.

"You can tell him you're his grandpa."

I smiled up at him. With the sunlight behind him, he looked like an angel, glowing from the inside out. I wondered if he had been sent to save us. They exchanged a look at my words, and both began to smile and cry simultaneously.

"Rebecca, you don't understand how much this means to us." He choked out.

"You don't understand how much I appreciate your support today—both of you. I was mad, honestly, when I found out you were coming here. I thought it was a major imposition. But I am so glad you are here. And I am excited for you to meet Dustin. He's going to love you both."

"We're glad to be here too, sweetheart. Now, let's get the show on the road. You have a mom to check on, and I have a boy to meet!"

We all rode back upstairs together. Dean collected the bags and went to catch his Uber.

Rae and I made our way to the ICU Waiting Room. Rae settled herself in one of the comfortable chairs and began to watch whatever daytime soap was on the television set bolted high up in the corner. It gave an impression of a prison visiting room.

"Would you mind terribly if I took a little catnap while you visit?" She asked, bunching up her sweater for a pillow.

"Not at all. I'll take your purse with me into Mom's room if you want so you can sleep without worrying someone will snatch it. Not that theft is a huge issue in this area, but I will if it makes you feel better." I offered.

"That would be great. Thank you! You wake me up when you need me. I'll be right here." She leaned her head against the wall, slid her phone into her pocket, closed her eyes, and went to sleep.

A nurse came out and brought me back to see Mom. When I saw her, my first thought was that she looked old, for the first time in her life. She would hate to be perceived that way and had paid handsomely on many occasions to make sure it wouldn't happen, but she did.

She was shrunken and shriveled in the bed. She was pale, thanks to the blood loss, and lying very still. She had a clear tube snaking over her face providing her with oxygen.

I held my breath as I entered the room. I pulled the chair close to her bed.

The nurse checked her vitals, recorded some numbers on the unwieldy computer she rolled from room to room and then left, thumping the computer against the wall as she went. Mom didn't even stir. I held her hand, careful of the IV that stuck out of the back of it. I wasn't sure how long I sat there, but I drifted off, my head resting on Mom's lap, her presence calming my frayed nerves.

I woke up to my hair being stroked.

"Good morning, Sleeping Beauty! Did you have a nice nap?"

I sat up and stretched.

"I am so sorry! I didn't mean to fall asleep. How are you feeling?"

She smiled.

"You're allowed to sleep. You've had a long day. Are they here? Did you talk to them?"

"Hold on, you just went through a major surgery, and all you want is the gossip about Rae and Dean?" I laughed and shook my head. "I love you, Mom."

"I love you too, baby, but you're not giving me the dirt."

"They're great. Well, Dean is great. Rae's nice, but she's a bit pushy. But she is here now. She didn't want me to be alone. Dean went to the condo to get Dustin settled in. We didn't want your neighbor to be stuck with him all night."

"What time is it? What happened? Were there complications?"

I took a deep breath. "Did the doctor come in to talk to you?"

She shook her head impatiently.

"Well, there were some surprises with the surgery. It was successful, but you had a lot of bleeding. That's why you're in here. They had to give you a blood transfer because you hemorrhaged. They got it under control, but you need to be monitored."

"So, that's it. Did they get it all? I'm cured?"

Her voice was so hopeful and childlike in its innocence.

"Mom, do you remember what Dr. Price said? This surgery would probably have been curative when they diagnosed you, but now it's just a measure to try and slow things down to be able to treat most effectively. This was never a cure."

"But he got a lot of it? How much more chemo does he think I'll need?"

"Mom, I saw him after your surgery, and he let me know that the scans didn't have the most accurate picture of your cancer. It was a lot more advanced than they expected. Mom, you're not going to get better. Dr. Price said you're terminal."

She made a wet, strangled noise.

I continued. "But they have a plan, Mom. I met a really nice lady from the hospice program, and we're going to make a plan for you."

"Hospice?" She whispered, a single tear sliding down her cheek.

"It's going to be okay, Mom. We can talk about it later. You need to rest."

She hit the button on her pain pump, and I watched as she slid back into unconsciousness. I watched her sleep peacefully for a few minutes. A nurse stuck her head in and saw me watching.

"Everyone okay in here?"

I stood up and sighed deeply. "I'm okay. Overwhelmed and exhausted, but okay. I think she'll be sleeping on and off for a while. I think I am going to head home. I live about fifteen minutes away and can be here fast if she needs me. I will be back first thing if she asks. Can you put this in her file, please?"

"Absolutely."

I jotted down my number for the nurse and wrote it on the whiteboard opposite Mom's bed in case she needed it. I checked that her cell was plugged in and within reach.

I put socks on her feet, made sure her water was full, and pressed a kiss to her cheek. Her eyelids flitted, and she smiled a soft, dreamy smile.

"I'll see you in the morning, Mom."

I roused Rae out of her sleep, and we made our way home. Conversation stalled in the car. Rae surrendered first, cutting her own thought off and falling silent.

She pretended to be absorbed in the scenery that flashed by as I navigated the highway. I could see her excitement grow as the GPS navigated us closer and closer to home. She was anxious to meet Dustin.

I was anxious to see him myself. Since his first flutters inside of me, he was the thing that most effectively soothed and centered me. After today, I needed to smell and hold him.

I don't know if all mothers and babies shared such a powerful connection, but simply holding Dustin's cheek to mine transferred his spirit and energy to me, and they settled into my cells, smoothing and calming me. He was the best medicine.

When we got home, it was dusk. Dustin usually loved to swim at this time of the night, but the pool area was quiet. Rae's head swiveled around, taking the complex in.

"This is lovely!" She gushed.

"Here we are," I announced unceremoniously.

The door flew open, and Dustin stood in the middle of the doorway.

"Mamaaaaa!" He crooned.

I knelt as he threw himself into my arms.

"Oh, Dusty Boy. I missed you."

As I embraced him, I felt a sense of calm wash over me. I saw Rae convulsing with contained sobs out of the corner of my eye. She leaned against the wall, overcome. Dean came out from the kitchen.

"Rae. Come on. Breathe, baby. Come meet your grandson." He soothed, holding his arm out to her for support.

She sobbed savagely now. Even with Dean's guidance, she was hunched over almost in half. Her hair hung over and stuck to her face, mingling with the tears and saliva and snot smeared across it.

I saw a mama wolf in my mind's eye, her head lifted towards the heavens, howling, staking her claim. She made a noise, a sort of howl, guttural, broken, primal. Dean leaned over, his mouth working at her ear. After a few moments, her wails shifted to sobs.

A few minutes more, and she had pulled herself together, her red and puffy eyes and face the only evidence that remained. Her eyes zeroed in on Dustin, and she produced a watery smile.

"May I?" She asked, bending down.

I nodded.

"Hi Dustin," she whispered.

He looked up, hesitant and frightened after her intense reaction. His eyes searched her face. Suddenly, his face bloomed with a smile.

"You?" Dustin spoke a shorthand of his own.

He was asking who she was.

"Dustin, this is your Grandma Rae," I said simply.

He clapped and smiled. Since we had arrived to find my mother transformed, Dustin understood the traditional perks for children where grandmothers are involved. Dustin would be up to his neck in perks soon if my mother's usual coping mechanism of power shopping was still the same as before her character transformation. I had no doubt Rae would hold her own in the spoiling category as well. "My Grandma!" Dustin trilled and held out his arms to Rae.

She looked at Dean incredulously, as though she couldn't believe that this moment was finally happening.

RAE

I bent down and swept Dustin into my arms. I buried my head into the nape of his neck. He smelled like all little boys of his age- like Sean once had. It was a heady, intoxicating blend of sweat, dirt, apple juice, and crayons. The baby powder smell of small children didn't cling to him anymore.

"I love you so much," I choked out. "It's so nice to meet you finally."

I didn't know who I was crying for, this child or the one I had carried and lost, or both. My body began to shudder again with deep sobs. Dustin was wriggling, trying to get away. Even though I recognized this, I physically couldn't let him go.

I felt his strong, quickening heartbeat through his shirt. A heart half Sean's pumped blood that was half my son's throughout his tiny body. I couldn't believe how much Dustin resembled Sean so completely- not just his looks, but even his voice and personality. I felt parts of me cracking and expanding out of the hard shell despair had encased them in as he relaxed into my touch.

My body responded, reliving memories of Sean coming home nearly every day and throwing his arms around my waist. First, he buried his head in first the expanse of my thighs, then as he grew, my soft stomach, and then into my neck as a teenager. My tears fell hot and fast. My breath came in stops and starts. Dean had moved behind me, presumably because I had developed a penchant for fainting since this whole thing had started.

As I cried, Dustin squeezed me harder and harder. Then, he reached his chubby hand up and started to pat and rub my shoulder lightly to comfort me.

"Is okay. Is okay." He mumbled, pulling away to look at my face with concern.

"Oh, I'm not sad. These are happy tears. I'm just glad to meet you." I assured him.

"You happy?" He smiled, obviously pleased to have that effect on me.

"Oh, yes." I hugged him close again. "I brought you some things to show you how happy I am to meet you."

I managed to extract myself from the tangle I had created of our limbs. I dug around in my carry-on bag. Finally, I found the box, wrapped in sparkly red paper.

Dustin made quick work of the wrapping paper, ripping it off in record time. I helped him lift the lid off the box. Even though I knew what was inside, it still laid me flat.

My tears came hard and fast, my throat aching with the effort of trying to contain them. I surrendered completely when Dustin lifted the Ramones tee shirt.

Seeing it held in front of him felt like I had traveled back in time twenty years. But then, in the next instant, I realized Sean was gone and would never know Dustin. I had to sit down; the air completely emptied from my lungs.

Dean, sensing my needs as always, navigated us to the couch. Dustin clamored up next to me. He pulled out the shoebox then.

"Converse?" Rebecca asked, surprised and delighted. "I love Converse."

"Your daddy wore these all the time. And now you can too." I nodded to answer Rebecca while explaining to Dustin.

I smacked a kiss on the top of his head, meeting Dean's eyes as I did. His enormous smile and tear-stained cheeks matched mine. The rest of the world fell away as I stared into the eyes of the man who I had loved most of my life with my son's child tightly in my arms.

As I marveled at the enormity of this moment, Rebecca broke through my thoughts. I looked up, breaking my stare with Dean, startled.

"I'm sorry, I forgot you were there for a second!" I stammered.

"Apparently," she said, her voice thick with sarcasm.

She looked uncomfortable and what I could best assess as aggravated or even angry.

"Are we ready to eat?"

"Can't wait!" I replied.

Rebecca and I both leaned down and reached down to pick up Dustin and put him in the highchair simultaneously. Her expression was openly hostile as she gave him a light, possessive tug, moving him closer to her.

"I got him," she snapped.

I immediately released my grip on him, took a step back, and held up my hands in a surrender pose.

"Sorry, I meant no offense. Just trying to help."

Her face softened, and she looked sheepish.

"Of course, you were. It's just been a long day. I'm still reeling over Mom. I'm sorry."

"Let's eat!" Dean said as Rebecca strapped in Dustin between us.

We all wordlessly heaped pasta onto our plates. I tried to meet Rebecca's eyes, but she busied herself with preparing Dustin's plate. My appetite had diminished as I began to worry about Rebecca's reaction to me meeting Dustin. Did I threaten her? Anyone could see how Dustin adored her. She was the sun and the moon in his world.

But I also knew the protective nature of mothers, especially mothers of sons. I hoped Rebecca wasn't starting to view me as a threat or competition. I began to retreat inside of myself, deep in thought. Dean's laugh broke through my fog.

"Excuse me?" I asked.

"What? Oh, I was talking to Becca. Sorry, Rae!" Dean said distractedly, turning back to Rebecca and their conversation.

I felt left out, just as I had that morning. Dustin began to rock back and forth in his high chair next to me. Then I heard a sound that pulled me back to my son sitting in his highchair, fists filled with whatever his favorite food was that week. Giggling. Sean had always giggled when he liked his meal. It was like his own personal chef's kiss.

Dean and I had marveled, bursting into excited and thrilled laughter, the first time he had done it. When he had stopped, around the time he went to kindergarten, we had mourned. It had felt like the closing of a chapter, the last of his infanthood slipping away right before our eyes. And now, Dustin giggled.

He sat beside me, his hands red with pasta sauce, and sloppily shoved noodles into his mouth. His laughter tumbled out in bursts as he chewed and swallowed. I felt the tears come to my eyes once again and looked up to see that Dean had stopped, fork mid-air, to stare at Dustin as well.

Rebecca chatted on for a moment, oblivious. When Dean didn't respond, she stopped abruptly.

"What's wrong?" She asked anxiously.

"He's giggling," Dean said as he sat down his fork and dabbed at his eyes.

"Oh yes, he's giggled when he eats since he was a tiny baby." She smiled. "My mother gets a kick out of it. She said it's joyous. Her vocabulary is so flowery now that she is sick."

She chuckled softly.

I found my voice. "Sean used to giggle when he ate."

"You're kidding!"

Rebecca looked back and forth between us in disbelief.

Dean nodded. "He did."

Dustin continued to giggle away, oblivious to the adults and the charged emotions around the table. He was making a glorious mess. Rebecca looked like she wanted to say something, but she didn't know exactly what.

She opened and closed her mouth a few times. She raised her hand as if she was going to start to speak when the phone rang. She jumped up to grab her cellphone off the counter.

"It's the hospital!" She said, worry clouding her face.

"This is she." She said into the phone. She listened for a moment. "Ok, ok. I will be there soon. Can you please let her know?"

She hung up the phone, and when she turned to us, she looked exhausted and aged. My heart went out to her immediately. I had lost both my parents within four months of each other when Sean had been a baby. The grueling pace of caring for them and then mourning while caring for an infant had nearly destroyed me. As with every other time in my life, Dean had been my savior then, stepping up and caring for Sean and making me sleep and eat.

"I have to go. Mom woke up again and is really anxious and won't calm down. Not that keeping her calm has ever been my specialty, but we'll see." She reported glumly.

"Do you want me to go back with you?" I asked.

"No, no! I would really appreciate it if you stayed here and got Dustin to sleep, if you don't mind. And he'll need a bath."

She smiled as she looked at him. He had taken his hands and raked them through his hair. He coated his curls in a salad dressing/ pasta sauce mixture.

"Oh, boy! He sure does!" I laughed. "I am more than happy to stay and take care of him. That's why we came- to be of help! Do you have a special routine you follow for him for bedtime?"

Dean began to attempt to clean Dustin off as Rebecca and I went to their room. She showed me the soap and shampoo, laid out a diaper and wipes, a pacifier, and some pajamas.

"I usually let him pick the book. There's a bunch in the basket right there."

She motioned to a wicker basket on the floor next to an upholstered glider.

"Okay, I think that's it. Do you have any questions? I have to get to Mom." She paused for a moment and sank onto the bed. "God, I am exhausted."

"I know you are. Being a caregiver is sometimes harder than being the one who is sick." I said, sitting next to her and rubbing her back soothingly.

"I didn't think she would die." Her voice cracked, and she began to sob. "It's not enough time."

"It never is, sweetheart. It never is."

Sean's face came to my mind and my own tears started to fall. I let a few tears leak out of the corners of my eyes and then began to gather myself. Rebecca didn't need to worry about my feelings when her own were so raw and consuming. I had come here to help her and to get to know her. I would do just that.

"Are you sure you want to go over to see your mom? Maybe you should get some sleep. I can call and have the nurses give her something to calm her down." I asked.

Her sobs ceased. She straightened her shoulders and swiped at her cheeks.

"No, Mom needs me." She said in a way that made me confident she needed her mother just as much as her mother needed her.

She stood up and went into the bathroom. The toilet flushed, and I heard the water running. Rebecca came out a few minutes later, with her face washed and her teeth freshly brushed.

"I'm going to go say goodbye to Dustin." She said.

"If you want, you can have Dean move the pack and play up to your room. Or you guys can sleep in here. When I get home, I can sleep on the couch or in Mom's room. Whatever you guys want. Just text me if you end up sleeping in here, so I don't disturb you when I come home."

"Okay, we'll figure it out," I said.

With that, she turned and was out the door. I heard her saying goodbye to Dustin. I admired the intricate mural of a Disney movie I couldn't quite remember on the wall in front of me. Dustin tore in suddenly.

"Potts! Potts!" He shouted.

"What? What do you want, Dustin?" I asked, confused by this shorthand that only Rebecca seemed to understand.

"Potts!"

Dustin leaned on the wall, his hand slapping down on a cartoon teapot. His hand and head resting on the wall smeared sauce across the colorful display.

Dustin was already half-naked and turning the faucet knobs by the time I rounded the corner to the bathroom. I finished undressing him and adjusted the water. I added some bubble bath and eased Dustin into the frothy mountains it formed. He immediately began to play with the toys lined up neatly on the ledge of the tub. One by one, he knocked them off, and they plunged into the white foam of the water. His laughter and splashes filled the bathroom. I felt Dean's presence watching from the doorway. He moved silently next to me and put his hand on my shoulder.

"It's been a long time since we did bath time." He said.

"I know."

"It feels pretty damn great." He said. "This is unreal."

"I know." I couldn't manage more than that.

We watched in silence for a few minutes. Dustin dipped his hand into the bubbles and emerged with a fistful of glistening iridescent spheres, running it through his hair and making a mohawk.

I took out my phone and snapped a picture. I wanted to send it to Patti later. I also wanted to add it to the wall at home, where Sean was displayed with his matching foamy mohawk.

"That was your dad's favorite thing to do, too," I told him as I doused his head to rinse out the soap.

"Rae, maybe we shouldn't talk about Sean with him until we talk to Rebecca. She looked pretty shaken by your gifts." Dean said.

"She wouldn't have let us come this far or even do the test if she wasn't open to him knowing his father and our family." I countered.

"Maybe so, but let's err on the side of caution until we talk to her. I don't want to do anything that would make her angry or cause her to keep him away from us. I don't want to lose another child." Dean said thickly.

"I know, sweetheart. We won't."

As Dustin played and splashed, nearly soaking the floor and us in the process, we hashed out the details of our sleeping arrangements. Dean made quick work of bringing his Pack and Play upstairs to the attic suite. I texted Rebecca, letting her know where he would be. I also asked how she and her mother were doing.

153

This could be a long night. She's agitated. Thank you for taking Dusty. I will talk to you in the morning. Please give him a kiss for me.

As I lifted Dustin, glistening and slick with water and bubbles, it was like long atrophied muscles were coming alive. My body reacted to the simple tasks of a mother getting her child ready for bed without me thinking about it. My mind and body were waking up from a long sleep, excited to be useful again after a long and painful break.

I toweled him off and smoothed lotion on his skin. The scent was just the same as it had been all those years before, when I had applied it on my own son's skin, dreaming of the days when he would do the same for his children. I swallowed the lump in my throat and helped Dustin into miniature dinosaur pajamas.

"Come on! You want to sleep upstairs with Grandma and Grandpa tonight?" I smiled down at him.

He jumped up and down and clapped excitedly. "I sleep with Grandpa! Snack?"

"You want a snack? I bet Grandpa does too. What should we have?"

We made popcorn in the microwave and brought it upstairs to Dean, who had changed into his pajamas. His face brightened at the sight of us.

"Popcorn! My favorite!"

He sat down on the bed and patted the mattress next to him.

"Come on, buddy, come sit over here. Want to watch something while we eat our snack?"

Dustin darted onto the bed eagerly and crawled up towards the pillows, settling against them, directly in the middle. The image reminded me of a king ruling over his subjects from his bed, comfortable and sated.

I giggled to myself as I handed over the bowl. They dove in eagerly.

I went into the bathroom to get myself ready for bed. I yawned. I was finally letting myself feel how exhausted I truly was. I brushed my teeth and slid my nightgown over my head.

When I came back into the room, the lights were dim, and a show about what appeared to be problem-solving cartoon dogs was on the television.

"This will be over soon, and then he'll go to bed," Dean said.

"It's good to know you're as much of a pushover as a grandpa as you were a father." I teased, recalling the many nights I got over-ruled for bedtimes, special treats, or movies I wouldn't let Sean watch by his father.

We had always agreed on the big stuff, but Dean was more laid back about the little things.

"Hey now, twenty extra minutes on a special day like this won't hurt him."

He sounded almost defensive, but he had a smile on his face.

"I know, I am just joking. Don't get your knickers in a knot." I said.

The glow of the television illuminated the room as we finished the popcorn. Before the show was over, Dustin was already cuddled into Dean's side, fast asleep. Dean and I met eyes over his sleeping form. He reached his arm out to me, and I slid over, closer to Dustin.

Our bodies all meddled together, our breath and hearts syncing almost instantly. Dean planted a kiss on the top of my head. *Complete*, I thought as I drifted off to sleep.

REBECCA

I heard her before I saw her. A long, piercing primal scream echoed down the stark white hallway as the elevator doors slid open. I hurried down the hall, terrified but also drawn to the noise.

My heart pounded as I ran towards the room. When I got to the ICU, I saw the nurses clustered together around my mother through the glass. Everyone crowded around her bedside turned to look at me at the same time. Mom continued to writhe and scream.

"Mom! Mom! Shhh. It's okay. Let's calm down." I said as I moved closer to her.

As she spotted me, her screams quieted.

"Where have you been?" She said tearfully.

"Mom, I told you I was going home for the night. Do you remember? I had to get Dustin. It's okay. Come here."

I leaned into her, hugging her. I was taken aback that her smell- the expensive perfume she dotted on her neck faithfully every morning mingled with lilac and sweet mint from the mints she always carried in her purse- was gone. It was replaced with a pungent, sterile smell of alcohol and adhesive.

"You haven't even been here. You left me alone." She sobbed. "You didn't even stay for me."

"Mom, I was here when you came out. Do you remember? We talked about Rae and Dean?"

A plump nurse with a gray-streaked bob and kind brown eyes touched my arm softly. "Sometimes, the medicine they use from surgery can be dis-orienting. It can make them lose moments of time. She's been pretty out of it."

Her words hung there, and she looked like she wanted to say more.

"But?" I supplied.

"But sometimes, it could mean that something is going on neurologically, like a stroke. It could also mean her cancer has spread. Her doctors have already been in, and her test results are all still pending. Right now, we can give her something for her anxiety so she can get some rest. You're welcome to stay as long as you like. You seem to have the magic touch."

She smiled.

"I can bring you a pillow and blanket if you would like."

"Yes, let's try to get her calmed down. Mom, they're going to give you some medication to make you feel better."

At that, the nurse standing next to me nodded to another one on the other side of the bed. She took a syringe filled with liquid out of her pocket and pushed it into her IV. in a few moments, Mom stilled, and a look of peace transformed her face. She opened her eyes and smiled weakly.

"I love you, baby girl." She said as she began to doze off.

I staggered into the hallway, barely able to make it out the door before I doubled over with grief. Silent sobs wracked my body. I was nearly on the floor, as every cry sent me sliding further down the wall when a strong set of hands lifted me.

"Not here." The nurse with the kind eyes whispered. She led me by the elbow to a deserted office. "I'll be right back."

I put my head down on the table in front of me and sobbed. My mother was dying. My secret was out. I was alone. My life was falling down around me, and I felt absolutely powerless to fix anything.

I heard the door open and the rustle of a wrapper close to my head. I calmed myself and lifted my head.

A packet of graham crackers, a pack of saltines, and a miniature can of ginger ale lay on the table. The nurse stood next to me and reached out to rub my shoulders. She held three popsicles in her other hand.

"When I'm upset, snacks make me feel better. Obviously." She gestured to her curvy waist with the popsicle hand. "But I didn't know if you would want salty or sweet. I also didn't know your favorite popsicle flavor. I have red, purple, and orange."

"Red, please," I said miserably, wiping tears away. I also popped open the can of soda and took a swig. "Can I keep these for later? I have a feeling I am going to be here a while."

"Of course, I brought them for you. I'll stick the popsicles back in our fridge, but I will tell the other nurses not to touch them, in case you want them later." She smiled. "They're vultures for unclaimed food."

"What the hell am I going to do? She doesn't even know what's going on. We had an entire, coherent conversation before I left earlier. Now she can barely string a sentence together. This surgery was supposed to help improve her life, not make it worse. At least before, she had her memory." I sobbed.

"This is the tough stuff. The not knowing. I don't know about you, but for me, I like to be in control. Most of us gals do, if we're honest, and not being the one steering the ship is scary. All of this is scary. But you both will get through it. The good news is she is stable. It looks like the transfusion did its job. And since we know she will be transitioning to hospice and that she wants to be home, barring any complications, she should be home tomorrow."

"And then what?"

"Did they walk you through the process this afternoon?"

I nodded as I made tidy work of the red popsicle. We chatted idly for a few minutes, the guarded banter of a negotiator trying to talk a suicidal person off the ledge. When I finished my snack, we left together. She went to deposit the popsicles back in the freezer, and I headed to Mom's room.

She was still asleep and likely would be for the rest of the night. Even knowing that, I hesitated to leave. I felt an urgency suddenly, to spend every moment I could with her, even just watching her sleep. I pictured an hourglass in my mind, with the fat layer of sand on top dripping faster and faster into the chasm below. My mother's sand was almost done.

I pulled out my phone charger and plugged it in. I sent a quick message to Rae letting her know I would be staying here tonight but got no response. I sat down in the crinkly plastic chair, pulled the blanket over me, and drifted off. A few hours later, I heard Mom stirring next to me.

"You ok, Mom?" I went over to her bed and saw tears pooled under her eyes,

"No, I'm not okay. I'm dying! And I messed everything up. I wasted so much time." She cried harder now. "I was just laying here thinking that I'll be gone soon, and then what happens to you and Dustin? He'll only know me through photos. I didn't even want to be a grandmother. I was mad. Furious at you for making me one. And now, it's all I can think about. All I want to be for as long as I can. I made my mistakes with you, but I thought I had time to fix them with him. But I'm out of time."

I perched on her bed and slipped her hand in mine." Mom, you're here. You have time to spend with Dustin. But right now, you need to rest so you can fight. You'll be home with Dustin tomorrow."

" Yeah, for a few more days. And then you'll go back to Boston and leave me to die alone."

" Mom, we're not going anywhere."

I hadn't thought that far ahead. I had only intended to stay a few more days until nursing services were in place and Mom was on the mend. But now, there would be no getting better. In fact, things were going to get a hell of a lot worse. No matter what hurts we had suffered at each other's hands, my mother deserved to die surrounded by her family. We needed to be here till the end.

" What?" Her Botoxed face couldn't register her surprise, but her voice did." What about work? What about your apartment?"

" A job is a job. They come and go. You're my mother. I will just extend my leave. If they can't wait, screw them. And my neighbor can feed my plants. I can pay my rent online."

" I don't want you to rearrange your life for me," she objected, but I could tell how touched and desperate for us to stay she was.

" You gave me my life. It's the least I can do. But you rest now." I said, pressing a kiss on her cheek.

As she drifted back off, looking more peaceful, I tapped out a quick email to Megan and our HR department, letting them know I needed to extend my leave indefinitely. I hoped against hope that Mom would defy the odds and heal. I didn't want to think about living in a world where she did not.

As it had many times during this visit, a wave of loss washed over me. I leaned my head back on the chair's headrest, gathered the blanket around me, and looked out at the city dotted with lights below. I cried myself to sleep.

The nurse coming in at 5 am woke both of us up. She took Mom's vitals happily and informed us Dr. Price was making rounds and would be in soon. About 6:30, Dr. Price and a cluster of young and eager-looking people I assumed to be interns came in. Mom turned on the Bernie charm, receiving her guests with a smile, batted eyelashes, and some hair twirling.

" Well, hello everyone! How are you all this lovely morning?" She trilled.

" Good morning, Bernie! I'm glad to see that smile!" He paused and smiled broadly. "Your coloring looks better. It looks like the transfusion did its job."

"I'm a bit sore but doing okay. The pain meds make me nauseous, though. I'm ready to go home. Can I go today?"

"Let's talk before we make any decisions." He came to her bedside and took her hand. Once again, I thought that she looked frail. He pulled no punches.

"Your tests all show that your diagnosis has now moved to terminal. Bernie, I'm so sorry."

Mom, prepared for the blow, waved her hand breezily, as though death sentences were handed to her as readily as samples at the makeup counter. She didn't flinch or cry. Her Stepford smile, the smile of my childhood, was fixed on her face. If he was waiting for tears, protestations, or pleas to higher powers, Bernie Malone would offer none. She was stone now.

Dr. Price paused for a moment, taken aback, then asked if she had any questions. I held my breath, praying that she wouldn't ask the same one I had.

"How long?" She said as casually as she asked women where they bought their shoes while we were out.

"6 weeks, at most. But again, we have talked about the mind/ body connection. You're the only one who can decide how long. And your spirit is very much alive, Bernie."

He looked at me. "And you have your daughter and grandson here. Enjoy your time with them. I'm ok with you going home today if you feel up to it. A worker will call you to set up a hospice intake. I think you'll find them invaluable."

She smiled the plastic smile and nodded. A man who obviously knew when to quit, Dr. Price gave her one last look and said goodbye. I waited for Mom to cry, but she didn't. Instead, she turned to me and chirped, "Let's get out of here!" brightly.

A few hours later, we had completed the paperwork and packed her belongings. The nurse insisted Bernie leave in a wheelchair. Mom put up a good fight, but they were unyielding.

When she couldn't get them to budge, she disappeared into the bathroom, emerging with a full face of makeup. She covered it with sunglasses, and a headwrap which she had informed me earlier was her "new look" until she found a wig that satisfied her.

She rolled through the halls like a parade grandmaster, her head and chest thrust forward to be admired by her public. The show for public consumption lasted until she was safely in the car with the door closed behind her. I saw her wilt again, and she slept most of the short car ride home. I had texted Rae, letting her know we would be there soon. I was surprised to see one of the complex's security guards and Dean sitting on a golf cart, waiting for us.

"What's all this?" I said, getting out and coming to Mom's side to help her out.

Dean smiled broadly. "We're the welcome wagon. I figured Bernie might not feel like walking to the house, so this young man and I found a solution."

He opened the passenger side and swept his arm out like a cartoon chauffeur. "Your chariot awaits, my dear."

Mom's smile triumphed over her fillers and danced across her face. "Thank you! You must be Dean. I've heard a lot about you."

Her hands flitted around, unsure of themselves since she was used to flirting by twirling her hair, which was tucked up under her head wrap.

"In the flesh. It's a pleasure to meet you, Bernie. Welcome home!"

He enveloped her into a hug and pressed a kiss onto her cheek. I could tell she was smitten with him instantly. She blossomed under his touch. He eased her onto the golf cart gently. She looked hesitant for a moment about the young security guard driving, but Dean picked up on it and soothed her.

"I am going to leave you in his capable hands. I drove this thing here. He had to take over after I drove us into a shrub."

Mom laughed. "That settles it! You're driving, young man. But be careful. You have precious cargo on board."

The driver nodded, obviously charmed. He was cute, tanned in a way that was probably from working outside on the property and swimming in the warm Florida waters but reminded me instantly of a farmer, rippled and shirtless, glistening in the sun while he bailed hay. Despite my sober mood, something inside me stirred as he smiled. *Not the time*, I scolded myself as Dean and I hopped on the back, cradling her overnight bag between us. As we motored through the complex,

I noticed a familiar head bobbing in the pool. Dean saw me looking and smiled.

"It seems your son and my wife have something in common. They're both water babies. I made pancakes and it was all I could do to make them eat and let their food settle. They've been in there for about an hour."

We both lifted our hands to wave to them. Rae spotted us first and pointed us out to Dustin. I heard his squeal of excitement at my arrival. His tanned arm waved furiously. I waved back.

The maintenance worker chuckled at Dustin's reaction. "Looks like you have a fan club." He called back to me.

"The best fan club," I replied.

"I'll get my bathing suit on and come swim!" I called to Dustin.

Mom said something from the front, but the wind and the whir of the motor made it hard to hear.

"What was that?" I asked her as we stopped abruptly in front of her door.

"I said I would like to go sit by the pool. That should be ok, right? I can't swim, of course, but some fresh air should be good."

"As long as you keep yourself hydrated, I think it would be fine for a bit."

"Well hell, if you're both going to the pool, I will too." Dean chimed in. "Let's all change. Meet back in 15 minutes?"

"I'll wait here, and we can go over together." Our designated driver said. "I have to cover a lifeguard shift anyway."

"Thank you, young man. You're so kind." Bernie enthused, placing her delicate hand on his muscled forearm and batting her eyelashes.

Fifteen minutes later found us all gathered by the door. Mom had a black tank suit on with a gauzy, oversized white button-down over it and an enormous straw hat and sunglasses. She looked exotic and classic, like a movie star snapped by paparazzi while on holiday. My suit didn't feel chic and sophisticated anymore, in the shadow of the megawatt brightness that was Bernie. Story of my life. But instead of being resentful as I had been my entire life, all I wanted to do now was bask in her glow for as long as I could.

The three of us climbed back aboard the golf cart, and we whizzed to the pool. Dustin shot out of the water and wrapped his dripping body around my legs as the driver climbed the lifeguard stand behind us. I noticed the flex of his calves as he climbed. When he reached the top and peeled off his shirt, revealing a broad, tanned chest, I gaped over Dustin's head. Mother of the year.

"Miss you." My son mumbled into my neck.

"I missed you too, baby boy," I said, scooping him up and hugging him hard.

I felt foolish to have felt jealous about him loving anyone more than me. It was apparent even with two eager and doting grandparents taking care of him, he had been waiting for and missing me.

We eased down the pool stairs into the warm water; Dustin slung on my hip and holding on tightly. Rae hovered closer to the deep end, where Dean sliced through the water after a nearly perfect dive off the diving board. It appeared Dustin and Rae weren't the only swimmers in the family.

"It's good to see you back. Dustin missed you. You must be exhausted," Rae said as she swam over to us. "I know how uncomfortable hospital chairs can be. And how early they like to get the party started there."

"You've spent a lot of time in hospitals?" I asked.

"Unfortunately, yes. I lost both my parents within four months of each other. It was terrible."

For a moment, her eyes went far away from me, back in time to people and places I would never know. Her face flushed with such pain that it broke my heart. Sympathy for her surged inside of me.

"That's why it was important for me to come when I heard your mom was sick. No one should have to go through something like this alone."

"I know I haven't always acted like it, but I do appreciate you being here. This is way more than I bargained for. I thought I was coming home for Christmas and now, I'm here to stay."

"You're staying here?"

She looked confused and alarmed.

"For the time being. I can't imagine leaving her here to die alone." My voice broke then, and I paused. "We're going to stay with her until the end. I extended my leave. My landlord is happy to hold our apartment, as long as I pay rent, of course."

"Well, I would think he would have to hold it if you're paying for it."

"True, but you know people do all kinds of unsavory things when people are at their weakest."

"You're not at your weakest, Rebecca. I know I'm virtually a stranger, but from what I've seen of you, you don't have a weak bone in your body." She smiled genuinely.

I was touched. I reached out to take Rae's hand, made pruny by the pool, and squeezed it.

"Thank you. You don't know what that means to me. I'm trying hard to stay strong for Mom. Glad to know it's working."

"I mean it, Rebecca. It seems impossible, but you will get through it."

Her voice caught then, and her chin quivered. I followed her gaze to Dustin and knew she was thinking of Sean. I saw her pull herself together. Her face smoothed out, and she smiled again. My heart broke for her again, even as I marveled at her strength. I gave her hand another squeeze.

"I think I am going to go work on my tan. That little man wore me out!"

She grinned as Dustin floated by on a raft pulled by Dean, who was rocking it. Dustin dissolved into laughter every time Dean bobbed under the water, holding his breath until he popped up, spraying water everywhere and snapping his arms like the treacherous shark's jaws.

I watched Rae climb out of the water and make her way over to the chaise lounge where Mom was holding court. I couldn't hear them from here, but I saw Mom reach up and Rae take her hand, then bend down into a hug. She sat down on the chaise next to her, and they began to talk like lifelong friends.

I'll be damned, I thought. *She's starting to grow on me.* I leaned back into the water, throwing my feet up and floating aimlessly. I could hear Dean and Dustin playing, their splashes traveling through the water. The sun was hot on my body. It felt good. It was almost like I was in a womb, isolated and protected. The tension of the past few weeks was slowly falling away. I felt eyes on me.

I looked up, poking my head out of the water like a lazy turtle. The driver turned lifeguard was staring at me, a smile on his lips. He caught me looking, grinned openly, and gave me a little wave. Unnerved, my face burned. I lowered my head back down, not sure how else to react. I floated there for a few more minutes. I felt a small, slimy hand grab my toes and looked to see Dean and Dustin at my feet.

"Play!" He commanded simply.

"Of course!" I exclaimed and sent a spray of water at him.

I looked over my shoulder to check on Mom, but she was absorbed in conversation with Rae. Joy filled me at the sight of the two chatting animatedly. Seeing that she was tended to, I devoted my full attention to Dustin and Dean. We spent the next forty-five minutes splashing and laughing together. Rae appeared at the side of the pool suddenly.

"Rebecca, your mom needs to go back now. Do you want me to bring her, or are you guys ready to go?"

I looked at Dustin, rosy and yawning. Dean also stifled a yawn. "I think we're ready to get out. Come on, Dusty. You can take a bath before dinner."

Dean took the bag as I carried Dustin, who was already starting to doze in my arms. I wrapped a towel around Dustin and gathered everything in the bag while Dean and Rae helped Mom up. The security guard with the golf cart was suspiciously but also conveniently driving by at the same time and stopped as soon as he saw Mom. Without a word, he stopped and held his hand out for her to sit down. She smiled gratefully and settled onto the seat.

"Anyone else?" He asked.

The three of us shook our heads. We trudged the short distance home, where Mom sat in the golf cart chatting with the guard. They regarded us as we came around the corner. His eyes swept me up and down. I could feel them rolling over my hips and cleavage, on display through the thin cover-up I wore.

"Slowpokes," she teased and elbowed the guard, clearly the co-conspirator in her joke.

"Well, we all can't be hell on wheels." I joked. "Come on in."

I opened the door, and Rae linked her arm through Mom's to help her off the cart and into the house. Dean was off to the side whispering with the driver.

"Bye, Todd!" Mom called over her shoulder.

"Who's Todd?" I asked, coming in behind her.

"The driver, Rebecca."

As I closed the door behind us, she turned and grinned. "He's too young for you to date, but a fling would be okay. Want me to set it up?"

"Mother!" My eyes widened in horror and shock. "Rae, I apologize for her. She doesn't have boundaries."

Rae grinned and exchanged a look with Mom. "I don't know. A little fling could be just the thing to help manage all that stress."

I shook my head at both as they dissolved into a fit of laughter. Dean came in the door and looked from one to the other, then at me.

"Do I want to know?"

"No. We're going to have our hands full with these two." I said jokingly. "What was that about?"

"Man talk!" He joked, puffing out his chest.

"I give up on all of you! I'm giving this boy a bath." I laughed and started towards the bedroom.

"I'll cook." Rae offered. "Chicken, okay?"

"Sounds divine, although anything is better than hospital food." Mom said as she moved towards her bedroom.

As I sponged Dustin's pink skin, my thoughts drifted to Rae. I wouldn't have predicted changing my feelings about her, but they were, and quickly. I had seen almost immediately that Rae had lived a life bogged down and cast grey by a cloud of tragedy and sorrow. Yet, she still shone as intensely as the sun with love, calm, and compassion. She drew you in, much like Bernie, but in a quiet and unassuming way that perfectly complemented Bernie's charismatic and animated one.

Where Bernie popped and fizzled like a magnificent fireworks display, Rae burned intense and steady. The hot fire of her love for Sean had almost burned my life to the ground, but Bernie's love for me was saving it. Each woman's complicated love of their children, and my own for Dustin, were all tangled up together now.

Loving my son was to love his father and the woman who loved him with a ferocity not even death could subdue. Right then, as Dustin splashed various marine animals in the glossy water, I waved the invisible white flag and surrendered. Rae was winning me over, despite my absolute best efforts to resist.

About half an hour later, everyone was bathed and changed and gathered around the table. My mouth watered at all the good smells that filled the room. We all oohed and ahhed over the meal and dove in. We all talked over each other and laughed, as though we were old friends or even family, instead of nearly strangers.

A knock at the door interrupted the meal. I rushed to open it. The golf cart Maintenance worker who I remembered was named Todd stood before me. He smiled, making my heart leap against my will. His smile faded when he saw we were eating. Todd cleared his throat.

"I just came to see if you left these in the golf cart." He said, holding up a pair of sunglasses. "But I see I interrupted dinner. I'm so sorry. I'm going to go."

Impulsively, I spoke. "No, no! Stay! Come sit down. We'll be excited to have you. We're having some delicious chicken Rae made. Do you like chicken?"

"Who doesn't like chicken?" He replied, moving forward almost involuntarily, drawn in by the smell of the food.

RAE

"We're going to put Dustin down for bed," Dean said suddenly, seeing Dustin's empty plate and Becca and Todd's starry eyes.

"Come on, Dustin." I held out my hand, following Dean's lead. He grabbed it eagerly and climbed the stairs happily.

Dustin settled down and drifted off quickly. Dean lay on the bed. I joined him, curling up with my head on his firm chest.

"So, how soon before those two jumps in the sack?" Dean asked.

"Let the girl have a little fun. She is losing her mother, and we rocked her whole world. She needs to blow off a little steam."

"Pretty sure my boy Todd is hoping she blows something other than steam." Dean teased.

I swatted at him.

"So vulgar!"

But I was laughing along with him as we both started to doze off.

About an hour later, Dustin stirred, crying for Rebecca. Dean didn't move, but no surprise there. He had always slept like the dead. Dustin wouldn't settle. We went downstairs in search of his mother's arms.

Bernie was still awake, folded into the couch with a blanket slung over her legs, regaling Todd with stories. Todd sat in the armchair, his deep laughter punctuating the air.

"He wanted Mama," I said, sliding Dustin off my shoulder and onto Becca's waiting one.

"Come here, my sweet boy." She said, smiling at the sight of him.

He immediately reached his hand up, cupped her cheek, and snuggled into her. He was asleep almost instantly. She kissed the top of his head, and her face smoothed, at peace.

As she sat rocking Dustin, I noticed Rebecca's gaze lingering on Todd for just a moment longer than was usual. I shared Bernie's fear that she was lonely. I also hoped that she would find a partner- strong, steadfast, selfless in their love and time- like the man sleeping above us one day.

However, watching her watch Todd like the treasured picnic basket to her hungry Yogi Bear made me remember some words I had always known to be true: sometimes a solid romp in the hay was the salve for what ailed you.

"Todd, would you like to stay for a drink? We're all going to watch a movie. I'm sure we can find a spot for you." Bernie said.

He smiled, catching Rebecca's eye and staring openly.

"Why, yes, I think I would."

"Excellent," Rebecca said, surprising both Bernie and me. She caught my eye and smiled quickly. "I'm going to put him in bed." She motioned towards Dustin, still sleeping on her lap, with her chin.

As she walked away, I noticed a bit more swing to her hips. I looked at Todd, and apparently, he had as well. It looked like he appreciated the view. As if channeling her mother, Becca turned slightly and looked over her shoulder through heavy-lidded eyes at Todd. Bernie beamed with unrestrained pride.

Rebecca emerged a few minutes later, her face pink after a fresh washing and her hair piled on top of her head, a few curls falling onto her neck. She had changed into a flowy cotton camisole tank top with matching shorts peeking out underneath. The hem of both was trimmed with matching lace, which accentuated the subtle cleavage Rebecca had on display. At the sight of her, Bernie turned to me, a smile lighting her face. Todd cleared his throat several times.

"Do you need a drink, dear?" Bernie asked him.

"Oh yes, please. My mouth is dry." He managed.

"A mixed drink or something non-alcoholic?"

"Soda is fine, thanks."

Being closest to the fridge, I leaned in and produced the drink, tossing it to Todd. Todd cracked it open and took several small sips.

Rebecca made quick work of pulling out the sectional, which transformed to a full-size bed with just a few tugs. Bernie settled on one side and then looked at me expectantly to fill in the spot on the other side. I did just that, pulling a blanket onto my lap as I lay against the cushions.

We rolled an old film from the 80s I vaguely recollected seeing before, but none of us seemed too invested. Bernie dozed first, about half an hour into the movie. I hadn't noticed that Rebecca and Todd were making eyes at each other in the darkness, but when the television screen illuminated the room, I did.

"I'm beat," I said, faking a yawn.

I made a hasty exit. Once I was upstairs and under the covers, Dean swept me into a deep, passionate kiss, moving stealthily in the night.

"What was that for?" I asked with a laugh. "Sorry I woke you."

"A man can't kiss his wife?"

"A man can always kiss his wife. I just didn't know if there was a special reason."

"Well, I love you, so a kiss for that. But I also haven't had one moment alone with you, so a kiss for that. And I want you, so a kiss for that."

"Ah, so this is seduction. I see." I joked.

"Hey, if you don't want to be seduced, I can do a crossword and take a cold shower."

"I didn't say that. Get over here."

I pulled him to me, kissing him this time. We ended up with mouths and hands roving. We paused when we heard Rebecca's laughter below, Todd's deep voice, and the front door closing. I expected to hear Rebecca go into her room, but the sound of her door closing never came.

"Oh, my goodness, do you think she left with him?" I asked breathlessly, not only from the kissing but from delight for Rebecca.

"Todd, my boy. Well played, sir." Dean mumbled into my neck, still kissing and nuzzling me. "Well, it appears that everyone is either asleep or out. No time like the present."

I didn't need any convincing. Dean had always been wildly attractive to me. He had to put forth almost no effort to get in my pants. I had lost my virginity to him much sooner than I had ever sworn I would, my desire for him accelerating the timeline.

My thoughts returned to the present as Dean entered me, hard and fast, taking my breath away. I lost time as we moved together, savoring each other and bringing each other to the brink of frenzy masterfully, in the way that only people intimately familiar with each other's bodies can. Soon, we both tumbled over the edge, coming to a shuddering and gasping end together.

We laid there for a long time. Unexpectedly, I began to cry silently. Dean turned to me with a giant, content smile on his face, but it quickly faded when he saw my tears.

"What's wrong?" He asked, alarmed.

"Nothing. That's why I'm crying."

He looked confused. "You're crying because you don't have anything to be sad about?"

"No, I'm crying because I feel happy."

"Rae, you're allowed to be happy."

"My son died. I don't feel like I should ever be happy again."

"No, you feel like we don't have the right to be happy again. There's a difference. You feel like every moment should be shadowed by our loss, and it's simply not true. Sean's death doesn't mean there will never be more joy for us." He paused. "Sean wouldn't want us to spend our lives unhappy. He wouldn't want us to cry anything but happy tears. You know that as well as I do."

"I just haven't felt anything even close to joy since the day Boston PD called us. Being here, every moment is happiness. Bernie dying is terrible, but Dustin makes it better for all of us."

Now it was my turn to pause.

"I'm almost afraid to love him," I confessed.

Dean's brow furrowed. "What?"

"The only other boy I have loved completely and totally, with a love that would make me slay dragons or lay down my life without hesitation, was Sean. And I lost him. And then I lost me."

"And that's not going to happen again. Even just being here this short of a time, I can already tell that Rebecca has accepted that we will be in Dustin's life. She isn't taking him away from us." Dean reassured me.

"Okay, but what about drowning in a pool? Or getting hit by a car? Or a brain tumor? Or a kidnapper? Or a murderer?"

"You would close your heart to our grandson based on a set of highly improbable what ifs? That doesn't sound like the woman I married." Dean chided gently.

"Logically, I know you're right. But that voice is always in the back of my head. Warning me to enjoy it while it lasts."

"Or how about just enjoy it? We beat some incredible odds to get here. You can relax and just bask in your grandchild. You're a grandma. Enjoy the benefits of the title."

He kissed my cheek softly, his stubble scratchy but erotic on my skin. "You've earned some happiness, my love. Let's just soak it all in as long as we can. But now, you've tired me out, and I am ready for bed. Good night."

"Sweet dreams," I murmured as his snoring started almost instantaneously.

I lay awake for a while longer, still unable to sleep. I first wandered downstairs to check on Dustin and then Bernie, who I discovered cuddled into the couch. I made sure the covers were snug around her. As I was adjusting the blankets, Rebecca came in, smiling and dazed, her face flushed.

"I-i just had sex with Todd. On a golf course!" She blurted, sounded amazed, and appalled at the same time.

I said the first thing that came to my mind, which was, unfortunately, the least grandmotherly thing I could say.

"Was it good?"

Rebecca's eyes widened. My heart lurched, thinking I had shattered the fragile peace she and I had danced around since our arrival. Her face went from surprise to amusement, and she started to giggle. She locked the door and moved to the kitchen, still laughing.

"Best I've ever had." She admitted. She shook her head. "I'm way too old to have just figured out what all the fuss about sex is about."

She fell silent. When she spoke again, she sounded dream-like but resolute.

"I feel like being here is changing me. Sex with Todd has woken me up. Not just my lady parts, though God knows they needed it, but the parts of me that had just been sleep-walking through life." She paused, thoughtful. "For a long time, I've fallen into a pattern- wake up, take care of Dustin, be at Megan's mercy for 8 hours or more, go home and take care of Dustin and fall into bed as soon as he's asleep. I'm a zombie stumbling through a life I intentionally chose. I've never realized how heavy the weights of motherhood and responsibility were on me until I got here, and life slowed down enough for me to breathe and think. I had a child to make my life fuller, and I can't even enjoy him because I'm too busy balancing all the plates in the air. I've been simply surviving for so long."

She stopped again, thinking some more. When she spoke again, her voice was soft and introspective. "This was the catalyst for change I needed. All of it: you and Dean and Sean and my mother's impending death and even Todd. You're all helping me grow and change. Awaken."

She paused again. I swallowed the lump in my throat as I opened my mouth to thank her for opening up to me. But before I could speak, she began again.

"I haven't been fair to you, Rae. I was so angry at you for finding me. I maybe even hated you. Your presence threatened me because it meant my lie would come out. I thought Dustin would love me less by loving you. So, I held you at arm's length and acted like a bitch. I've been unappreciative when all you have tried to do is help. You've been nothing but generous and kind. I've never met anyone like you. I just want to say thank you and apologize. I'm not the easiest nut to crack, especially when I feel threatened, but my guard comes down now. You came into our lives for a reason, and you're stuck with us now."

She stopped. I reached across the counter and squeezed her hand, too overcome to talk. Again, she chuckled.

"Sorry, I'm all excited. I'm talking too much." She said.

"Don't you dare apologize," I replied.

She slid off the seat, fished a bottle of water out of the fridge, and headed towards her room.

"Good night, Rae. I'm glad you're here."

REBECCA

Todd's kiss was fresh on my lips, and his smell, Irish Spring and sunscreen mingled with aftershave lingered on my skin. I marveled at myself, at the impetuous and unexpected turn of events.

After Rae's unceremonious exit, Todd asked if I would like to make sure everything was quiet on the property. I knew it wasn't his responsibility, but I agreed, without over-analyzing, stressing, or thinking for once in my life. It felt good to be with someone in my age bracket, not just the "infants and elders." We whizzed through the night on the golf cart, Todd's voice punctuating the dark.

"Look at that lizard! I didn't know they mingled with humans until I moved here."

"The Rothstein' flower beds look a little overgrown. I'll have to issue them a citation tomorrow."

We stopped at the golf course on the outskirts of the property. The lake that spanned across the back of the course was still in front of us, the moon magnified and luminous in the canvas of the water. The sky above us twinkled with millions of points of brilliant light.

The scene seemed like a plotline from an 80's teen movie, complete with the heartthrob. The teenage girl inside of me squealed with anticipation and delight. The woman in me felt slightly ridiculous but also swept up in the romance of the moment.

"It's gorgeous." I breathed, taking it in.

"It certainly is," Todd said, but he wasn't looking at the view. He was staring straight at me, his gaze unwavering.

"Thank you," I said, not quite sure how to respond to such an overt flirtation.

"You're quite welcome, darlin."

And with that, he had sealed his mouth over mine, probing the recesses with an experienced touch. When his lips touched mine, I realized how starved I was for romantic affection, passion. How much I didn't believe I was due these things. I kissed him back with what I hoped was the same amount of intensity and passion.

When we pulled away from each other, we were both breathless and grinning.

"Wow," he said fervently.

"Yeah, I'd say," I said.

"That was something else."

"Again, I agree."

"Let's do it again."

And with that, he had planted another lingering kiss on me. He worked his mouth down to my neck next, taking his time kissing and licking the thin skin there.

"I feel your pulse. Someone's excited," Todd teased. "You smell incredible."

My thoughts flickered to Bernie and the obscenely expensive Chanel perfume she had gifted me several Christmases before.

"Men find this scent so alluring." She had purred.

Now, I could see the wisdom in her words.

His teeth gleamed in the moon's light as he smiled. He began to kiss me again. As our hands began to roam over the landscape of each other, beginning the process of learning the curves and scars, I felt his excitement through his pants. Without thinking, I tugged at his belt. He stopped his roving for a moment, surprised, and pulled back.

"Hey, no pressure here. You don't have to do that. I just needed to kiss you. I haven't stopped obsessing about it since dinner."

"Well, what if I need to do this?"

"Then, don't let me stop you." He held up his hands in surrender, a smile on his lips.

That was all the permission I needed. Things moved rapidly from there, a blur of motion and wetness and skin. I had intended to stop, but something inside me, the same place that was numb with a loss so profound I couldn't breathe to think of it, craved more. It felt good to be wanted.

The desire burned down through the icy sadness, consuming me. I was heady with the power of being the one to elicit such a reaction in a man. I was finally the girl who got the guy, not the one watching from the sidelines, while the other girls made love connections. I was feeling for the first time since I heard the words terminal and hospice.

And so, I cast aside my personal code of conduct and surrendered to my carnal impulses, right there on the green. After such a long dry spell, I was worried that I had forgotten how to do it or that it would be painful. I worried about being able to satisfy someone, whether Dustin's delivery had impacted my physical structures. As it turned out, all my concerns were unfounded. As he entered me, Todd's face told me all I needed to know about the state of my lady parts. I also discovered sex was like riding a bike, the motions and the sensations coming back with each touch and movement. It was like I was outside myself, watching another woman, one desirable and even a bit wanton. A woman men wanted so bad they had to have them right on the golf course. I surrendered control as an orgasm rolled over me.

I cried out, my voice carrying across the deserted course and mixing with Todd's guttural moans and grunts. When we were done, we laid there, fingers laced, looking up at the stars. The air felt heavy like Todd wanted to say something.

"Thank you," I began but was cut short by rustling in the bushes near us.

Todd jumped up, on high alert. "It could be a gator, but we're not sticking around to find out. Let's go."

We made quick work of putting our clothes back on and took off in the golf cart. We jetted through the night, our laughter bouncing off the buildings like a fun house's ghoulish cackles. We reached my mother's unit, and we sat there for a moment, my anticipation mounting. After what seemed like forever, he leaned over and kissed me, a soft, chaste peck.

"I picked up a lifeguard shift tomorrow. See you and Dustin by the pool?"

"Of course, he doesn't miss a day."

"Good night, darlin'," He said.

"Good night," I replied and slipped in the door.

My phone ringing jerked me awake. I didn't recognize the number, but it was local. I answered it.

"Hello?"

"Hello. Is this Ms. Malone?"

"This is Rebecca Malone."

"I was calling about Bernie Malone. May I speak to her?"

"This is her daughter. She's asleep right now."

"This is Lynn Balboa, your mother's caseworker with Hospice. I was calling to set up your mother's intake appointment."

"Ok," I managed, momentarily overwhelmed with how fast this was moving.

She heard the tone change and paused. Her voice was soft when she spoke again. "The faster we start services, the quicker your mom will have the freedom and peace of mind to enjoy the time she has left. I have time tomorrow, and I would love to meet with you and your mother. The nurse assigned to your mother will be coming with me. We will add or change people on the team based on what your mother needs. Since she's stable right now, we'll stick with me and the nurse. We're here to help. However you need."

"Of course, of course. Tomorrow is fine. How about 11 am?" I managed.

"Perfect. See you then."

I sighed, fighting to compose myself. I heard sounds of life on the other side of the door. I wiped my tears, threw a satiny robe over my pajamas, gave my hair a check- yup, still crazy- and opened the door.

"Good morning, everyone!" I said, a fake smile plastered on my face.

Rae and Mom both stopped in their tracks with one look at me.

"What's wrong?" They both asked, their faces identical masks of worry.

I slid into a seat at the island. "Nothing. Well, nothing new. I just got a call. Your hospice workers want to come tomorrow to meet with us."

Mom's eyes dimmed, but she pasted a smile on her face. "What time?"

"11 am. A social worker and your nurse." At the last word, she turned even more into herself.

"Well, let the good times roll, I suppose." She said after a beat. Rae reached over and rubbed her shoulder.

"You got this, Bernie." She said soothingly.

Bernie shrugged, not convinced. "Coffee, Bec?"

I nodded, eager for the change of topic. "What's that delicious smell?"

"That would be French toast," Rae replied.

"I haven't had French toast in years! I never have time to eat a nice, big breakfast. And I rarely have childcare to escape to brunch with Kieran anymore." I sighed, momentarily wistful for the freedom of my childfree days, filled with nothing but endless time to spend how I wanted to.

"So, you'll take a plate then?" She asked.

I nodded vigorously. "I make it a policy never to turn down carbs, especially when they're covered in syrup."

I waited for the inevitable cutting remark from Bernie about not needing the calories or carbs, but it never came. I looked up, pleasantly surprised. I was shocked to see her applying a liberal amount of syrup to her French toast. She saw me watching and smiled.

"What? I don't need to wear a bathing suit where I'm going." She tried to laugh, but it came out brittle and bitter. She sighed and took another bite. "Do we have any bacon?"

"You really are a whole new Bernie!" I said.

"Hush and eat your breakfast." She retorted.

I was saved from Bernie's faux wrath by Dustin and Dean, who burst into the living room, whooping and hollering. Dustin made a loop as the three of us begged them to settle down and stop before someone got hurt or something got broken.

Finally, Dean called a time-out and got Dustin to the table to eat his breakfast. He was adorably funny. He and Dean riffed off each other like they had been a comedy duo for a decade. As I chuckled at yet another joke they had cracked, I caught Rae with her head down.

"Are you okay?" I asked, alarmed.

"Ugh! I'm sorry! I'm prone to spontaneous tears." Rae apologized. "Sean and Dean used to cut up at our table. I just had a flashback. Hit me out of nowhere. I'm better now."

She dabbed at her eyes as Mom reached over and patted her hand. Dean looked serious and sad.

"Is it okay to talk about Sean?" Mom asked softly.

"Excuse me? What do you mean?" Rae looked confused.

"I was asking if it hurt too much to talk about him."

"It hurts too much not to," Dean broke into the conversation.

"Good, because I want to know everything I can about the young man who helped create my grandson." Mom became emotional. She looked up at me suddenly. "How do you feel about it?"

"Me? This isn't about me. If you guys want to tell us about Sean, I want to listen."

"But do you want Dustin to know? Can we talk about Sean with him?" Rae was almost pleading in her questioning. I knew they had discussed this privately and feared the answer.

I chose my words carefully.

"I never intended for Dustin to know anything about his father. I was taking my secret to my grave. I may have wanted to do it alone, but I don't anymore. I realize now how stupid and selfish my choice was. Dustin deserves to know his whole family, especially his father. I want you to talk about him as much as you want. Tell us all everything."

Rae and Dean visibly relaxed. Their smiles stretched across their faces.

"You don't know what you're in for," Rae warned. "I could talk about my son all day, every day."

"So, start talking." Mom said.

RAE

"Sean was amazing, just an extraordinary human being. Better than we ever thought we'd create." I recalled, making a face at Dean. "He was the kid who didn't worry about his own Christmas list. He worried about gifts for everyone he loved and worked tirelessly to find the right gift for each one."

"He once made me go to seven Targets looking for a specific color of socks he wanted to give this one. And he tracked it down. I was half-dead in the parking lot, and he charged through, knowing right where he needed to go. He was a force." Dean recalled.

Bernie smiled, spoke. "Just like his parents, it would seem to me."

I smiled, touched by her words, and continued.

"Sean was the kindest boy. He saved the ants instead of burning them. He cried when kids bullied the kids that weren't just like them. He was just the best."

"And he loved trivia. He was like an encyclopedia of history and music. Everything. But especially classic rock and punk." Dean interjected.

"The Ramones?" Becca guessed.

Dean nodded. She smiled.

"Now the shirt makes sense. I assume he also loved Converse?"

"You assume correctly. But really, we started him wearing them. They were the first thing I bought when I found out I was pregnant. But he loved them and never stopped. Rain, snow, sleet, beach, mountain, funeral, baptism, wedding… Converse. It's all he ever wore. We couldn't get him to wear anything else. No amount of begging, pleading, bribing, or yelling worked." I explained.

"You see, he was as stubborn as his mother." Dean supplied.

I shot him a withering look, and Rebecca and Bernie cracked up. Dustin clapped, wanting to join in on the fun without knowing why.

"You know what this breakfast needs, Dustin? Some ice cream!" Dean said to change the subject.

"Yay! Ice cream! Ice cream!" Dustin chanted.

The trio of women at the table gasped then sighed in unison.

"Dean Baxter! Ice cream for breakfast?" I said.

"Hey, grandmas don't have a monopoly on spoiling grandkids." He shot back, smiling an impish grin that turned my insides to mush.

"Oh, Grandpa!" Rebecca pretended to scold him.

She stopped, pretending to think. After her dramatic pause, she smiled. "Okay, Dustin. I guess you can have some ice cream."

Dustin wrapped himself around her neck in an enthusiastic hug. "Fank you, Mama!"

"You're welcome, sweet boy. Just try to be careful with your clothes."

"You all enjoy your breakfast sundaes. I'm going to go freshen up and take my meds." Bernie interjected.

Apparently, breakfast ice cream was too far out of the rigid comfort zone she was struggling to break free from.

"You okay, Mom?" Rebecca asked, instant concern springing to her face.

"Oh yes, I'm fine. Just already stuffed to the gills. No room for ice cream."

Bernie patted her flat stomach.

"I'll help you, buddy." I offered, stepping to Dustin and picking up a spoon to help him start eating the sundae Dean had assembled during Rebecca's mock protest.

Rebecca smiled gratefully and began to build her sundae.

"Ah, what the hell. You only go round once, right? Ice cream for breakfast it is." She said, unrepentant as she heaped her bowl with scoops of ice cream.

"That's what I like to see. No man likes a damn bone." Dean commented.

Color rose to Rebecca's face, but she was smiling.

"Well, bones or curves, there are no takers."

"Well, then, all the men of Boston are damn fools." Dean proclaimed earnestly and immediately.

197

It warmed my heart.

"It must be difficult to date as a single mom," I commented.

"Dating, in general, is hard enough. Dating apps should be illegal. I never had any luck before Dustin. But dating as a single mother is something other-worldly that happens only with a solid foundation of magic, unicorn tears, and Spanx. I don't think I have had three dates since he was born, which is fine. He's the only man I need in my life." She said.

I felt immense sadness for Rebecca. Her tone was light and proud, but wistfulness lay underneath. I looked at Dean and thought about just how empty my life would have been without him in it. How empty Sean's would have been not to have had a father.

"My dating life isn't for lack of Kieran trying. He tries to set me up all the time. I just would always rather give Dustin my time than some random guy." She went on.

"Kieran?" Dean asked.

"Oh, that's my best friend. He works in my office in Boston. He and his mom, Dianne, are kind of well-known there."

"How did that happen?" I asked, amused.

"I will tell you when little ears aren't around." She promised.

Dean nodded, as eager for good gossip as any woman I had ever known. I chuckled under my breath.

"Okay, I'm done! Come on, Dus, let's brush your teeth! Would you like to go for a swim?"

Rebecca stuck her bowl and Dustin's in the dishwasher and shuttled him off to her room.

Bernie came back, her hair encased in a floral-patterned head scarf wound to look like a turban. She settled onto the couch.

"Are Becca and Dustin going to the pool?" She asked.

I nodded. "Thinking about joining them?"

"I want to spend every moment I can with them, but I am just too tired. And it's only the beginning." She made a pained face and sank back, pulling her feet up.

"Well, I will stay here with you. Too much sun causes wrinkles, and I don't need any more of those." I said, laughing.

"I don't see one wrinkle!" She insisted.

"We need to get your eyes checked," I said.

We burst into laughter together as Dustin came tearing out of the bedroom. Rebecca was hot on his heels. He threw himself onto Bernie, wrapping his arms around her as tightly as he could.

"Bye, Mimi. Wuv you." He said, smacking a kiss on her cheek. "I go swim now."

"Gamma!" He called to me.

My knees buckled at his tiny voice calling me grandma.

"Yes, buddy?" I managed.

"Ganpa come swimming wif me?" He asked.

Dean materialized, as was his way, already in his suit. He smiled as he slung a brightly printed beach towel over his shoulder.

"Go kiss and hug your grandmas again, and then we can go to the pool." He said to Dustin.

Once the trio was out the door, Bernie and I started talking. Our words were a constant stream of stops and starts, memories, hopes, and regrets. We talked until her voice became froggy, and I had to retrieve her a bottle of water.

Then, just as quickly as our words had begun, they ended. We fell into companionable silence. I felt, like me, Bernie had gleaned the knowledge that not all moments needed words. I reflected on the two vastly different lives we had led, which had by a series of highly improbable events had intersected. I felt grateful, not only for a lasting connection to my son, but to know this woman- these women, Rebecca included.

I was smiling to myself when my phone chimed, jarring me back to the moment. I looked over at Bernie, propped against the pillows, sleeping peacefully. Quickly, I retreated to the attic so I wouldn't wake her.

I hit the video chat icon on my phone, Patti's face filling the screen.

"Well, look what the cat dragged in!" She crowed. "How the hell are you?"

"Oh Patti, it's incredible. HE'S incredible. He sounds and acts just like Sean. And seeing him and Dean together, it's like being in a time machine and going back twenty years. Oh, and Becca said we could tell him about Sean. Her mother and her both want to know about him too. She also is letting him call us Grandma and Grandpa."

I felt like I was talking a mile a minute, jumping from one thought to the next in rapid succession, just like Bernie and I had done just a short time ago.

"How is she?"

"Rebecca? She's a sweet girl. Overwhelmed. Insecure in her mothering like you and I both were with Sean and Liv."

"No, Bernie! Is she just like Cami? Hoity toity as all hell?"

"Rebecca said she used to be just like that. But cancer has changed her. She's lovely. We have spent a lot of time talking. She is trying hard to keep a brave face after her surgery. They told her she's terminal. Only weeks to live."

Patti frowned deeply. "Oh no. That's so terrible. How's Rebecca doing with it?"

"She's also trying to keep a brave face, but this is a lot for her to deal with on her own. Between her mom and Dustin, she's running ragged. She told me today they are staying here until her mother passes. She took a leave from her job."

"She sounds like a decent kid. A good daughter, at least."

"She is a good mom too. But she seems lonely, even if she would rather die than admit it. Kind of like someone else I know."

"Who, this old gal? Only certain parts of me get lonely from time to time, and I have a cure for whatever ails them on standby." She laughed.

201

"Is Bryan part of that cure?" I joked. "Was there a second date?"

"Yeah, when you were being a jerk and accusing me of adultery. You broke up date three, sister."

"Well, excuse me, madam. Did you ever get to finish the date?"

"We did last night."

"And?" I leaned forward like we were at my kitchen table, with tea or tequila, gossiping about our sex lives.

She held up her hands, palms together, as in prayer, and moved them almost a foot apart. She waggled her eyebrows over the wide space.

"No! Bry-an!" I laughed, not knowing whether to be impressed or horrified. "What do you even do with something that big?"

"It's not the size of the wand. It's the magic in it." She said. "And Jes-us, there was magic in that wand. I think I either created a new language or spoke in tongues."

"Patti!"

I was laughing with her as Dean emerged from the stairwell.

"I thought I heard you, Patti. What are you two going on about?" he asked, moving into the frame.

We both just laughed harder. Dean shook his head. "I just give up."

"I'll let you go. I love and miss you both. I am so happy the visit is going well." Patti said.

"Love and miss you too."

We hung up, and I turned to Dean. "How are you doing, Mr. Baxter? How was the pool?"

"Just fine, Mrs. Baxter. How about you?"

"Wonderful. Bernie and I talked for a long time while everyone was at the pool. She's so happy we are here. She's worried about Rebecca and the effect her death is going to have on her. She asked me to watch out for her."

"Of course, we're going to look out for her."

"Dean, I think I need to stay."

"Come again?"

"Bernie only has weeks left to live. Yes, she will have a nurse, but that's still so much on Rebecca. I want to stay and help her care for Dustin. And it would be a great way to get to know all of them."

"Rae, it's not your job to help everyone."

"It is my job to care for my loved ones. That's part of the role of a mom. I don't have my kid to take care of anymore, but I do have his son."

Dean sighed. "I can't stay with you. I have to be back at work."

"I know, sweetheart. But it won't be long. Bernie told me they told her six weeks if that."

"I'm not worried about being without you, though I don't relish that thought. I'm worried about what watching someone die will do to you."

I knew he was thinking of my short stint on the mental health floor when Sean died.

"That was Sean. This isn't the same. Didn't you just tell me not very long ago that you should always listen to me and that I am always right? I feel like this is the right thing."

"I don't recall saying those words per se, but if I did, it's not fair play to use my own words against me. I would, however, be willing to admit that you rarely lead me wrong."

"Rarely?" I said, scooting closer to him and molding my body to his.

I nibbled and licked his neck, savoring the saltiness of his sweat and the tang of the pool chemicals still on his skin. I toyed with his waistband.

He tilted my head up, kissing me deeply. As his tongue tangled with mine, my nipples tightened against his bare chest. He responded, flipping me over and pinning me under him. He propped himself up on one elbow, gazing into my eyes long and hard. My stomach flipped.

"God, I love you." He said.

I arched up to meet him, already panting, craving. He reached down between my legs, unsurprised to find me already wet and wanting. He slid his mouth down to my neck, then my chest. I drew in a sharp breath as he took a nipple in his mouth, sucking it, then rolling it in his teeth. I felt his lips turn up into a smile against the silky skin of my breast as he suckled the other nipple. His hand came up to find my hair, weaving a chunk through his fingers. He tugged, sending shivers of pain mingled with pleasure from the top of my head to my toes, which curled involuntarily.

He moved down further, over the doughy slope of my stomach. He paused, kissing my belly button. His stubble was like the friction to the fire building inside of me, spurring me on and making me grow hotter and hotter. Finally, he moved between my legs. His tongue found my opening expertly. I hitched my legs over his shoulders and lost myself in the sensations.

I cried out softly, finding his salt and pepper hair with my hands and running my hands through it as I came. He stopped, moved up, and positioned himself over me. He closed his eyes as he slid into me slowly. After all this time, to know he still savored the experience- my body, me- warmed my heart and revved my engine. I came again, surprising both of us. And then he did too, leaning down and kissing me as he did.

He slid off of me, spent.

"God, there's nothing like a nooner," Dean said.

We laid in sweaty, sated silence. I was drifting off when Dean spoke.

"If you need to stay, stay." He said, sliding out from under the sheets and padding into the bathroom.

We spent the evening playing Chutes and Ladders with Dustin. Morning dawned early. I had decided to make brunch for the hospice meeting. I was working on my grandmother's famous coffee cake recipe when Bernie came out. Her face looked puffy

205

and creased from sleep, but her eyes looked alert and radiant beneath her bright pink turban. She wore a tight-fitting tee shirt dress that stopped right under her knee in the same vibrant pink color. Her feet were bare, with pink polish.

"You look better with cancer than I do on any day, perfectly healthy." I gushed.

"Oh shush!" She scolded. "You are beautiful, and you know it. And just as importantly, Dean knows it too. He looks at you like you're a sex goddess. It's ridiculously hot."

She smiled conspiratorially as she slid onto a stool at the island with a cup of coffee.

"Yes, I am lucky in that aspect. Passion has never been lacking in our relationship."

"Passion or sex?" She teased. Her eyes were round over the rim of her mug.

"Both," Dean said, startling us both.

I gasped and clutched my chest. "Jesus Christ, you scared the shit out of us!" I gasped.

"Sorry," he said, not sounding sorry in the least. "Is that your Nanny's coffee cake?"

He sounded hopeful as he took in the various dishes in progress. The coffee cake was a longtime favorite, but I had stopped making it after Sean died, just like I had stopped doing so many other things.

"Not for you!" I scolded.

"Well, maybe for you." I immediately relented. "I can serve it sliced on a platter, so no one will see a piece cut out."

"If you're not making this for all of us, who is it for?"

"Well, it is for some of us, just not *us* us. Rebecca and Bernie have their hospice meeting today, so I thought some brunch might make the meeting a bit easier."

"How thoughtful of you!" Bernie interrupted. "You are so sweet. And Dean, you can have some of the coffee cake."

"Why, thank you, Bernie." He made a show of hugging her and smacking a kiss on the side of her head.

"Kiss her all you want, but just remember, I am the keeper of the coffee cake."

"Okay, okay. I'll play nice." He immediately backed off.

"You would make a terrible prisoner." I teased.

"Oh yeah, all the state's secrets, gone, just like that." He snapped his fingers, and we all laughed together.

We all were drinking coffee and chatting while I continued to prepare things for brunch for a long while, till Dustin came out of Rebecca's room like a shot.

"Isn't he just amazing?" Bernie asked me. "I can't believe I hated being a grandmother for so long."

"He's terrific." As he zipped around the room, I sighed. He was a blur of dark curls and red fire engine pajamas.

"Well, good morning, everyone," Rebecca said dryly, trudging from the bedroom bleary-eyed, her hair a chaotic tornado of curls.

She pulled Dustin into her as he tore past her and squeezed, smothering him with kisses. "How are you this morning, my boy?"

"Good!" He said, leaning into her with the security of a child well-loved. He reached up and stroked her face lovingly.

"What's that delicious smell?" Rebecca asked.

"Rae is making brunch for our meeting today," Bernie explained.

"It smells incredible," Rebecca said, turning to me. "Do I have to wait till the meeting?"

"A woman after my own heart," Dean said. "Rae is holding out on letting me at her famous coffee cake."

"I am going to throw a lasagna in after breakfast, so you have some variety. It's not brunching if you have just breakfast items. I'm going to make some chicken salad finger sandwiches too. Oh, and a quiche." I told them.

"You're going to so much trouble." Bernie protested.

"It's my pleasure!" I reassured her.

"Rae finds cooking therapeutic," Dean explained.

"Unlike you, who finds it a declaration of war, my love," I replied.

Everyone started laughing.

The rest of the morning flew by. Bernie lounged on the couch, chatting with me as I cooked. Dean and Dustin ping-ponged around the house, getting so rowdy that we forced them outside for a walk. Rebecca lingered in her room, taking a long shower. She seemed to be floundering to find a place where she fit among the elders and the toddler.

I was putting the finishing touches on the spread when there was a knock at the door. As if she had been waiting just offstage for her cue, Rebecca emerged in a loose v neck grey tee shirt and oversized black jogger sweatpants, her feet bare and hair slightly unkempt. She opened the door as the second round of knocking sounded.

REBECCA

I pulled the door open, filled with dread at our impending meeting. A reedy woman with long, wavy brown hair parted down the middle stood on the doorstep, smiling beatifically. She was wearing a loose dress, a billowy scarf, and a load of handmade jewelry. She stood next to a tall, broad-shouldered man with smooth dark skin. He wore simple green scrubs with a white tee shirt peeking out of the top. Sinewy bulges in his chest and arms strained the thin material. His hair was dark and close-cropped. As I looked into his eyes, shockingly green, like the Caribbean waters, my heart stopped. Every part of my body responded to him. I willed myself to stay still and not betray the fireworks shooting off inside of me. When he smiled, straight, white teeth flashing, I had to fight from jumping him on the doorstep.

"Rebecca?" The woman broke into my thoughts.

"Uh, oh yeah. Yes, that's me." I stepped aside, letting them enter.

As he went past, the man turned his face towards me, so close it should have been uncomfortable, met my eyes, and smiled again. I looked down quickly, realizing in that instant I was barefoot and wearing workout clothes. I had dressed for comfort, thinking a social worker and a nurse, who saw people at their worst, would understand. No part of me wanted this man to see me at my worst.

I was mentally kicking myself as I closed the door when Dean and Dustin came in.

"Hey there, everyone, so sorry to interrupt. We're off to go bowling. Rae, you coming?"

Rae looked from me to Mom and back, unsure what she should say.

"Please stay," Mom asked simply. "You two are welcome as well, though I think distracting Dustin is a good idea."

"Sorry, Bernie, we have a hot bowling date. We're off. We will see you ladies tonight. And enjoy my wife's coffee cake. It's her specialty and a personal favorite."

He stared towards the table, spread with the fruits of Rae's labor, wistfully.

"Looks delicious. You didn't have to do all this on our account." The man spoke.

His voice jolted through me, settling in the warm, throbbing place I had long considered dead or very deeply asleep—first Todd and now this man. Maybe Sleeping Beauty was coming out of her slumber.

Mom was eyeing me knowingly from across the room.

"Please come, sit down. I'm Bernie. The...patient." She faltered at the end of her spiel but recovered with a luminous smile.

"It's a pleasure to meet you. I'm Lynn Balboa. I'm going to be your caseworker while you are involved in our program."

She stuck her bracelet-filled arm out to Mom. Mom shook it warmly but not enthusiastically. I knew how hard she was working, not just to keep it together but to maintain the Bernie Malone caricature.

"And who might you be?" Mom said, looking around the broad-shouldered guest to me pointedly.

He stepped closer to her, wafting a delicious-smelling cologne towards me. I took a deep breath as my hormones started doing somersaults in my nether regions.

"I'm Malachi. I'm going to be your nurse. It's a pleasure to meet you, Bernie."

Mom extended her hand, her lips pursing into a flirty pout reflexively as she peered up through heavy-lidded eyes.

"The pleasure's all mine." She practically purred. "Meet my daughter, Rebecca. She's come home to care for me."

"Rebecca. Nice to meet you." He turned and smiled that blinding smile.

"You can call me Becca. Thank you for being here to help my mom." I stammered awkwardly as my mom and Rae stared on, amused.

"Please sit. This is Rae, my grandson's other grandmother. She made us all this lovely brunch."

"Oh, that's nice. You and your mother-in-law came to help your mother. Your families must be tight." Malachi said.

"I'm not her mother-in-law," Rae interjected a bit sadly but quickly. "She doesn't have a husband."

I gaped at her, horrified by her blurted confession. She looked at me apologetically. My face burned, and my eyes went to Malachi to gauge his reaction, hating how much it mattered. I noticed his eyebrow raised. Before I could wonder what that meant, my mother was snuggled in her armchair, and Lynn was on the couch. Malachi was at the table, loading his plate.

"Would you like a drink, Malachi? Lynn?" Mom asked from her chair.

"Water would be great," Lynn said. "Oh, is that fruit organic?"

"Yes, it is," Rae said. "Here, let me bring you a bowl."

"I'll take coffee, please," Malachi said.

Mom had a sudden surge of energy as she scrambled out of her chair and motored over to the coffee pot. I turned from the fridge to retrieve the water when she crashed into me, sending warm coffee all over me. She pulled her head back slightly, a smile playing on her lips. She had spilled on purpose.

"Oh, my goodness! Clumsy me! I am still a little shaky from surgery. Oh, sweetie. You'll need to change that outfit. I am so sorry."

"No problem, Mom. Here, sit down." I played along, enjoying being swept into a caper with Bernie.

Malachi was at her side in an instant. He took the nearly empty cup in one hand and her elbow in the other, steering her back to her chair and making sure she sat safely. He came back and re-filled the cup. He smiled at me.

"We got this." He reassured me.

The response inside of my body was like being struck by lightning, everything firing and fizzing and popping, smoldering on a slow burn. I attempted to smile but felt like it came off more as a smirk.

"I'm going to change. Start eating. Don't wait for me." Short sentences were the best I could manage.

"Yes, ma'am." He responded.

It turned me on so much; I practically staggered dead-legged into my bedroom. I fell onto my back on the bed, careful to avoid soaking my comforter with the spilled coffee on my shirt. I groped for my phone charging on the nightstand. I found it, disconnected it from the charger, and went into the bathroom.

I tapped in Kieran's work extension quickly. My heart was pounding, and I felt sweaty.

"Go for Kieran."

"Kieran!"

"Becs? What's up? Are you okay?"

"No. Yes. No... no."

"Is this the part where I am supposed to read your mind? I can only do that after a few margaritas."

"Kieran. I am hiding in the bathroom at my mother's house."

"Are you about to be killed? Am I about to be the hero? Who are we going to get to play me in the Lifetime movie? I got this, boo. Give me your location so I can call the authorities."

"Kieran! Focus! There is no emergency. There's a man."

"OHHH." He stilled, the silence between us pregnant with anticipation.

"We're meeting with my mom's hospice team. This crunchy former hippie is her case manager. Her nurse is a tall, chocolate-skinned Adonis with muscles and Jackson Avery eyes."

He left out a small gasp. Jackson Avery from Grey's Anatomy had been our mutual crush for many years.

"What are you wearing?"

"I don't want to tell you," I said glumly.

"Oh Rebecca, no. Tell me."

"A baggy tee-shirt...and sweatpants."

His grief at this confession was palpable. He remained silent but managed several deep, disappointed sighs.

"Mom spilled coffee on me, so I had an excuse to change," I reported.

"Thank goodness for Bernie. She's the only one with any damn breeding. Here's what you're going to do. Take some of D's baby wipes, get off that coffee smell, spritz on the Chanel."

"I hardly think it warrants my Chanel."

"Rebecca- you're in a baggy tee-shirt, for Christ's sake. Sweatpants! What the actual fuck? What shoes do you have on? Not flip flops?"

"Barefoot."

"Fuck! I could punch you in the face! Two spritzes of the perfume. Do it or so help me! Take a picture of your hair and send it to me right now."

I did as I was told. I heard Kieran's alert go off.

"Ok, it's not terrible. It's like tousled sex hair. Adonis thinking about sex could work out very well for you."

"Stop! He's my mother's nurse!"

"You called me to report this man sighting. I was innocently minding my business until you involved me. And you're not the patient. There's no law against that."

"There probably are rules. Besides, I am a hot mess. I look like I was about to go jogging! Or worse- gardening. And I have a toddler. And I haven't had sex since the first Obama administration. Who knows if it even works after Dustin shot out of there like a tee-shirt out of a cannon?"

"You're spiraling. There is only one question I need you to answer."

"What? I called you for help, not an interrogation."

"Bitch, please. You can't get one without the other. You know this. Now, tell me. Does your kitty have a heartbeat when you look at him?"

"It has a heart attack when it looks at him."

"Oh shit, you're about to get dickmatized." He said gleefully, without even a hint of remorse.

"I won't get anything if I don't get back to this meeting. Now, what should I wear?"

"Put on a sundress. I would go with the chambray, that makes your eyes pop. Keep your hair up so Lover Boy can see your neck. Put your thick straw belt with it. And I swear to God, I will come to Florida and slap you myself if you don't put on shoes. Those cute sandals from Marshall's. You have them, right?"

"Yes. I have all that."

"I know, I helped you pack. Okay, girl. Go get your man. Call me later."

I followed all of Kieran's instructions, marveling at his bossiness. Malachi was on the couch next to Lynn, facing me. Rae and Mom were deep in conversation with them, but his eyes flickered to mine when I reappeared.

"Welcome back." Mom cut her sentence off to greet me. "Are you eating?"

"No, I'm good. Keep going. I'll catch up."

"We were just getting started," Lynn said. "We were just sharing information about your mother's health. Next, we're going to discuss her end-of-life wishes."

I swallowed thickly as I perched on the wide armrest of the chair Mom sat in, noticing with satisfaction that Malachi's eyes flitted to my legs gracefully crossed as they peeked out under my dress. I was happy I had thought to lotion them at the last moment.

"I know it's difficult, but we need to set all the expectations right from the start. Sometimes, people can decline quickly, and we want to be prepared to honor their wishes. We get them right upfront, so we don't have to guess or put the family in the position of choosing during a time that's already incredibly difficult."

"I don't want anything," Mom spoke up. "No feeding tubes, no life support, no keeping me on machines. Give me something for pain, and let me go."

I turned to her, surprised. "Mom, surely you don't mean that."

"Rebecca, I don't want machines keeping me alive. I don't want to lay in a bed and be a vegetable and have people pitying me. No feeding tubes. When my body gives up, let me go."

Rae made a strangled noise next to us. I turned to her and reached out to squeeze her hand.

"Excuse me for a moment." She said, smiling a sad smile.

She went upstairs, and I heard faint sobs and her blowing her nose.

Lynn looked at me quizzically.

"She suffered a loss. She is still grieving." I said, not wanting to get into the overly complicated backstory.

"Oh, I see. Will she be able to handle the upcoming weeks? Caregiving is a thankless and grueling job."

"I'll be here. Rae and Dean are leaving next week."

"But she just said-"

Mom cut Lynn off.

"While you were getting changed, Rae discussed the possibility of staying on with us. Dean has to go back to work. We both think it would be a smart move, especially for you and Dustin."

"I have Dustin and me," I said, feeling defensive even though I wasn't opposed to Rae staying and helping. In fact, I was filled with gratitude and relief that she would offer to be here to help me shoulder this enormous load. "I can take care of you and him just fine."

"I am sure you can, but who takes care of you?" Malachi interjected.

Heat bloomed from my core. *You can take care of me*; I wanted to say.

"In situations like this, the more people to support each other, the better." He reasoned.

"I'm fine with it if that's what you want. I'm doing whatever you want and need, Mom." I relented.

"Ok, then she stays."

"Ok, great."

Both Lynn and Malachi smiled.

"So, can I add her to the team roster?"

I noticed a stack of papers piled on Lynn's lap. She was scribbling notes furiously.

"Yes, please." Mom said. "And can we make Rebecca in charge? I don't want to worry about keeping track of appointments and talking to doctors. Just have everyone talk to her."

I felt lucky I had managed Megan's life for so many years. Balancing all these balls was going to be easy after dealing with her. Lynn asked me for my cell phone number.

"I'm going to add it to the care plan, so all providers have it."

She returned to her paperwork. Rae came back in, composed but tear-streaked, and bent over to speak to Mom, leaving Malachi and me to chat. Our eyes met expectantly

"Do you prefer texting or calling?" Malachi asked.

"Excuse me?"

"I usually contact you the day before every appointment just as a reminder. I also will contact you directly if I have to cancel for any reason."

"Oh, I see. Texting is usually best for me. My son makes the phone almost impossible sometimes."

"That little man who tore through here earlier?" He asked.

"Yes. Dustin. He's two." I smiled, thinking about him.

"He's gorgeous." He said softly.

My vagina clenched.

"You guys live in the area too?" He asked.

"No, we live in Boston normally. We came home to visit for the holidays, and things kind of came to a head, so now we're here for the duration."

"You're not going back?" I couldn't gauge what was behind his voice as he asked.

"Not for the immediate future. I took a leave."

"What do you do?"

"I work as a personal assistant for an architect."

"Ah! Is that the dream or the thing paying the bills till you reach the dream?"

"The latter."

"So, what's the dream?"

Before I could answer, Lynn broke in. She began to talk in detail about the coming months, the stages of death. The steps they can take to keep Mom comfortable as cancer overtook her body. As she talked, Mom's smile became dimmer and dimmer.

She perked up when Lynn said she was approved for four visits a week with Malachi, but that could be adjusted as her needs increased. She looked at me and smiled slyly.

We talked for a long time. I was reassured that this was a logical and smart next step. Mom would need these services sooner rather than later. It would be easier to have familiar faces around when the end came. Mom even seemed to warm to the idea, if only for the opportunity to have attention and time devoted especially to her, a life-long love of hers.

Lynn finished discussing things Mom may consider unfinished in her life or something she wanted to do before her passing.

"So, a bucket list?" I translated.

"Yes, for all intents and purposes."

"Do I have to tell you now?" Mom asked.

I could see her wheels working. I was equal parts intrigued and frightened.

"No, of course not! Some people will have a list automatically. Some will have none. Just like life, death is an individual process. No person has the same one. You think about it and let me know. You can email it to me if you decide you want to act on it."

She handed Mom a glossy business card.

"Thank you. Now, if you'll excuse me. I'm ready for a nap."

"Let me help you to bed," Rae said instantaneously, standing up.

"Can I come see the bedroom? So that I have a mental picture if we end up needing to bring in equipment down the line." Lynn asked. "We also want to make sure it will be suitable for your needs."

"Of course. Right, this way." Mom leaned on Rae as they led the way. "You guys coming?"

"We have information to go over if that's okay," Malachi said. "I want to set up your visit schedule."

"That's just fine. See you soon, Malachi."

She fluttered her fingertips at him. *Oh, Bernie, you're doing too much*, I thought. Malachi smiled that megawatt smile at her, and I resisted the urge to fan myself. Mom clicked the thermostat down a few degrees as they entered the hallway. She glanced over her shoulder at me meaningfully.

"I printed this out for you," Malachi said, handing me a blank calendar page. "People usually like to post them on the fridge so everyone in the house can be kept up to date and know when I'm coming. It's handy to have it visible if the patient panics. I wrote my number on top. Any of you can call me at any time."

He paused for a moment.

"Your mom is one of my only clients right now. I'm just starting back full-time. I was finishing my MSN courses."

He paused again and smiled, obviously proud of himself. I was impressed with his achievement.

"So basically, you guys get first pick at hours." He finished.

"What do you suggest?"

"She's approved for four days to start. Based on what I saw today, she's a hell of an actress, but she also doesn't need four days quite yet. Why don't we start with Monday, Wednesday, and Friday and see how we do with that to start? I am scheduled for eight-hour shifts, but again, those times can be adjusted as needed."

"That all sounds good. Hopefully, we can keep it that way for a while."

"In my experience, once we start needing to make changes, we will be on a slippery, downhill slope. Your mom will decline, probably sooner rather than later." He was matter of fact but gentle.

I drew in a sharp breath as his words sank in.

"Hey, hey. I'm sorry. I was just trying to prepare you. But the good news is, I'll be here to get you through it." He grinned.

"Is that so?" I said, my eyelashes fluttering against my will. I was feeling very much my mother's daughter as my dwarfed flirting skills began to emerge.

Before he could respond, Lynn and Rae re-joined us. They chatted softly.

"She's asleep," Rae said.

"Great," I said. "I know this was stressful for her. I can't thank you enough for all the time you took to answer our questions."

"We can't thank you enough for all the delicious food. Thank you again, Ms. Baxter." Malachi said.

"Please, it's Rae. And here, take this leftover coffee cake."

"Really? That's so generous. Thank you so much."

Rae moved the remaining slices onto a disposable plate. She started to wrap it, but Malachi stopped her. He put two pieces back on the plate. We all looked at him curiously.

"For your husband." He said, shrugging. "I will see all of you in a few days. If you need me before then, my cell is on the fridge."

When the door closed behind them, Rae turned to me with raised eyebrows.

"So?" She prodded.

"So what?" I asked.

"Malachi? HOT."

"Stop! I mean, yes, he's extremely attractive, but he's out of my league, and my plate is way too full."

"He is NOT out of your league!" She looked at me with dismay. "You are a beautiful woman."

"Well, thank you, but I sure don't feel like that a lot of the time."

"I mean, Todd certainly thought so. And it looked to me like Malachi did too."

I cut my eyes at her, doubtful. "Ok, okay, I'll spare you the lecture about enjoying being young and beautiful, okay?"

"Thanks." I smiled at her to let her know there were no hard feelings.

Suddenly, the door burst open, Dustin darting in like a shot, Dean and Todd hot on his heels. Rae and I both immediately shushed them, me plucking Dustin up mid-stride, his legs still in motion.

"Bernie's sleeping!" Rae chided.

Both men had the good sense to look sheepish and tried to settle Dustin quickly. His voice dropped to a normal volume, and he stopped moving. He looked at me.

"We rode the golf cart!" He said in a stage whisper.

"Well, of course. It's yours." Todd said.

"Um, excuse me?" I said. "We don't own a golf cart. The company you work for does."

"Actually, Todd and I made a deal. His cart is for exclusive use by Bernie for as long as she needs it. So, yes, essentially, the cart is indeed ours. I rented it. I thought it would make things easier and keep her mobile a little bit longer." Dean explained.

He rushed through his explanation in a way that made me realize he had not discussed this idea with Rae before implementing it. I looked over, and her eyes shone with love for him. I think he was safe from the doghouse for today.

"You guys are just so amazing. I can't ever repay you for all the ways you've helped us through this. You staying and you being so thoughtful is so appreciated." I stopped, emotional.

I pulled them both into a hug. Within the comfort of Rae and Dean's arms, I realized how exhausted I was. As we pulled apart, I stifled a yawn and stretched.

"While Mom is sleeping, I think I am going to take her lead. Would you guys mind watching Dustin?" I asked.

"Actually, we have a pool date," Dean said. "We're all going to swim, so things should be nice and quiet for you here."

"Thank you so much. Have fun. Dustin, listen to Grandma and Grandpa and be a good boy. And don't run next to the pool."

Dustin nodded, already chomping at the bit to swim. When the door closed behind them, I checked one more time on Mom then retreated to my bed. I was exhausted after our meeting. There was just so much to process. My head swam, darting from one topic to another- Mom, hospice, Todd, Dustin, Rae, Malachi.

My mind lingered for an extra moment on Malachi. The man was, in a word, fine. Fine in the way that probably made him the homecoming king and head quarterback or an underwear model or someone's someone. Or an annoyingly perfect hybrid of all of them. Except he was light on the annoying and heavy on the perfect.

One thing I did know was that he was a nurse. My mother's nurse. Which made things way too complicated and him strictly off-limits. We all had one primary focus- Bernie- and getting her to the end of this journey and onto the next with as little pain and as much love as possible. There wasn't room for anything else. *Damn it,* my inner voice sounded.

And now, as I lay there analyzing the current state of my life, I realized I needed an outsider's perspective. I dialed Kieran's cell and waited.

"You better be under a man right now." He said as a way of a greeting.

"No, that was last night." I demurred.

His response on the other end was explosive.

"Whatttttt! Come again? You told me NOTHING of this when you called about Adonis earlier. What is even happening?"

I realized I would have to unfurl this story with care, leaving out what seemed like the significant roles of Dean and Rae since Kieran had no idea I had a secret or that the secret had caught up with me and was living with us here.

"My mom befriended a security guard from her complex. He came to dinner and then stayed for a movie. Then, he offered to take me for a ride on his golf cart."

"His golf cart? Girl, I don't know about that."

"It's part of his work perks."

"I think a golf cart can hardly be counted as a work perk."

"It's not Boston. Golf carts are like Benz here."

"Okay, if you say so. So where did he take you in this magical golf cart?"

"We went to the golf course."

"How very Dirty Dancing of you. Sex on the 9th hole."

"We weren't on the 9th hole!" I protested.

"But on the golf course? Who is this girl? Because I know that's not my Rebecca. Florida must have something in their water because you're completely different. And not different bad. Different good. But I'm still mad that you held out on me, you bitch."

"Well, if my mother can change, so can I. I kind of feel like Bernie these days. Flirting and fornicating!"

"Such language!" He pretended to be shocked.

"Do you want the details or not?"

"Does a bear shit in the woods?"

I laid out every detail for Kieran. He chortled at points, gasped at others. In the end, I heard enthusiastic applause.

"Ok, wiseass," I said. "Enough. Tell me what to do?"

"What to do about what?" He sounded genuinely confused.

"About these men! I mean, maybe I am overthinking this. Maybe neither of them even wants me. But Jesus. Malachi is HOT. I look at him and imagine twenty-five varieties of freaky shit I want to do to him. Todd's cute and so wholesomely nice, but I'm pretty sure he was a one-off."

"A hole in one on the golf course! It was a hole in ONE, right? Dear God, Becs. I can't bear to think of what that gator could have seen." He teased.

"Shut up!" I snapped. "You're really no help with my problem."

"What a problem to have. Two hotties to choose from."

"I can't date Malachi! He is my mom's nurse."

"So, there are no rules about fucking a resident's daughter on a company-owned golf course?"

"Shut up." I laughed.

"All I will say is, you are known to play it safe. You have been putting up with Megan's shit for all these years, not because you want to but because it's the easiest and most secure choice. You settle. It's not a judgment; it's just a fact. But here's another fact. You don't deserve to settle. You're a catch, and you deserve all the love the right man has to give. Just don't settle for the one that seems easiest. You have played that shit out."

"Well, damn, tell me how you really feel."

"Did you want honesty or smoke blown up your ass? I'm not Willy Wonka. I don't sugarcoat things. You don't deserve to settle. So, I got your back whoever you choose, as long as he is who you truly want."

"And this is why I love you," I said. "Thank you."

"Anytime. Now, let me get back to my date." He affected a Southern accent. "I got a man waiting for me."

"Oh, my goodness, why didn't you tell me to shut up? Why did you even answer?"

"Because I don't get the dirt that way. I've been waiting since you called me earlier to hear what was going on. This plot twist was better than I could have dreamed up. I can't believe you held out on me before. The nerve!"

I laughed, "Go already! Don't make him wait anymore."

And with that, I was alone with my thoughts. I rolled over and snuggled into my covers. I fell into a dreamless, heavy sleep almost immediately.

I was woken up by Dustin bounding into the room and catapulting onto the bed. The smells of dinner danced through the air, compelling me to get up.

"How long was I asleep?" I asked Bernie, who stood in the doorway watching me.

"Forever," Dustin said.

"Not quite that long, but it's around six."

"Why did you let me sleep so late?" I said, sitting up and shaking off the sleep.

"You needed the rest," Bernie said. "Come have some dinner."

I tugged on a hoodie and headed into the living room, where I spied Todd in the kitchen. I looked quizzically at

Bernie, who had settled back onto the couch next to Rae. She shrugged.

"He wanted to make us dinner." She paused, took a sip out of an oversized pink mug. "You must have bewitched him with your lovely lady bits. That's my girl."

I stared at her, equal parts horrified and shocked. "Jesus Christ, Mother!"

Rae chortled next to my mother. "I swear, I didn't say a word!"

"You didn't have to. A mother knows!" Bernie said. "Was it the full show or just the preview?"

She took in my ever deeper reddening skin and sat back, smug. "Rebecca Malone, you make a mother proud."

"Well, if I had known all it would take to make you proud is sex with a stranger, I would have done it years ago." I laughed.

She became serious in an instant. "I am so proud of you, Rebecca. Please know that."

I put my hand on her cheek. "I do, Mom. I know."

She opened her mouth to say more, but Todd came bounding out of the kitchen and announced that dinner was ready. I picked at the simple pasta and salad. Talking to Kieran then seeing Todd in our home attempting to become a part of this trauma forged family clarified my feelings. Our one night would be only that- one charmed night.

After dinner, Todd suggested going for a walk. I agreed, steeling myself for the conversation that was to come. We walked in silence for a while, admiring the clear, star-pocked sky. Finally, we settled on a small patch of sand with a view of the beach sprawled before us.

"What a gorgeous view," I said.

"I feel like I have Deja vu," Todd said, his voice deep and sensual, recalling moments of our night spent together.

I laughed uncomfortably. "About that night…."

"It was great, right?" He interrupted, clueless still as to where I was trying to steer the conversation.

"For sure," I assured him. "But I want to make it clear to you, even though it was wonderful, it was a one-time thing. I hope there are no hurt feelings, and we can stay friends." I rambled on in a rush.

He sat in silence for a few minutes. He looked deflated and sad. Then, he took a deep breath and shrugged.

"Guess a tan and some muscles don't get the ladies after all." He said.

"Excuse me?"

"I moved here to Florida from the Midwest. I was a dork. Pale and skinny and lanky. I had glasses and braces. People never looked my way, especially not girls. And I really wanted a girl to look at me. I just wanted someone to love and to give my love to. I still do. And I knew it would never happen with the same people and their same small minds. They would only see me as the dorky pale, skinny kid. So, I came here. I wanted to be different, to be the person I always felt like inside. I went to the gym. I started bulking up. And I got a job here. I get a tan on the lifeguard stand every day."

He paused for a moment and smiled.

"Then, you got out of that car with Bernie, and my heart dropped into my stomach. I was instantly attracted to you. And I know I'm younger than you, but when you flirted back, I was so happy."

"I know it's going to sound so cliche, but it's truly not you. It's me. I have way too many balls in the air right now. It's not fair to you." I took the easy way out, blaming it on circumstance and sparing the fact that I just didn't feel that way or picture being with him.

What I had told him was true. I couldn't take on any more or anyone. It just also was a convenient cover for the larger truth. Before Rae had arrived in Boston, I was hard-pressed to imagine building a life with anyone but Dustin and maybe some cats by my side.

"I like you, Bec, but I'm okay with just being friends." He bowed out gracefully, respectfully.

There wasn't much to say after that. We headed back to the condo, silence as thick as the humidity in the air. Todd gave me a friendly hug after a moment of uncertainty on how to proceed-kiss on the cheek, hug, high five, handshake? I showered the sand away and slid under my covers, tired but relieved.

The next few days passed in a blur of sunshine, chlorine, laughter, and hugs. It was like Bernie wanted to cram in as many memories with Dustin while she still felt well enough to do it. We visited the museum, the aquarium, the planetarium. Dustin was exhausted, and so were the rest of us. Yet, we pushed on, not knowing what to expect or how much of our time would be consumed once hospice care started. We took tons of pictures, ate lots of junk food, and shared enormous amounts of love. Missed sleep didn't matter when mortality hung over us, dark as a rain cloud.

One balmy, grueling day, we spent the morning at the zoo, then an afternoon poolside. I was wiped out. I showered quickly, then threw on whatever was closest and clean from an ever-growing jumble cascading out of my suitcase. I snuggled into Dustin, who had fallen asleep while reading him a story, and I didn't have the heart to move. I breathed him in, feeling calm and peaceful.

The following day, Dustin beat me out of bed. I heard him and Rae and Bernie in the kitchen, along with sounds of breakfast preparation. Compelled by the smells and sounds, I wandered into the kitchen, not worried about my bedhead or the ratty pajamas I had thrown on last night. Rae was at the stove, cooking pancakes. My mother was at the kitchen island and regarded me with a look of pure horror. Before I could figure out why she looked so stricken, I heard a voice to the right of me.

"Good morning, Rebecca."

My stomach dropped as I realized in a split second why my mother was horrified. I knew without looking that my hair looked like Doc Brown in Back to the Future, wild and unkempt. My shirt was old and faded, a high school relic spotted with hair dye and holes, worn almost bare in some spots. I wondered fleetingly if it was so bare as to show off my breasts underneath. My shorts were baggy men's basketball shorts, stolen from my college boyfriend as a display of ownership. This was an outfit I alternately slept or cleaned in. Only Dustin and once the UPS man had ever seen the unflattering ensemble. Yet, here stood Malachi, regarding me with barely concealed amusement.

"Oh, uh, hi Malachi. Good morning. I forgot you started today."

I knew my face was as red as a tomato with unconcealed embarrassment.

"Apparently." My mother said, her eyes wide over her coffee rim.

"I just got here. Sorry to catch you off guard." He said. "You got my appointment reminder text, yes?"

"Yes, yes! Total oversight on my part. I'm just going to go freshen up before breakfast. Rae, are you able to keep an eye on Dustin for me? I can find Dean if not."

"He's on a call for work upstairs. I can watch him." She replied.

"We'll all keep an eye on him." Malachi offered.

"I couldn't ask you to do that." I protested.

"He has two grandmothers here ready, willing, and able to take care of him. Come sit with me, Dustin." Mom trilled, pulling out a stool for him at the bar.

"Just watch him sitting up there," I warned.

"Rebecca, I managed to keep you alive for this long. I am fairly certain I can keep my grandson safe on a stool while you get ready. He wants to go to the pool after breakfast. Was that on your agenda?"

"I was going to stick around and get Malachi familiar with everything while Rae and Dean took him to the pool."

"Nonsense! I am perfectly capable of showing him the lay of the land before my nap." She argued.

"We'll be fine, really. Go enjoy some time with your son." Malachi interjected.

"Thank you. We won't be far if you need us." I smiled, grateful for the time with Dustin. He met my eyes. The fireworks of our first meeting went off, and I blinked, trying to clear them. "And he'll have to nap at some point so we can sit down then and go over anything Mom doesn't get to or that you have questions about."

"Sounds like a plan." He said, smiling his dazzling white smile.

My breath hitched in my chest, and my nether regions pulsed. I turned and went back into my room. I laid on the bed for a minute, vowing to either get dressed before that door opened every day or to get cuter pajamas.

But for the moment, I had to get myself together.

Maybe I could redeem myself with Malachi by putting my bathing suit on full display, I pondered. After two experiences of him seeing me in disarray, displaying a little confidence may be a refreshing change. And besides, we're going swimming after breakfast.

I still wasn't confident enough to saunter out in just my suit, so I threw a long, filmy sarong on, adjusting it to show a maximum amount of leg and thigh. My bathing suit top was a halter and framed my breasts nicely if I did say so myself. I added a pair of jeweled slides and coiled my curls into a bun on top of my head. I brushed my teeth, slicked on some lip gloss, and added some waterproof mascara as an afterthought. Here I come, ready or not, I thought, heading back to the living room.

RAE

The door to the bedroom where Rebecca was staying opened, and she stepped out. From her perch at the kitchen counter, Bernie gave a slight, surprised exclamation under her breath. Rebecca was trying hard to maintain an air of confidence as she strode out of the door, but she faltered slightly, her movements faintly jerky. It was apparent to me that she was putting on a show for Malachi. She could deny it all she wanted, but the air between them hummed with charged attraction.

I glanced at Malachi, and it looked like her display was having the desired effect. His eyes were trained on her, sweeping head to toe. His gaze danced over her curves appreciatively. I knew Rebecca felt his stares. A smile filled with satisfaction but also mingled with wonder played on her lips.

"Ready for the pool, Dustin?" she asked, lifting him off the stool and heading back to the bedroom to get him changed and wipe away the remnants of breakfast that clung to his pudgy cheeks.

Rebecca's hips were loose again today as she swayed seductively past him. As she turned around, giving Malachi a full frontal view he hadn't benefitted from before, he choked, coughing and covering his wide grin instead. Bernie and I exchanged a knowing look.

"Pancakes?" I finally broke the silence as I offered Malachi a plate.

"Oh no, thank you! I had to step up my workouts to work off the food from last time." He said.

"You look just fit as a fiddle to me." Bernie demurred.

He smiled broadly, unembarrassed by the compliment.

"I have to stay in top form to deal with you." He said jokingly.

"Isn't that the damn truth!" Bernie laughed.

Rebecca and Dustin re-emerged then. Dustin had on his swim trunks, and he wore water wings. Rebecca struggled with the enormous tote bag she always took to the pool.

"Ok, we're off now." She said, opening the door, which Dustin darted out of without hesitation.

Her voice calling for him to slow down and wait for her traveled as she closed the door.

Malachi laughed, a deep, booming baritone.

"She has her hands full with that little man." He commented.

"She sure does. Dustin's sweet as pie, though." Bernie replied. "Do you have any kids?"

"No. My sisters both have kids, so I see my nieces and nephews a lot, but I haven't had the pleasure myself."

"Do you and your wife want children?" She asked, clearly fishing for information to pass to Rebecca later.

"No wife for me."

"Husband? Girlfriend? Boyfriend?" She pressed on.

"None of the above. Now that you've eaten let's take these meds." He changed the subject swiftly and efficiently.

Bernie pulled a face, displeased at not only being deterred in her mission but also because she was being treated as a patient. I slid my hand across the countertop and put my hand over hers in support and acknowledgment. She took the medications, one for pain and one to combat anxiety, without protest. Soon, she would be asleep again, the heavy, dreamless sleep of the sedated.

Malachi made some notations on a colorful chart. "Let's do some vitals while we're at it."

He made quick work of taking her blood pressure, measuring her oxygen, and listening to her lungs and heart. As he recorded them on another chart, I noticed she was starting to fade.

"Are you ready for a nap?" I asked her.

Bernie nodded. Malachi immediately reached out to her, holding his arm out for her to take and slipping her tiny, pale hand into his large, darker one. She slid off her seat and followed him. Silently, they went towards her room together.

Malachi emerged several minutes later as I was finishing up the breakfast dishes.

"She's out." He announced.

"That's good. She's sleeping more and more." I said.

"Unfortunately, as the cancer takes over, that will happen. Eventually, Bernie will be sleeping more than she is awake. All we can hope for after that is for a peaceful end."

"I've been on death watch before. I lost both my parents." I paused, drawing in a breath to fortify myself. "And my son."

"Oh, no. That's so terrible." His sympathy was evident. "He must have been young."

"He was nineteen," I told him. "He was in college in Boston. A drunk driver hopped the sidewalk when he was walking home."

I stopped, taking long, deliberate breaths to keep the gripping pain I felt whenever Sean came up in conversation at bay.

"He never saw it coming. He was gone before he hit the sidewalk." I finished in a whisper, tears sliding down my cheeks.

Malachi shook his head and rubbed my back.

"My God. I am so sorry. He and Rebecca dated?"

You could see him trying to figure out the relationship, how we all fit into this puzzle. This new family, built on loss, would never fit anyone's family model, but here we were.

"No. You won't believe me when I tell you, but hand to God, it's all true."

"You have me on the edge of my seat."

"Dean and I live in the same neighborhood as Bernie's sister, Cami. She throws a huge Christmas bash every year. When we were at the party, I saw a card from Rebecca with Dustin's picture on it. I instantly knew he was my grandson. He looks just like my son at his age. So, I set out to find him and find out if he really was Sean's son. With the support of no one, I went to Boston, found Rebecca, and convinced her to give us a DNA test. No one believed it would come back a match. But it did."

"So, Sean had a fling with Rebecca?" He said, still confused.

"Oh, sorry! No, Sean and Rebecca never even knew one another. She conceived him using artificial insemination."

His eyebrows shot up, obviously surprised.

"Why would a woman like that need to use a sperm donor?"

His tone was telling, almost defensive, or maybe protective.

"A woman like that?" I teased.

He was still serious as he turned to me.

"A beautiful woman. Real. Who cares about everyone else above herself? Who would uproot her life to come care for her sick mother?"

"Sounds like you've thought a lot about her." I speculated.

He faltered a little. I saw his mind working, unwilling to reveal his thoughts or perhaps to appear unprofessional.

"I have." He admitted.

"Interesting," I commented.

I was just about to delve deeper into the specifics of his thought process when Rebecca and Dustin came bounding through the door.

"Gamma!" Dustin said, spotting me.

He threw himself, soaked trunks and all, on me, dampening my clothes as he did. Rebecca dropped her unwieldy bag at the door. She worked next on untangling herself from the towels she had snaked around her arms. When she was finally free, she readjusted her bathing suit, gave a deep sigh as if to gather her composure, and smiled.

"We're back." She announced unnecessarily. "Dustin, you got Grandma all wet! Let's go get you out of your suit and ready for a nap."

"No nap!" Dustin announced, drawing a chuckle from Malachi and me.

"Yes, nap. Come on, little man." She reached out her hand, and he took it without protest, sliding off my lap. He left me with a giant wet spot. I looked down sheepishly.

"Guess I need to change too," I said. "I'll be right back."

He nodded, his eyes fixed on the door that Rebecca had gone through. I headed upstairs, where Dean was working on his laptop.

He looked up from his screen. "What happened to you?"

"Dustin. He came in wet from the pool and sat on me."

"Oh good, I thought you needed Depends." He teased.

"You'll need Depends before me, old man."

"The only thing old about me is my age. I still got it." He said, pulling me to him and planting a long, lingering kiss on my lips.

"Penny for your thoughts?" Dean murmured into my hair.

"I was actually thinking about Malachi."

"Great. You have my replacement all lined up and ready to go." Dean joked.

"He has designs on Rebecca. I don't stand a chance."

"Good. She's going to need a strong man to help her through this. Especially the next part."

Dean fell silent, and I knew he was thinking about the way we leaned on each other, not only in the first moments of tragedy but still now. If Malachi could be even half as steadfast for Rebecca as Dean had been for me, I knew she, as well as their relationship, would thrive through all the hardship ahead.

"I love you." I looked up into his eyes.

"Right back at ya, babycakes." He said, tracing my lips with his finger.

We shared another long kiss. I changed quickly. Dean returned to his computer, attempting to meet a deadline.

I went back downstairs, where Malachi and Rebecca sat on the couch lost in conversation, the charts and information splayed between them forgotten, their bodies angled toward one another, and their arms flung over the back. From where I stood, I could only see Rebecca's face.

It struck me that for the first time since meeting her, she looked young. Usually, she wore her responsibilities and obligations like heavy garments. Her spine rounded under their weight, and her shoulders drooped. Her face always wore a perpetually exhausted and anxious look. But right now, watching her with Malachi, I saw no evidence of any of the burdens she carried. Her face glowed under his attention. And could it be? Yes, she was batting her eyelashes! Bernie would be proud, I thought.

They didn't notice my entrance into the room, their eyes never leaving the other's face. As I was moving towards the kitchen, someone knocked on the door.

" I got it." I said, the conversation stalled by the interruption.

I opened the door, and Todd stood there. Looking at him reminded me of a character in a Disney movie I had recently watched with Dustin. The character had a pet reindeer, floppy dirty blonde hair, a broad chest, and affable nature. There was no pet reindeer in sight, but everything else was spot on. He grinned at me.

"Hey there!"

"Todd! What are you doing here?"

"Just stopping by to check on Bernie." His eyes looked behind me, searching for Rebecca. At least that was my guess.

"She's sleeping now, but I was just about to make some sandwiches. You hungry?"

He patted his stomach and looked unrepentant. "I can always eat. But I can make my own sandwich. You don't have to serve me. In fact, let me make you one."

Todd moved into the house with a self-assuredness that reminded me suddenly of Dean. He brightened when he saw Rebecca on the couch. His face fell slightly when he noticed Malachi.

"Hey, Rebecca! Sandwich?" He was keeping his voice neutral but upbeat. I could see how he was trying to keep himself from jumping to conclusions.

"Todd!" Rebecca's voice came out shrill and thready. "Sure, I'll have a sandwich."

"Great! What will it be?"

"We have turkey, chicken salad, or roast beef," I interjected. "Here, I'll help. Malachi?" I asked.

Malachi stood up, looking almost guilty. He smiled.

"I'm going to gain fifty pounds working here." He said. "But I'll take turkey."

"You work here?" Todd asked.

"I'm Bernie's nurse," Malachi explained.

Todd looked incrementally more comfortable. "I'm Todd. Nice to meet you."

"Malachi."

The two men shook hands, both feeling the other's intentions out wordlessly. Rebecca looked like she might faint at any moment. I repressed the urge to giggle. Men and their egos. Jealous before they even knew if there was something to be jealous about.

Todd and I worked together to make lunch. As he finished the sandwiches, I added potato salad and a thick pickle to every plate. Todd made small talk easily as the four of us sat at the table, recounting the very sordid tale of two other elderly members of the complex caught making love in the pool after hours.

"I just took Dustin swimming in that pool!" Rebecca laughed; mock horror fixed on her face.

"Does chlorine kill sperm?" Todd wondered aloud.

We all looked to Malachi, the only medical professional among us, for the answer. He paused from eating and regarded all of us with a raised eyebrow.

"Are you asking me? I have no idea!" He laughed.

"The American education system at work! A Master's in Nursing, and they don't even tell you if chlorine kills sperm." Rebecca teased him.

"Well, I learned plenty of other useful information." Malachi laughed again, holding up his hands.

"What's all this? Having fun without me." Dean came into the kitchen. "Good afternoon, gentlemen."

"I didn't realize you were done with work! You hungry?" I stood up to fix him a sandwich.

"Sit! Eat! I can make my own sandwich. Not that I don't appreciate the offer, darlin'." Dean leaned over and kissed me softly and quickly, then turned to make his lunch.

We heard Bernie call out, weak and disoriented, and Rebecca and Malachi were both on their feet in an instant, darting into her room without a word.

"Should I go too?" I asked.

"Looks like they have it under control," Dean said. "Finish your lunch. They'll let us know if they need us."

I took his advice, even though the impulse to rush in and help still nagged at me. A few minutes later, Rebecca reappeared, sober but calm.

"She's okay. The meds are making her a little loopy." She explained. "Malachi is going to sit with her."

We all finished our lunch, more subdued now. Eventually, Rebecca heard Dustin stirring. Dean sprang up to get him. They emerged just a few minutes later with a newly changed and outfitted Dustin, who immediately sat on Dean's lap and reached for the remains of a sandwich on a plate.

"Looks like someone's hungry. I got you, buddy." Todd said, moving to grab the bread. "What does he like?"

"Turkey is fine," Rebecca said.

Todd worked quickly. "Pickle?"

"Yes," Dustin spoke up, clear as a bell, looking right into Todd's eyes and sending us all into peals of laughter.

"Pickle it is then," Todd said.

Malachi appeared in the doorway, a stern look darkening his face.

"Can you all keep it down just a little? Bernie's having a difficult time."

Rebecca looked immediately guilt-stricken and sick. Her eyes darted wildly, cutting a track from the hall where Bernie's room was to Todd, then Malachi. I knew, without having to ask, that she felt immense guilt. I could almost feel her remorse, thick and heavy, for flirting while her mother lay dying.

I also knew her mother's fervent wish that she would spend her time just like this. She wanted Rebecca to see herself as beautiful and desired, worthy. Bernie hoped that flirting with Malachi and Todd would help her find that.

"Not because her worth needs to be determined by or given to her by a man, but because a man will make her find those things inside herself." Bernie had said. "She IS beautiful, desirable, and worthy. Becca should know that, inside of herself, every day. So that when the right man comes along, she demands nothing less. I want to help her find the things I never gave to her, the things no one ever thought to help me find inside myself. But I won't be able to because my time is running out. All I can do now is try to give her the tools to do the work."

Bernie had cried then, her hands knotting and twirling the delicate fringe of the blanket spread over her lap. The moon had streamed in through the window, making her look luminous, like she was already an angel, orchestrating and overseeing the happenings of us all.

"We didn't realize we were too loud. Did we upset Bernie?" I asked.

Malachi's face relaxed, and his body language became more casual, not the stiff, business-like demeanor he had come out of the bedroom with.

"She didn't complain, but that's my job. I get to be the bad guy."

"I don't think you could be the bad guy if you tried." Dean intoned.

"We'll have to agree to disagree on that," Malachi said. "I didn't mean to act like a jerk, but it's my job to take care of Bernie."

"Of course, it is, and we appreciate it," Rebecca said. "We'll make sure to keep it down from now on. Do you or Mom need anything?"

Malachi brushed past her, their arms skimming one another, and opened the fridge. He took out a bottle of water and smiled broadly.

"For Bernie." He said, disappearing back into the hallway towards Bernie's room.

I looked at Rebecca and noticed that she was rubbing the small patch where Malachi's arm had touched hers gently. Todd regarded her with curiosity and concern.

REBECCA

"Wanna go for a walk?" Todd asked, distracting from the tingles dancing across my skin from Malachi's velvet touch.

"I should stay, with Mom not doing well."

Todd looked crestfallen but brightened.

"How about dinner tonight? As friends..." He trailed off like the words left a bad taste in his mouth.

I hesitated. What the hell was I doing, having random hookups with virtual strangers on golf courses and lusting after another? I wasn't here for sex and love triangles; as intriguing and intoxicating as they promised to be, I was here to take care of my dying mother. Yet, love affairs were precisely what my mother wanted for me. It would be poor form for anyone else, but for Bernie, my sexual escapades were her perfect sendoff.

"I really can't. Dustin will be ready for bed by then."

His face flashed disappointment again, but he shrugged casually. "Ok, I guess I will see you guys by the pool. I'll let you relax."

He let himself out. Once I was alone, I splayed on the couch and began to scroll through my phone. I was texting with

Kieran, laughing aloud at his latest dating debacle, when a voice startled me.

"What's so funny?" Malachi asked, his eyes filled with humor.

"Ohhh, you scared me!" I shot up and tried to gather myself into some semblance of attractiveness. "I was just texting with someone back home. He was cracking me up. Well, you know that part."

"Your boyfriend?" he asked, sounding not as casual as he intended to and not meeting my eye.

"Oh heavens no. I am single as a pringle. Kieran is my best friend. I'm not exactly his flavor." I paused, laughed. "He's gay. Gold star gay."

"Okay, we've established he's gay." He chuckled and shook his head. "Single as a pringle, huh? And ready to mingle?"

He looked at me, innuendo heavy in his gaze. The air crackled. My insides felt like molten lava. I wobbled as my limbs shot hot and cold. I had hoped he didn't notice, but Malachi reached out to steady me.

"You, okay?" he asked, face concerned.

"I'm fine. Just got dizzy for a minute there." I looked up into his beautiful eyes. I started to blush as the fuzziness descended again.

"Oh no, we can't have this. Here, sit down."

He guided me to the armchair, then sat on the couch and cupped my knee with his hands in comfort. His very large, masculine, sexy hands.

My pulse scrambled as heat bloomed under his touch and began to spread, slow like honey, through my veins. His touch was heady, intoxicating. I never wanted his hand to move, but I would require some serious medical intervention fast if it didn't.

Reluctantly and with effort, I moved his hand off my leg and again met his gaze. Once the connection between our bodies was broken, my head started to clear.

Malachi looked down as I returned his hand to his lap. He looked confused, maybe even hurt.

"I don't mean to hurt your feelings." I began. "But I couldn't think with your hand on me."

His face went from rejected to excited. He smiled broadly, an air of confidence infusing his demeanor.

"Nice to know the effect I have on you." He said quietly, heat rolling off each word.

" I didn't think it was much of a secret. I haven't been able to keep it together whenever you're close to me." My eyes widened, shocked at the words that had tumbled without thought from my lips.

" You don't have to keep it together for me." He said quietly. "My entire career is built on helping people at the worst moments of their lives. Every single one is coming apart at the seams by the time I get on board."

" I'm not falling apart at the seams." I protested, my pride fighting against my attraction, grief, and loneliness, creating a chaotic storm inside me.

" Of course not. If you spend two minutes with you, you can see how strong you are. You must be to be a single mom if I were to wager a guess. But I'm here if you need to lean on someone. I don't just want to guide your mother to the next chapter. I want to help you too." He said earnestly.

My heart thudded in my chest, and my head swam with tears that I refused to let fall. I didn't trust my voice. I took some deep breaths and willed my voice not to wobble.

" I've never had anyone offer to help me. Ever." I felt like a child, feeble and timid.

" You and Bernie seem so close. She hasn't been there when you needed her?"

" My mother and I have barely had more than a formal, cordial relationship before this trip. Growing up, she was more concerned with her social obligations than she was with me. Cancer changed her whole perspective. That's the silver lining of all of this."

" That may not be the only one." He said, locking his light eyes onto mine.

Before I could reply, my mother emerged from the hallway, moving slow and bleary-eyed.

" Did Dean already leave?" She asked, confused and disoriented.

She appeared unsteady. Malachi moved to her side.

" No, he's upstairs with Dustin and Rae. He's not flying out till NEXT Friday, remember?" I explained." Would you like me to call him?"

She smiled, the genuine smile I loved but also mourned, knowing the light it brought would be extinguished, too soon and forever.

" No, thanks. I'm going to lay back down. Good night, Bec. Help me, Malachi?"

He nodded. "Of course! Here, nice and easy."

He led her by her increasingly thin arm down the hall. In a few minutes, he emerged.

"She's all set. I gave her some sleeping meds. Dean's leaving?"

I nodded as a wave of sadness suddenly overtook me. We had all intertwined our lives; Dean had become a trusted friend and confidante. I would miss him and his calm presence.

"Yeah, he has to get back to work."

"At least you'll have Rae to help. It can get pretty heavy." He said.

"Yeah, that's what I'm afraid of," I said.

"Don't be. Death is a part of life. And you have me as your tour guide, as I said before."

"Well, keep my life jacket ready because I feel like I'm drowning." I looked down, shocked at allowing myself to be vulnerable in front of this man. I drew in a deep breath to fight the tears.

When I looked up, Malachi was staring at me. His jaw worked, clenching and unclenching. He seemed deep in thought as he held my stare. Unexpectedly, he reached up, his hand closing in on my face. I didn't flinch or even breathe. He brushed the pad of his thumb along my cheekbone, then followed it up past my ear and into my hair.

He smiled faintly then as his fingers danced and played. He wrapped a curl around his finger, letting it go and watching with satisfaction as it sprang back to its original form. Then, his hands fell to his sides again, as though the intimate moment had been nothing but a figment of my imagination.

He cleared his throat, suddenly looking sad. "I'm going to go. See you tomorrow."

And then he was gone, out the door and into the night, leaving me to wonder what the hell had just happened.

True to his word, Malachi arrived bright and early. Taking no chances, I had risen even earlier. By the time he arrived, I had showered, taking extra care with shaving and exfoliating. I slathered my body in body cream. I smelled like a cupcake and was as silky smooth as a rose petal.

I strolled out of my room, feeling beautiful in my own skin for the first time in a long time. My confidence soared when I saw Malachi's eyes widen. The corners of his mouth wobbled up and down, fighting the smile that I inspired.

"Good morning, everyone," I said, getting coffee.

"It's a good morning indeed," Malachi said, making Bernie and Rae whip their heads so fast to look at him that I was surprised they didn't get whiplash. "Do you have plans for the day, Becca? I wanted to introduce you to another one of my coworkers who will be filling in if I am unavailable or if we end up needing to add another caretaker as things progress. She's going to stop by after she's done with her client this morning. I'm not sure what time, so you'll be stuck here, I'm afraid."

"I think Dean is taking Rae and Dustin out, so I am all yours," I said.

Bernie immediately perked up. She wore a dusty lilac-colored turban with delicate white line drawn flowers all over it. She had paired it with a fitted white tee shirt and a pair of wide-legged dusty lilac capri pants. She stretched and made a show of yawning.

"I'm feeling a bit run down today. Malachi, is it okay if I take my medication and go back to bed?" Her voice was too innocent, but he didn't catch it.

"Of course, whatever you need." He said.

I sighed, aware of her scheme. Even on her literal deathbed, Bernie's persistent, meddlesome nature took over. She blew me a kiss and mouthed, "You're welcome."

"Let's go get you settled," Malachi said.

A few minutes later, he returned, shaking his head and laughing. "Your mother is something else."

"Oh God, was she being inappropriate?" I asked, horrified. "She has no filter."

"No, not at all. And Bernie may have no filter, but she's a sweetheart. She's already becoming one of my favorite patients."

"Didn't you tell me that you didn't have too many patients right now?" I joked. "Not hard to be the favorite when you're the only."

He held up his hands in surrender, laughing. "Guilty as charged. But she's still my favorite."

"I don't think you're supposed to have favorites."

"I love coming here. Great patient, tasty food, and a beautiful view." His voice was soft, unsure.

My stomach felt full of gravel. I felt it tumbling and shifting, like when you went on the Scrambler at the carnival as a kid, sling-shotting out into the open air and whipping back before your stomach could catch up. I held my breath, head down. Finally, I couldn't stand the suspense any longer.

"Beautiful view?" I asked, looking up from under a curtain of curls.

He met my eyes, held my gaze. It felt like we were teetering on a line, one we both knew we should not cross. I bit my lip and sighed. He looked like he wanted to say something but didn't. His eyes just stayed trained on mine, intense and unnerving.

We stood like that, neither of us willing to be the one to step over the boundary for what seemed like forever. Finally, he moved back, taking a giant step that sent him halfway across the room from me. He shook his head and frowned.

"I'm sorry. I'm unprofessional." He paused, paced, agitated. "I can't do this. I'm your mother's nurse. This is my career. I shouldn't be coming on to you."

"Who are you trying to convince? Me or yourself?" I asked him softly, the sting of rejection prickling on my skin like wasp bites.

He stepped closer, inhaled deeply, closed his eyes. "Mmmm, you smell like a cupcake. I love cupcakes."

He paused, stepped back. He stopped, then spoke.

"Rebecca, you are a wonderful woman. You're smart and selfless...beautiful. But your mother is my patient, and I have an ethical obligation to care for her to the best of my ability, undistracted. We have to stop this before it starts."

My heart leaped at him, calling me beautiful. It was so bittersweet to know what we felt was mutual but would never be acted upon.

"This?" I questioned.

"This- this flirtation, this dance, this attraction between us."

I chuckled, and my mouth cranked into a smirk. "I don't think you get to choose who you're attracted to."

"But you can certainly choose to have the willpower not to act on it." He said.

I laughed again. Malachi tilted his head, confused.

"You're all muscles and steel. My entire body looks like a down comforter. One of us obviously lacks any type of willpower." I spat out.

He balled his fists at his side. "Don't talk about yourself like that." His voice was fierce, anger, white-hot with emotion. "You know what a down comforter does? Yes, it may be soft and pillowy and maybe even lumpy sometimes, but it keeps you warm at night. It provides you comfort and protection, makes you feel safe. Hell, it could even save a man from freezing to death."

He stopped, looked at me long and hard. "Maybe you are like a down comforter after all."

I resisted the urge to stride through the distance between us and kiss him. Instead, I laughed self-consciously and spoke.

"I don't think talking about our bodies is going to help the attraction die down," I said.

"I know." He said. "And it has to die down and to stay dead. Your mother needs us."

I nodded vigorously. "So, friends, it is."

I stuck my hand out. It hung there, suspended in the air, awkwardly. Finally, Malachi sighed, stepped forward, and extended his hand. We met eyes, the same waves of lust rolling off of both of us as steady and strong as the tides of the ocean.

"Friends." He whispered.

The day Dean had to head back to Connecticut came quicker than any of us wanted to, Rae and Dean most of all. But Dean had already begged, borrowed, and pleaded vacation time to extend his trip, and his boss wasn't feeling generous any longer. The day he left, Bernie stumbled out from her room, where she had taken to spending more and more time, leaning against her pink headboard, a queen ruling her public.

"Dean?" She called, squinting in the brightness, fuzzy because of the painkillers.

I rushed to her.

"He's upstairs. I can call him for you."

"Can you ask him to come to see me in my room? I need to lay down. I'm so tired, Bec. Just so tired."

" Of course. If you're tired, though, I am sure Dean will understand a quick goodbye." I said.

Mom paused for a moment. Her eyes went somewhere else. Her chin quivered, and a tear cut a wet path down her face.

"The last goodbye can't be a quick goodbye. I have things to discuss with him. And no more time to do it. The next time he sees me will be in my casket."

I fought hard the urge to sob. Instead, I managed a weak smile. Malachi shepherded her back to her room as I called up to Dean. He appeared almost instantly, brushing past me with purpose.

Malachi appeared a few minutes later.

" She kicked me out." He laughed and shook his head.

" I'm not surprised. When she's on a mission, as she appears to be, nothing and no one deters her. How is she doing? Did you do her vitals?"

" I did. She's stable."

" Stable is good." I proclaimed, grasping to the word like a child with a lollipop.

"It's certainly better than unstable." He replied, but he didn't sound as hopeful as I had.

"What are you not telling me?" I asked.

"I just think we're seeing a small shift in her health. I think the disease is progressing a bit. Or it has been for a while, but she's getting too tired to mask it anymore. Either way, changes are happening." He paused, then finished in a rush. "I could be wrong. But since I have been working with her, there are some definite changes."

My body felt numb and heavy. So many words and emotions bubbled up into my throat, but none would come out. Finally, one surfaced.

"Fuck." I murmured.

The withheld sob overtook me then, and I doubled over, my body shaking with each cry. Malachi moved to me. He sat me on the couch, then folded himself down next to me. His hand made small, slow circles on my back. He didn't offer empty platitudes or shush me. He let me cry. He let me feel. He was silent and strong, a rock anchoring me in the storm of grief.

Finally, I stopped. I felt empty and crumpled like the tissues that dotted the coffee table, damp with my tears. He finally spoke.

"I know you're going to take Dean to the airport when he's done with Bernie. Would it make you feel better if I stayed till you got home so your mom won't be alone?"

"I can't ask you to do that! I wouldn't want to be a bother or interfere with your personal life." I rambled, trying to talk my heart out of singing at his selfless act.

"It's not a bother. I offered. And the only plans I have for tonight involve takeout and mindless television. At least if I stay, I am almost guaranteed a home-cooked meal thanks to Rae." He smiled then.

"Oh, I see, so this isn't a purely selfless act." I teased." Despite your nefarious intentions, I will take you up on your offer, as long as you're sure we're not messing up your plans."

" I'm sure. Let me help." He said.

" You don't know how much this means to me. Thank you."

" It's no trouble, really." He assured me.

Dean emerged from the direction of Mom's room. His eyes were puffy and wet, but his face broke into a wide smile when he saw us. He chuckled and shook his head.

" Your mother is something else, Becca." He said.

"That's the understatement of the century." I agreed. "Everything okay?"

"Just saying my goodbyes and getting my marching orders."

"Marching orders? Is she micromanaging her funeral?"

"Something like that. I'm going to grab my suitcase. You ready to go?" He changed the subject abruptly.

"Whenever you are, though, I will be sad to see you go."

"I'm sad to leave. I worry about Rae going through this without me. All of you, for that matter."

"I'll be here for them every step of the way," Malachi spoke up. "Try not to worry, though; in my experience, that's like telling ice not to melt."

Dean's face flashed several emotions at once. Before I could ask why him why Dean spoke.

265

"At least I'm leaving you in capable hands." He said. "Let me go rally the troops."

As he headed to the attic, Malachi moved past me to go sit with Mom. Dustin bounded down the stairs, followed by Rae, who looked sad and already lost without her husband. Dean brought up the rear, hauling his suitcase down with him.

We made our way to the parking lot in silence, except for Dustin, who chatted in a nonsensical stream. He and I were in the back. Dean manned the wheel, and Rae rested her hand on his thigh and her head on his shoulder. Their combined sadness was palpable.

Dean pulled up to the curb marked for Departures. Rae reluctantly opened the door onto the busy sidewalk. Dustin strained against his straps, ready to go on an adventure with his grandfather.

"Grandpa! Grandpa! I go?" He called.

"Not this time, buddy. Just me today." Dean said, lifting Dustin out and up onto his shoulder.

He squeezed him tight. I could see him inhaling his scent. I saw his face slacken as he lost composure. He wept openly, clinging to him. I knew he was not only saying goodbye to my son but his own as well.

Rae's tears were flowing as we stood together and watched the tender scene. She moved in, embracing both of them. I stood there, feeling like an interloper during the intimate moment.

Dean opened his eyes and moved to envelop me into the fold.

"Come here. I'm going to miss the hell out of you, young lady." He talked into my hair.

We were a wet mass of emotion, clinging to each other as strangers moved around us. Finally, we broke apart.

"Come on. You'll miss your flight." Rae said reluctantly. "Do you want us to go in with you?"

"No, I can't say goodbye again."

He gave us all a strong, lingering hug. He brushed a kiss on my cheek.

"Stay strong, kiddo. But let people take care of you when you need it. And if you need me, I'm on a plane. Take care of our boy."

I nodded my head as he bent to tickle and kiss Dustin, who squirmed in my arms. Rae was last. He held her at arm's length for a moment, an unspoken conversation in their eyes. Then, he pulled her close into a hug that was so tender but strong that his biceps flexed under his thin sweater. She convulsed with a solitary sob as she laid her head on his chest. He pulled away, brushed a tear off her cheek, and consumed her mouth with a passionate kiss.

I placed Dustin back in his seat and climbed behind the wheel, not wanting to intrude on their private goodbye. Rae entered the car, her eyes puffy and watery, but her lips arranged in a smile for Dustin's sake. He eyed her curiously. I navigated us back onto the highway home.

When we got home, we found Mom had woken up and moved out to the couch, where she sat with Malachi.

"Did Dean get off okay?" She asked, halting mid-sentence.

"He's not in the air yet, but he's on the plane. He just texted me." Rae said. "I think I am going to take a little swim. Dustin, do you want to go with grandma to the pool before dinner?"

"Yay!" He screeched, running straight into our room and to the bathroom where his swim trunks hung over the shower rod.

"Wait for me!" I called, hot on his heels.

He was already naked when I reached him, his clothes a puddle on the floor. I grabbed the trunks and stooped down. He quickly thrust his legs into them and set off in a run to meet Rae.

"You forgot this, silly monkey," I said, handing Rae his beach towel as I came into the living room.

"We'll be bac-- oh, shit. Where's my head? What about dinner?"

"Let me take care of it," I said. "I can cook...or at the very least call for takeout."

"Sounds good to me." She smiled, but her eyes were dull with sadness.

"You're not our maid or cook. I can share the duties. Go, enjoy your swim." I replied.

And with that, they were off. I turned around to Malachi and Mom looking at me expectantly.

"What are you going to cook?" Mom asked.

"What do you feel in the mood for?" I asked her.

She paused to analyze my question. Then, she laughed.

"Wonton soup and lemon cake with fresh raspberries."

"Interesting combination," I said. "So, Chinese. I can run to the store for dessert." I turned to Malachi, grinning. "I know we promised you a home-cooked meal for your service, but I will have to give you an IOU."

"I would have it no other way. Bernie should get whatever she wants. I love Chinese, though we should probably order more than just soup. I'm a growing boy, and so is Dustin." He patted his stomach playfully.

"We can order whatever you like." I pulled the menu out of the drawer and handed it to him. "I'm going to run to the store for dessert."

"Actually, I'm coming with you. We can call in the order while we're in the car."

"I can manage the grocery store by myself," I said.

"You're not going to the grocery store."

"I beg your pardon?"

"My gran owns a restaurant not too far from here. One of her specialties is her lemon cake. And she always serves it with fresh raspberries and whipped cream."

"Oh, my goodness, does your gran own Fern's?" Mom exclaimed.

"Yes, ma'am! I grew up in that place. I drove my cars down the aisles of booths and colored the menus. I even learned a recipe or two. Though not that one. Gran guards it with her life."

"Well, is it any wonder why? That cake is amazing. I've been dreaming of it. I thought the place had closed."

"Gran had some health issues, and her stubborn self wouldn't allow anyone else to make the lemon cake or anything else for that matter, so we had to close. But she's doing better. She's been up and running for a few months now."

"Well, thank goodness she's doing better. Her cooking is a gift."

"That it is." Malachi agreed.

"Well, now I am excited to try this legendary cake." I broke into the conversation. "You ready? Mom, can you manage for a little while on your own, or do you want me to send Rae and Dustin back?"

"I think I can manage on my own for a bit. They should be back soon anyway. It's almost dark."

After a quick stop to collect Rae's Chinese food order, we were off. A few minutes into the ride, an R&B song I had loved as a teenager came on. Without thinking, I turned it up and started singing. Malachi eyed me, amused.

"I'm glad you made yourself comfortable." He said, sounding sincere.

"I'm sorry. I didn't mean to dominate the radio. I just used to love this song."

"Used to? I still love it." Malachi said and joined in singing with a rich baritone that my body began to react to almost instantaneously.

We sang together, our voices mingling to create a harmony that rivaled the ones coming from the radio. The song continued for a few minutes. When we were done, we were both breathless from the high, long runs in the music.

"We don't sound half bad together," I said. "That might have been perfect harmony."

"I wonder what other magic we could make," Malachi said, the flirting tone back in his voice.

My stomach flipped.

"I thought we agreed to be friends," I said in a quiet voice.

He laughed, sending ice then heat through my veins. "I guess you're right about that. But I'm not a particularly patient man. When I find something I want, I like to have it as soon as possible."

"So, you want me?" I asked, my heart plummeting into my stomach. "So much for willpower."

He laughed again. "Rebecca, my attraction to you wasn't a secret from the moment you opened the door. But spending time with you, in your house, with your mother and your son, over these past few weeks has been like torture."

"Torture?" I asked.

"Yes, because I see with each passing moment what an amazing woman you are, how much love you have to give for everyone in your life. And I can't help but want to be on the receiving end of it. I go home at night, lay alone in my bed, and think about what it would be like to lay next to you. For Dustin to bust in and do a running leap, knocking the air out of us."

I was quiet for a long time. I was stunned by his words, trying to catch my breath and think without being distracted by the pulsing between my legs.

"Penny for your thoughts?" Malachi broke into my thoughts.

"I just thought that I hadn't expected our flirtation to come to anything more than that."

"You didn't expect it, or you didn't want it to?" Malachi asked.

"Oh, I definitely wanted it to." My voice became seductive effortlessly, my body again reacting to him without my consent or forethought. I coughed, my usual, pragmatic voice returning. "But it's not that simple."

"Explain."

"Even if our flirtation is more than that on both sides, you're my mother's caretaker. Not to mention we BOTH agreed that we had to keep it friendly so that you could focus on giving Mom the best care possible. There are rules in place about dating clients or their families, I am sure. I won't let you risk your career over me. And I don't want to hide from anyone. If we date, I won't be a dirty little secret."

"I would never do that to you. When we start dating, I want the world to know." He said fiercely.

"When, huh? You're pretty confident." I said.

"That I am."

"Interesting." I managed.

"Is that so?" He laughed again, and my lady parts pulsed. "And don't worry about my job. I'm a big boy. I can handle whatever comes."

"You won't need to do that. I won't do that to you." I protested.

"Relationships aren't just about what one of us needs or wants. It's not just your call if we're just going to be friends. I get a say too."

"Why are you so willing to throw away everything you have worked for so easily? I'm not worth it."

"So, that's what this is about." He said, navigating the car to the side of the road in front of a small purple building with cheerful yellow flower beds and a giant neon sign that blinked "Fern's" with a giant, steaming pie on it.

I reached my hand out to open the door, but he reached across and stopped me.

"Hold on just a second. I want to finish this." He said quietly. "Rebecca, is that how you think of yourself?"

"Think what about myself?"

"That you're not worth taking a risk for. That you're not worthy of love or a relationship."

A lump rose in my throat, and a heaviness bloomed in my chest. Malachi had cut to the quick, picking up on my most profound insecurity before even I fully recognized it. When he said it, I knew it fit. I knew it was stomping down the excitement trying to erupt out of my heart like lava. With each pounding of its foot, it was warning me against opening up, trusting his words, getting hurt, the lava charring its heels.

"How did you do that?" I asked thickly.

"Because I listened. I observed. And I can tell you you're wrong. You are more than worthy of every good thing in this world. Especially love."

"Love?" I asked playfully to distract from the emotional impact his kind words had on me. I arched my eyebrow and wiggled it.

He laughed at the face. "That does remain to be seen, I guess. I told you, I'm not patient."

"Well, one word that could describe me is patient. Cautious to a fault would be more accurate. I don't make decisions lightly. I over-analyze. I work out every worst-case scenario in case it happens. So, love, to me, is a slow process fraught with anxiety and panic."

"It doesn't have to be. And we don't have to rush anything. I just want you to be open to the possibilities."

"Possibilities?"

"Yes, as I see it, this could go a few ways. We could get to know one another, see where things go, maybe have some fun."

My heart thudded so hard against my chest, it physically hurt. I drew in a deep breath.

"Option two?" I said breathlessly.

"Oh, option two...that's simple." He paused and put his hand over mine on the console. "Forever."

Before I knew what was happening, Malachi leaned over and kissed me. His lips were just as I had imagined since I had first seen them- amazingly soft and supple. Gentle at first, testing the waters. Then more urgent, deeper. His scent, the expensive cologne, woodsy cologne, and slight antiseptic smell enveloped me. My head swirled.

Between his words and his touches, his lips on mine, I was lost in him. I reached up, traced his strong jawline with my finger as he kissed me again and again. I looked into his beautiful eyes and tried to regain my ability to speak and breathe. Even though I wanted desperately to believe his words and even more to savor his kisses, my insecurities wouldn't allow me to. Pulling away from him, I sighed deeply.

"You can't possibly know me well enough even to consider that."

"I know more about you than you think. I saw the life we could have the moment you opened that door. You didn't even need to parade past me in your bathing suit to inspire the vision." He grinned broadly. "But if you need time, I'm willing to move at your speed. But right now, we should get inside. We have attracted an audience."

I turned and looked out my window. Two women, who looked a lot like Malachi but with more delicate, ladylike features, squinted out the window, observing us from a distance. When they spotted us watching, the younger of the two quickly started sweeping, and the older woman scuttled away from the window.

"Your family?" I guessed.

"Oh yes. That's my aunt CeeCee and my gran, Fern."

I was stepping out on the sidewalk as he came around the side of the car. He held the door open to the restaurant. I walked inside, a bell tinkling as the door swung behind us.

"Sugar!" The older lady called from behind the register next to a display case of baked goods. Her face lit up as Malachi smiled at her.

"Hi, Gran! Aunt CeeCee. How are you both doing? This is my friend, Rebecca."

CeeCee approached. Up close, she was striking. Tall and thin with creamy chocolate skin, she had shiny, fat braids cascading down her back. She reached out her arms to fold me in them. She smelled like lemons, frosting, and a hint of sandalwood. It was intoxicating and comforting.

"Rebecca! It's nice to meet you. To what do we owe this pleasure? My handsome nephew doesn't make it over here too often these days. Too busy for the likes of us." She teased, elbowing him affectionately.

"Don't start on me, Auntie. You know I've been busy working. Rebecca's mother had a taste for Gran's lemon cake. And Rebecca is new in town and wanted to try it for herself."

Malachi's grandmother had been in motion while we chatted with CeeCee. She came around the counter, a thick slab of cake on a plate in her hand.

"Here you go, baby. I just baked it a few hours ago." She set it on the table and opened her arms for a hug as CeeCee had. "I always like to watch people when they eat my cake for the first time. It brings my heart such joy. It's a pleasure to meet you. Where has my grandson been hiding you?"

"I've been busy caring for my mom. That's how I know Malachi. He's Mom's nurse. He's been a godsend."

CeeCee and Fern exchanged a subtle look, but I still spotted it. I wondered if they had the same worries about Malachi's career as I did. Fern recovered first. She pulled a chair out and patted the lavender-colored tablecloth.

"Sit and eat!" She insisted. "And grandson, come here and hug your gran."

Malachi did as he was told, dwarfing the small woman in his massive arms. I took a bite as ordered. My mouth instantly exploded with flavors. The tart lemon danced with the sweetness of the sugar and creaminess of the whipped cream. The raspberries exploded on my tongue, fresh and bright. All the flavors played together well. The cake was divine.

"Mom was right. This is a gift!" I said.

Fern laughed. "Your mother is giving me too much credit, but I thank you just the same. Would you like another piece?"

I looked down. I was surprised to see only a few bites left. I had only meant to eat one bite and save the rest for dessert, but I had been unable to resist.

"No, thank you! I didn't intend to eat that whole thing, but it was too good to stop."

"I will take that as a compliment to the chef," Fern said, smiling proudly.

"Absolutely," I assured her. "What do you think, Malachi? How many pieces should we get? One for each of us?"

"Nope, we need at least a whole cake," Malachi said. "If Bernie will eat it, encourage her. Her appetite could wane at any moment. Let her enjoy what she wants while she can."

"Well, then we will take a whole cake," I said.

"I just took one out of the oven. I'll go package it up so you can get it home for your mama." Fern scurried off.

"How is she doing?" Malachi asked CeeCee.

"She'll outlive us all out of pure stubbornness. Mama's something else, plain and simple. She'll die with a stack of lemon cakes beside her, warm from the oven."

"Just try to get her to rest. I know she puts up a fuss, but she needs to put her feet up and relax sometimes."

"Don't you start on me." Fern chided as she handed Malachi a box with a purple ribbon tied on it.

"How much do I owe you?" I asked.

"Your money is no good here," CeeCee said, smiling warmly. "And if your momma wants more, you just tell Malachi."

"Well, the next one I'm paying for. I insist."

"We'll see," Fern said beatifically.

"Do you want to grab some cookies for Dustin? Gran's are as good as the cake." Malachi asked.

"Who's Dustin?" CeeCee questioned.

"My son," I answered.

Another fleeting look passed between the women. Fern went over to the display case and pulled out half a dozen chocolate chip cookies, thick as a slice of bread and as big as a compact disc, a forgotten relic from my youth.

"And you say that you're going to gain weight hanging out at our house. I don't know how you're not five hundred pounds growing up with all these delicious treats around you." I said to Malachi.

"They lose their appeal when you can have them whenever you want." He said, shrugging.

"I wouldn't know. Sweets were worse than drugs in Bernie's house. I made up for lost time." I gestured to my hips and stomach.

"You stop that. A man needs a little cushion to pad him when he falls." Fern declared. "Those skinny girls can't keep a man warm at night."

"Hey!" CeeCee protested, gesturing to her slim frame.

I giggled as Fern said, "I rest my case," though she had provided no argument against CeeCee.

"Okay, enough, you two." Malachi broke in, shaking his head. "Can you behave if I leave you here alone?"

"Of course. I've been tolerating Mama all my life. Today is no different." CeeCee assured him.

"Ok, then. It was great to see you. Thanks again for the cake and cookies, Gran." He gave her a long, hard hug filled with tenderness.

"It was wonderful to meet you both," I said.

"Don't be a stranger," Fern commanded.

"I'll be back," I vowed.

When we got home, Rae was laying out the Chinese food. Mom was perched on a stool at the counter, talking animatedly.

"Just in time!" Rae said.

Malachi set the cake box on the table next to Mom.

"A whole cake? For me?" She said, delighted.

"Well, you have to share, but I will limit everyone to one piece. And Fern said to let Malachi know when you want another, and she will send it over."

"That's so kind." She said. "Please thank her for me, Malachi."

"I certainly will." He said. "Do you need help with anything, Rae?"

"Nope. Just grab a plate and get your food."

"No, ladies, first. Becca?" He handed me a plate. "Would you like anything other than wonton, Bernie? I can get it for you."

"No, you won't. You're off the clock. I can make her plate." I said.

Malachi held his hands up in mock surrender and grinned. Bernie and Rae looked back and forth between us. I wondered if they could sense that something had changed, even if it was just a declaration of intentions.

RAE

That must have been some car ride, I thought. Malachi hadn't stopped smiling the entire night, and Rebecca looked like the cat that ate the canary. I wondered if she would indulge Bernie and me with girl talk and wine later and let us share in her life and excitement.

My mind went to Olivia, cuddled under a blanket on my couch, tears flowing down her face either from laughter or sadness, aggravation or panic, spilling her heart out to me. She and Patti were close, especially for a teenage girl and her mother, but Liv had a different relationship with me. I was her sounding board and her safe haven. She was the daughter we had so fervently wished for and never produced. A wave of longing for her and Patti bubbled up inside me.

Dustin started chuckling as he thrust his tiny fists stuffed with lo mein noodles into his mouth. Malachi looked at him, surprised. A smile spread across his face.

"Whatcha doing, little man?" He asked.

"It's good," Dustin replied, dipping his finger in the red sauce.

"Would you like some of that? Don't dip your fingers in there, though. That's what the chicken is for." He held up a chicken finger, dipped it in the sauce, and took an enthusiastic bite. "Yum yum! Good stuff! Now you try."

Dustin watched Malachi with studied appreciation and admiration. Then, slowly, he dipped his chicken in the sauce, even wiping the excess sauce off with the rim of the bowl as Malachi had done.

"There you go! Great job, buddy!" Malachi praised him, holding his hand up high for a high five, which Dustin returned enthusiastically, his small hand dwarfed by Malachi's larger one.

Rebecca's face changed as she took in the scene. Malachi was tousling Dustin's curls affectionately.

"You done, little man?" He asked, standing and starting to extract him from the highchair.

"Here, let me do it," Rebecca said, snapping out of her reverie.

"No, no. You sit and finish eating. We're both done. And Dustin can show me where the bathtub is, right Dustin?"

At the word bathtub, Dustin was off like a shot, eager to show Malachi he could be a helper and to submerge himself into the fluffy white bubbles.

"It's not your job to do that, you know," Rebecca said, looking Malachi in the eye, neither speaking the conversation passing between their gazes out loud.

"It could be if you let me." He said, and I had to stifle the urge to fan myself as the temperature in the room seemed to shoot up suddenly.

I looked to Bernie, who had dropped her soup spoon, and stared open-mouthed and wide-eyed at the interaction. I caught her eye and hooked my finger under my chin in a silent reminder for her to mask her surprise. She snapped her mouth shut, making me laugh inwardly. Malachi went off in search of Dustin as Rebecca sat down, her face carefully arranged to appear calm but her eyes blazing.

"What is going on with you and Malachi?" Bernie asked, unable to contain her curiosity one second longer.

"Can we talk about this later, like after he leaves?" She asked in a whisper. "He can hear us."

"Okay, okay. But we ARE talking about this later." She said.

"That's fine! Can I finish my dinner, please? I have to get Dustin down soon."

"Don't let me stop you. I'm going to lay down myself. Rae, could you help me to my room, please?"

I rose quickly, linking my arm through hers. I noticed instantly how bony Bernie's arm had become, seemingly overnight. We made our way, slowly and methodically, to her room.

This room was one of my favorites in the house. Whereas everything else was washed in shades of gray, Bernie's room bloomed with different tones of pink. Her walls were a pearlescent

284

pale, pale pink. Her expansive headboard was blush pink fabric and spanned almost to the ceiling.

Her bedding was darker, a beautiful dusty rose, plush and extravagant. A delicate chandelier hung from the ceiling, giving the room a perfect feminine last touch.

Bernie sat on the edge of the bed, looking impossibly small. She slid her feet out of her slippers and swung her legs up. I settled in the armchair.

"So, what do you think is going on with them?" She asked as she cuddled down into the pillows. "First Todd, now Malachi!"

I chuckled. "Most moms would be horrified to find their daughter in the middle of a love triangle, you know."

"Well, I am not most moms." She laughed. "I never was. But she deserves it."

She was quiet for so long; I thought she had fallen asleep. Then, she spoke.

"It's my fault, you know."

"Excuse me?"

"I never loved Rebecca the way she needed. The way she deserved. So, she just stopped believing in it. I was a terrible mother. She had every material thing she could want and need but not my time, my attention. My love. I never taught her what she was worth."

"Bernie, you did the best you could. Think about your mother. What was she like?"

"My mother was hard as stone." She immediately replied. "We had nannies, all the toys, the finest dresses. We were at the top of the social food chain. She had better things to do than raise us."

The sadness in her voice tore at me and made me flush with pity for her and Cami.

"I bet she thought providing for you in the physical sense was being a good mother."

"But we wanted her to read with us, put us to bed. We had nannies, wonderful women whom I love and respect to this day, but we wanted our mother. And she treated us like houseguests long overstaying their welcome."

"You mothered like you were mothered. But Bernie, you broke the cycle. You changed your course with Rebecca."

"Just barely. And if cancer hadn't kicked me in the teeth, would I have come around at all?"

"We can't operate in the what-ifs. I know better than anyone how counterproductive that can be. We just have now, and, at this moment, you are doing a wonderful job. And Rebecca is opening herself to love."

"You think she's going to date Malachi, right?" Bernie asked, brightening again. "I mean, my god. Look at him."

I laughed. "She would be crazy not to. The way he looks at her--"

"Is the way Dean looks at you."

And there it was. That's what I hadn't been able to place. Malachi loved her. In the way that ran hot, weathered cold, healed hurts, restored. Saved. Just as Dean had loved me throughout my life.

Rebecca was facing a loss that was unlike any other, indescribable. One that weighed you down and never completely freed you. A daughter losing her mother is like losing half of herself, losing her dearest, most intimate friend in the world. The world seems dimmer permanently.

Rebecca would need someone who understood the science of loss and grief, with compassion and knowledge to get her through the times when the loss bent her over at the waist and enough passion for keeping her mesmerized and craving. Dustin would need someone to learn from, ask questions to. Her partner would need to make sure she didn't ignore herself while she tended to the needs of others.

"They're perfectly suited. Or at least appear to be." I said. "But we have to let them come to that for themselves."

"Not my style. And I'm working on borrowed time. Before Dean left, I told him what I would ask the hospice for my bucket list. Now, I need you to help me."

"Bernie, that's why I stayed. To help you. I would be honored to help complete your bucket list. Anything, you name it."

"I need you to help me plan Rebecca and Malachi's wedding."

"WHAT?" I gasped. "Bernie, we can't do that. Marriage is serious. And it is a commitment that they need to decide to make, not us."

"Ahh, if it doesn't work, they'll get a divorce." She laughed, shrugging. Then, she again grew serious. "I don't have much time left. I want to leave this world knowing I had a tiny part in her happiness. I want to right the wrong I have done to her in her life. I want Malachi's love, the security, and joy a marriage to him will afford her and Dustin to be my final gift to my child."

"So, you want Malachi to marry Rebecca so she can be taken care of?"

"Not monetarily. Rebecca will inherit the entirety of her late father's estate when I pass, plus the money I inherited from my parents and this condo. Money isn't something she will ever have to worry about. I worry about her emotional wealth. She needs to be as rich in love as she will be in money."

"But how do we know they aren't both just gunning for a romp in the hay? What do they call it now?" I asked.

"Friends with benefits. I had a few of those before this all happened." She preened. "But I can tell, they're not just enamored of each other. I saw it the second Rebecca opened the door. Sadly, I don't know my daughter well, but I know her enough to know she's never acted or experienced something like that before. It's like there is just this energy going through the space between them, like invisible strings tying them together."

"I feel it too, but again, they have to feel it, not us."

"I'm going to get to the bottom of this." She sat up. "Ask Malachi to come in here."

"Bernie--"

"Just get Malachi, please. And start a Pinterest board. We need to get this underway as soon as possible. Small, intimate. We can do it in the clubhouse here. I think I can manage that."

"I don't know about this."

"You promised me anything. I want to be a part of Rebecca's happiness when I spent so much of her life being the source of her misery. Please, help me." She paused. "By the time she comes to her senses, I won't have much energy to plan. It needs to be ready to go."

I sighed deeply. I knew Bernie would push on with or without me.

"Okay, I'll send him in," I said.

I found Rebecca, Dustin, and Malachi in the living room. Dustin sat on the couch sandwiched between them, Malachi reading a book in his deep voice. Rebecca's arm was stretched across the back of the sofa, her hand resting on Malachi's shoulder. She looked relaxed and happy. Together, they all looked intimate and familiar, a family.

Tears sprang to my eyes at the thought of it. I sniffed back the tears, and Rebecca stiffened as if she was doing something wrong by enjoying a quiet moment of happiness.

"Rae! Is Mom okay?"

"Of course. Finish his story. Malachi, she wants to talk to you. I'll go sit with her until you're done."

I turned quickly, admonishing myself for interrupting. Bernie craned her neck as I entered, looking for Malachi behind me.

"He was reading Dustin a bedtime story. He'll be right in."

She looked pleased with my report. "Rebecca can get Dustin down while we talk to him. Perfect."

"We? Oh no, this is a conversation for you and him. You're her mother. I'm just the unwilling wedding planner." I teased, but Bernie didn't laugh.

"I'm turning it over to you." She said tearfully.

"What?"

"My role as Rebecca's mother."

"You can't be replaced, Bernie. But I will always be there for her. I will always try and guide her, help her and do what you would have done."

"No, you do better than I've done. You're a remarkable mother and woman, Rae. Becca needs to have a relationship like that, a person like that, in her life."

"You are too, Bernie."

"Hush. Rae, you went against everyone in your life- your husband, your friends- because your mother's heart just knew Dustin was Sean's son. Without regard to yourself, you risked so much to find a small piece of what you lost. I admire you, the way you love your son, the way you talk about him. You speak of Sean like he was your lungs or your heart, vital for your survival."

"He was--is." I began, the tears starting. "When you talked about the invisible strings, a wordless, unbreakable bond between Becca and Malachi, it felt like Dean and me, but also me and Sean. I have always wondered why I didn't know he was gone before the call. It just seemed like our bodies have been in sync since he grew inside of me, a small spark growing to a roaring inferno of a kid ready to burn the world to the ground. When that flame was extinguished, my world should have dimmed immediately; our cosmic connection fanned out and cold. But it just continued to flicker, smaller but still there. And then, I saw Dustin on that card, and it started roaring again. I wasn't brave. I didn't risk anything. I needed to find Dustin, to know him. I needed that spark so that I could exist again."

"I'm so glad you found us all," Bernie said, crying openly. "Becca's going to need you both to help her through. And you deserve to watch Dustin grow up and live his life. You've lost too much already."

"Am I interrupting?" Malachi interjected, looking at both of us, crying with a concerned expression.

"No, no. We're fine. Just two old ladies having a good cry."

"I'm no old lady! Speak for yourself!" Bernie objected.

"There is no good description for this stage in our lives. We're not middle-aged anymore, but we're not senior citizens either." I lamented.

"We're...elderly lite." Bernie finished, sending all three of us into peals of laughter.

When we finally settled down, Bernie motioned for Malachi to sit at the bottom of her bed.

"Malachi, I wanted to ask you something. It may sound presumptuous, but I want to know what your intentions are with Rebecca."

His face registered evident surprise.

"And here I thought that you were going to lobby for an extra sleeping pill." He said.

"I know you haven't known each other very long, but you both seem to have some kind of interest in each other." I tried to explain.

"It's that obvious?" Malachi said. "I guess I don't have a poker face."

"So, Vegas is out." Bernie shrugged. "I know enough about men to know you're interested, but what I want to know is if it's just a physical attraction or if you want an actual relationship with my daughter."

"I can assure you my intentions expand beyond the bedroom. The minute she opened the door, I was captivated by Rebecca."

"Does she know that?"

"I made it very plain what I wanted when we were in the car today."

"And what is that, exactly?"

"I want a life with Rebecca and Dustin."

Bernie fell back against the pillow, but I leaned forward, skeptical, feeling protective of Rebecca and Dustin.

"How can you know that already?" I questioned.

"When did you know with Dean?" He challenged, making me remember the day we met.

I had looked up from picking up my textbooks scattered across the school hallway and into the kindest, most steadfast eyes I had ever seen and never stopped. Malachi was right. It hadn't taken but a moment to love Dean.

"We're going at her pace. She's scared. There's a lot of complications too." He explained further.

"Well, would you be willing to pick up the pace?" Bernie asked.

"I'm impatient, but not so much that I am willing to risk losing her. If I push her, she'll run. She doesn't believe my affections are true or that she is worthy of me." He replied.

Bernie winced. "That's my fault. I made a lot of mistakes as her mother. But I want to repair some hurts before I go. If you're serious about wanting to be with Rebecca forever, I am going to ask the hospice to help me give you a wedding for my bucket list. I want to be a part of her happiness after bringing her so much sadness."

Malachi's eyes widened, and his eyebrows shot up in surprise. He gaped openly at Bernie. He sat at the foot of the bed, shaking his head in shocked silence.

"It's not that easy. Rebecca was right that there are many factors to consider before we even start dating, let alone consider marriage. She lives in Boston, and I live here. She has Dustin to watch out for. I work for the hospice you're asking to help make this happen, which violates a lot of rules. It's just too much even to consider marriage right now. I care about Rebecca enough to wait for her and to work through all the challenges in good time."

"But couldn't you do private nursing? I will hire you as my nurse. You can quit the hospice." Bernie persisted, then sat back, satisfied with her solution.

"I'm not prepared to do private nursing quite yet." He protested.

"Money is no issue. I can more than make up the difference for any other clients you have."

"It's not about the money. I don't have the resources and connections to keep you comfortable. I haven't established enough relationships to leave the hospice on a bad note, either. Leaving dying clients high and dry is a surefire way to end up with a ruined reputation." Malachi went on.

"What if my doctor worked with you directly?"

"I don't know that they would be willing to do that." He said.

"You leave it to me." She assured him. "I'm emailing him now. And here…"

She reached over and fished in the nightstand for something.

"This is my financial advisor's card. He will arrange to pay you." She paused for a beat. "And for whatever start-up costs you will incur to become a private nurse."

Malachi and I both gaped at her.

"You can't be serious." He said incredulously. "I just told you I am not ready to start out on my own."

"Is money the reason why?"

"Among them."

"Then let me take it off your plate. I'm trusting you to provide for my daughter and my grandson. Me helping you is an investment in them just as much as you."

"I can't let you do that."

"I'm not doing it. The men I was forced to endure for all my life, who thought I was nothing more than a sparkly jewel in their crown, a doll for their amusement, gifted it to me. And it will all be hers when I go. And yours when you marry. So, use some now. Make her happy. Give my grandson a father." She paused, no doubt for dramatic effect as she enjoyed doing. "Don't make me pull the dying card. Just say yes, come work for me, and live happily ever after."

I could see Malachi warring in his head. She had oversimplified the complicated situation. Even if the logistics of combining two lives across the country from each other and jobs could be worked out, the fact remained Rebecca simply wasn't ready.

"If it means losing her or scaring her away, I won't do it. I will quit my job at the hospice and work for you exclusively, but only if the doctor agrees. I'm not taking your money for my business, just my salary."

"Okay, but what day would you like to move in? I'm going to call Habitat for Humanity and have them come pick up the furniture down the hall." She said breezily, as though she hadn't just strong-armed Malachi into getting her way.

"Come again?" Malachi said. "I'm not moving in here."

"You most certainly are. You're my private nurse, and you need to be here 24/7. I will make sure there is a housing allowance to cover your rent for your current apartment."

Malachi stood speechless, shaking his head at Bernie. His face betrayed him. He knew he was outsmarted. She smirked triumphantly from her pillows.

"You win." He said. "I'm going to head home. It looks like I have some packing to do."

"Why don't I show you the room before you go? So, you know how much space you'll have for things." I said.

"Thank you. That would be great."

"Oh, and let me know if you want it painted, dear. Whatever color you like. My home is your home." Bernie purred, pleased with herself. "I'm going to rest now."

"Oh yes, you've had a hard day plotting. Get some rest." Malachi joked, bending to brush a kiss on her cheek.

"Goodbye. I will see you in the morning." She said and clicked off her light.

"I can't believe I agreed to that." He lamented as we left. "She got me hook, line and sinker."

The glam room that was to be a bedroom was next to Bernie's room. A Jack and Jill bathroom connected the rooms.

"I know Bernie uses that bathroom. Maybe you can designate this one for you." I said, gesturing to the bathroom across the hall from the room.

"Sounds like a plan." He said.

His eyes widened as I opened the door to the glam room.

"What in the actual hell?" He said in mock horror.

"It is something." I agreed.

Glam was the perfect name for this room. The walls were silver glitter. Clothing racks filled with clothes, mirrored chests, and a floor-length mirror took up the rest of the space. There was a large vanity with a plush armchair. On the floor, there was a fluffy, thick white fur rug.

"Um yeah, so we have some work to do." Malachi said. "When you find out when they can clear this place out, let me know, and I can come over and paint. Can you even paint over glitter?"

"I guess we're going to find out." I laughed, making a mental note to ask Dean later.

Rebecca was coming out of her room when Malachi and I entered the living room.

"You're still here?" Rebecca asked. "Is everything okay?"

"Your mom is fine, but I have to talk to you." He said. "Come sit with me."

She hesitated for a moment but then eventually sat next to him on the couch. He immediately put his hand on hers.

"I'm quitting my job with the hospice tomorrow." He began.

She immediately opened her mouth to protest, but he held up his hand and looked at her.

"Let me finish. I am quitting so I can be your mother's full-time private nurse. Her live-in, private nurse."

Rebecca immediately began crying, surprising both Malachi and me.

"She's sicker. She needs more care." She whimpered.

He reached for her, crushing her into a hug.

"Calm down. Shhh. It's okay. Let me explain."

Rebecca stilled and pulled away to meet his eyes. "She's okay? Why would she need a private nurse if she is holding steady?"

"She's as good as she can be with terminal cancer. She IS getting sicker. But she asked me to sign on as her private nurse, and I accepted. It was her choice to increase her care. It doesn't mean she's worse."

"You're going to live down the hall from me," Rebecca murmured, sounding both dismayed and enticed at the same time.

"You know how much your mother enjoys being the center of attention. She just wants Malachi all to herself." I chimed in, trying to soothe her.

She looked up and smiled at me. She then turned to Malachi.

"You're sleeping in the glam room? I didn't picture you living amongst all that glitter." She teased.

"If I have my way, I will be painting over that as soon as possible. The sooner, the better. But right now, let me bid you good night."

He brushed a chaste kiss on Becca's cheek, then strode over and did the same to me.

"Good night!" We both chorused.

As soon as the door closed, Rebecca jumped up. She locked the door then turned to me.

"Have a drink with me." She said, her eyes wild. "I need some lubrication to wrap my head around this."

I opened the freezer, pulled out the vodka, and gestured to it.

"Or would you rather have wine?" I asked.

"That's fine." She said gratefully. "Are you tired? I know Mom is asleep, but I really need someone to talk to."

I pulled a tub of French onion dip out of the fridge, grabbed some chips, and put them on a tray with the drinks.

I brought the snack over to her and sat down.

"I am not tired at all. I would love to listen."

"Malachi wants to be with me, and I am too afraid to admit that I want the same thing."

"What are you afraid of?"

"Everything."

I bit back a laugh. "Care to try and narrow it down for me?"

"Look at him. And look at what he does. He is a beautiful man with a good career. He's the pick of the damn litter. I'm an overweight single mother with a job and not a career. I'm damaged goods. It's like he's trying to hitch a fourteen-karat gold cart to a broken-down aged mule."

I paused to breathe through the anger the negative words she had spoken about herself sparked within me. Rebecca saw herself so differently, so inaccurately, from what she was. It was astounding and maddening.

"Rebecca Malone, I better never hear you describe yourself that way again. Any man, especially Malachi, if that's who you choose, would be lucky to have you. You're afraid you're not good enough, and it is simply not true. Please stop selling yourself short." I spoke sternly but with what I hoped was love underneath.

She looked at me, her eyes cloudy pools of uncried tears and doubt.

"I didn't have a mom like you, who told me I was beautiful inside as well as out. Maybe if I had, I would believe it now. I'm trying to change, Rae. It's just not second nature yet."

"I know. But you ARE beautiful, and more importantly, you are worthy of whatever man you choose." I replied, more tender now.

"It's Malachi." She said softly. "Todd is a nice guy, but Malachi...." The way she said his name was like a maiden exalting her hero, her savior.

"So, you told Todd it's not going to happen?" I asked.

"Oh yeah, a while ago. We're trying to be friends, but I don't want Malachi to find out about our encounter, and I don't think it's nice to flaunt Malachi in front of Todd."

"Of course. Was Todd upset?"

"No, he was fine. But he's from the Midwest. He has those manners. I probably wouldn't know if he hated me. All I do know is if Malachi and I can ever have a chance, I can't have any more complications in the mix."

"You did the right thing," I assured her. "If my opinion matters at all, I know Malachi really does care for you. And I think you're adorable together."

REBECCA

"Ok, I think that's the last of it," Malachi said, setting the box he held down on the dresser.

His muscled arms flexed appealingly. He wore a tight-fitting black tank top and black basketball shorts. He lifted his arm, wiped the sweat off his brow. I licked my lips. He looked good, covered in sweat. Very, very good. I handed him a bottle of water from my perch on his bed. He lingered as our fingertips brushed.

"That's everything? Not bad. It looks like you will have more than enough space. What did you do with all your furniture and stuff?" I rambled on and on, nervous.

"My cousin DeVon is subletting from me while I'm here." He said. "I left everything there."

"That worked out well then," I said.

It had been over a week since our conversation in the car. That time had been filled with movers and painters and a floor guy and a tile guy—none of the guys I wanted to see. I only wanted to see one guy. Malachi.

He had been there, of course, but never alone. We never got to discuss the car or the move or what we were going to do about the fact that not touching either other felt more horrendously torturous with each passing moment.

"So, I guess I am gonna go start dinner," I said. "Pasta, okay? It's made from chickpeas, but you can't tell. Don't tell Dustin or Bernie."

He grinned and raised his hand. "Your secret is safe with me."

He reached down to pull me up off the bed. I accepted his hand, and he hoisted me effortlessly. I came up fast and immediately teetered, off-balance. He steadied me.

"Hey, you want to go for a swim after Dustin goes to sleep?" He asked. "A nice swim to cool down after moving all day sounds amazing. And this is the first place I've ever lived with a private pool. May as well take advantage of it."

My mouth went dry at the thought of Malachi in a bathing suit, chest wet and glistening in the moonlight. I gulped and nodded. He smiled.

"It's a date then." He said.

My heart thudded at his words.

It was after nine o'clock when Dustin finally settled, and Malachi and I set out. Rae had taken the baby monitor to listen for him gleefully.

"Go, go! Have fun. Relax! I have them both." She had insisted, settling by Mom's bedside and scrolling through Netflix to find a tearjerker for them to watch.

The gate of the pool creaked loudly in the silence of the night. The crickets chirped, and I could hear the ocean nearby, lapping at the white sands of the shore. The sounds comforted my nerves, which were increasingly frayed thinking about being near Malachi in a bathing suit without the benefit of distraction. He held out his arm to me.

"Ladies first." He said.

I walked through the gate. I sat my towel down on a pool chair and took a deep breath. *Be bold;* I encouraged myself. I turned away from Malachi, pulled my dress over my head, revealing my swimsuit, and turned to him. I gasped.

While I was undressing, so had Malachi. His body, in its most natural state, was a thing of shocking beauty. I couldn't stop myself from staring openly. When I collected myself, I noticed he was staring back. His eyes were wide, admiring.

He closed the gap between us. "You're so beautiful."

And then, he was kissing me. He kissed me like a man starved for the one thing he longed for. His tongue danced with mine. His hands rested on my hips, his thumb making small circles on the silky fabric there. His mouth slid down to my neck, kissing and licking there.

"Oh God, that feels go--" I began.

My words were cut off by the water rushing around me as I fell into the pool. I came up sputtering and coughing, my hair a heavy veil over my face. Malachi was doubled over, contorted with laughter. He didn't make a sound, just shook. Suddenly, he let out a loud whoop which echoed off the surrounding buildings. My cheeks burned with embarrassment.

"I guess I stepped too close to the ledge," I said.

"I guess you did." He said, wiping the tears that had formed under his eyes. "But here, if it makes you feel any better,"

He took a deep breath and cannonballed into the water, sending a tidal wave of spray at me. When he emerged, he was directly in front of me. Water coursed off him in shiny rivulets. He smiled- his teeth almost neon in the darkness.

"I like everything I know about you, Rebecca Malone." He said, tracing my lips with a wet fingertip.

Arousal sparked within me. I felt hot, even surrounded by cool water. I reached up, cupping my hand behind Malachi's head and rubbing the border between his short, cropped hair and his smooth neck. He shivered.

"And what do you propose we do about those feelings?" I said what I hoped was seductively, even though I felt silly and unsure.

"I think it's time we acted on them." He said, sliding his hand underwater to my back and drawing me close. "Be my girl."

I snorted, breaking the tenderness of the moment. "You're still Mom's nurse. I still live in Boston, and I haven't been a girl in an awfully long time." I said.

"You can be my girl." He said, kissing me long and hard. "Everything else we can figure out together."

I pressed against him, feeling him grow hard. He moved, forcing me gently to the side of the pool. His mouth never stopped kissing me, sliding from my neck to my mouth, dipping down to my breasts. Small moans of pleasure escaped me. He grunted, stopped only long enough to lift me in the air, and lay me on the edge of the pool. My skin stung from grating against the rough concrete around the pool, but I ignored it. He looked at me, asking my silent consent. I nodded. He grinned and gave my shoulder a tiny shove, motioning for me to lay back. He disappeared over the edge of the pool.

I felt his long fingers moving over my stomach. I resisted the urge to suck in, to minimize the loose skin there. He moved lower still, resting his hand on the swollen mound between my legs. I trembled, only a thin piece of fabric separating my most intimate area from his touch. He danced over the material, his fingers beating a rhythm as I throbbed my own pulse beneath him.

I squirmed, needy. Malachi pulled the thin fabric aside. He paused. I arched my hips up, trying to meet him. He laughed, low and throaty.

"I thought you told me you were patient." He said.

I couldn't even form words. I wanted this man more than I had ever wanted anyone in my life. Every one of my nerves was raw, waiting for his touch. I felt like my entire body was filled with tv static.

I felt his heavy, smooth fingers spreading me, the ridges of his fingertip as it touched my sensitive, thin tissues. He finally dipped his finger in, slow but firm. I gasped, bucked against the sensation, needing more. He obliged, inserting another finger and beginning to move them inside me.

Then, without warning, he moved down and pulled the strip of fabric aside. I felt his fingers slide out, to be replaced by his tongue. He made varied licks and strokes, causing me to cry out. It was my voice that echoed in the complex now. I came, hard and fast.

I sat up on my elbows, ignoring the scratching of the cement under them. I struggled to regulate my breathing. Malachi dipped under the water, then came up, propping himself up to meet me on the ledge. He kissed me, and I tasted myself there, a combination of salt mingled with a bit of chlorine. He pulled me into the water, both of us going under at the same time.

He reached out underwater, pulling me to him. As we came up, I crushed against his chest. He leaned down, kissing me. We were back up against the edge of the pool. He was still hard against my stomach. Heady after my orgasm, I reached down and cut a path between us. I met his eyes as I stepped out of my bikini bottoms and set them on the edge of the pool.

His eyes grew large and milky with desire. I smiled. I reached up, letting the halter tie of my top fall. His hands darted out to catch the heft of my breasts before they hit the water. He made tight, rough circles on my nipples, sending me into a frenzy. My hands roamed the expanse of his chest, then traveled down. He dropped one of his hands and tugged his shorts over, whipping them above his head like a lasso and sending them shooting off into the darkness beyond the pool. We laughed together.

"Great, I'm going to have to risk getting eaten by an alligator to find those for you later." I teased.

My laugh was cut short by his kiss, a bit rougher and more urgent than before. As we kissed, I navigated us towards the stairs. When we reached them, I bent forward, forcing Malachi down. He laid back, head resting on the pool ledge, body sprawled across the stairs. He gripped the rail as I took him in my mouth.

"Damn, that feels amazing." He said.

I took his entire length in my mouth, raking my nails down the steely plane of his abs. He drew in a sharp breath, and his other hand came up and tangled in my wet hair, spurring me on.

"This is even better than I imagined." He managed between fevered pants.

I continued for a few minutes until his breath was ragged and shallow. He held out his arm suddenly to stop me.

"Stop. Our first time isn't going to be like this. I swear, I just wanted to come for a swim so we could talk. I wasn't planning all of this." He said.

"Yeah, right," I said. "That's what they all say."

I said it like I knew. Like another man had ever liked me enough to even kiss me in a pool, let alone think about screwing me. He pulled a face.

"You should know by now. I'm not like everyone else." He said.

"Oh, believe me. I know that." I said, pulling him in for a kiss.

After I retrieved Malachi's trunks from a shrub, we walked hand in hand back to Bernie's. We kissed at the door, "like a proper date," Malachi said, smiling.

We kissed again in the living room before retreating to our bedrooms. Right before I dozed off, my phone pinged. I looked down, temporarily blinded by the bright screen.

The text was from Malachi.

Thank you for a beautiful night. Sweet dreams, baby girl.

The days passed quickly, a blur of neediness and caretaking. Mom was wasting before our eyes, her skin growing taunt and sallow over her bones. She barely left her bed anymore, and when she did, an unwieldy oxygen tank had to be carted along with her. Alarmingly gaunt and pale, she wore a turban constantly, her hair patchy. Sparse wisps clung to her scalp after the trauma of chemo, aided by the process of death.

Keeping my promise to know her before she left, I was discovering Bernie. I was trying to soak up every morsel of her, recording her stories on my phone. She strained and struggled as her voice came in gasps, cracked with exhaustion and emotion. We spent hours, our heads together under the covers in her bed, Mom's words filling the space in between us and inside me. All the chunks she had chipped away in me as I had grown up were being filled up again with the honey of her voice; the spun sugar stories of her life.

I saw her now, the woman she had been forced to tamp down, make smaller. All she had ever craved was more, bigger, excess. To be put on a shelf and made meek in exchange for what she felt necessary for her survival was the ultimate punishment.

"The Universe, God, Mother Nature, Karma. I don't know who I pissed off, but they got me good. I had every single luxury and more money than should be allowed, and all I wanted was to have an opinion and talk about something other than the weather, fashion, and the news. My life was a cosmic fuck you." She managed, her oxygen and words coming out in alternating breathy puffs.

I wanted to share Bernie's stories with Dustin when he was older. *And Fern, too.* My inner voice chimed in, putting words to my heart's secret desire to share Malachi's fantastical daughter, a beauty with wayward curls and his eyes.

He and I had been lying in my bed one night- maybe days, maybe weeks ago. Who knew anymore? Seconds blurred into minutes into hours and eventually days into weeks as we focused all our energy on Bernie. The moonlight illuminating our faces, Malachi lifted my chin to look into my eyes.

"Do you want more kids?"

"Of course, I want more." I paused, considered. "Wait. How many more?" I questioned.

"At least one more. I've dreamt all my life of having a little girl. She has eyes like mine and curls. Which, as it turns out, look a hell of a lot like yours. I just never realized that until now."

He raked his hand through my chaos of curls, winding one around his finger and watching it bounce back. He smiled and kissed my head. I realized with a start that my face probably resembled the expression Rae wore around Dean, safe and secure in the knowledge that a man loved me wholly and completely. Now, whether I was willing to accept that or admit it to anyone else was a whole other story.

"You know what she looks like?" I asked, a bit incredulous.

"She's visited me in my dreams since I was a boy. She's never talked, but I know it's her. My Fern." His voice caught then, and a tear slid down his face and onto mine resting below.

"After Gran?" I asked.

He nodded. "She's the only one who ever gave a damn about me. Gran saved me. Kept me out of the system, off the streets, in school. I owe her everything."

"She's not the only one anymore," I said, kissing him with all the pain and love that filled my heart as he spoke. "You've got me now."

In the weeks since Malachi had moved in, Gran and I had grown closer. When Mom's appetite was still hearty, Malachi and I stole a few private moments retrieving Gran's lemon cake each week. In the first few weeks, we visited almost daily, Bernie resolving to die fat and happy.

"That's as close as I'll come to giving the finger to the patriarchy." She said, fork in hand, devouring Gran's cake as fast as her body would allow.

Fern always had something to share with me when we arrived. Sometimes a story, sometimes a photo of Malachi as a boy. Occasionally, a recipe.

As Mom grew sicker and her appetite waned, our visits to the restaurant dwindled, then stopped. Then, one day Fern showed up on the front step, and she had never stopped coming.

She and I, alongside Rae and Malachi, played cards and talked for hours as we took turns caring for Bernie.

That first day, she accompanied Todd, who had a giant stock pot on the golf cart seat next to him.

"She stopped me to ask where your unit was, and it looked like she could use some help." He paused, turned to Fern. "This is as big as you are, ma'am."

He laughed. Fern waved her hand at him, exasperated.

"Young man, that's nothing! Here, let me carry it if you're going to fuss."

She reached out, and Todd curled the giant pot into himself, shrinking away from her.

"No way! I got this." He said. "It smells great."

"Chicken rice soup. I figured Bernie might like it." She explained.

"Would you like to stay and have dinner with us?" I asked them both.

Malachi came in from Bernie's room to find us all in the kitchen.

"Gran? What are you doing here?" He asked, doing a double-take.

"I brought my chicken rice soup for Bernie."

"And I hope you'll stay and enjoy some with us." I prodded again.

She nodded, moving to find bowls, already making the kitchen her own. Todd looked from me to Malachi, who had pulled me against his chest and was resting his chin on my head. He seemed torn. Finally, Todd shook his head no.

"I think I'm going to have to skip it." He said, his voice tinged with wistfulness.

"You sure?" I said. "It does smell good."

"No worries. Here's some for the road." Fern said, thrusting a Tupperware I wasn't even aware had been in the cupboards at him.

"Thanks!" He said enthusiastically. "Malachi, is Bernie awake? May as well stop in and say hi while I'm here."

Malachi nodded. With a silent nod to us, Todd lopped off to the bedroom. I had to admire him. True to his word, he had accepted my rejection gracefully, and we had remained amicable. He stopped by often to check on Mom.

In Dean's absence, he had taken responsibility for taking Dustin on adventures. They had begun swimming lessons in the complex pool. Todd had gifted Dustin tiny red shorts, a whistle, and a visor. Together they sat on the lifeguard stand or the edge of the pool, watching and waiting, their noses matching white zinc slopes.

When I thanked him for helping keep Dustin away from the chaos unfolding inside the condo, he shrugged.

"No biggie, Becs. I lost my mom young. She had cancer too. I watched her just fade away before my eyes. I hated every second. Dustin is too little to see that. I'm glad to distract him."

I hugged him then, long and hard. To his credit, Todd didn't try to cop a feel. He squeezed me back warmly and without malice, his hands in the safe zone of the center of my back.

"Thank goodness what happened between us didn't ruin anything," I mumbled into his shoulder.

"What kind of man would I be if it did? I mean, I admit the night you dumped me, I went out and tied one on, cried over our great lost love, but I think things worked out how they're supposed to. As much as I hate to admit it, you and Malachi seem pretty good together."

"Thank you, that means a lot," I said sincerely.

"Even though you said you weren't ready for a relationship." He teased. "But you must have forgotten the "with you" part."

"I know, I know. I was sincere when I said it. But you and I weren't a right fit. But I think we make pretty great friends." I said by way of explanation.

"Yes, we do. That being said, if things don't work out, I call dibs- first in line for the rebound."

We laughed together.

Malachi's deep voice vibrated through his chest, snapping me back to reality, the chaos of the past few weeks falling out of my head.

"What was that, baby?" I said, rolling over onto my back and stretching, accidentally on purpose letting my camisole ride up and expose the soft curve of the underside of my breast.

"Huh?" He mumbled, distracted. "I don't remember."

I nodded as his thumb began to stroke the soft, exposed skin. Then, he leaned down and his tongue, raspberry pink, darted out. Its tip on the thin skin sent shivers through me. He did it again, sending shockwaves to my nipples, which puckered in response. He smiled, seeing them poking through the thin material of my shirt. He moved his mouth over one, sucking it through the fabric. I moaned softly, pleasure radiating from where his mouth worked at my breast. It slid down like a snake to my lower belly, coiling there, waiting to be fed.

He made a face.

"This is in my way." He said, reaching up and pulling the neck of my camisole, exposing my breasts.

He sighed, a content and playful smile. "Good God, what a beautiful sight."

"I'm glad you appreciate the view, sir." I practically purred.

"I don't just appreciate; I worship at the altar." He mumbled, taking my other nipple into his mouth.

His fingers traveled the length of my body. He paused as he skimmed the curve of my hip. For all the hardness of his body, he loved the softness of mine. I rose to meet his touch. His touch danced across my skin, moving ever closer to my core. He found it, slipping a finger inside with a smile.

"Ain't nothing sweeter." He said, beginning to move inside me while he paused his ministrations on my nipples to kiss me hard and long on the mouth.

I responded, arching up, begging with silent, wide eyes for more. Malachi inserted another finger, pausing to let me get used to the fulness. I savored the sensation as his fingers danced a figure eight around my most sensitive spot. The sweet tension started to build. I was getting closer when he stopped. I grunted, frustrated, causing him to chuckle.

"You need to develop an appreciation for delayed gratification." He teased.

In one fluid motion, he pushed off the bed, looming over me on his knees. He stopped, stared down at me, and grinned. "You're fucking perfection, babe."

I chortled. "Hardly."

"No, don't do that." He scolded.

He knew my whole story, the parts that made me look desperate, lonely, and sad. He saw my imperfections- the rolls, the cellulite, the scars. And he wanted me anyway. Despite, maybe even because of, all the things that had made me complicated and strong and flawed. He chose me. And I still didn't believe it.

His gorgeous face moved between my legs, his tongue replacing his fingers. As he dipped and delved into, licked, and sucked every one of my intimate crevices, my entire body spasmed and clenched. My fingers grasped at the sheets, almost tearing them with my steel grip. My feet and toes were stiff from being held at attention for so long. And just when I couldn't take it anymore, I came.

Malachi sat up then and, while I was still spasming, flipped me onto my stomach. I brought my knees up and arched my back almost without thinking. He entered me fast. The sudden new sensation sent me over the edge again. Malachi moved slowly at first, teasing. I writhed under him, frenzied and sweaty, but he was undeterred. I was almost feral with desire. He took his time, dipping in and out of me like ink in a well, telling me a story each time our skin touched.

"God DAMN." He whispered over and over.

Then, as slowly as he had started, he increased the pace. His hips pumped over me. His sinewy arms bulged and popped. He moved like a well-oiled machine, bringing both of us to the finish line before he collapsed, slick with sweat from the exertion, onto my bare back.

I pulled the covers around me as I struggled to regulate my breathing. Malachi moved under the covers and pulled me to him. We laid together in satisfied silence. He weaved a piece of my hair through his fingers.

"I love you, Rebecca Malone." He said.

My heart felt it, but the words bubbled up, then faded in my throat. I gulped, placed a hand on his cheek, and kissed him hard.

It was a Friday morning, almost eight weeks after Bernie's terminal diagnosis. She had defied all the odds and hung on past the six-week yoke Dr. Price had laid around her neck. There was a knock at the door. I regarded Malachi, who was reading with Dustin, with surprise.

"Are we expecting a delivery or something?"

"Nope." He said, rising. "Let me get it in case it's an ax murder."

"I don't think killers knock."

"Smartass," he smiled, bumping me aside with his hip.

His face broke into a wide smile when he opened the door and saw who was on the other side.

"Get the hell in here!" He ordered.

Dean came in, arms overflowing with flowers.

"Oh, my goodness! What are you doing here? We didn't know you were coming! Dustin, look!"

Malachi ran to Mom's room to get Rae. They came around the corner, Rae's face registering concern and fear. She spotted

Dean and froze. Their eyes locked, and after a beat, she burst into tears. Dustin tore across the room, tackling Dean at the knee. Her trance was broken, and her feet flew to him. Before she could crush the flowers by pinning them to his chest, he held them out.

"I brought flowers for my three favorite ladies."

"Patti would kick your ass to hear she's not on the favorite ladies list." She laughed, taking her red roses and the pink ones.

"Pink for Bernie. And these for you." He handed some lavender-colored roses to me.

"Oh, my goodness, they're beautiful. Thank you so much. You didn't have to do that."

"The hell I didn't. But it looks like someone beat me to the punch." He said, noticing the many vases of fresh flowers scattered throughout the space.

"Yeah, you're taking a play from my playbook," Malachi said. "Should I worry about you moving in on my girl?"

He pulled me close, my back against his steely chest, his voice vibrating through both of our bodies. Dean looked surprised at the display of affection but said nothing.

"No worries, I only have eyes for Rae. Always have, always will." He pulled Rae into a lingering hug. I could see her whole body relax under his touch.

They pulled away, and you could see the smoldering heat in their eyes.

"You must be tired. Why don't you go upstairs for a nap?" I suggested.

Both looked at me gratefully.

"I could use a nice, long... rest," Dean said, his tone loaded.

"Well, I think we will take Dustin out to a movie," I said. "Give you time to *rest*."

"I should stay with Bernie. I'm waiting on a call from Price." Malachi said. "But you should take him. And I'll have my headphones on so that I won't disturb your *nap*." He laughed.

"I think I will. A little time out of the house could be nice." I said.

"We will see you when you get back," Dean said, planting a kiss on my cheek and bending to hug Dustin.

I made quick work of getting ready to go. Malachi was in Mom's room when I was done.

"We're heading out to the movie," I said, leaning over to kiss him.

He lingered for a moment, kissing me deeper than a quick goodbye kiss normally would be. I lost myself in it for a moment. Mom's voice broke our spell.

"Do you have a kiss for Mommy?" She teased.

We broke apart and laughed. Mom was snuggling with Dustin on her bed, smothering his face with kisses.

"Of course," I said, leaning down to kiss her cheek.

Dustin enjoyed the movie, a cartoon about some singing animals. It seemed like I had just leaned back in my seat, enjoying the moments of peace and stillness, when it was over. Life was moving faster than it ever had before. I wanted to savor Mom's last moments, Dustin growing up, falling in love with Malachi, but time was slipping like water through a sieve. There wasn't even any time to think since Dustin was back on the move, demanding a swim before dinner and a snack.

When we got back to Mom's house, we were greeted with a locked door. Confused, I fumbled for my key. Suddenly, the door opened, and Rae slid out, blocking the view behind the door.

"Come here, Dustin." She said, taking his hand and opening the door, and depositing him on the other side.

"You stay here." She said authoritatively.

"What's going on? Is it Mom?" I asked, suddenly anxious.

Rae immediately reached out to put her hand on my arm. "Oh no, sweetie, nothing like that. This is all for you."

And like magic, the door opened. Dustin came back out, outfitted in an adorable black suit and his tiny Converse that put tears in my eyes.

"What in the world?" I gasped.

He held out his hand, and I took it, Rae following behind us. He led me to a red-carpet runner laid out in the living room strewn with flower petals and lined with candles. Malachi stood in the middle of the living room, also dressed in a suit. He looked so devastatingly handsome that I momentarily stopped breathing, and my knees buckled. Dustin, oblivious, dragged me on to where Malachi stood. Dean stood off to one side. Rae joined him. When Dustin finished leading me to Malachi, they ushered him away upstairs.

"You two have a great night," Dean called.

I couldn't even reply. My mind was thinking a million thoughts at once. *God DAMN, he looks good in a suit. What is he doing? Is he proposing? What about Dustin's dinner? Is this really my life?*

"Hey, beautiful." Malachi smiled his brilliant smile down at me.

"Hey there yourself, handsome. What is all this?"

"I'm taking you out tonight."

For just a split second, disappointment shot through me. Had I actually been anticipating a proposal? Was I insane? Then, I got excited.

"Where are we going?" I asked.

"We're going to a fancy restaurant deserving of a woman as gorgeous as yourself, and then I got us a suite at a hotel. The night is ours. The *entire* night." He said, meeting my eyes and stirring my hormones into a frenzy.

"Two things."

"Anything."

"Can we go to Gran for a lemon cake for dessert? And what's the dress code?"

He laughed. "We can go wherever you want to go. Rae picked out a dress for you. It's on your bed. Other than that, just bring your toothbrush. You won't need anything else."

"Presumptuous, aren't we? Let me change, and we can go. Is Mom ok to be without you for the night?"

"I briefed Rae on her meds, but my friend Shanda, a girl I graduated nursing school with, is coming by to spend the night. I told her she could sleep in my room."

"Oh really? That better be the last girl in your bed beside me."

"Does it count if I am not even in the bed, let alone the house?"

"Well, I guess you get a pass. Just don't make it a habit." I joked.

"Thanks, I appreciate that. Now go, get ready. I won't say get beautiful because you already are." He said.

"Charmer." I smiled over my shoulder as I headed into my bedroom.

Rae knew me better than I gave her credit for. She had laid out a black dress, dangling gemstone earrings, and matching black heels—classic, timeless, elegant. *Bernie-esque*, I thought. I tugged on my shapewear, thrilled for a night with Malachi away from the heaviness of daily life.

I also pulled a fistful of lingerie out of my drawer along with a satin robe Mom had gifted to me a few weeks ago from her collection. I threw my bathing suit and a change of clothes in the bag, along with my toothbrush.

I did my makeup quickly, playing up my lips with red lipstick, and twisted my hair into a high bun, with some curls falling. The effect was alluring but romantic.

I was just admiring the fit of the dress, made of a flattering material that skimmed over my Lycra'ed curves beautifully when the phone rang. It was Kieran. We talked frequently but usually by text. If he was calling, it would mean he had news of some sort. My heart beat a bit faster as I clicked on the button to pick up.

"Hello?" I asked, hesitant.

"What's up bitch?" Kieran responded, immediately putting me at ease.

"Are you okay?"

"Of course, I just wanted to talk to my best friend. I miss you. When are you coming home?" He asked.

"I don't know," I answered honestly.

I had a sinking feeling as I realized Malachi and I would need to figure this out sooner rather than later. Mom was nearing the end. That was evident. But what happened then? My life was in Boston. I had a job and friends there. It was only a few hours from Rae and Dean so that they could see Dustin often.

But, on many levels, Florida also felt like home. We had a richer, more active life here. Malachi's whole family was here. His career was here. My mother and the memories of her were here. She would be buried here.

"How's Bernie?" Kieran broke into my thoughts.

"Sicker by the minute," I replied. "It won't be too much longer, I imagine." My voice caught, and I blinked back tears. "Damn it, Kieran. Don't get me crying. I just did my makeup."

"Makeup? Makeup for what?" He was instantly curious.

"I have a date with Malachi tonight," I said.

He was a faraway cheerleader of our romance. He had been so excited when I had finally confessed that we were dating. He had sent me a giant box of lingerie, some innocent and some X-rated. He had enclosed a note. "Get yo freak on."

"Ohhh! What are you wearing? Facetime me."

I hit the button, and his face sprang onto my screen.

"We're going to a nice restaurant," I explained, stepping into the view of the floor-length mirror so he could see the full effect.

"You picked out that dress?" He said, immediately skeptical.

"No, if you must know," I said. I still hadn't told Kieran about Rae or Dean and their role in our lives, so I thought fast. "Bernie picked it out."

"She got it just right." He said appreciatively.

"I think so too," I confessed, pleased.

The dress came down to mid-calf, tight the whole way down, but was off-shoulder, the top ending in a v at the top of my cleavage. It was sophisticated and sexy. It made me feel like Audrey Hepburn.

"Are you ready for a night alone with no potential children or elders to wake up?"

"I have all the slut wear you sent, so yes."

"Very good. You've pruned the garden?"

"God, you're so nosey."

"Is that a no?"

"Shut up! Yes, if you must know."

"Are you excited?"

"Yes, but scared too," I confessed. "I think I'm in love with him."

"Baby girl, you think? I think that ship has sailed. The first time you told me about him, I knew. I was just waiting for you to get a clue, but you're taking too long. Haven't we discussed your tendency to deliberate to death? You've spent every day for weeks on end with him. He's hot. He has a job. He's great with Dustin. Hell, if you don't, I will." He laughed. "Seriously though, you know by now what you want. Just leap. Your mom doesn't have all the time in the world. Maybe you should let her go knowing you have someone looking out for you."

My breath hitched. I knew Kieran was right; I was still holding back.

"Don't get in your head, girl. Go enjoy your night and put that lingerie to good use."

"I love you, and I miss you like crazy. I'll text later, okay?"

"I'll be pissed if you text me tonight. The only thing you need to be doing is focusing on Malachi's delicious self all night long."

"Oh, I fully intend to believe me."

"That's my girl! Oh, and that dress needs a necklace. Bye bitch!"

Kieran's face dissolved. I took a deep breath, grabbed my bag, and stepped into the living room. Malachi stood there where I had left him. When he saw me, his mouth fell open. Feeling suddenly shy, I did a twirl.

"Gorgeous, baby." He came to me and kissed me hard and long, making me want to turn and drag him into my room.

We heard someone clearing their throat behind us and broke apart. I grabbed a tissue and tried to repair the red smeared across both our mouths.

"Maybe red wasn't the best choice."

"Yes, believe me, it was," Malachi said, his voice husky with desire.

Mom sat in her wheelchair, manned by Dean. I could see the great effort she was putting forth to sit up, breathe and stay awake. A deep sadness cracked through the happiness of the moment, thinking that Mom's time was growing ever shorter. Rae held Dustin. They were all watching us.

"Well, this feels like prom." I laughed.

"Becca, I, I...have...something. For you." Mom wheezed out, expending maximum effort.

"Mom, you need to rest." I knelt to kiss her, spotting her cheek with red.

"Here. For the dress." She held out a diamond necklace, brilliant and glittering.

I gasped. "Mom, I can't wear this. This is yours from Daddy. You've told me the story a hundred times."

"It's yours now, so you should wear it. Please." She puffed out, barely able to finish.

Teary-eyed, I allowed Malachi to clasp it around my neck.

We posed for pictures. I had to admit the necklace was the finishing touch. I sent some photos to Kieran. He texted back fire emojis. After tucking Mom back in, giving her some meds, and kissing Dustin good night, off we went.

"Do I get to know where we're going?"

"Right now, I want to go to the hotel. You look amazing." He slid his hand over and up my thigh.

"Not yet!" I protested.

"Okay, fine then." He pretended to pout. "Dinner it is."

He steered us into a valet line. We stopped, and he jumped out, almost sprinting to get to my door before I did. He handed a man his keys and a tip and thanked him.

He ushered me into the restaurant, which was as upscale as he had described. Every table had thick, spotless white linens, deep red roses, and velvet seats. The place settings were gold. The walls were swagged with crimson material. A giant crystal chandelier was the focal point of the room.

We didn't stop in the main dining room, though. The hostess escorted us to the rear of the restaurant, then pulled back a curtain, revealing a private room filled with white roses on every available surface. Lit candles were in the candelabra on the round table set for two. The room's entire back wall was glass, the whole beach and ocean spread out before us. Boats dotted the horizon as the sky exploded in an array of sherbet hues.

"Sunset." I breathed. "It's so gorgeous."

"I thought you would like it."

"How long have you been planning this?"

"I have wanted to get a night away with you for a long time. I needed backup and enlisted Dean as part of the surprise. His being here made it happen. I didn't want to leave Rae with both Bernie and Dustin. And Shanda doesn't know Bernie well enough not to need Rae. It would be too much. At least with Dean, Dustin is covered."

"He idolizes him for sure," I said.

"Boys need male influences." He said.

"Yeah, I didn't understand that when I chose to have him. I thought it didn't matter, but seeing how he has responded to Dean and you has made me see a new perspective."

"Well, it is my hope I can change your mind on a few other things too." He said.

"What else?" I asked, stomach sinking. Was this dinner a romantic gesture or an attempt to butter me up for whatever inevitable bad news or question was to follow?

"Moving." He admitted quickly. "Before you freak out, just hear me out."

I nodded, noting that I wasn't as resistant to the idea as I thought I would be when he made this argument.

"Well, first, and my main, selfish argument is I want you to move here so I can see you and Dustin every day. Grow our relationship, move to the next stage, start our life together. But I can't get us to the next stage if I move to Boston. I can transfer my nursing license, but it could take a while, and I could have to start over, working shitty shifts at city hospitals, exposing you and Dustin to God knows what. If we stay here, I can grow my private nursing company and make more than enough to support you while you write. Oh, and the cost of living is much lower here, and there is no snow. And you already have a house here so that we could save even more money." He finished in a rush like he didn't want to forget all the key points to his argument.

"What home?" I asked, unbelieving that Bernie had also shared her plans with him about leaving me everything.

"Bernie is leaving you the condo. Surely, you knew that."

"Well yes, which also, frankly, should take the whole money piece of your argument off the table. If you don't want to transfer your license and start over, or you are drawn to private nursing and want to follow that path, it's fine. We will have money to take care of us while we both chase our dreams." I paused, thinking about seeing a novel I wrote on a store shelf. "And about the house, I was planning on AirBnBing it. But plans could be subject to change. I wouldn't mind moving, honestly. My job was just that, a job, not a career. I could write here; Dustin has the pool and sunshine every day."

"But?" He said, correctly identifying my hesitation.

"But, in Boston, Rae and Dean live about two hours away from us. They could see Dustin all the time. Living here, it would be a plane ride. That's a lot to put on them."

He thought for a long moment. "What if we asked them to stay with us? That suite upstairs could be fitted with a kitchen. We can turn it into an in-law apartment for them."

"Dean has a job back home." I reminded him.

"Doesn't hurt to ask them." He said mildly.

"We can, but what if they won't consider it?" I asked.

"What about splitting our time? We live in your place in Boston six months out of the year and here the other six. We Airbnb both places when we're not there." Malachi suggested.

"How do you propose holding a job when you move around that much? And what about when Dustin goes to school?"

"I can find private clients just as easily in Mass as I can here, I'm sure. And sweetheart, Dustin is two. We have lots of time to figure out where we will settle before he starts school."

"Well, don't you just have all the answers?" I teased, pulling him close for a kiss.

He looked at me seriously again as we pulled apart.

"What's up?" I asked.

"Please consider staying here, not just for six months at a time. I want to stay here for Gran. I want you to get to know my whole family better, but especially her. And I can't be halfway across the country when she dies." He dipped his head to his chest, blinking away his tears.

In an instant, I made my decision. "Of course, we'll stay," I said.

He lifted his head, his green eyes glistening. "Really?"

"If that's what we need to do, that's what we'll do. Fern needs you. I get it. This time with Mom is hard, but it's a privilege to witness this process and help her. I would never begrudge you that opportunity. But, please, let's ask Rae and Dean to consider moving."

333

"Anything you want. I love you, Rebecca Malone."

I took a deep, jagged breath. Anxiety surged within me, but I tamped it down. I lifted my hands to cradle Malachi's beautiful face.

"I love you too, Malachi Anders."

He made a slight noise in the back of his throat and smiled widely.

"You don't know how good it is to hear you say that." He said, closing the distance between us.

Our phones beeping at the same time interrupted the moment. I cursed technology inwardly as Malachi read the message.

"Don't panic." He said immediately, sliding my phone off the table and into his pocket. "We have to get to the hospital. Bernie's on her way there in an ambulance."

RAE

One minute, Bernie and I had been debating bouquets, and the next, she was seizing. Her eyes rolled in the back of her head. I started screaming for Shanda and Dean. Bernie continued to seize, her mouth foaming. She stopped suddenly but wasn't coherent.

Shanda skidded in. "What's going on?"

"She just seized," I screamed. "She's not conscious!"

She came to Bernie's bedside and took her pulse. "Call 911 now."

"Okay," I said tearfully.

As I was giving the dispatcher the address, Bernie started seizing again. "Please hurry!" I cried.

"What the hell?" Dean said, finally hearing the commotion after coming down for a snack.

"Keep Dustin out!" I yelled.

"He's sleeping. Calm down, Rae. She's going to be okay. Shanda, can I help?"

"I got it; she's breathing, so I don't need to do CPR. Hopefully, the ambulance is close."

"They're three minutes away," I reported tearfully.

"I'll go let them in," Dean said immediately.

After what seemed like hours, with Bernie still seizing, Dean led the paramedics inside the room.

"Stand back, please." A small woman with brown hair swept into a messy pile on top of her head said, plunging an injection of some kind into Bernie's thigh.

Her seizure stopped, and they loaded her on the stretcher. Shanda ran around, gathering her medical chart, which Malachi had organized in a thick red binder, in case of emergency.

"Do you want to stay with Dustin, or should I?" I asked Dean, shaken and still crying.

"You're in no condition to go alone. Let me go run and see if the neighbor can keep him."

He was back in just a few minutes. I had run upstairs, thrown on jeans and a tee-shirt, and stuffed my feet into sneakers.

"We're in luck. The neighbor's granddaughter was there. She'll stay till we get home."

"Thank god. Let's go."

Dean grabbed our sweatshirts, and we headed to Bernie's car, which had mainly sat unused as Bernie got sicker, all of us isolated on an island of grief. We made quick time to the hospital, following the ambulance, its lights and sirens blaring the whole way.

When we got into the waiting room, I was surprised to see Malachi and Rebecca already there. I realized with a start that in all the frenzy, I hadn't even texted them. Dean caught my eye and squeezed my hand. Once again, my husband had picked up the pieces of me and made sense of them.

"I am so glad to see you guys." I hugged them both tightly.

"What happened?" Malachi asked.

"She had two seizures. One minute we were talking, and the next, she was jerking around with her eyes rolling around. Do you think she'll be okay?"

Malachi's expression looked grim. "I don't know. I will have them page Dr. Price and see if I can talk to the ER doc. You ok?"

He touched Rebecca's elbow and regarded her with concern.

"Yeah, I'll be fine. Go help Mom." Becca's chin wobbled.

"I have her," I assured him. "Come sit down."

Rebecca, Dean, and I sat together, waiting for any news. I remembered our first day in Florida, waiting for Bernie to come out of her hysterectomy. It seemed like another lifetime.

"Dustin and I are going to be living in Florida. When Mom dies, we'll inherit the condo. I'm leaving my job, leaving Boston, and raising Dustin here, with Malachi. He needs to be here for his gran, so we're moving here." She said in one long breath.

Dean and I looked at one another. I wanted to cry again. How would we ever grow closer to Dustin? I didn't want to watch him grow up on social media, never touch his skin, or attend school events. I wanted to be as present in his life as I had been in Sean's. I had promised Bernie I would be a grandmother for both of us.

But now, Becca was moving halfway across the country. Boston was two hours away, but Florida was a plane ride.

But I also understood that Rebecca had to do what was best for her and Dustin. Dustin would have a childhood filled with sunshine and water instead of screeching subway cars and trash heaped on sidewalks and honking taxis. And Rebecca and Malachi deserved to love one another and an opportunity to build a future together. Rebecca was finally opening her heart to love. She was finding her worth. I would be sad in private, but I would support her choices. I smiled at her and squeezed her hand.

"Dustin does seem to love it here. We'll work out some visits." I said bravely.

"We want you to move in." Becca blurted.

"Excuse me?" Dean said.

"We want you to move to Florida too. Malachi and me. It's important to us that Dustin has his grandparents in his life. We know you have a job in Connecticut, Dean, but we would love for you guys to consider it. We want to make the suite upstairs into an in-law apartment, so you have your own space. Just think about it before you say no. I understand it's a huge decision and there is so much going on right now. Talk about it later." She talked and talked, afraid to meet our eyes. I assumed she thought she would find flat-out rejection there.

She stopped abruptly. "I have to walk. I'm way too anxious. You guys want coffee?"

"You want company?" I asked.

"No, actually, I kind of need a moment alone. My mind is going at super warp speed."

"Okay. I'll take a tea, two cream, two sugar."

"Black coffee for me, please," Dean said, standing up to peel a bill off his stack.

Rebecca waved him off. "Put that away."

Dean didn't argue, which let me know just how thrown off he was by her offer. When she had headed off in search of drinks, he turned to me, his eyebrows raised.

"Well, that was unexpected." He said.

"Yeah, tell me about it," I said. "But what do you think?"

"I can't say I hate the idea of having daily access to Dustin. We missed so much of his life already. It's nice to be able to be there for the rest of it." Dean said, uncharacteristically putting the cart way before the horse.

"But no Patti and Olivia across the street." I lamented.

"But we would get Dustin and Becca every day." He said as a counterpoint. "And no snow and ice and shoveling."

"Or chopping wood," I added. "I don't know. Maybe it's worth considering."

My heart skipped a beat, thinking of never having to say goodbye to my grandson as I had to do with Sean.

"I think we should get our own unit if we do this, though," I said. "They'll be newlyweds at some point. They're not going to want to have to keep quiet for the benefit of not scandalizing the grandparents sleeping over their heads. They need privacy."

"Who are you kidding? You need privacy. You like being loud." He teased.

I tried to act indignant, but I couldn't muster it.

"It will be nice to have a place for Dustin to go to give them some truly kid-free time, too," I said. "But what about your job?"

Dean held up his phone, where he already had a job site pulled up.

"My company has several Florida branches, but if they don't transfer me, there are plenty of options from what I see right now."

"So, are we just considering this, or are we doing this?"

"We're seriously thinking about it. We'll need to sell the house." He cautioned.

I paused. That house was where I had raised my son. The only home Sean had ever known. Every corner contained a memory. But I knew what my son would say. "Mom, you have me in your heart. You don't need the house. Go make memories with my kid."

"We can. It's going to break my heart, but it would make the most sense. Should we see what's available for condos?" I asked.

"I already found a unit that I think is a few down from Bernie's online. I already sent an email to the realtor."

"You know, sometimes I forget just what a force my husband is."

"Only because my wife is an even bigger one." He kissed me deeply. "I'll follow you anywhere. I'm yours."

"And I'm yours," I assured him, resting my forehead on his forehead.

"I found some provisions," Becca announced, rounding the corner.

She passed out our drinks along with bananas. We sat in silence for a few minutes, drinking and eating. Finally, Malachi appeared, along with the ER doctor. Rebecca shot up, her banana peel tumbling onto the floor.

"What's going on?" She asked Malachi.

"Baby, sit down." He replied.

He sat in the chair next to her, tugging her down and sandwiching her hand with his.

The doctor sat on the armrest of one of the waiting room chairs.

"So, she's had another seizure. She's having a harder time coming back, so we are not sure if there is some neurological issue or just the progression of her disease. We have called Dr. Price, and we are doing an MRI to get a better picture. I hesitate to say much more, but if she has family who may want to say goodbye, you should call them."

Rebecca shuddered and let out one sob, then pulled herself together.

"Can I see her?"

"I'll go with you," Malachi said. He kissed her. "We're in this together."

"I thought you were the patient's nurse, but it looks like you're her boyfriend." The doctor observed.

"I'm both," Malachi said, shrugging.

I saw Rebecca flush at him, saying he was her boyfriend. They stood and followed the doctor into the unit.

"I should let Cami know what's going on. She may want to come to say goodbye." I said.

"You sound thrilled to be calling her." Dean teased.

"Well, you know I don't much care for her, but it is her sister."

"Very true. I'll leave you alone to do that. I have a few calls of my own to make."

A few minutes later, Cami's shrill hello vibrated through my ear. I adjusted my phone's volume, took a deep breath, and plunged ahead.

"Hi Cami, it's Rae."

"Rae! How lovely to hear from you. Are you back?"

"No, I'm not, actually. That's kind of why I called. I'm still with Bernie, and her health has taken a turn for the worse. She's had some seizures today, and they're not sure how much damage they've done and if she'll pull through."

"What are you talking about?"

"I'm saying if you want to say goodbye, you need to come."

"No, Rae. The last time I talked to my sister, she didn't say a word about being sick. This is the first I have heard of it, and now you're telling me she could die!"

Shit. I didn't know that Bernie hadn't yet told anyone but us about her cancer. I had unintentionally violated her privacy.

"I'm sorry you had to hear it this way, Cami, but Bernie has ovarian cancer. She's terminal. You should come. Soon."

I heard her sniffle discreetly on the other end. "I'll text you with my flight time. Can you pick me up?"

"Yes, and you can plan to stay at Bernie's. There's room."

"Okay, thank you. See you soon."

"How's Cami?" Dean asked, settling into the seat next to me.

"On her way. I just was the bearer of the bad news. Neither Rebecca nor Bernie told her about the cancer."

"Some people are private," Dean said. "Others, like us, wear our pain like a coat. We roll it around on our tongues like a pill. It's the song running through our heads relentlessly. We can't judge their choices just because they grieve differently than us."

"I know, but I still feel terrible springing that on her."

"I know. But I have some good news. I got an email back about the condo. It's down two and across from Bernie's, which is plenty close enough. We can see it tonight or tomorrow. The realtor lives in the condo complex, so she can show it whenever." He said.

"Let's wait and see if Bernie is okay," I said.

"Of course." He said. "Now, come here and let me hold you. You always make me feel better."

We stayed like that for quite a while until Malachi and Becca returned, holding hands and eyes swollen from crying. Rebecca looked devastated.

"The cancer's spread. It's all in her brain." She cracked at the word brain.

Malachi slipped his arm around her shoulder. "Come here. It's going to be okay."

"Will they let us stay with her tonight?" Dean asked suddenly. "You two still have that suite waiting. Bernie would want you to finish your date."

"I agree. She's stable now and medicated. She won't know which one of us is here. Go enjoy that big bed, take a bubble bath, talk. Things are going to get difficult very soon. You need to recharge your batteries." I chimed in.

Becca looked uncertain. "It feels wrong to be running off to a hotel to cavort with a man while my mother is in the hospital."

"We're not cavorting. And we can come back later. I did this for you. You deserve, hell, you need a break, my love." Malachi said. "Let's go to the hotel. You can take a bath. We can get room service. And if you want, we can come back in the middle of the night and relieve Dean and Rae."

"Dustin is with the neighbor's granddaughter, sleeping. One of us will head home to be with him by morning. You guys, please, go. Try to salvage what's left of your evening. You know that's what Bernie would want you to do." I said. "And if you waste a perfectly good hotel room, she'll definitely kick your ass."

Rebecca laughed.

"We can come back if I want?" She asked Malachi.

He made a cross over his heart. "I promise."

"Okay, let's go then. I don't want to hear it from Bernie if I waste a little black dress, a hotel, and lingerie."

"Lingerie?" Malachi questioned, and Dean and I laughed.

"We'll see you two tomorrow," Dean said, clapping Malachi on the shoulder.

"Text us if anything changes," Becca asked.

"Of course," I said.

As the elevator doors closed on them, I headed to the nurses' station to find out what room Bernie had been moved to, Dean behind me. It promised to be an exceedingly long night, and not in the way I hoped Becca's would be.

Once I was settled next to Bernie's bed and bid Dean goodbye, I reached for my phone. The decision to move to Florida, to sacrifice the life we had always known for a child we could have never known, weighed heavy on me. I knew what life in Connecticut was. But that familiar life held little appeal without my grandson.

Patti's face popped up on my screen. Her smile made longing bloom in my chest.

"Hey, lady, what's up?"

"You alone?" I asked.

She nodded, then swung her phone around and showed me her empty living room. "You have my undivided attention. Liv is

345

off, probably making me a grandma in some senior's backseat, and I got ghosted. Again."

I chuckled. "You know damn well that's not what she's doing. And as for the ghosting, that's his loss. What happened to what's his name with the magic wand?"

"He didn't rise to the occasion in his repeat performance. Anyway, enough about him. Why is it so dark?"

"I'm at Bernie's bedside. She's had a bunch of seizures. It looks like this is the end." I said, starting to cry.

"Oh, Rae. I'm so sorry. How's Rebecca holding up?"

"She's a wreck. Devastated. And this couldn't have happened at a worse time. Malachi planned a special night for them, though I'm sure you know since Dean flew in as his accomplice."

"Who me?" She demurred. "I may have been roped into fetching the mail and keeping watch on the house. It sounds like he pulled out all the stops. It sucks it got cut short."

"It didn't get cut short."

"Pardon?" The surprise was evident on her face. "That's cold, chasing ass while your mother is dying. Malachi must have some kind of magic wand himself."

"Dean and I insisted they go. It took some convincing, but we all know this is precisely what Bernie would have wanted."

"It seems wrong, insensitive." She said.

"Tonight plays right into Bernie's plans. She would come and haunt us all if her death was the reason Rebecca didn't get her happily ever after."

"Or her happy ending, as the case may be," Patti said.

"I'm sure Malachi had a few happy endings in mind." I laughed. "And honestly, sex is a good coping mechanism in my book."

"Yes, I know. You woke up the neighborhood multiple times a night for a year after Sean died. You two were worse than in high school." Patti chuckled.

"It was the only way to feel anything. We were zombies except when we were making love. And I tend to believe Rebecca's going through much of the same. She's feeling so many things at once. She has to turn it all off just to get through. The only time she can feel it all is in her safe space- with Malachi. Unless you've been there, you won't get it."

"I get it. It's just a little taboo, and that's saying something coming from me." She smiled, chuckled under her breath. "I do hope they have a good night, as impossible as that seems. At least someone's getting laid around here."

She laughed but stopped short when she saw I didn't.

"That's not what you called to tell me, is it?"

"Nope. Becca dropped a bomb on us before she left for the hotel, and I need to talk it through."

"What's going on?"

"Becca decided to move to Florida to try and make a go of it with Malachi. They've asked us to move too. Well, they asked us to move in with them, but we would want our own space."

"So, you're considering it then?" Patti said, quiet for once. Her face was mournful.

"We want to be close to Dustin. I want to be part of his everyday life, not the grandma he talks to on the phone once a week and sees on holidays."

"But with modern technology, you can be part of his life. Look at us right now. You could video chat every day."

"You can't smell his smell or feel the warmth of his skin on a screen. It's not the same."

"What will happen to Liv and me if you move away? She's had you countering my crazy every day of her life." She looked sad, almost pitiful.

"You ladies have survived this long without me." I tried to make light, even though my heart broke incrementally.

"And it's sucked. I don't have anyone to do a post-date play-by-play with, gossip, and drink with after work. Liv's always off with her friends. I'm a lonely spinster without you. And then when Liv leaves for college, it's really over. I'll just start collecting cats and wearing my bathrobe all day."

Inspiration struck. Without thinking, the words came out of my mouth.

"Well, Liv's off to college in a few months. Why don't you think about a change too? There are tons of eligible bachelors here. You would be in hog heaven."

"That's not a half-bad idea, but I'm going to have to think about it. I think you're acting a little rashly, and I don't want to make the same mistake."

"Fair enough, but Pat, whether you decide to come or not, I think we are. I can't be that far from my grandson. I don't have the choice with Sean, but I do with Dusty."

"Rae, I get it. But I still think you're moving too fast for such a major choice. But at the end of the day, you know I'm here no matter what you choose. Whether I like it or not, I'm stuck with you, you pain in my ass." She laughed tenderly. "So, you think I can compete with the Florida beach bunnies?"

REBECCA

Malachi had gone all out with the hotel too. Even in my black dress and diamonds, I didn't feel fancy enough to walk into the lobby. Our suite was luxurious, with a giant jetted tub, plush carpet, and more ocean views. Despite my guilt about leaving my mother's bedside, I was glad I had allowed myself to come. I had never stayed at such a lovely place before.

"This is amazing. You didn't have to do all this." I said to Malachi.

"Yes, I did. I'll do anything I can to keep you happy. You deserve the best, and that's what I intend to give you, now and for as long as you and the good Lord let me."

"It feels like a fairytale when you say things like that," I told him.

"Then just call me Prince Charming. And this is just the beginning." He drew me in for a scorching kiss.

When we pulled apart, his pupils dilated with desire.

"I want you." He said, his voice rough and sexy.

"Five minutes," I said.

His response was a kiss, more passionate, more tantalizing than the previous. Desire soared within me. I tried to move away, so I could go to the bathroom and slip into the lacy underthings waiting in my bag. Yet, every time I moved, Malachi kissed me deeper, bringing me to new heights of frenzy.

He slipped his hand to my bare shoulders, sliding his hands down my arms and sending the top of my dress down to my waist. I stood there, feeling lumpy and awkward in my strapless bra.

"Hold on, wait, please!"

"Sweetheart, you do realize that I have seen you naked before. And I want you so bad, you would be wearing a trash bag, and I'd rip it off with my teeth."

"Believe me when I tell you Spanx are less attractive than trash bags."

"Not from where I stand." He said, coming up behind me and unstrapping my bra.

He slid his hands to the front, catching my breasts as they fell free. He sighed as he thumbed my nipples, the sigh of a reverent man experiencing something akin to a religious experience. I moaned, the sensations rippling through me, creating a delicious tension. Once my top was bare, he slid his hands down again, giving my Spanx a hard tug. He stopped for a minute to examine them, fascinated by their construction.

"What are these made out of?"

"Is that what you want to focus on right now?" I asked, rolling onto my back on the large, downy bed.

He looked up from his inspection and saw me. He tossed the garment over his shoulder and lowered himself over me, kissing me.

"You're wearing entirely too many clothes," I said.

He stood up and started removing his clothes quickly.

"My God," I said appreciatively.

"Do you like what you see?" He said, spinning on his heel, his impressive erection bobbing.

"Very much," I said, standing to meet his mouth mid-spin.

As our mouths collided, I took him in my hand. He drew in a sharp breath. We fell onto the bed, still entangled. Limbs were flailing everywhere. His tongue was licking the salt off my skin as he teased me with his fingers. I climaxed quickly; my inhibitions tossed aside. He continued down my body with his tongue, coming to the center of me and tasting me.

"Delicious." He proclaimed and started a masterful oral performance.

I climaxed again and then again. "You're going to use me up before we even have sex." I panted.

"There's no such thing as too many orgasms." He said but moved up and positioned himself over me.

He leaned down to kiss me at the exact moment he entered me. I gasped, shocked at the way my body stretched to accommodate him as he entered me to the hilt. I shivered at the delicious fullness when he was finally completely inside.

"Are you okay?" He asked. "We can stop."

"Do. Not. Stop." I ordered.

"Your wish is my command," Malachi said, smiling down at me.

And we were off. Our bodies moved in sync, already familiar with one another. I felt him pulse inside me as his body shuddered. He took me over the edge, again and again, my most sensitive muscles flexing and clenching around his steely length until I begged for a reprieve. He didn't break my gaze as he finished.

"I love you." He murmured. "I love you. Marry me."

I froze. Malachi's eyes grew wide, immediately realizing what he said. I didn't know how to respond. He had probably just gotten caught up in the moment. Emotions were running high today. It was just a mistake, I told myself over and over, so I wouldn't be disappointed when he claimed it and took the words back.

"Hey, look at me." He said as I cuddled into him, the little spoon to his big. "You're in your head about what I said."

"Oh, you mean the marriage proposal while you were coming?" I said, trying to make a joke but coming out snarky instead.

He cringed. "Yes. Becca, I was already planning on asking you tonight, just not like that. I'm sorry. You deserve better than that. I just got so caught up in you."

"Nice save. How am I to believe that you had already planned to ask, and you didn't make that up to save your ass?" I was teasing, but he took the bait.

He sprang from the bed, rooted around in his bag, and came back. He had a small black ring box in his hand. My heart was pounding. I was glad I was lying down.

"Rebecca Malone, let me tell you how this was supposed to go. We were going to come in here, you looking amazing and highly fuckable, might I add, in that black dress, me handsome and all that in my suit. They had candles and rose petals everywhere, but they removed them after everything with Bernie happened. I wasn't sure we would get here after that."

"So that's why Dean was so gung-ho for us to come here even with Mom," I said.

He smiled. "Yes, he and Rae both knew my plan."

"I also invited them to stay with us permanently, but they wanted to talk about it first."

"Live with *us*? I love the sound of that."

"Well?"

"Well, what?" He looked at me, confused.

"What's the rest of it? I am picturing this proposal. You in the suit, rose petals, candles. Then what?"

"Then I would take you out on the balcony, under the stars, looking out over the ocean that is almost as blue and beautiful as your eyes and ask you to be my wife." He said. "Rebecca Malone, I love you. There is no one else I would rather spend my life with. Will you do me the honor of being my wife?"

He cracked open the box, and a simple, elegant diamond solitaire sat in the velvet.

"If this isn't your style, we can get something else." He said.

I began to cry. I knew I would say yes, but my natural-born pragmatism took the wheel for a moment. "Are you sure? We have only been together for like six weeks."

"Bec, six weeks or six years, we have experienced, dealt with, and survived more than some couples deal with in a lifetime. And I believe, when you know, you know. And I know what my heart wants, what my head wants, what every part of me wants. So please, just say yes and be my wife."

I took a deep breath. He was right. It was quick, but I didn't need any more time to figure it out. Malachi was my destiny. He would be my husband. Dustin's father. A father to our daughter and whoever came before or after her.

"Yes," I said. "I will marry you."

He smiled broadly and pulled me to him. "You've made me the happiest man on the planet."

"I can't believe it. Men like you don't really exist, and if they do, they don't love women like me." I blubbered, ugly crying.

"Yes, we do. And I'm yours. Forever." Malachi said softly; his green eyes fixed on mine.

I kissed him. I felt him grow hard again against my leg.

"Well, well. Let's see what we can do about this." I said, swinging my leg over his torso.

His eyes widened.

"Oh, hell yeah." He whispered.

After Round Two and okay, maybe Three, we lay there, spent and sweaty. It was quiet, except for the sound of our unregulated breathing. As he caught his breath, Malachi spoke.

"We've got to get in the shower and head over to the hospital."

"Why? Did they call you? Did Rae text?" I sat up on one arm, alarmed.

"No, no. We need to tell Bernie about the engagement. She has something for you."

"She knew too?" I asked.

"She's been conspiring for this to happen since the day I first walked in the house. The day we went to Gran's for the cake, she asked me what my intentions were with you- if you were just a booty call or more."

"She didn't!" I said. "I'm so sorry."

"I'm not. I knew then how much Bernie cares about you and Dustin, and it made me even more determined not to let you or her down."

"I am a grown woman. She doesn't have a right to butt into my personal life."

"Well then, you're probably really not going to like the next part." He said, hesitant.

"Oh no. What?"

"When I told her I wanted to be with you, to build a life with you, she asked if she could start planning a wedding."

"What?" I sat up, all my tension and anxiety flooding back in. "Whose wedding?"

"Our wedding."

"And you okayed this?" I said, beginning to get angry. "You presumptuous ass!"

"No, I told her I wanted to respect your need to take things slow and that I wouldn't risk losing you by pushing you to get married too fast just because she wants to be a part of your wedding."

The reality that my mother would not be at my wedding hit me then. I would have no one filling the reserved seats in the front. I wouldn't get a special moment with my mom where she passed me some token from her own day with tears in her eyes. I wanted to look over and see her face as I entered this next phase of my life. After so many years of strain between us, we had mended fences. I needed her there when I married the man I had taken so long to find and even longer to love.

"So, did she plan the wedding?" I asked. "Even when you told her no? That's her claim to fame. Never taking no for an answer."

"Yes, she did. I wasn't sure, but she showed me the binder this morning." He paused, then plunged ahead. "And it's gorgeous. Small, tasteful. She has the clubhouse at the condo on standby, same with the florists."

"Dresses?" I was almost amused now.

Of course, my mother would plan my wedding on her deathbed. The gall of that woman made me chuckle. Her steadfast faith that we would all find the way to the right path, her path, never failed to baffle and aggravate me.

"They're in her closet—the one in her room. I didn't look at them. I just know where they are."

I was stunned into silence. It looked like Mom hadn't overlooked a single detail in true Bernie Malone fashion.

"Rebecca, she doesn't have much time left. I won't be upset or try to change your mind, and I won't leave if you say no, but what do you think about getting married tomorrow?"

I gasped. Surely, we didn't need to move that fast. We had been engaged for mere hours. I wanted the complete experience- the celebrations, the toasts, my own planning binder. But did any of it really matter if my mother wasn't there to enjoy it too? It was because of her I had found Malachi. I owed her a debt I could never repay.

"Mom should be there. She is the one who brought us together after all, but I'm sure we have a little time."

Malachi looked hard into my eyes and reached over to stroke my cheek. "Becca, if you want her there, we should get married tomorrow."

A huge lump formed in my throat. "This is it?"

"Yes, baby, it is. I am so, so sorry. But I got you. We'll get through this together."

He held me as I sobbed. After a little while, I stilled. I turned and kissed him. I nuzzled into his neck, breathing in his scent. I sighed deeply.

"Where's my phone?" I asked.

"Why?"

"If we're getting married tomorrow, Kieran needs to get a flight tonight," I explained.

He grinned widely. "Really?"

"Yes. I can't imagine not having my mother there when we get married. We can have a big party later, but we should get married like it started- with Mom, Dustin, Rae, and Dean. Oh, and you need to invite your family! Can Gran make a lemon cake for a reception?"

He regarded me, amused. "You really are Bernie's daughter. Party planning runs in your blood."

"You don't witness a master at work your whole life without picking up some tips along the way." I joked, then grew serious. "I don't think we can manage to get Mom home. We'll have to see if the hospital has a meeting room we can use. Maybe they can wheel her down for the ceremony. Hell, we can do it at her bedside for all I care."

"No more dragging your feet and holding me at arm's length?" He asked.

"No. I know what I want- have known what I wanted. That's you. A life with you. And now I want to start it as soon as possible." I said, honestly and without fear.

"Your wish is my command, madam." He said, sprinkling kisses on my naked shoulder.

"Hey, none of that. I'm calling Kieran!" I tugged the sheet over me in the nick of time.

"Bec! What's up? What are you wear- OH MY GOD! You're not wearing anything! Sluuu-t! So, which one did he rip off with his--"

Kier!"

"What? Is he right there?"

I moved the phone over so Kieran could see Malachi lying next to me, bare-chested. Kieran's eyes grew wide, and his mouth gaped. Malachi grinned and gave a little wave.

"What's up, man!" He said to Kieran.

"I'll give you one guess," Kieran responded, drawing laughter from Malachi and me.

"Behave! And listen, I need you!" I said.

Kieran shook his head as if to clear the images of Malachi shirtless. "What's up?"

"I need you to book a flight."

"You're coming home?" He was excited and confused.

"No, a flight for you to come here to Florida. I'm getting married tomorrow, and I need my Man of Honor."

There was silence, then a long, loud whoop and wolf whistles. I heard him start tapping on his screen.

"There's a red-eye. I'll text you. Can I bring a date?"

Malachi started laughing.

"Sure. Anyone I know?" I asked.

"Maybe." He said mysteriously.

"Why am I scared?"

"Don't be scared. Oh, and I'm proud of you." He said tenderly.

"Text me your flight info, and I'll pick you up."

We hung up, and I sat up.

"I've got to go see a lady about a dress. Can you please go check on Mom for me and see if there is a space there that we can use?"

"Anything for you." He said, kissing me again. "On one condition."

"What's that?"

"Join me in the shower."

RAE

I was half asleep, slumped in a chair next to Bernie's bedside when Malachi came in. I assessed him, trying to gauge his mood and whether his proposal had been successful.

"I'm here to relieve you." He said. "How is she?"

"She's heavily sedated. Why are you relieving me? What's going on?"

"You're needed at home for a dress fitting." He smiled then. "She said yes. But we're doing it tomorrow. And we will need to do it here. Bernie won't be stable enough to come home, I'm afraid." He regarded her sadly.

"Congratulations!" I crowed, hugging him. "I couldn't be happier for you both."

"Thank you. You don't think we're crazy for getting married so fast?"

"You have to be a little crazy to be in love," I said. "But you both are old enough to know what feels right for yourselves."

"I appreciate that." He said. "You go help Becca and get some rest. I'll be here."

"I'll send Dean over soon to give you a break."

I squeezed Bernie's limp hand as I leaned in close to her.

"I'm going to go take care of your girl, just like you'll take care of my boy till I get there. But you better not report for duty until after we get this done, do you hear me? Hang on for Rebecca, Bernie. I know you can do this. I'll see you soon."

I hugged Malachi again and was gone, an Uber shuttling me through the town. I arrived at the condo to find Dean and Dustin fast asleep. Light spilled out into the hallway from Bernie's room. I headed towards the glow. When I got to the door, I saw Becca staring incredulously at herself in the mirror. She was a confection of white tulle and sequins.

"You look gorgeous." I breathed.

She looked at me, her eyes filling with tears. "I do, don't I? I never thought I would wear a wedding dress or even get married."

"And look at you now. Did you find one you like?" I asked, moving over to the closet.

"I was enjoying a bit of dress-up before making a decision." She said.

"I don't blame you. Try on all of them five times if you want. Have a little fun. It is your wedding, after all."

"It feels a little indulgent to wear a wedding dress to a ceremony at a hospital. Do you think I should just wear a white suit or a sundress?"

"Again, it's your wedding. You can do whatever you want to do. Why don't you finish trying these on before you make a final decision?"

I handed her one dress after another. She grew more amazed and confident with every one she tried. Watching her, I saw her inner light glow stronger. She was evolving into the woman Bernie had begged me repeatedly to help her become. Finally, there was one dress left in the closet. I had saved it for last for a reason, but I wanted to let Rebecca make up her own mind before I told her.

She slid the dress up, and a look came over her face.

"Can you please zip me up?" She asked softly.

I did, and we both stood in the full-length mirror admiring her.

"You are exquisite in that dress." I choked out.

The dress was simple, crepe material, with a high neck that flowed into a mermaid silhouette at the bottom. It had no embellishments. No glitter, lace, or sequins. As I took in Rebecca in the dress, I saw that it accentuated not only her stunning curves but her personality. She became the dress- its strong lines matched her steely internal strength. It's simple and unadorned surfaces mirrored her own face, often un-fussy and without makeup. Rebecca smiled and ran her hands down the sides of her body.

"This material is great. It hugs instead of clings." She marveled. "It's very classy. I feel like Carolyn Kennedy or something."

"Bernie was right." I laughed.

She looked at me, confused.

"What?"

"Your mother knew the day I found it that it was your dress. She bet me this is the one you would choose. It was also her favorite."

Rebecca smiled. "I hate to make you the loser of the bet, but you are. This is my dress."

"It's a wonderful choice. Now for shoes and jewelry...." I began, flipping to the coordinated pages in the binder Bernie had insisted we keep.

"I already know the jewelry." She said, padding over to her mother's jewelry box and routing around.

After a moment, she produced a pair of sapphire earrings and a matching bracelet. They were simple yet stunning. When she put them on, we both nodded our heads.

"Something old, something borrowed, and something blue." She said.

"You can count your dress as something new," I assured her.

"That covers it then. Mom didn't leave shoes?" She smiled.

"Check the shoe boxes on the top shelf. I vote for the metallic ones."

She examined all the shoes and ended up choosing the ones I had suggested. She stood before the mirror. She kept staring at herself.

"Something is missing." She said. "I can't put my finger on it."

"I know what it is," I said, rooting around in the back of the closet.

I finally found what I was looking for, a long, cathedral-length veil.

"This was your mom's," I said. "Let's see how it looks."

Rebecca's lip trembled, and she threatened to cry. She composed herself almost instantly and pulled her hair into a bun. I secured the veil on her head and fluffed it out behind her.

"Bingo," I whispered. "Bernie never misses the mark, huh?"

"No, she doesn't. This is perfect." She said, still not taking her eyes off the mirror.

I hugged her. "I'm glad we had one you liked. I thought planning your whole wedding was risky. I was so worried you would hate everything."

"Well, if this is any indication, you hit it out of the park." She said.

We both yawned simultaneously. "Okay, time for bed. We'll have a long day tomorrow."

"You won't get any argument from me," she said. "I'm going to call Malachi and check on Mom."

After she was satisfied that Bernie was resting comfortably and that Dean would be taking over for Malachi so he could rest, Becca finally settled down.

The day dawned like many others in Florida, warm and breezy. Dean had slipped out from under the covers a few hours after I laid down, leaving the bed cold and empty beside me. I woke up before Rebecca and Dustin. I had emailed the florist and officiant we had enlisted to help execute the wedding last night and given them the green light and the updated venue. The florist had called as soon as the sun rose.

"I have an idea, but it's going to cost more, and I'll need your permission to bring in another vendor." She said.

"Do whatever you need to do to make this wedding beautiful," I said, dollar signs already filling my head.

A text popped up on my phone. It was Cami. *I will be coming in on a flight this morning.* In all the chaos of the rushed wedding and Bernie's worsening health, I had forgotten she was coming.

I was trying to work out logistics when Rebecca came out of the room she shared with Dustin, her hair a wild tangle and her eyes heavily ringed in shadows.

"Did you sleep at all?" I asked, aghast.

"No, not really."

"Second thoughts?" I asked fearfully.

"No, not at all. Malachi is the only thing that I am sure about."

"That's good, especially when everything else is so unsure," I said.

"I've been up half the night worrying what's going to happen when Kieran touches down and the other half crying my eyes out about Mom."

"Why are you worried about Kieran?"

She looked guilty. "I haven't been particularly forthcoming with the details of my life."

"So, he doesn't know about Dean and me? Does he know about the real circumstances of Dustin's conception?"

"He knows what everyone else knows- nothing."

"He's walking into a situation blindsided. That's not very fair." I commented.

"I'm going to tell him the minute he lands."

"There's a minor snag in your plan." I paused. "Cami is coming to say goodbye to your mom and now, apparently, your wedding."

"And you want me to pick her up when I get Kieran?" She guessed. She sat down on a stool and heaved a sigh, then started laughing. I regarded her with curiosity.

"Are you okay?" I asked.

"It just serves me right. I lied, and now it's coming back to bite me in the ass. Even this wonderful day- my wedding day- is sullied by it. I won't ever think of the good thing without the bad thing. And I deserve that because I chose to lie. And the real bitch of it is, I didn't even need to in the end. I know now Kieran will be upset only because I lied, not what I lied about, same as Mom."

"Rebecca, you made a choice, the right one for you with the information you had at the time. The good news is, now that it's out in the open, it doesn't have to be the black cloud hanging over everything. You can heal and move on."

"I know. I just wish I had just been honest, especially with him, in the first place. He's the least judgmental person on the planet." She sighed again. "Oh well, what's done is done. All I can do is confess and apologize."

"Very true."

"I came out here to ask you something important, and we got sidetracked."

"Yes?" I asked.

"Do you have a makeup artist lined up for this wedding, or do I need to stop at Sephora on the way back from the airport?"

"Knowing your mother, you already know the answer to that question. She will be here at noon. She does hair too."

"Thank goodness. I'm going to hop in the shower and head to the airport to face the music. And to collect Cami."

She pulled a face like the one I made whenever Cami's name came up. Before I could reply, there was a knock at the door. I moved to answer it.

Malachi stood on the step, his back to the door.

"If it's you, Rebecca, don't look. I can't see you on our wedding day."

"It's Rae," I said, laughing. "She just got in the shower. What are you doing here at the crack of dawn?"

"Well, all my stuff is here, and I need a shower. I can use Bernie's bathroom so that Rebecca won't see me. I want to take Dustin and get ready with him today. Could you do me a huge favor and get him ready to go? I'll be done in 20."

"Of course, I'm here to help."

"You're the best." He kissed my cheek and headed towards his room.

A few minutes later, I heard Rebecca get out of the shower and wake Dustin. I knocked.

"Come in!" She called.

When the door opened, Dustin streaked by, naked. Rebecca stood in her bra and black leggings, a towel coiled into a turban on her head.

"Come here, please!" She called, obviously frustrated.

"I've got him. Finish getting ready. Oh, and Malachi just got home. He's in the shower in Bernie's bathroom."

Her face softened and relaxed at his name, just as mine did when Dean's name came up in conversation. I hoped again that they would have the same strong, stable marriage we had always enjoyed. From what I had seen, they would.

She threw an oversized sweatshirt over her leggings.

"I can't tell how much your help and support is appreciated. I am so glad that you're here. And that you found us." She threw her arms around me. "Sorry, I am an emotional wreck today."

"You're allowed to be. I am so happy I found you and that we're here for this." I paused, overcome. "And I am so touched you want us to move here and be a part of your lives."

"Have you made any decisions?" She asked.

"Not yet, but you and Malachi will be the first ones to know when we do."

"Thank you. I'm going to go get our guests. And confess my sins."

I gave her a lingering hug. "Are you bringing Cami right to the hospital?"

"I was hoping you could when we get back. I'll need to start getting ready by then." She said. lol

"That's fine. Malachi wants to get ready with Dustin so Cami and I can make sure everything is on track at the hospital."

Tears sprang to her eyes. "I forget that Dustin gets a dad when I get a husband. Our whole lives are going to be different after today."

"Isn't it wonderful?" I said, snagging Dustin and hugging him close.

Dustin was as much of a wonder to me as Sean had been. Every time I held him, I marveled at his seashell pink ears, his little boy smell of sunshine and chlorine, his hands, his laugh. I kissed him again as Rebecca came over. She, too, kissed the top of his head, reminded him to behave, and was gone. She hesitated for a moment, needing to leave but pulled by the invisible threads that bound her to Malachi. Pragmatism won out, and she left, off to the airport to collect Kieran and Cami and face the music.

REBECCA

"Becccccccccccaaaaaaa!" Kieran's voice pierced the air of the airport terminal, causing even the hardest of hearing travelers to turn and glare at him.

He remained oblivious to their stares and made his way to me. He threw his arms around me and swung me several times, creating a wide berth around us.

"My God, girl, I have missed you like crazy. Florida agrees with you! Or is it just Adonis? You have a tan in winter!" He talked a mile a minute while checking his phone and the incoming flights simultaneously.

"I've missed you too. But I am working on zero hours of sleep, so you'll have to forgive me if I lack some enthusiasm. What are you looking for?"

"Adonis keep you up all night?" He asked. "That's an excellent reason to miss a little sleep."

"I was up worrying about your arrival."

"So sweet of you to worry about me!" He exclaimed. "But I'm fine."

"I wasn't worried about you flying. I worry more about the other passengers having to deal with you than you having to deal with them." I teased. "I have to tell you something, and it's kind of big."

He stopped mid-stride as he power walked to an unknown destination. "Oh my god! You're preggers!".

"No, no. I'm not pregnant. Why are we going this way? We have to pick up my Aunt Cami. She's coming in to say goodbye to Mom." My voice broke, and he pulled me into a hug.

"I have a surprise for you." He said. "Turn around."

"What in the--" I started but was cut short.

"I can't believe you thought you could have a wedding without me!" Dianne crowed, barreling into Kieran and me and folding us into a hug. "Come here, my babies! Where's Dusty?"

"I can't believe you're both here!" I said.

I started to cry, right there in the middle of the airport. Soon, my tears turned to full-body sobs. Dianne and Kieran ushered me into the closest bar. Kieran ordered me a rum and Coke and a shot.

"Here, you need this." He said, "Drink it down."

"I have to drive us all home!" I protested.

"My driver's license is valid in all 50 states," Dianne assured me. "And I can follow directions with the best of them."

"I have time to sober up anyway. Cami's flight won't come in for about an hour. Which gives me time to talk to you."

They both leaned forward; their curiosity peaked.

"Is everything okay?" Dianne asked.

"It will be once I say this," I said. "Before we go back to Bernie's condo, I want to let you know that some other people are staying with us."

"Oh my God, was Bernie running an elderly commune? A swingers club?" Kieran took the ball and started rolling with it.

Dianne read my expression and shushed him, "Let Becca explain."

"Nothing like that," I said. "Their names are Rae and Dean, and they are Dustin's other grandparents."

Kieran and Dianne both sat back at a loss for words. So, I continued.

"They've been here since about a week after Christmas. They live in Connecticut, the same neighborhood as Cami. That's how they found me. Rae saw Dustin on a Christmas card and knew he was related in some way to her son. Cami told her where I lived and that I was a single mom. She came to Boston and found me. We did a DNA test, and it turns out she was right. Dustin is their grandchild."

"Hold on, where is the dad in all this? Why didn't you tell me? Did they disown him for abandoning his lovechild? And how in the hell did they end up staying with you guys?" Kieran fired a million questions at me.

"Their son, Sean, Dustin's dad, died four years before he was born." I began.

"You mean four months?" Dianne broke in.

"No, four years."

"Um, that math doesn't add up, or is it just me?" Kieran said, swirling his celery in the Bloody Mary he had flagged the waitress down for.

I took a massive gulp of air and bowed my head, unable to meet their eyes for the next part.

"I haven't been truthful with either of you about how I conceived Dustin, and I'm sorry. I used artificial insemination to conceive Dustin. Sean was the donor."

I looked up, scared. Dianne and Kieran both wore identical masks of surprise, but I plunged on.

"Sean went to college in Boston and donated sperm, apparently for date and drinking money. He was hit by a car two years before I chose him. They came to Florida when Mom had her surgery because they really couldn't wait to meet Dustin. They also wanted to help me with her. It was Bernie who asked them, well, Rae- Dean had work- to stay and move in until...the end."

I paused, gathered my composure.

"They've been in hell for the past four years, mourning their son. This way, they get to be a part of Dustin's life, know him, be with him. Be a part of our family. And truthfully, that's what they are now. They're not just his family, they're mine too, and they will be yours by the end of all this. They're amazing. Rae has stayed on to help Malachi, and I take care of

Mom. She and Bernie are like best friends. They don't think I know, but they stay up all night talking. Dean is the nicest guy in the world."

"But, like, why did you lie?" Kieran asked, clearly hurt by my dishonesty.

"I felt ashamed of it. I'm a mousy nerd who couldn't even get a man to give her a second look. I felt like a complete loser. I wanted you to think I was cool and desirable. Even if you don't desire me." I chuckled, but it fell flat.

"Becca, you're the only one who sees yourself like that. Do you see the hot ass man you're about to marry? According to the state of undress you both were in last night, he desires you. He thinks you're cool, just like I always have. And neither he, I am sure, nor I associate with losers, so you're clearly not one of those, baby girl. I would have supported you no matter what. Hell, I would have shot the turkey baster up in there."

Dianne made a face at his comment, but she reached her hand out and patted mine.

"I don't care how he got here; I am just happy you had that baby boy. Your reasons are your reasons for doing it how you did. As long as there's room for me to spoil him rotten too, then I'm good." She smiled. "And please, just know you can be who you are with us. You never need to lie or change."

Her kind words made me start crying once again. Kieran jumped up and fetched another drink.

"I'm so sorry I lied. And I am so happy you're here. And I'm so sad. My mom is dying."

My words were a watery jumble as I sobbed, all the things I had pushed down to function- to survive the tragedy every day had become- raw and exposed.

Dianne moved next to me and just held me. "It's okay, sweet girl. We're all here. Everyone's here for you. We're all going to get through it together." She whispered it over and over, like a chant.

Once the rum took hold of my feelings, I calmed down. I wiped my eyes and splashed water on my face in the bathroom.

"It's time to get Cami. She just found out Mom is sick. She's pissed I didn't tell her, so the car ride could be fun."

"Wonderful." They said in unison, making the three of us laugh.

We were still laughing when my aunt Cami stopped in front of us. She wore head to toe black, with a sleek patent leather suitcase on wheels, also black, trailing behind her. She wore enormous black sunglasses. Her hair was cut into a bob. She looked like a Russian spy.

"Cami! Over here!" I called.

She pushed her sunglasses up and pulled a disapproving face as she took us all in.

"Rebecca, I didn't know our reunion would have an audience." She said, holding me at arm's length and air kissing my cheeks.

"Holy Housewives of Fairfield County," Kieran whispered, and I elbowed him.

"Cami, this is Kieran and Dianne. They're friends of mine from Boston."

"Pleasure." She said, even though her face very clearly said it wasn't.

"We're here for the wedding," Dianne explained. "It's great to meet you."

"What wedding? What the hell is even happening here? My sister is dying. Someone is getting married. Rae has moved in with you. And I'm just sitting in Connecticut, clueless." Cami's hair shook with indignation, and I waited for her to stomp her foot. "So, kind of you to include me in your plans. If Rae hadn't called me, would you have even let me know Bernie was gone?"

"Well, in my experience, the phone works both ways. I am sure Becca would have gladly filled you in if you had bothered to call. Did you?" Kieran said, his tone icy.

"Okay, enough, enough. I'm sorry I didn't let you know, Cami, but I had my hands full dealing with all of this. I was as blindsided as you. And I'm getting married today, in just a few hours. I'm glad you will be able to be here for it." I said, my tone placating and saccharine.

"I didn't even know you were dating anyone." She said.

"I met him here. Malachi is Mom's nurse."

"Rebecca, that's just not proper!" She flitted her hands around.

"And yet, it's still happening," Dianne said. "It's not up to us. We're here to support Rebecca and your family. If you don't want to be involved, that's fine, but your opinion doesn't change the plan."

"Well, I've never." Cami huffed, but she was quieted by the look that Dianne shot at her. That look had caused burly, tough men to cower and back down. I laughed inwardly at the fear such a kind woman could inspire with a menacing look.

"Let's get you guys to the car," I said. "Cami, Rae is waiting for you at the house. You can go see Mom while I get ready. Kieran and Dianne, you guys can help me get ready for the main event."

"Where are you holding this wedding?" Cami asked.

"Mom's room," I said, starting to get emotional again. "She brought us together. She needs to be there."

"And be there, she shall. Let's go get you ready!" Dianne said, sticking out her hands for the keys.

The afternoon went by in a blur. Hair and makeup done, champagne drank, Lycra shimmied into. My dress drew tears from both Kieran and Dianne. He had snapped so many pictures of it and me that I felt like a celebrity.

"This is straight-up Meghan Markle reception dress vibes. I can't. I'm dead. I'm dying." He gushed.

"Meghan Markle after a mishap with a bike pump, maybe," I said.

"Meghan Markle has nothing on you, kid," Dianne said, patting my hand soothingly while Kieran zoomed around us, snapping photos from every angle.

"Those better not end up on your Instagram before I post the announcement," I warned as we slid into the back of an Uber to the hospital, anxiousness, and excitement bubbling inside of me.

"I would never!" Kieran promised. "For my eyes only until you say go."

When we arrived, Dean met us on the sidewalk. He looked handsome in a gray suit with a crisp white shirt and a navy-colored tie. At the sight of him, Kieran drew a sharp breath.

"Damn, where the hell has he been hiding?"

"Down, Tiger. He's straight and married. And very much in love with his wife."

He made a face. "You never let me have any fun."

Dean opened the door.

"I hear there is a bride who may need an escort down the aisle." He said, his charming smile instantly calming me.

"I would be honored, Dean. Thank you."

Dean and Kieran helped hoist me out of the car, Dianne pushing from behind. Finally, me, my dress, the train, Kieran, and Dianne were all on the sidewalk and ready to go.

"How's Mom?" I asked, wanting to prepare myself for the worst.

"She hasn't woken up at all. And her breathing has changed. The nurses say that usually means the end is near." He said, his voice husky with sadness.

"I'm so sorry, Bec," Kieran said. "Is there anything you need or that we can do?"

"Just help me get inside. It sounds like time is of the essence. How are things looking in there?"

"Gorgeous, but not nearly as beautiful as the bride," Dean replied. "You look stunning, Rebecca."

I smiled, genuinely touched. "Thank you. How are Malachi and Dustin?"

"Impatient, but also quite dapper. Malachi's family is here too. His gran, his aunt, his sisters, and their kids, and his cousin. The nursing staff is about done with us taking over their waiting room."

We stepped off the elevator. Everyone at the nurses' station stopped what they were doing. Some smiled, a few called their congratulations, and one scowled.

"Thank goodness, the bride. Let's move this along so we can get all these people out of here." She snapped.

"Aren't you a joy?" Kieran said, waving his fingers at her as we went by.

Right outside the door of Mom's room, Rae stood, radiant in a jumpsuit of pale, pale pink silk, sleeveless with a shimmery jeweled belt at the empire waist. She had a sheer white wrap threaded around her elbows and held a giant bouquet of white roses. I gasped at the sight of it.

"This is stunning! Just what I would have chosen." I said. "Another home run."

She looked at me, pleased. "You look amazing, Rebecca. Your mom will be so proud." She paused for a moment. "But sweetheart, you need to prepare yourself. She's extremely near the end."

I breathed in and out, trying to stave off the tears. "Then let's hurry."

"Okay. We're ready. Wait for the signal, Dean."

Rae went back in, and I heard the first notes of an instrumental version of "Can't Help Falling in Love with You" begin.

Dianne, already inside, was standing with the other witnesses. Kieran smoothed his suit and walked into the room. At the sight of him, Dustin yelled, "Kiewan!" and clapped his hands.

"Our turn. Ready, kiddo?" Dean said.

As we walked arm in arm, I regarded the room with amazement. The walls were covered in faux white roses threaded with tiny twinkling lights. The ceilings had soft white fabric swagged off them. The lights had been turned down, and flameless candles were creating an aisle and all over the windowsill and any available surface.

"This is incredible!" I whispered.

But even more beautiful than the room was the man waiting at the head of the aisle for me. Malachi stood tall and handsome in a black suit that hugged his body in every complimentary way. He was smiling and crying, shaking his head in wonder at the sight of me.

Dustin stood next to him in the same tiny suit from the other night, looking excited but slightly confused. His eyes lit up at the sight of me. I couldn't hear him, but his mouth formed the words, "Mama pretty."

His little feet danced a happy jig. The black Converse Rae had gifted him that first day kissed the shiny floor, making tiny squeaks. *Sean*. I owed so much to a stranger, a teenager, never to grow into a man. As I glided towards the man I would spend my life with, I marveled at how an impulsive donation made by a college student looking for beer and book money changed the course of my life. Of Rae and Dean's life. It had given Dustin life. I knew I had Sean to thank for all the ways I was blessed right at this moment.

Mom's illness had set into motion another series of events that had changed everything in my life almost instantly. What Sean's influence hadn't touched; Bernie's had. In welcoming Dean and Rae, she thrust us all together and forced us to bond. It seemed she knew, even then, how close we would get and how much I would need them when her time came.

Thanks to her, I had found, and fell in love with, Malachi. I had found myself underneath the self-loathing and insecurity. She was leaving, but she had given me all the tools she knew I would need to survive her absence.

Thanks, Mom.

I swallowed the lump in my throat and looked to the left before I got to Malachi, where Mom lay. She looked grey and old, her skin sagging off her bones, despite the makeup and bright turban I was sure she had instructed Rae on. An elegant white faux fur blanket was spread over her. It looked almost like she was a wedding prop with it there. She didn't move and had tubes going in and out. Her chest rose sporadically, and each one came with a wheezy rattle. Cami was in a chair at her bedside, clasping her hand and watching the wedding.

We should have done this sooner, I thought, as I reached the man who would become my husband. Mom was here physically, but her spirit was gone, somewhere else I wasn't privy to. I hoped wherever it went, a piece of her was here, omnipresent.

But Malachi was here, alive and in love with me. We would be each other's family now. I looked over to my right and saw Gran and CeCe. They waved and smiled, along with the rest of Malachi's family. Dianne, Rae, and Dean stood together next to them, all crying openly. Dianne held her cell phone. On the screen, I saw Mia and Betty. I fought back the tears of pure joy. Everyone I loved in the world was sharing this moment.

Malachi squeezed my hand and looked into my eyes.

"You look amazing." He said.

The justice of the peace, a tall woman with teased red hair and long red nails and an odd, shiny gold robe, welcomed everyone and began. I didn't hear the words. I just focused on Malachi. He had chosen the vows earlier, so I would be the only one hearing them for the first time. Soon, we reached that part in the brief ceremony. He started.

"Because of you, I laugh, I smile, I dare to dream again. I look forward to spending the rest of my life with you, caring for you, nurturing you, and being there for you in all life has for us. I vow to be true and faithful for as long as we both shall live."

He paused and then continued.

"I, Malachi Anders, take you, Rebecca Malone, to be my partner, loving what I know of you, and trusting what I do not yet know. I eagerly anticipate the chance to grow together, getting to know the person you will become, and falling in love a little more every day. I promise to love and cherish you through whatever life may bring us."

My throat thickened with tears as I struggled through my vows. Dean had picked up wedding bands for us earlier, a thick silver band for Malachi and a delicate band of small diamonds for me. He produced them, and we slid them onto each other's fingers. And then, we were kissing. I was kissing my husband.

Everyone clapped and cheered. We pulled apart and thanked everyone for coming. A photographer who had melted into the background emerged and started taking pictures, both formal and candid. Malachi introduced me to his sisters, Cherish and Tasha. Cherish was the younger of the two and the more skeptical of our relationship. I tried to reassure her.

"I know it's fast, but I really do love your brother. I can't wait to get to know you both better too." I said, smiling at her. "I'm excited for Dustin to have some cousins his age."

Cherish scowled, but Tasha responded kindly. She smiled the same broad smile as Malachi and offered to host a day of treatments at the spa she worked at as a massage therapist. She offered her husband, who couldn't get off work on such short notice for the wedding, as a babysitter for the kids. I accepted immediately, grateful for the chance to forge a relationship with the women and for Dustin to get to know his new cousins.

While I was meeting Malachi's cousin, DeVon, Kieran strode over. He eyed him hungrily. To my surprise and delight, DeVon reciprocated the attention. I made a quick exit. When I looked back, they were deep in animated conversation.

"Good. My plan worked." Malachi whispered in my ear.

"You planned that?" I asked, incredulous.

He just nodded and smiled. "Everyone deserves love. Besides, who doesn't love a meet-cute?"

"Is a quickie deathbed wedding in a hospital a meet-cute?"

"Come on, look around. Would you know this was a hospital? No. The event people pulled out all the stops." He said, pulling me to his chest and slinging his arms over my shoulders.

"It really is beautiful. I can't believe all this fuss is for me."

"Well, get used to it. I'm going to make a fuss over you for the rest of my life." He sprinkled kisses down my hair, over my ear, onto my neck, then my shoulder.

"Is that a promise?" I said, turning to face him and slipping my hands around his waist.

"Always, my love, always." He said, kissing me.

RAE

We did it, Bernie, I thought. *You can go if you need to. Malachi has her now. We all have her and Dustin. They'll be okay.*

The crowd in the room was starting to thin. Fern and CeCe had to get back to the diner for the dinner rush. Malachi's sisters had kids to get off the bus and babies to put down for naps. Only his cousin DeVon remained, still deep in conversation with Kieran. Dianne watched their exchange with delight.

Rebecca and Malachi hadn't taken their hands or eyes off one another since they were pronounced husband and wife. Dustin was in Malachi's arms, practically asleep on his shoulder. I looked over at Bernie, her essence gone, leaving just a shell, weakening more every moment. Cami sat with her, talking to her in a low whisper with few pauses.

" We should take Dustin home. Let's let Rebecca have some time with her mom." I said to Dean.

He nodded. " I can take him home. You would stay. Bernie would want you here when…." He stopped, unable to say the words that hung unspoken in the air.

He finished with humor, his preferred method of distraction." Becca will need someone without ice in their veins and a stick up their ass when the time comes."

Dianne joined us and heard the tail end of the conversation. She smiled and jerked her head towards Cami.

" You talking about Elsa the Ice Queen over there?"

I shushed them both." I know she's hard to deal with, but she's losing her sister. We have to be empathetic."

" You're right...but she makes it so easy." Dianne lamented.

" That she does." I agreed." Why don't you start making the rounds and say goodbye? I think I will stay."

" You're heading out?" Dianne asked Dean.

" Yes, Dustin needs to go to bed, and I wanted to give Becca some time with Bernie before…." He trailed off and struggled to compose himself." I'm sorry. I just have come to love that lady. It's hard."

Dianne regarded us both with sympathetic, kind eyes.

" No apologies needed."

She paused for a moment, debated with herself.

" And I am terribly sorry to hear about your son."

With loss and grief and death already so thick in the air, thinking about Sean almost took me to my knees. I wobbled. Dean's hand shot to the small of my back and kept me upright. Dianne moved closer and rubbed my arm.

" I'm sorry. I can't keep my mouth even if you pay me. Blessing and curse." She said.

" It's true. She's hopeless." Kieran said, joining us with DeVon." I don't know what she said, but I can guarantee she didn't mean to hurt you. She only uses her words as weapons against Republicans and other bad guys."

All of us laughed at that, resulting in a dirty look from Cami. Malachi and Rebecca joined us then, their joy radiating from them like rays off the sun.

" Every wedding has a rowdy group, and I believe we just found ours." He teased, smiling his dazzling smile.

" Well, you won't have to worry about us for much longer. I'm taking my grandson home to bed." Dean said, transferring Dustin from Malachi's shoulder to his own.

" And I'm going back with you. I'm exhausted." Dianne said." As long as that's okay with you."

Dean nodded." Of course."

" You can stay in my room." Malachi said." Well, I guess it's the guest room now."

" We're heading out too, cuz." DeVon said." I'm going to give Kieran a tour of the city."

Dianne's face brightened and split with a giant smile, thrilled to hear of her son's impromptu date.

They both kissed Becca on the cheek and hugged Malachi.

" Text me if you need me. I'll come running." Kieran said, then he grinned. "But if you don't need me, don't wait up."

" God, I've missed you." Rebecca laughed." Go enjoy yourself. I'll text if there's news."

Dean, Dianne, and Dustin made quick work of their goodbyes and headed back to Bernie's. I promised I would call with any news. Then, it was just Rebecca, Malachi, Cami, and I, waiting for the inevitable.

Malachi straddled the line, monitoring her vitals, helping us understand what was happening and what was to come. He was also working hard supporting Rebecca as her husband. Cami sat stony and silent as if we had intruded on her private mourning or her lambasting of herself about her lacking relationship with her sister.

Rebecca was also silent but clung to Bernie's hand and laid her head on her shoulder, crying without making a sound. I stood at the foot of the bed, waiting for the other shoe to drop.

It was hours later when Malachi roused me from the light sleep I had been in on the windowsill of Bernie's room.

" Let's take a walk and get some coffee. You too, Cami."

We walked into the hallway, all of us blinking like newborns adjusting to the shock of emerging from the dark to light. Cami ducked into the bathroom, no doubt making sure her makeup and hair remained impeccable even at a time like this.

While we waited for her, Malachi spoke.

" I wanted to give Becca the chance to have some alone time with Bernie. To say whatever, she needs to. It won't be long now."

" I know." I spoke.

Cami came out of the bathroom, looking tear-stained but stoic.

" Coffee?" Malachi asked, guiding both of us through the abandoned hall of the unit.

As we stepped onto the elevator, we heard Rebecca call out.

" Help! I need someone in here!"

Malachi held the elevator door open, and we sprinted down the hall. Nurses flooded into Bernie's room. Rebecca stood with her mother, holding her hand, tears ruining her makeup.

There was a juxtaposition that momentarily paralyzed me. Becca in a wedding dress, Bernie's veil still cascading down her back, crying and clinging to her mother's wasting, gray form as Bernie struggled for her air.

People moved around me as I stood rooted at the end of the bed, taking them in, mother and daughter. I recovered quickly and reached out to hold Bernie's ankle.

" We're here with you, Bernie. Cami and Malachi, and Rebecca. We're all going to be okay. I'll take care of them just like I promised, always." I spoke loudly and calmly, so she wouldn't be scared to make her final transition.

" Mom, no one will ever forget Bernie Malone. Every day, I'll tell Dustin about you. I love you, Mom." Rebecca sobbed.

Malachi reached and cupped Bernie's shuddering shoulder with his hand. He bent down close to her ear.

" Bernie, you changed my life. Thank you for raising the woman I love. I'll live every day in a way that would make you proud to have me as a son-in-law, I swear it. I'll raise Dustin to love and respect and honor you. I'll tell our kids stories about you. You rest now."

Cami struggled to keep her tears at bay as she kissed Bernie on the cheek.

"I love you, baby sister."

Rebecca leaned over and kissed her mother, her tears falling onto Bernie's slackened face. Bernie opened her eyes for a moment, wide and wild, gasped one breath, and was gone.

Rebecca collapsed into Malachi's arms at the head of the bed. Malachi scooped her up and carried her into the hall, the train of her dress flapping like an admission of surrender behind them. She wailed over and over, loud keening, her voice echoing down the halls. The nurses scurried up and down the corridors, closing doors, not wanting to disturb or alarm the other patients. Cami sank into her chair, silent and shocked.

I went to where Rebecca had stood at Bernie's head. She was radiant and beautiful, already peaceful and angelic. I smoothed her covers and arranged my hands on top of her crossed ones on the blankets. I kissed this woman who I had come to love as a sister on both her cheeks.

" Give one of those to Sean for me." I spoke.

ACKNOWLEDGMENTS

For Grandma Kay: Thank you for nurturing the talent you always believed I had. I love and miss you.

Kayla and Chayse: Everything I do is for you. Thank you for being my constant inspiration. I love you.

Ricky: Thank you for being the happy ending to my story. There's no one I'd rather do life with.

DQ: You inspired this story. If there is still a piece of you wandering this world, we are blessed indeed. I miss you, bro.

My amazing friends and family: Thank you for the endless support. If you liked a post, shared a link, or left a comment, I appreciate you. If your eyes read a word of this at any stage in the writing process, thank you! I took every word everyone gave me and used it to make this book better and stronger. You all helped me make this something I am so proud to send out into the world.

To my beta readers, editors, formatters, website master: a million thanks!

Made in United States
North Haven, CT
02 November 2022

26212717R00217